Gren
Guardian of the Flying Tigers

Betsy K. Haydon
2021

Gremlin (1945)

Dedication

To my family and friends;

To the dogs I've known and valued
For their unconditional love:
Rusty, Jamie, Susie, Squeaky,
Orion, Beauregard, Klaus,
Kyria, Keyboard, Capo, Tex,
Cedar, Russia, Astro-tini; and

To the memory of Dad's puppy,
Gremlin

Foreword
By Kerry Keithcart, Ph.D., Col. (USAF-Retired)
Former Vice Wing Commander and Instructor Pilot

Lt. George Haydon, my wife's father, served with General Claire L. Chennault and the Flying Tigers of China during WWII, defending the Chinese people against Japanese forces. In *Gremlin: Guardian of the Flying Tigers*, the author, whom I call my "Beautiful Bride Betsy," tells their story—from a puppy's perspective. This novel follows the dachshund named Gremlin and his best friend George on their missions for the U.S. China Air Task Force and the Fourteenth Air Force.

The founders and members of the Flying Tigers Historical Organization believe in "Honoring past friendships by strengthening future relationships," the theme of this historical novel. The story of these relationships forged between the American and Chinese military units as they fought a common enemy convey how much we have in common and that we have much to learn from each other.

Gremlin transported me back in time and inspired me to be kinder to dogs because they know what is happening. My father served as a career Navy pilot, and I served as an Air Force pilot for twenty-nine years and change. After reading this book, I want to learn more about my own Dad's experiences during WWII, get back up into the air, and, like Gremlin, have fun.

Table of Contents

Chapter 1: My Mission

Major General Claire Lee Chennault and
Doreen Davis (WWII)

I want you to be everything that's you,
Deep at the core of your being.

Confucius

The long, silky blanket of Mom's ear barely covered me as my two littermates and I snuggled in our basket. Mom sighed with a *whiffff* and moved onto her side. Hungry again, I crawled aimlessly, whimpering, until Mom pushed me toward her warm tummy where I found her milk.

Once my eyes opened, I could see Mom's fur, blurry at first and then clearer after she licked my face with her moist tongue. Nestling closer to feed again, I felt the short, soft hairs of her underbelly on the pads of my feet as I kneaded her skin.

I stopped nursing when I heard *rat-tat-a-tat*. Mom perked up her ears. She made a rumbling sound in her throat.

1

Mom's human reached down to pat her shoulder with her hairless fingers. "It's okay, Hedda. Maybe the general's returned. I wonder if Joe Dash is with him. Hmm?"

My mother licked her hand. The human moved away. *Click tap, click tap.*

My littermates whimpered, and Mom nuzzled them toward her belly. They edged closer to me. The fur of one tickled my nose, while the other wrestled between us, rolling me toward Mom's tail. We warmed each other, side by side, breathing heavily through our noses and snorting now and then as we drew in nourishment. Mom licked each of us in turn.

The door opened, and a breeze flowed over me, making my whole body shiver. I tucked my short hind legs and tiny tail and curled into a ball between my littermates.

"General Chennault. Good evening, welcome back." Her voice sounded louder than my mother's bark.

The man's voice was as gruff as Mom's growl. "Thanks, Doreen. Sorry to interrupt your evening. Just came by to check on Joe Dash's little dachshund family." The general coughed, something I did when a hair caught in my throat.

I opened my eyes, lifted my heavy head, and turned to see fuzzy shapes high above us. My nose twitched from an itchy feeling inside. I closed my eyes tightly and sneezed. *Chhhhooo.* Mom licked away the mess on my face.

"Of course, sir. Glad you came by. But that cigarette you're smoking isn't good for you—or Hedda's puppies. And one of the nurses in the next room is allergic to smoke." Doreen moved her arm toward us. "Now, I'm just your secretary and you're the general, but I have every right to keep you in line around these precious pups."

"Right, as usual, Doreen," he said. "I'll put it outside."

Why was Doreen shouting? *Hnnnnff?* Did I do something bad? *Hnnnnff?* I lay next to Mom, pushing up on my short, shaky legs to raise my long body. I tumbled down. After several tries, I stood again, my long ears dangling alongside my neck.

Doreen came closer and sat on the floor next to our basket. "Hedda dear, let's see who's making such a valiant effort to join the party." Picking me up under my tummy, she settled into her chair, held me close, and whispered, "Don't mind me yelling, my little friend. The general is quite deaf from all those noisy airplanes he's flown. I have to shout so he can hear me. No, my dear, you're not in trouble."

She poked my full belly and wiggled the ends of her fingers. "Tickle, tickle." Her dark eyes widened and the hair above her eyes moved up. I opened my mouth, stuck out my tongue, and smiled at her. She pulled me to her chin; I licked her cheek to say I understood, the same way Mom kissed my face.

Doreen cuddled me between her shoulder and neck, and I nibbled at her ear lobe to see what it would do. Her ears didn't move like ours—and they weren't furry, either. She giggled, and the sounds she made tickled me inside my tummy.

Chennault came back. He kneeled next to the basket, peering at Mom and my littermates. "How're they doing, Doreen? They must be, what—two-three weeks old now?"

"Two and a half weeks." Doreen held me up. "This one was born last, but he was the first to open his eyes. Runt of the litter, but there's something special about him." She stroked the top of my head. "You're my little friend, aren't you?"

3

"Good-looking pups," he said, nodding his head.

She rubbed my back. "They're adjusting well to life in Headquarters, sir. Since their eyes opened, I've been taking them to HQ. Thanks to Mac in the canteen and the base laundry, I've got lots of towels in the basket and for cleaning up. Hedda keeps them from straying around the office—for now, at least."

Mom looked up at me and wagged her tail. I sent her kisses by licking my lips, relaxing into the sensation of Doreen petting my fur. She showed her teeth, something she called smiling.

She gave me to the general. His hands felt much rougher than hers. I closed my eyes against the stinging, smoky smell as he rubbed my back. Cuddling against his chest, I felt warm and safe.

"They sure have grown," Chennault said. "Coming along nicely." He stroked my ears, and I melted into his hands.

"Hedda's an excellent mother, for her first litter," she said. "Sir, I've named two of the pups. The black male who looks like his sire is Tom, named after your brother. And the chocolate and tan female is Wench. She's a sweetheart—except she can be a bully, pushing her brothers away when she's hungry. As for this little chocolate and tan puppy, the last one born, I saved him for you to name."

Doreen cocked her head to one side, as Mom did sometimes. "But there's something about his eyes, sir. I think he understands exactly what I'm saying."

He turned me onto my back, near his jutting chin. The skin on his face wasn't smooth like Doreen's; he had deep lines near his mouth and eyes. I held still, my tiny paws in a prayer pose, the way Doreen held hers when she said certain words at night. His intense, dark eyes bored into mine, and I stared back at him in wonder. Who was this General Chennault?

I breathed in deeply. The scent of smoke from his hands made me sneeze. A moist spray landed on his chin. I licked my lips since Mom was too far away to clean up my mess. Would the general yell at me the way Doreen shouted at him?

Chennault held me in one hand, his lips pressed together. He slowly wiped off my puppy drool with the back of his hand. My tail tapped against his palm.

After a long silence, he said, "Runt of the litter, huh? Well, this one looks like a fighter, a real tiger. And we need a pup with a big heart to help us out in this long war."

"War... What can one puppy do?" Doreen frowned as she rubbed Mom's neck and chest. "We'd barely gotten over the 'War to End All Wars' when hostilities began again—even worse. We Brits joined the war in nineteen thirty-nine after the Germans attacked Poland. Who knows when it'll end?" She sighed. "Sir, forgive me, but I'm relatively new here. When did you arrive in China?"

"Nineteen hundred and thirty-seven," Chennault said. "The year Japan made a major invasion of China. Since the U.S. joined the fight in forty-one, we're having some success, despite the odds against us."

"What about your family?"

"My wife supports my commitment to the military. Our eight kids are in good hands. I'm here to protect millions of Chinese children. We make sacrifices to defeat our enemies."

Doreen took a deep breath, her shoulders shuddering. "Sometimes it all gets to me, sir. Hitler... Japan... How could

5

anyone invade their neighbors? Their friends? I'm sorry this is all tumbling out now, sir, but the situation here—and around the world... The Japanese occupy so much of China, and we're stuck in the southwestern corner, nearly powerless. What can we do?"

Chennault cradled me in one hand and touched each paw. Doreen picked up Wench and Tom, and they attacked her chin with puppy kisses. She sat in her chair and put my littermates in her lap, where they wrestled, growling softly. "Hedda and her puppies give me so much joy, amid all this terror. What kind of life would they have—or would we—if the war is lost?" A trickle of water slid down her cheek.

"Trust me, Doreen." Chennault said in a low voice. He frowned, and the lines seemed to deepen in the leathery skin across his face. "I'll give you my personal assurance. Number one: We've got innovative aerial tactics to combat the enemy's air raids. We haven't had any bombings here lately, right?"

Doreen nodded, me blinking and sniffing as the general continued. "Number two: Nothing secret here—yes, the Japanese have sewn up the coast of China and all the sea ports, but we've still got a thin supply line over the Himalayas, flying the Hump route through the passes."

I wiggled in Chennault's hand, and he handed me to Doreen. My brother, sister, and I tussled and bit each other, but when Chennault spoke again, I crawled onto Doreen's knee to listen.

"Number three," he said, "the American Volunteer Group—and now the China Air Task Force—is part of a multi-national effort. That said, we're not getting the parts and supplies we need over the Hump. Our fighters can't fly missions because we can't maintain them."

He picked me up again and rubbed my tiny chest with his fingernails. "But, you know, Doreen, we're determined to win with everything we do have." My back leg, smaller than his little finger, scratched at the air.

Tom yipped when Wench bit his neck. Doreen separated them. "Thinking it over, sir, British pilots and mechanics in India say that gremlins are tricksters. When they can't find what's wrong with the planes, they say it's a mischievous gremlin. How about naming this one Gremlin and giving him the mission of keeping away those troublesome pests?"

"All right, young pup," General Chennault said, holding me above Mom. He pressed one finger onto my forehead. I tried to look at it, but my eyes couldn't focus on it up close. I squirmed for a moment, hoping I wouldn't make water while he held me.

"I pronounce you The Gremlin, meaning the head gremlin, and you are charged with the mission of keeping any and all other gremlins away from the Flying Tigers. You'll be good for morale, Gremlin, you understand. No more mechanical issues. Every Curtiss P-40 fighter in tip-top shape. Our transport planes flying safely over the Hump, with you as our guardian."

He put me in the basket with Mom. I rolled onto my back and Mom licked my face. Doreen put Wench and Tom next to me. She scratched my chest, which I puffed out to meet her fingers, proud of the moment I had been named.

Chennault stood and opened the door, whistling. I scrambled to sit up and watch. The biggest dog I'd ever seen jumped into the room, sniffing the air. He had a huge head, long body, and short, sturdy legs.

7

"Joe—up." The dog with black, shiny fur sat up straight and tall, far above us. He lifted his front paws, raised his head high, and put his chin in the general's hand, holding the pose until Chennault said, "Down. At ease. Kids, meet your pop, Joe Dash."

Joe Dash, our pop—whatever that meant—snorted and stepped closer to us, his nails tapping the floor. Mom shook us gently out of her way and stepped out of the basket to nuzzle Pop's nose. Pop made the same whimpering sounds we made whenever Mom came back into our basket.

General Chennault and Joe
(WWII)

Mom wasn't quite as big as Pop, but she jumped up and ran under a chair, then stopped and looked at him, blinking her huge eyes. I heard Doreen and Chennault laugh as Pop chased after her.

Peering over the top of our basket with my brother and sister, I whimpered, *mmmrrrrff?* Mom and Pop ran in and out among the chairs and the human's legs. We pounced on each other until I tripped over my long ears and fell. I nipped Tom's tail. He yelped. Mom came back to the basket and growled. I let go and licked his face, then crawled over him to gnaw on Wench's neck.

Doreen asked, "Sir, why do you call him Joe Dash?"

I got up, panting, and cocked my head, listening for his reply.   He chuckled; his eyes glowing. "Joe was the name of a man back home who taught me how to hunt and fish and fight. Dachshunds are good hunters. Short legs, smart and agile. Always had doxies; always named them Joe."

"You do?" Doreen asked. "By the way, why does he have two names?"

"Even though his breed is pronounced *doc-son* or *daks-hoond*, I call him Joe Dash 'cuz he's a good retriever."

Chennault sat back in his chair, watching Mom and Pop. "Some of the men take him out hunting, always surprised at how good he is in the field. Call him Joe Dog."

He cleared his throat and picked up Wench, holding her against his chest and stroking her fur with his thumb. "I'd like to train his pups, too, if I have time. I usually watch them to learn their personalities. Ha—just like teaching schoolkids back in *Loosiana*."

"You, sir? A schoolteacher?" Doreen raised her eyebrows.

"Yes, ma'am. Comes in handy when training pilots. Good for instilling discipline, too. Well, night, Doreen. That's a fine litter of pups." Chennault put my sister next to me. Tom and I piled on top of her. I barked and chewed on the folds of fur on her back.

He called, "Joe Dash, attention. Heel." Pop licked Mom's nose one more time and trotted to the general.

I pounced on Tom. Mom whined and rushed over to nip me near my tail. Wench pulled on my ear and I yowled until Mom nosed us apart. Tiring at last from our playful fighting, we tangled up our dachshund bodies, legs, and ears, and fell asleep.

9

Chapter 2: Puppies in China

Three Dachshund Puppies in Kunming, China
(WWII)

Everything has beauty, but not everyone sees it.

Confucius

Doreen took us to what she called "work" in Headquarters or HQ. Nearly every morning after we slept and ate, and the world was light again, she loaded us into the basket. Mom trotted along, keeping an eye on us.

We had a good view of the Kunming air base on our morning walk, especially as Doreen climbed the steps to HQ. Rows of buildings and barracks stretched out before us. I blinked into the sun to see machines of different sizes buzzing in the air like flies, but farther away. Jeeps rushed past HQ, beeping as they bumped along the rutted roads. Groups of airmen and army troops ran next to the graveled roads with packs on their backs, chanting and stepping in unison.

Inside, airmen in green Army Air Corps uniforms filled the room, working at crowded desks and tables. Smoke hung in the air, and I always sneezed when we came through the door. Bright lights hung on black cords hanging from the low ceiling, making sunshine in the big room. Doreen placed our basket on her desk. I sniffed at her things there but didn't care about them. All I needed was Mom and my brother and sister.

Airmen walked briskly from one place to another. Some of them paused to talk with Doreen. "What cute puppies." "Beautiful brood, Hedda." "Joe Dash is such a good poppa." "Aww, will ya look at the baby Flying Tigers?" "Wonder who's lucky enough to get one of those pups."

They smiled and made kissing noises with their mouths as Mom sat proudly next to Doreen's feet, her head up, eyes bright, tail wagging. I didn't like it when people asked to hold me. I wiggled and squirmed to get back into the basket. What I found worked best was to make water on their scratchy-feeling clothes, leaving a dark spot behind. They always made a squeaking sound and passed me right back to Doreen and Mom.

~   ~   ~   ~   ~

Doreen put our basket under her desk and settled down to work. I nipped at a fold in her pants when her knee came close, growling and tugging until she peered down and shooed me away. "I've got to work, Gremlin. We'll play later," she said. She rolled her chair away so she was just out of my reach.

Chennault called for her. Doreen rolled back her chair

and dropped something into our basket. "Now where's my pencil? Have you seen it, Gremlin?"

She bent down just as I took a bite out of the thin stick, leaving little holes in it. "Now I'll know exactly which pencil is mine," she laughed.

I placed my front paws as high as I could, peering over the curved top of the basket, and watched her go. Doreen stood and clip-clopped into the general's office at the back of the long, narrow room. I worried that she might not come back. And that Mom might not come back, too, whenever she left us. What would we puppies do without them?

People walked by, and I wagged my tail, showing my tongue in a big puppy smile. Whenever I heard loud sounds, I shoved Wench and Tom aside to burrow under the soft towels lining our basket. When it was quiet, I poked out my head. Mom fed us until our tummies were full, and we played until we fell asleep.

For most of the morning, voices rose and fell throughout HQ, like Doreen's humming. Office equipment clacked and rattled and rang out. Finally, Doreen returned; she talked to people and made clanking noises on top of her desk. I sighed because she didn't give me any attention.

After a long time, Doreen took us outside for fresh air and sunshine. She sat in the grass in the bright sunshine and took us out of the basket one by one. keeping us close as we explored the itchy stems and leaves.

What little creatures hid there? I put my head down and followed my nose, tripping over my ears now and then. I rolled, feeling the textures of the grass on my back and sides. Standing, I shook myself, scratched at the ground, and

13

snuffled the scents there, with my nose close to the little plants. I propelled my long body across the grass, first on one side and then the other, snorting with joy.

The rest of the world faded away, until I heard the swishing sound of someone coming toward us. A tall man walked across the lawn, the sun above his head. Doreen put her hand above her eyes. I ran back to protect her, growling.

She picked me up and held me in her lap. "Oh, Colonel Hill, how are you, sir? Just in from flying a mission?"

"I'm fine, Doreen. Yep, another victory for our side," he said, kneeling next to her. "And please, just call me Tex. Say, ya mind if I hold one of those puppies?"

Doreen placed me in his outstretched hands. "This is Gremlin, Tex."

He stood, and I felt breathless, wiggling and squirming high above the ground, so frightened I couldn't even whimper to Mom. He held me firmly near his face, rubbing me under my neck. "You're a little tiger, aren't you?"

Those big noisy flies droned overhead and flew to a huge open field where they landed and rolled to a stop. "See those planes, Gremlin—with the tiger shark's mouth painted on their noses? That'll

Curtiss P-40 and Pilot
(WWII)

be the rest of my Twenty-third Fighter Group," Tex whispered to me. "Good ole Curtiss P-40 Warhawks. You remember that now, okay? I've heard from Chennault that you're the one to talk to about keeping the gremlins away. The Twenty-third, now. All right?"

He scratched me all up and down my back. I stretched my head up and sighed in delight, determined to watch over the Twenty-third, that big squadron of noisy flies. Planes, he called them. Fighters.

A woman in a white uniform and cap came up to us. "Hey there, Tex—cute puppy you're holding." She sat on the grass near Doreen and Mom, who seemed to watch everyone, especially us three puppies.

Tex nodded. "Yeah, Red. He's a good pup." I licked his fingers.

Wench pinned Tom on his back and bit his neck, snarling in her high puppy voice. Mom growled at Wench, a much deeper sound, and Doreen picked her up. Wench gnawed at Doreen's hand while Tom shook himself and walked to Red, lifting each paw up and over the grass before setting it down again.

"Glad to meet you," Doreen said. "But I thought your name was Susan."

"Just call me Red. Everyone back home does." She petted Tom, who rolled onto his back.

Red's hair was pulled away from her ears, the way Doreen wore hers. Her face had brown speckles on it. And her hands had spots, too. Would her skin—and her ear—taste the same as Doreen's?

Tex set me down on the grass near Mom, who licked my mouth in greeting. "Ladies, I've got to mosey along."

"Bye, Tex," the women said together.

"Well, little tiger. Maybe when you're bigger I'll get a chance to take you flying, high into the air."

Rrrrrmmmff? Tex had already taken me up into the air. How much higher could we go?

Doreen held Wench upside-down on her lap, her long fingers tapping Wench's nose, mouth, neck, and paws. Wench nibbled at Doreen's fingertips wherever they touched her. It looked like a fun game, and I wished Doreen would play with me like that.

"I heard from the general you'd found vaccines for the puppies," Doreen said. "Thanks for bringing them over. Should I hold them while you give the shots?"

"Better let me do it." Red gave Tom to Doreen and held me firmly with her strong fingers. "I'd rather be the bad guy than for them to think you're the one causing them pain."

Pain? Like when Wench bit my leg? Or Tom pawed at my belly? *Yip-yip,* I cried out to Mom. She showed her teeth and gave a rumbling growl.

"It's okay, Hedda," Doreen said, putting Tom in her lap with our sister. Mom put her head down, keeping her eyes on me.

Red tickled my belly, and my hind legs wiggled in the air with joy. How did she know I liked that? I squirmed loose, trying to lick the back of her hand and taste her spots, but she pulled away before my tongue could reach it.

"I requisitioned the vaccine when I heard the puppies were born," she said. "Sure helped that General Chennault's dog is the sire, but it took this long for approval and to get it all the way out here over the Hump."

She put me in her lap and held my chin up, her green eyes looking into mine. "Well, you're a bright one, aren't you? What's your name?" I whimpered, not knowing how to tell her my name.

Doreen said, "He's Gremlin, named by the general. A long story."

"My, you're a good little boy." I opened my mouth and panted. I liked her tone of voice when she told me I was good. She picked up something shaped like Doreen's pencil and held it up in the air, tapping it and squirting out some liquid. Then she put my head down and squeezed my rear end onto her leg so I couldn't move.

"Just a pinch, little one," Red said. "Good boy."

Pain worse than Wench's sharp puppy teeth poked into my bottom. *Owwerrrg*—I howled. I wriggled as she lifted me up, my feet clawing the air until she put me back in our basket. Mom's eyes opened wide with concern, and she licked me all over. I whined. *Whirrrmmff? Whirrrff?*

"There you go, Gremlin. Safe and sound, back with your mum," Doreen said. Mom made the sting disappear with the gentle way her teeth combed my fur.

Red lifted my brother out of the basket, and Doreen told her, "This one's Tom."

"Good boy, Tom." Oh no. When Red said I was good, she hurt me. Was she going to hurt my brother, too?

"A shot for you, Tom," she said. "Good boy."

Tom wagged his tail and kept still. He gave one high-pitched bark—*yyiiiyiip*—then he licked Red's arm. When Tom came back to the basket, he wiggled his whole body like nothing had happened.

Red picked up my sister. "Who's this cutie pie?"

"Wench, meet Red." Doreen smiled.

"What a sweet puppy you are, Wench." Maybe Red wouldn't hurt Wench, since she didn't call her good, but she picked up the same kind of thing that bit me and Tom. "Good girl, Wench. You're the last one. Here's your shot. Be good."

Oh no—Wench cried out, yipping and squirming as Red put her in our basket. Mom curled around all of us. Tom wanted to play, while Wench and I whimpered and nursed. Mom licked away our pain.

"Say, will you do me another favor?"

"Sure. Glad to help."

Doreen pointed to us. "I'd like to get a photo of the three puppies. They're growing so quickly. I want a memento, before they're big enough to be given away."

"Sure." Red sat cross-legged and picked up Tom.

"Okay, I'll be right back with my camera." Doreen went back to HQ. Would she come back for us? Or leave us with someone who hurt us? I whined—*hhhhnnnnnn*—*hhhhnnnn*?

Red picked me up, and I chewed on her thumb. "Ouch— sharp teeth, Gremlin. But it's okay. You're all so cute."

Doreen returned with a small black box and knelt on the grass in front of us. She gave Wench to Red, and we poked our heads through her fingers. Mom sat next to her, wagging her tail.

Doreen twisted a button on the camera. Then she held it in front of her face and said, "One, two—"

Red said, "Good puppies."

Good? Was she going to hurt me again? I panicked, squeezing through her fingers, and jumped out of her hands, falling upside down onto the grass. I cried out with a *yyyyippp*.

Red gathered me up again. "Come on back, Gremlin. This won't hurt a bit. Stay still, now."

I trembled all over when Doreen's camera made clicking noises. My ear rested on Red's hand, close to her spots, but I

18

didn't want to taste them anymore. At last, she put us back into the basket and said goodbye to Doreen.

Shaking my head, I pounced on Tom. Mom whined and nipped me near my tail, then curled up with us. Tiring at last from our big outing, we fell into a huddle of dachshund noses, feet, and ears. I pawed my way toward Mom's belly and wedged myself between Tom and Wench. After nursing, I rested my head against her chest, my paws wrapped around my brother's neck. I barely noticed when Mom hopped out and Doreen picked up the basket. The swaying of our basket rocked me deeper into sleep.

Chapter 3: My Family

Hedda, Gremlin's Mother
(WWII)

To know what you know
And know what you don't know
Is characteristic of one who knows.

Confucius

We grew quickly at the Kunming Air Base. We ate as much as we could, relieved ourselves, usually outside but sometimes inside, and learned how to behave with our human friends. I learned the names of the people, places, and things in our lives. For me, mealtime and outside time made up the best part of each day. If we weren't eating, we were hungry. If we weren't playing, we napped—or ate some more.

21

Every day, Doreen carried us in our basket from the barracks, where we slept at night, to Headquarters, where she worked at a desk all day. Our basket sat next to her feet. We nipped each other's tails, growled, snorted, and yipped almost as loud as the machinery and human voices in HQ.

When we were little, we stayed in our basket most of the time. If we tumbled out, Mom growled at us. She'd pick us up by the scruff of the neck and put us back into the basket.

Doreen reminded us constantly about where to make our water and piles—outside, not inside—and told us to sit and stay and heel. Although I heard the words, I didn't understand what they meant, even though Mom seemed to know. I just wanted to play with my littermates and eat everything I could get ahold of.

Each of us wore a collar like Mom and Pop, but smaller. Doreen put leashes on our collars. We three excited puppies spin around, barked, and chased one another before we went outside. I liked the way she laughed, but sometimes she sighed and called our names loudly while rounding us up.

One cool morning, we squeezed through the barracks door with our puppy *yippppees* while Doreen held our leashes. She carried us one by one down the stairs onto the cold, moist ground. We put our noses down and went in different directions, sniffing to find out who visited during the night. I chased the dried brown leaves falling from the trees, skittering from the wind on the moist ground.

When Mom finished doing her business under a bush, Doreen said, "Hedda, heel." Mom ran to her, head up, and her human reached down to stroke Mom's neck and back. "Good girl. Try to keep these little guys in line now, dear. It's a good thing HQ isn't too far away, but—oh, my goodness—those pups always get into a tangled mess. And that's exactly how I feel when we arrive at HQ—a tangled mess."

Tom, Wench, and I picked up our favorite scents, all leading in different directions, pulling Doreen's arms into different directions. "Oh no, not again," she said. "Come on, everyone. This way."

We chased each other to get ahead of Doreen. Then Tom stopped to poop. Wench squatted to pee. I chased after a fly. Mom waited. Doreen sighed, then tugged on our leashes again, pulling us toward HQ. We growled at each other, stopped to sniff at every new scent and bumped into each other, crisscrossing our leashes.

When we got to the steps to HQ, Wench ran in circles, wrapping her leash around Doreen's ankles. Twisting around to untangle herself, Doreen said, "Wench, you little stinker, what have you done now?"

Jumping over Wench's leash, I helped Doreen the best way I knew how, by giving her kisses on her knees. She laughed, saying, "All right now, my dears. Enough horsing around. I've got to go to work."

Tom jumped on me. I rolled over and pinned him, nipping at his shoulder. He got up to chew on my neck, then jumped away with an *arrrrggghh*. As I prepared to pounce on him, Tom gave a *yiiiipppp* and sat down, lifting his front paw. Doreen stumbled over him and fell onto the bottom step, dropping our leashes. I licked his leg, whimpered, and sat down next to him, nuzzling his neck. Mom and Wench joined us; Mom licked the top of Tom's head, while Wench sniffed his paw.

"Tom—are you all right?" She picked him up while we barked and huddled around to comfort him.

"Down, everyone," Doreen said, brushing us away. "Let me have a look. I know, I know. Oh, poor dear—you have a big sticker in your paw. Stay still—I'll get it out."

I jumped up to see better, barking into Tom's ear so that he would know I worried about him. Tom wiggled and whined, squirming on Doreen's lap.

"Down, Gremlin. I've just about got ahold of it. Be a good boy, Tom." I barked louder, telling Doreen not to hurt him.

Yyyiiiipp! Tom cried out as Doreen said, "Got it! Maybe now you'll mind me." My brother tilted his head up and closed his eyes as Mom licked his paw and face.

General Chennault came out of HQ. "Morning, Doreen. What's the commotion? Everything all right?" Pop followed the general and rushed down the stairs to Mom. They touched muzzles; we barked at our parents. When Mom and Pop ran in circles on the grass, we chased them, even Tom, who seemed to have forgotten about his sticker. I rolled over onto my back, hoping Pop would play with me, but he and Mom licked noses and ran away together.

"Good morning, sir. Well, Tom got a sticker, so we just took care of that." Doreen sighed as she pulled a loose strand of her brown hair behind her ear. "*Hhmmph.* It's just that the puppies are becoming a bit much to handle." She looked around the grass at her feet. "Now—where'd you go, Tom?"

Wench and I chased each other around the general's feet. Chennault picked up our leashes and gave them to Doreen. He found the end of Tom's leash. "I do believe Tom is under here. Come on out, you rascal."

Reaching under the stairs, he pulled Tom out from under the bottom step. Holding Tom against his belly, the general inspected his short legs. Tom whined when the general touched his sore paw.

Doreen sat with her head in her hands. "They're just into everything, General. I hate to say it, but it's high time to get them into their own homes."

"I've got some ideas about that," he said. "Time for them to graduate."

A few days later, while we chewed on little white bones in our basket, General Chennault introduced a new man to Doreen, Staff Sergeant Andy Chavez. He had dark hair and eyes and was almost as slender as Doreen. I licked my bone three more times and burrowed under the towels to hide it from my littermates.

When I shook the towels off my head, I saw Andy sitting at the desk next to Doreen's. They talked in soft voices, then she went back to work on the noisy machine they called a typewriter. Andy answered the clanging telephone and shouted into the radio with its buzzing noises. He talked with humans who came into HQ and said who could see the general and who needed to wait.

Doreen *clip-clopped* into the general's office with her pencil and paper. When she came back, she typed, making clattering, ringing, and dinging noises. She rolled the paper out of the typewriter with a thrumming noise and took it to Chennault. When she came back, she put it into a smaller paper, licked it and put it on the counter for someone to take it away. I wanted to taste whatever it was she licked, but she never let me get close to it.

25

Pop passed by our basket with General Chennault, but he didn't stop to play with us. Since we didn't get much attention, we played games with Mom. I started it by jumping out of the basket, followed by Wench and Tom. We kept Mom busy chasing us under desks and chairs. As soon as she got us all back into the basket, one of us climbed out again.

"Such naughty puppies," Doreen told Andy, but she laughed, so I thought she liked our game.

Late in the afternoon, my littermates and I put our paws on the rim of the basket to look at Andy. We wagged our tails to let him know we were ready to play. He stopped working and said to Doreen, "How are you doing?" He gestured at us. "Need any help with the little dachshund family?"

Doreen's fingers clattered on her typewriter keys. Then she stopped and took a deep breath. "We're managing, Andy. Thanks, though." She continued her clicking and ringing.

"I dunno, Doreen." He leaned back in his chair and scratched his head. "You have a lot to do, and I see those puppies playing tricks on you and Hedda." Andy smiled and turned his head to one side. I moved my head to the same side to show him I was listening. "I don't mean to butt in, though, wouldn't want to interrupt your training program. But I do have some experience with dogs."

"Really?" Doreen propped her elbows on the desk.

"Sure. Always had dogs on our farm. When my wife Graciela told me she was expecting a baby, I trained a puppy. That dog's a perfect companion for our son. So, I'd be glad to give you a hand—if you'd like me to."

"Truthfully, Andy? As dear as they are to me, these puppies are wearing me out. Frankly, I'd love your help."

Doreen paused. "You have a little boy? How old was he when you left home?"

"He was a year old when war broke out and I enlisted. He's nearly three now. Graciela writes that he and his dog Amigo are inseparable." Andy smiled. "So, it will be my pleasure to work with Hedda and her puppies, Doreen— anytime. It'll take my mind off how much I miss my family."

Andy became a good friend for our dachshund family. Several times a day, he took all of us outside. Sometimes he carried me, cradling me next to his chest as Mom walked beside him. I always smiled, my tongue lolling in my mouth, whenever he sang a song, repeating the words *de colores*.

"Gremlin, this song reminds me of home and rocking my baby boy to sleep," he told me, tickling my belly. "And so, here in China you are my Mexican *hijito mío*, my little boy. I'll call you *mi hijito*."

That night in the warm barracks, I rolled onto my back, looking up at Mom's best friend. Doreen always talked to me in ways I understood, teaching me the names of people and things.

I rolled over and whacked my head against Tom's shoulder. He woke up with a *rrrwwwgg?* and shook his head, then went back to sleep. I put my chin on my paws and sighed, wondering what it would be like to have my own best friend. But I didn't want to think about that yet. My family of dachshunds and our human friends was all I knew. And that was enough.

Chapter 4: The Flying Tigers

Original Symbol of the Flying Tigers
(WWII)

What the caterpillar calls the end,
The rest of the world calls a butterfly.

Lao Tzu

Mom and Pop stood with their humans while my littermates and I nosed around the ground outside Headquarters. Big, puffy clouds took turns covering the sun, and I shivered each time the world became darker.

I followed a small creature with a long body and more feet than I had, inching its way across the brown grass. My ears dragged on the ground as I trailed the fuzzy thing, wondering where it came from and where it was going. I pulled my leash out of Doreen's hands to chase it under the flowering bushes.

Chennault cleared his throat and crouched next to me. "Ah, so you're tracking a caterpillar, huh? You might turn out to be a good hunter, like your sire. See the butterflies?" He pointed to bugs with colorful wings fluttering around the flowers and stopping for a moment to lay tiny round eggs on leaves and curling tendrils.

A big butterfly perched on a leaf flapped its wings and joined the others flying circles in the air. Wagging my tail, I wished I could ask General Chennault questions. Where did the caterpillars go? Did butterflies come from dead leaves? Could they fly as high as the Flying Tigers?

The general picked up my leash. "Come on, Gremlin. We need to get a photo before we break up your little family." I gave the butterflies one last look and trotted to keep up with him.

"Andy should be here any time now to take us out to the airfield," he told Doreen. "We'll take the pups on their first Jeep ride to meet an old friend."

"A bit chilly today, but at least it's not raining," said Doreen, steering Wench and Tom to the road. Mom stayed by her side, as always.

Andy came up to us in a loud desk kind of machine and slid to a stop. I hid behind Chennault, but Tom ran forward, surprising Doreen. She pulled back on his leash, saying, "No, Tom. Heel."

Chennault knelt next to my brother, rubbing his chest. "General purpose vehicle, spelled GP. Dangerous, understand? Jeep."

Tom panted and whined and wiggled. Mom stood between Tom and the huge machine.

Andy jumped out and put his hand up by his face. The general lifted his hand, too, saying, "At ease, Andy. We'll load up the Jeep and head out to the airfield." I scratched at my eye

29

with my paw to do what they did, but no one seemed to notice.

"Yes, sir." Andy ran around to the side of the Jeep. "Here you go, Doreen." She sat in the front seat of the Jeep.

"Joe Dash, in the back," Chennault commanded, and Pop jumped into the seat behind us. The general picked up Mom and gave her to Doreen, then picked us up one by one until we were all on her lap.

By the time the general got into the back of the Jeep with Pop, we wiggled around on Doreen's lap with Mom, licking each other and sniffing the cool air. Andy sat next to us. When he turned a key, a noise startled me, louder than any machine in HQ.

I jumped down, landing on Doreen's feet. "It's just the Jeep's engine, Gremlin," she said.

Chennault had told me gremlins could hurt plane engines. Maybe there was a gremlin in the Jeep's engine. I had to scare it away. I barked as loud as I could—*brrrrkkk-brrrkk-brrrrrkk.*

I scooted backwards on the slippery floor every time I barked. Doreen moved her feet to one side of me. "Don't fall out, Gremlin. This Jeep doesn't have doors. Stay in the middle."

I felt scared. Couldn't do anything right. How could I protect anyone? I crept over toward Andy's feet. Maybe he could help me, since Doreen's hands were full.

"Oh no, you don't," said Doreen, moving one foot between me and Andy's feet. "Gremlin, you stay there."

I put my front paws on Doreen's seat, wagging my tail and hoping to jump up again into her crowded lap. Mom cuddled Tom and Wench, their heads bobbing with the bouncing of the Jeep. The wind made my eyes sting, and I blinked nonstop.

"Sorry, Gremlin. You lost your spot," she said. I curled up behind her feet, partway under the seat, cringing with every lurch and bump, afraid that a litter of gremlins would eat us.

When the Jeep stopped, I stood up and peered out the opening. Big machines flew in the air and rolled on the ground in a huge open space. Doreen picked me up and held everyone's leash. I licked Tom's face, but he didn't lick me back. He squirmed and wiggled, ready to run and play.

Chennault jumped out of the back of the Jeep and picked up Mom, putting her on the ground near the Jeep. He picked up Tom and me, holding us tight as my brother shivered with excitement. Once we were on the ground, the general kept our leashes tight, and we stayed close. He whistled, and Pop jumped out of the Jeep to join us.

Doreen put my sister next to me, and we touched noses. "General, I know we're meeting someone who's flying over the Hump from Karachi. Care to fill me?"

"My old flying buddy from the States, Luke Williamson. He's been training Chinese pilots in Hangchow for the past several years. He's taking a break to work directly for me."

"Andy, would you mind taking Wench?" Doreen gave my sister's leash to him and pulled something out of her jacket. "I'll take notes if you don't mind. I brought my things just in case."

"Sure, take a few notes for the record," Chennault said. "When I was on active duty at Maxwell Field in Alabama, back in the thirties, Luke Williamson, Bill McDonald and I developed tactical aerial maneuvers in our biplanes. We wanted to show the top brass of the Army Air Corps that

31

airplanes could be used in fighting situations, especially that we could fly in formation in innovative ways. We became the 'Three Men on the Flying Trapeze.'"

"Haven't heard this story," Doreen murmured. "Sounds like a good one."

"Well, we tied our three planes together with twenty-foot lengths of rope. Then we took off, flew our rehearsed patterns of aerobatics, and landed, without ever breaking the rope. The officers were so impressed, we performed at military airshows for the general public. We showed off our flying skills and recruited new airmen."

Doreen looked at Chennault, her pencil by her half-opened mouth. "That's amazing! We didn't hear about that in Great Britain. Wish I had."

The general cleared his throat. "Actually, the top brass thought our display was as outdated as the dogfights of the First World War. Thing is, they kept me from promoting these aerial pursuit tactics in any meaningful way. They retired me. Not that I wasn't ready to go."

He pointed his chin at the sky. "Madame Soong Mei-ling asked Luke and me to train their pilots to counteract the Japanese aggression, as it was called in the late thirties. I jumped on the chance to put my ideas into place with the Chinese Air Force."

"How did she hear about you?" Doreen asked.

"A Chinese general saw our trapeze show and recommended us. Well, war was declared between China and Japan before we started training. The Chinese flight students weren't ready for missions. Too dangerous. So that's how we got the American Volunteer Group out here—the AVG."

"No wonder China needs you here. Do tell me more about the flying trapeze act. That's brilliant," Doreen said.

"My favorite trick was dressing up as a stooped old woman, pretending to be a paying customer waiting in line for a ride in Luke's biplane. While he helped a passenger out of the back, I sprinted from the line and jumped into the pilot's seat. I took off, with Luke chasing the plane. A real show-stopper."

Chennault moved his hands through the air. "Oh, I did all kinds of maneuvers, barrel rolls, stalls, and a couple of loops. Even high above the crowd, I heard everyone scream for that old lady. Once I landed, I'd shake off the dress and stand up straight in my uniform—fooled them all."

Chennault and Doreen looked up as machines flew overhead and rolled to a stop on the ground. Butterflies didn't do that. What were these machines? Flying Jeeps? Typewriters with wings?

The general motioned to the airfield. "Luke will be my personal pilot, taking me around China when I have business off base. You'll come with us and take notes at meetings, unless it's a dangerous situation. Then I'll take someone in the military unit."

He scanned the sky, squinting. I heard a noise that sounded far away and got louder. "Ah, there's his transport plane," the general said.

I lifted my head. The loudest noise ever rattled my ears as the huge noisy thing flew past us, tipping its wings one way and then another.

"Well, I'll be." Chennault's voice was deep and gravelly. "That's Luke's signature move. He was known for barnstorming and all kinds of stunts in his home town.

33

Excellent pilot. And I here thought he'd be a passenger." He placed me on the warm hood of the Jeep.

The plane turned and came back toward us again. My short legs trembled, and I let out a high-pitched *yyyippp— yyiiippp*. I tucked my tail between my hind legs and tumbled backwards.

Chennault's strong arm steadied me. "Hold on, there, tiger." He chuckled. "He'll be coming around again to land that Curtiss C-46 transport plane. You'll get used to the Kunming Airfield, Gremlin. Our planes are noisy, but I've gotcha."

He held me close against his chest. I looked up at a strange animal on his jacket and growled—*grrrrwwwff*.

"Oh, you see this?" He pointed to a circle on his jacket. "Our emblem, a tiger with wings, made by an artist from Walt Disney studios. Not that you know much about that yet. The Chinese call us tigers of the sky, *Fēi Hǔ*, the Flying Tigers."

The noisy thing he called a plane came closer, bumping onto the wet landing strip and rolling to a

Chennault with Flying Tiger patch (WWII)

stop just a few feet away from us. It had a huge mouth with lots of teeth. I tossed my head from side to side, backing into Chennault's belly as he laughed.

Wishing I could hide under the Jeep or in a pile of towels, I stood still and held my eyes open, like Pop. I showed my teeth and growled. *Grrrrrff.* The hair on my back raised as I protected Chennault and the flying tiger on his jacket from the giant gremlin.

"It's OK, boy," the general shouted above the noise. "Those whining engines will sputter to a stop. Hear that swishing sound? They're gradually slowing down. Once the door pops open, we'll see our flyboy emerge from the cockpit, like a butterfly from a cocoon."

Several airmen piled out of the plane. They swarmed around the opening of the plane. One of the last to leave the plane was a tall man, who was hugged by each of the waiting men.

He came up to us. "Hiya, Boss. Well, I declare, the world-famous Brigadier General Claire Lee Chennault of the infamous Flying Tigers is here to greet me." He raised his hand to his cap.

The general raised his hand, too, and they dropped their arms at the same time. The men reached over the Jeep's hood to shake hands. "Welcome to Kunming, Luke. This is Doreen, my secretary for personal correspondence."

"Nice to meet you, ma'am. I look forward to working with you." He took a step toward Doreen and they shook hands. Luke towered over both of them. "Nice flight jacket, sir—Flying Tigers. Will I get one of those?"

Chennault pointed to the plane. "Depends on what kind of job you do. And–what was that all that commotion around the plane?"

"Flying over the Hump, through those high Himalayan

passes... I've never seen anything like it. Wreckage on the mountainsides making a silver trail." Luke shrugged. "Well, our C-46 had a little engine trouble. Nothing that couldn't be remedied in the air. One engine out and the other on its last gasp. The Hump pilot was still wet behind the ears. Said to put on our parachutes and bail out."

He shook his head. "No way I was going to let a perfectly good aircraft go down. Didn't want to add to that path of steel at the base of the mountains. I shoved him out of the pilot's seat and got the engines going again. I swear, there must have been a gremlin on that plane."

I perked up my ears when I heard my name. Doreen and Chennault chuckled.

Luke said, "I gave him back the controls after clearing the last pass. I got lots of hugs when we landed, but I imagine his shorts were brown."

Chennault laughed. "Okay, Luke, you get a jacket. Maybe with a little decoration to go with it, like a Distinguished Flying Cross."

"Nah," Luke drawled. He pointed at me. "Say, who's this?"

Chennault leaned against the hood of the Jeep. His hand caressed my front paws hanging over his arm. "This is Gremlin, one of Joe Dash's pups. He was a little shook up by your fly-by, but he's all right now."

Luke rubbed the top of my head with two fingers. "Hi there, little guy." I crouched and peered up at him, trying to sniff his hand, but his fingers kept moving away from my nose. "Gremlin, huh?"

Chennault slapped Luke on the back. "He'll be fierce in

keeping those gremlins away from our planes. Can't get the parts for maintenance and repairs, so we've got Gremlin here for protection and prevention. You had a safe landing, so it looks like he's already gone to work."

I was learning what my name meant. My job was to keep gremlins away from the planes, but I didn't know what gremlins were. Or how to hunt them. Although I didn't like noisy airplanes, I'd have to get used to them to do my duty. Whatever gremlins were, they couldn't be as scary as the flying tiger on Chennault's chest.

Chapter 5: Will I Ever Find My Own Best Friend?

General Chennault's Dachshund Family
(L-R) Wench, Tom, The Gremlin, Joe Dash, Hedda
(WWII)

No flower can remain in blossom for a hundred days.

Lao Tzu

"You remember Joe Dash, don't you, Luke?" General Chennault signaled, and Pop sat in front of him, his ears cocked forward in the cool breeze blowing across the Kunming airfield.

"Proud of Joe Dash and his family," Chennault said. "Doreen and I brought them here for a photo shoot. Time to get a family portrait."

They put Mom, Pop, Tom, and Wench on the Jeep's hood with me. We touched noses and wagged our tails. Tex Hill,

Nurse Red, Andy, and few other people gathered around us, talking and laughing.

I was in the very middle of my family, next to Pop. My brother Tom and I sniffed the air, wrinkling our noses. Wench held her head up, looking at Red, who was dressed in a white uniform. Red called to her, making kissing noises. "Look over here, Wench. You're so cute, yes, you are. Hi, baby. Look at me."

I backed away since I didn't want Red to get too close to me. I remembered how her shot stung and my cries for Mom to make the hurt go away. Wench seemed to have forgotten about it.

Doreen stood next to Red making a snapping noise with her fingers. I crept forward to see how she did that. The ground looked so far away, I whimpered. My tail drooped.

"It's okay, Gremlin." Doreen's voice soothed me. "Be brave. It's just for a moment. Good boy, Tom."

"Attention, Joe," Chennault said. Pop stood motionless, looking at his human. I wanted to stand as tall as Pop but felt afraid of falling off the Jeep. I kept my head down.

Andy held a small black box like Doreen's camera—*click-click-click*. Since Pop and Mom stood still, I did, too, except my legs shook.

Doreen wrote down our names on a slip of paper. She showed it to me. "This will go on the back of the photo once it's developed: Wench, Tom, The Gremlin, Joe, Hedda. Born September seventh. Pups are two months, three days old. November tenth, nineteen forty-two."

Chennault cleared his throat and spoke louder than usual. "Doreen tells me these Flying Tiger puppies are too much to handle any more. Kind of like what the enemy says about our fighters." He chuckled with everyone else. "Some of them are going to new homes today."

He picked up my sister and took her over to Red. "Nurse Red, here's your pup, the little Wench."

"Oh, thank you, sir," Red said as she held my sister next to her face, smiling at the general. "We'll get along fine, Wench. Oh, you are so adorable." My sister licked her new best friend's face and hands. Maybe she thought Red's spots tasted good.

Chennault called out, "Ralph, thanks for all you do servicing our planes. This is The Gremlin. He's going to keep away any gremlins, so your crew can maintain our P-40s without any break-downs."

"Hey there, Gremlin, I need all the help I can get." Ralph stepped close to me, and I smelled something on his hands and clothes. I sneezed, backing away from him. My eyes stung. I rubbed my face with my paws, and then gnawed at my back leg to avoid him. I nearly made a puddle on the Jeep's hood but didn't want everyone to see I couldn't control myself.

I heard the general say, "Sit, Tom." When I looked up, my brother Tom was dancing on the edge of the Jeep's hood near Ralph. "Sit," Chennault said again, pointing a finger at Tom's nose. Tom sat, wagging his tail. Tom's eyes looked wider than ever as he stared at Ralph. He lifted his head and licked the air between them.

Chennault picked up Tom. "And, Ralph, this is Tom, your Flying Tiger pup." Ralph took my brother in his hands and held him under his chin. Tom licked Ralph's face, snorting and wiggling all over.

"Thanks a million, Sir, I'll take good care of him. Good boy, Tom." Ralph carried my brother away to a big building.

"That's it for now." Chennault motioned to the Jeep. "Let's head back to HQ."

Doreen held Mom and me. I missed being with Tom and Wench. My brother and sister went off with their new best friends. Would I ever see them again?

Doreen wiped raindrops from her cheeks, but it wasn't raining. She stroked Mom's head. "Hedda, I know this is sad for you, too, but your puppies will be happy with their new families."

Mom looked away and sighed. I snuggled next to her to let her know she wasn't alone. I wrinkled my face and twitched my whiskers as I lowered my muzzle onto my paws. I knew I could be loyal but didn't feel ready to be anyone's best friend. At the same time, I wondered if I would ever have a human friend of my very own.

~   ~   ~   ~   ~

Curled up with Mom in our basket behind Doreen's desk, I burrowed under our towels and sighed. My sister didn't fight me for my bones anymore. My brother didn't chew on my leg. Andy rocked me like his baby. I had Mom's attention all to myself. But sometimes I wished for my littermates to come back. Although Mom's warmth was comforting, I paused in my solitary play, letting out another big sigh—I didn't have a human friend of my own.

Doreen lifted the towels and scratched the back of my neck. "It'll be your turn for a family soon, Gremlin. General Chennault will find just the right person for you. You're a special one, you know. You have a big responsibility."

41

"Doreen," Chennault barked from his office. "Get Casey Vincent on the horn. He's in Karachi. And bring in Joe's pup."

Doreen cranked what she called the radio and I heard a crunchy sound, like when Mom ate her dog chow. She tried again and I heard a crackly-sounding man's voice.

"Chennault for Colonel Vincent." Doreen's voice was loud and commanding, like the times when I made a puddle or a pile in the wrong place. I wondered who had done something wrong.

"One moment, please. I'll patch you through to Chennault's phone," she yelled into the radio. Doreen picked me up in her warm, soft hands, but she didn't cuddle with me for long. She carried me into the general's office. "Colonel Vincent has been alerted by his office staff. It'll be a moment before he can get to the radio. Lots of static on the line."

"What's the hold up, did you say?" said Chennault, cupping his ear.

Doreen stood close to the general, handing me over. "Static. Delays. I'll patch it through to your telephone."

"Thanks, Doreen. Please shut the door. In the meantime, this pup and I have got some negotiating to do."

Doreen's heels tapped on the floor and I heard the door close with a click. Pop greeted me by licking the air between us and thumping his tail on the floor by the general's feet.

General Chennault held me in front of his chest, his eyes locking onto mine. I blinked and stared at the star on his shoulder. Something about his eyes drew me back to his steady gaze. But after a moment, I shut my eyes, as if accidently looking at the sun. I glanced at his star again then watched his mouth as he spoke.

"We need a good man for you, Gremlin. And I need more personnel in HQ. Someone who knows how to work with people, all kinds of people. Someone who's not afraid of authority and who can get things done. I have a feeling you need someone like that, too." He set me down on his lap.

He pointed his finger at my nose. I pulled my head back to see it better. "You've got a big job to do, guardian of the Flying Tigers, master of the gremlins. You've gotta make them all mind and stop their shenanigans. No more gremlins running amok. No more glitches with our engines. No more loose connections. And you need someone who understands just how critical your mission is."

Chennault stroked my ears. The telephone on his desk clanged and I jumped. He steadied me with his strong fingers. The lingering smoky smell on his hands tickled my nose.

"General Chennault? Casey Vincent here." He picked up something shaped like a black bone and held it next to his ear. I put my nose close to it. Did it smell like a bone? No luck.

I heard a faint voice in the hissing static.

"Vincent. You gotta speak up, man. I'm nearly deaf. Can hardly hear you." Chennault lit a match above my head. I hoped he wouldn't light a cigarette. I didn't want to interrupt their talk with my spit flying onto his desk. *WWrrmmff?* I whimpered.

He looked down at me and chuckled. "Okay, buddy." He blew out the match. "Not now."

"Sir?" the crackly voice said.

"Vincent, I hear you're holding your own in India with the Tenth Air Force."

"Right, sir. Just marking time here, waiting for orders to fly and fight with you in Kunming. Really want to get to China, sir."

Chennault leaned back in his chair and stroked my back. "Sounds like you're getting some flying in there."

"Yes, sir. An honor to be here, sir. Named a P-40 after my wife—Peggy One."

Chennault leaned forward over his desk, and his tummy pressed down on me. "Good name. She'll bring you luck." I shifted my position but didn't whimper because I wanted to hear what they'd talk about next. When he sat back in his chair, I sat up and shook my ears. *Flap, flap, flap.*

"I'm working on getting you out here to Kunming. We can sure use you. Say, I heard about your office work, too—highest ratings from General Brereton's inspection of camps. And a commendation on administrative duties from General Brady recently."

"Yes, sir. I have a good staff. Plus, West Point drilled it into me. But my position is shorthand for one big headache. I'd rather be flying my P-40 than a desk." Vincent grunted. "I belong in the air—itching to engage the enemy, sir."

"Vincent, as you know, the Japanese have sewn up Hong Kong, Shanghai, Nanking, and Peking. Since coastal shipping is locked out, and we're not getting what we need over the Hump, we're fighting a losing battle."

The radio crackled before Vincent's voice became clear. "Understood, sir. What can I do for you?"

Chennault fingered a cigarette, tapping one end on the table. "Vincent, we're on the same page—I need you here. Let's hope General Bissell agrees to reassign you immediately."

"Yes, sir. I need to see action. Not only for our country—

it's also personal. My friends were slaughtered ruthlessly by the Japanese—Pearl Harbor... Manila... Bataan Peninsula. I know I can make a difference."

Chennault said, "I'm with you there, son. Orders are coming. Over and out." Chennault set down his cigarette, leaned back in his chair, and held me up, staring into my eyes again. I nearly peed from being so high in the air, but I held it, feeling proud of myself.

"Looks like you'll be getting a family soon, Grem. Still need to find the right one for you, though."

He brought me under his chin, and I licked it, his stubble tickling my tongue. Did General Chennault really say I'd have my own human soon? A best friend? He pulled me down to his chest and I felt his heartbeat. Squirming and whining, I licked the space between his face and mine.

"Doreen," he called. "Time for Gremlin to take a walk to the bushes." How did he know me so well?

Chapter 6: Field Promotions

Clinton Dermott "Casey" Vincent
(WWII)

Sincerity and truth are the basis of every virtue.

Confucius

Someone dropped a duffle bag with a thump, startling me awake. I crawled to the edge of the basket under Doreen's desk and poked my nose out. Doreen glanced up and continued typing with a clatter. Mom lay nearby, sleeping. She didn't seem interested in meeting someone new. A man with dark hair, bright eyes and a big smile stood in front of Andy.

"Casey Vincent, reporting for duty," he said, handing papers to Andy. "General Bissell's orders are for me to serve as the executive officer for General Chennault."

"Welcome, Lieutenant Colonel Vincent." Andy glanced at him as he shuffled through the papers. "Our current exec, Colonel Scott, is still here, but we'll get you squared away. The Old Man is ready for you—this way."

Once Andy closed the door of the general's office, I heard Chennault shouting. "You're to be the operations officer, Vincent. Can't believe Bissell set you up as exec. I need you in Ops."

Vincent's voice was muffled. I hopped out of the basket and walked closer to the door to hear better. "The position doesn't mean a thing to me. Look, sir, I've studied your aerial tactics and practiced with my pursuit pilots. We're ready to go."

Chennault cleared his throat. "Looking over your record, I see you made major and were on your way to Pearl Harbor when it was attacked." Chennault coughed. "Promoted to lieutenant colonel somewhere between Australia and Burma. Impressive—you're just a youngster at twenty-seven."

"Right, sir. Though I didn't hear about making light colonel until I got to Karachi in mid-April." Vincent chuckled. "Must have been more of a promotion at sea rather than a field promotion."

Chennault took a sip of coffee. "Anything you need, let me know. Might not be able to get it, but you may as well ask."

I put my paws on the rim of our basket to take another look at Casey Vincent. Would he be my new friend? The colonel strode through the door and brushed past our basket so quickly the side of his boot nearly touched my nose. I fell backwards into the basket and decided to stay out of his way.

~ ~ ~ ~ ~

Over the next several days, Casey Vincent came into HQ many times. Since Doreen worked directly with the general, Vincent

47

always greeted her and Andy, but they didn't talk much. He didn't pay any attention to Mom or me.

He frowned more often and was as stern with Andy and the others as Doreen was with me about my behaviors inside and outside. Maybe we all had things to learn from each other, especially the right ways to do certain things.

One day, Vincent gave a stack of papers back to Andy, telling him, "You might not like it, but any and all official reports need to be done right." He turned toward Chennault's office and I followed him, careful to avoid his boots. I walked under the general's big desk to rub noses with Pop, then sat with him near the general's feet.

After closing the door, Vincent said in a loud voice, "General Chennault, this transition from the American Volunteer Group to the China Air Task Force has its challenges, as you know. Some personnel have stayed on. We've got new folks coming in and they're untrained in the processing documents and reporting to commanders."

Chennault nodded. "Not my strong suit. That's one reason you're here."

Vincent shook his head. "General, we need qualified people—right now. Meanwhile, my 35th Pursuit Group administrative staff are waiting in Karachi, already trained in proper procedures and military protocol. They were with me in Hamilton Field, before Pearl Harbor. I want them here to get this office mess straightened out."

"Who's your chief clerk? A good one's worth his weight in gold." Chennault rubbed his chin with his hand.

"Technical Sergeant George Haydon. Typing, filing, good at communications. Currently taking a course in shorthand.

He's been with me all along, providing effective administrative support. Started out as a private. I'm telling you, General, this administration will run smoother with better support here in HQ."

Chennault picked me up and pressed me to his chest, rubbing my back. I licked his chin, tasting cigarettes and coffee. Gagging, I licked my mouth and lips to get rid of the unpleasant flavors.

"Vincent, I'm convinced Bissell tapped into your Military Academy background to get this administrative staff in shape. Let's bring your group over and make our China Air Task Force more effective."

"Thank you, sir." Vincent closed his eyes for a moment. "As you recall, though, I came here to fight. I want to be in the air."

Chennault stroked my ears. "You'll get plenty of flight time, son. I know it's important to you. Just dig us out from under this bureaucracy." He put me on the floor next to Pop, who sniffed my face and chest and yawned loudly.

The general sat forward in his chair. "The War Department has said we can elevate four enlisted personnel to officer status. As per my recommendation, promote this Sergeant Haydon to second lieutenant, you hear? You can't have an enlisted man as your chief clerk."

"Understood, sir." Vincent pointed at Pop and me. "By the way, sir, what's the story with these dogs?"

I wagged my way to Casey Vincent as the general motioned to me. "Gremlin's the last of Hedda's litter of three. He's the runt, about two months old now. My dog, Joe Dash is the sire. Know anyone in your group who's good with hunting dogs?"

49

"Doxies are hunters? Never knew that." Vincent scratched his chin.. He didn't smile at me or bend down to let me sniff his hand the way some people did.

"Yeah, sure," the general drawled. "Up, Joe." Pop rolled to his feet and raised up on his haunches, standing as straight as an airman at attention—and held the pose until Chennault said, "Good dog. Down." Pop sat next to Chennault's feet. "See, short legs and all—they're strong. Bred for burrowing after badgers. Some of the men take Joe Dash out hunting with them. They'll fly to a remote spot and bring back all kinds of game. Cook's getting a reputation for whipping up some pretty good Southern meals from it."

Casey Vincent smiled at me. "Don't that beat all. Doxie hunters. Tell you what, General, I'll check around for someone who has a way with dogs once my people get over the Hump and settle in here. I'm sure they'll make headway in no time, although there's a lot to clean up."

~　　　~　　　~　　　~　　　~

People dashed in and out of HQ. I learned to recognize the sound of Casey Vincent's footsteps on the outside stairs, as he took two steps at a time—*tap-tap-tap*. When he strode into the office, I backed under Doreen's desk to stay out of his way. Andy and the other staff members sat up straighter and worked faster than they had done before, even if Vincent *tromp-tromped* directly into General Chennault's office.

Sometimes Vincent brought people in to meet the general. One man brought something with an unusual and enticing aroma. I followed Vincent and him into the general's office. As always, I kept my head up and wagged my tail to let everyone

50

know that I belonged everywhere in HQ. He smiled as he held the door open for me, then closed it once I was inside.

They saluted the general, who remained seated as he raised his hand to his head. I settled next to the general's feet. Casey Vincent spoke loudly. "General, this is Second Lieutenant Haydon, my chief clerk. Been with me, as I mentioned earlier, since Hamilton Field, almost two years now."

Chennault swiveled his chair. I moved back and forth to avoid the swaying of his legs, then sat by the side of the desk where I could see everyone.

The general said, "Well, young man, I hear you've been getting our old AVG records straightened out. Leading the administrative staff in Operations. Setting up procedures for HQ. Fine job, son. A credit to the China Air Task Force."

"Thank you, sir. Just following orders." George blushed.

"Well, a bit more than that." Chennault rubbed his chin. I heard a scratchy sound as his fingernails raked through the stubble on his chin and neck. "I understand there was a field promotion in it for you."

George chuckled and said, "Yes, sir. An honor I d-d-didn't—uh—expect so soon."

"Although unceremoniously," added Vincent. "As you recommended, sir, I told George he was out of uniform. You should have seen his expression—then I tossed him his butter bars. Couldn't have an enlisted man as my chief clerk in Ops, now, could I, George?"

"Can't b-b-believe I'm an—uh—officer now. Thank you, sir," George said. I heard him repeat some sounds when he talked.

The general reached for a cigarette. "At ease, Lieutenant. Cigarette?" He held out a little box to the men.

Both shook their heads, and George sat forward in his chair. "I'm still getting used to my new rank. Permission to speak freely, General?"

Chennault nodded, and George reached into his pocket. "I have something—uh—for you, sir." What was that irresistible aroma? My nose twitched. *Sniff-sniff.* George handed the little package across the desk to Chennault. I ran around to the general's side, my nails tapping on the wooden floor.

He let out a loud snort and laughed as he held up something that sparkled under the bright office lights. "Lordy, look at the size of that hook—well I declare. Whew—smells like it's been rattling around in a fishing tackle box for a while. Son, how in the world did you come by such a big fishing hook out here in southwestern China?"

"My d-d-dad sent me my tackle b-box when I was—uh—stationed in India. I think he overestimated my prospects for fishing when he included that—uh—hook for deep-sea fishing. D-D-Don't think I'll ever use it b-but thought you might get a chance."

I sat up. Why did George's fishing hook smell so good? And what was fishing?

"I'll find an opportunity to use it." Chennault set down the hook and extended his hand. "Thank you, son. Good to meet you."

Vincent said, "Thanks, Lieutenant. I'll see you back at Ops." They saluted again, and I followed George to the office door.

Chennault cleared his throat. "Oh, one more thing, son."

"Yes, sir?" George stopped, his hand on the door knob.

"Ever go hunting? Worked with a dog for retrieving?" The general lit a cigarette and puffed on it, breathing out a cloud of smoke that covered his desk. I backed away from the stench, bumping into George's leg. Somehow, I felt safe next to him.

George's shoulders relaxed. He smiled at me. "Whenever I have a chance, General. Good d-d-day."

Chennault nodded, and George closed the door softly behind us. I tested the air to see if he had any other treats, maybe something for a puppy. But—no luck.

I followed George toward the outside door but didn't leave when he opened it, just as I'd been taught. Doreen called to me, and I raced back to her.

"Did you find a new friend?" she cooed, scratching my neck and back. She put me back into the basket with Mom, but I was too excited to stay still, wiggling with joy at meeting someone new. Gradually, as Mom licked my face and neck, I closed my eyes, wondering about fish and why they smelled so good.

~　　　~　　　~　　　~　　　~

Doreen or Andy took Mom and me for walks every day. Sometimes I buried things and dug them up later. One day, when Mom stopped to make a puddle, I rushed to a certain bush where I'd hidden a treasure. I'd buried it a few days before. I wanted to dig it up.

"Gremlin, out of the mud. Let's go. I've got to get back."

I heard her but couldn't stop, dirt flying between my paws. Mom growled at me. I ignored her and shifted my behind to dig in a new direction.

"All right, mister." Doreen dragged me out from under the bush by the scruff of my neck. I wiggled out of her grip and ran under the bush again.

"Aww, shoot. Come on, Gremlin." She grabbed my hind legs. I turned my head and saw Mom next to Doreen, ready to pounce on me. I knew better than to fight them both and went limp, feeling my belly and legs slide along the soil as Doreen pulled me away by my hind legs.

"Now look at my shoes, you little pistol." Doreen straightened, scooped me up, and walked across the grass, placing me on the top step. "Stay," she commanded. I looked down—too far for me to jump. *Wwrrufff*—I wagged my tail and panted to Mom, hoping she would find my bone for me, but she was busy gnawing between her toes and licking her paws clean.

Doreen pulled leaves from her hair. "What on earth am I going to do about you?" She put one foot on the bottom step and pulled a white handkerchief out of her jacket pocket. Bending over, she dabbed at one shoe and then the other until her handkerchief matched the color of her shoes.

Doreen straightened with loud sigh. Her shoe slipped on the slippery step, and she started to fall toward me. I barked for help—*bbrrkkk*—*bbrrrrkkk*. Mom yipped and backed away. An airman came around the corner of the building and caught Doreen's arm, helping her regain her balance. "Are you okay?" he asked.

"Sure, thanks. Say, weren't you in HQ recently?" Doreen smoothed her clothes and sat on the top step with me.

"Right. I'm George Haydon, in Operations with Lieutenant Colonel Vincent." He lowered his hand toward Mom, and she smelled it and licked his fingers.

54

He knelt and put out his hand to me. I sniffed over and under and all around his hand. *Sniff-sniff.* His thumb was bigger than my paw. I remembered the huge hook he gave Chennault and wondered if he brought a treat for me.

"I'm Doreen, Chennault's personal correspondence secretary. Thank you, Lieutenant, for rescuing me. This one's been a handful lately." She pointed at me with her dirty handkerchief, dangling it in front of me. I bit it and held on, shaking my head until I pulled it away from her. "Give that back. Gremlin, do you hear me?"

It smelled so good, like dirt and worms and dead things. I growled at it—*grrrwwwf-ggggrrrr*—and twirled my head and body around in circles. The cloth caught on my puppy teeth. I shook my head and my back foot slipped on the step. My hind end followed. I scrambled to hold onto the edge of the step, back feet pumping the empty air, whining, *wwwhhhrrff*? A warm hand caught me.

George pulled the handkerchief out of my mouth and handed it to Doreen. "Let me take him for a b-b-bit. It's b-been awhile since I've taken a d-d-dog for a walk, and he's a handsome little guy." He held me against his warm chest, my muddy paws facing Doreen. I reached around to chew on one of his buttons.

Relaxing in his arms, I realized I hadn't made my puddle yet. Wriggling, I turned to face him and felt myself dribble as I slid all the way down the front of his shirt before he set me in the grass.

"Oh, I'm so sorry, sir. Gremlin hadn't done his business yet." Doreen's cheeks turned brighter.

Since I didn't have any more water left to make a puddle, I scampered back to the bush and dug for that bone.

"It'll dry," he said. "Tell you what, I'll b-b-bring this little guy in when he's d-done."

"That could be awhile, the way he's been acting."

"It's A-okay. I need to stretch my legs anyway," he said.

I stopped digging long enough to enough to see the airman smile. He had a big lump on his nose that looked as painful as Tom's paw when he had a sticker in it.

"Thanks, George. Come, Hedda. Heel." Mom hopped up the steps after Doreen, and I turned toward my bone, digging, sniffing, growling, and digging some more.

He kneeled on the grass and folded his long legs into a crisscross. "Go get 'em, tiger," he told me.

My paws hit something hard. As I dug around it, I moved my rear in a circle, springing up now and then with a *brrrkk-brrrkk*. Finally, I could see the white of the bone. The man reached over me to poke his fingers into the soil and out it popped. I snatched it in my mouth.

I heard him chuckle as he picked me up. He pulled out his handkerchief and wiped off my feet and belly. My teeth held the bone tightly as he stood up, but he pried it from my mouth and held it in his hand. A tasty-looking milky-white bone, smeared with dirt, a hole in the middle. My prize.

George sat on the bottom step and set me down on the grass. I pranced by his feet, looking up at him—and the bone—wagging my tail and begging with my eyes. His large lips curled into a smile and his light blue eyes twinkled. When he talked to me, I felt like he was the boss of my little world.

"You can have this after you finish your business." George held the bone in the air and pointed to the grass. I sniffed around, made my circles, and squatted to make a pile.

I shook all over, scratched the grass with each paw, and gave him my attention.

"Come," he said, lowering the bone. I ran toward him and nabbed it.

"Nice going, Gremlin. You follow directions well." He wrestled the bone from me and placed me near the bush. "Stay," he said, holding the bone up in the air.

A game? He walked back to the steps; I waited for him to lower the bone. When he did, I ran to taste it again. After a few more rounds of this game, I stopped to make a puddle.

"Good dog, Gremlin," George said. But he didn't say it like Red did, with a shot in her hand. I thought he really did mean that I was being good. He picked me up and took me into HQ. I held my prize in my mouth, sitting up against his chest and looking down at Doreen, for once.

"Thanks, Lieutenant." Doreen looked happy.

The man put me in the basket with Mom, saying, "Here you go, little fella." I put my bone down and sat on my bottom, trying to sit up the way Pop did, but I fell over. They laughed, and he rubbed my head and ears. I felt happy, too.

"D-D-Doreen, General Chennault wanted to see me. Glad I got here early."

"The general's expecting you. I'll let the Old Man know you're here. Please check in with Andy."

Andy moved his hand in the same way he invited me to go to him. "Over here, George. I'll get you set up."

I lay down and cradled my treat in my front paws. Nosing it carefully, I glanced up at him between nibbles and licks. Mom turned her head toward me, and I growled to keep her away from my treasure. She jumped out of the basket and walked with Doreen. I breathed in the perfume of my bone as I gnawed on it.

Andy and George shook hands and talked in low voices. Doreen shouted at the general, something about George and me. I chewed on my treasure, feeling it scrape against my teeth and tickle my gums and tongue.

George pointed toward the general's office with his thumb. "Say, Andy, what's this about calling Chennault the Old Man?"

"Yeah, Chennault cares about everyone who works for him—calls us his men. So, he doesn't mind our nickname for him. He's also called 'Old Leatherface' at times." Andy scratched his chin. "Colonel Vincent runs a tight ship, doesn't he? He sure is getting us in shape."

George nodded, shifting his weight from one foot to another in front of Andy's desk. "He's b-barely older than any of us coming up through the ranks. I've gone halfway around the world under his command, from—uh—San Francisco to China. He's one fine officer who d-deserves respect."

Andy raised his eyebrows. "The colonel's discipline will make us look good when the big brass come around. The China-Burma-India theater commanders always made a stink about the way Chennault ran the American Volunteer Group. Uniforms and saluting weren't a big deal for the AVG. They focused on operations, running missions, and saving lives."

George nodded. "It's a d-different thing with the China Air Task Force that brought us here. Whatever I can do to help you out, just ask." He stepped back. "Well, anything I should know about b-b-before I meet… the Old Man."

"Sure, just don't call him that directly. Use 'General Chennault.' Oh—and look at him directly when you talk. Speak up. Don't turn your head away. You probably figured out he's pretty deaf, so it helps him to read your lips."

Doreen stepped out of Chennault's office and signaled Andy with a nod of her head. "He's ready for you, George," Andy said.

George walked into Chennault's office without looking at me. I stood on my hind legs, my front paws on the lip of our basket, observing my new friend. My tail hung limp as I cocked my ears, turning my head from one side to the other, watching and waiting. Would I see him again? After all, he helped me dig up my bone and I would never forget that.

Chapter 7: A New Treat

George Arthur Haydon, Jr.
Santa Cruz, California (1941)

Be content with what you have; rejoice in the way things are.
When you realize there is nothing lacking,
The whole world belongs to you.

Lao Tzu

I heard the general laugh, a deep gravelly chuckle. "George, I see by the wet stripe on your shirt that you're getting to know Gremlin."

Andy closed the door, so I couldn't make out what they said anymore. After a while, I got tired of standing up and waiting. I burrowed under the blankets, dozing off and on with my prized bone between my paws.

After what seemed like forever, I heard the general growl through the door, "Doreen—it's time." She chuckled, patting her hands over my towels and saying, "Where in the world did you go, little dachshund? Burrowing your way to China?"

I popped up my head and shook off the towels. My ears perked up as Doreen smiled at me, her warm brown eyes crinkling at the corners. I wagged my tail against the side of the basket—*swish-swish-swish*.

Doreen picked me up by my middle. "Gotcha, you naughty little sweetheart." Holding me against her shoulder, she whispered into my ear, "You're in for a treat." My heart beat faster in my ears. A treat? Another bone? What a lucky day.

Mom licked kisses in the air for me as we walked past. I knew she was smiling, like Doreen. I licked Doreen's cheek, hoping for a clue about my treat. She wrinkled her nose. "Stop that, you little cutie pie."

General Chennault sat in his chair behind his desk and George perched on a smaller chair near the door. Doreen carried me into the office like a special package from the States. I wiggled and waggled my way toward George, hoping he had the treat Doreen promised me, but she held me tight.

"George, has temporary lodging on base been okay for you?" Chennault asked.

"Yes, sir. Not as d-d-dry and d-dusty as Karachi," George said. "An honor to serve Colonel Vincent, sir, wherever he goes."

"That's fine, son. Listen, I know you've taken the lead to get our administrative records in order. We need you here. In appreciation, I want you to meet your puppy, The Gremlin." He nodded at George and me.

Doreen passed me to the startled young man. His hand was as long as my whole body. He held me close, and I could hear his deep, slow heartbeat, much louder than Mom's. "What? General, D-D-Doreen—I never expected to get a puppy in China."

I licked his hands, front and back and between his fingers, noticing the back of his hand had speckles and short, golden hairs. He smiled, saying, "Well, hello again, Gremlin."

The biggest day ever for a dachshund puppy—George was my treat, my new best friend, my own family. I wriggled in his arms, creeping up to his collar and licking his chin three times to tell him I was happy.

"He'll be just fine with you." Doreen sat in the chair next to him. She leaned forward and held my chin in her hand. "Congratulations, Gremlin. You finally have your best friend."

"Thank you, sir, ma'am. I d-d-don't know what to say," George stammered. I tried to lick his nose, but he moved his face away and lowered me to his chest. I found the button I'd chewed on earlier and tugged at it with my teeth.

"Been waiting for the right man," Chennault said. "I've given Gremlin a special mission."

George had a puzzled look on his face. "General Chennault, if I may ask? How d-d-did Gremlin get his name? What's this—uh—mission?"

"Humor me here, my boy. Since there are times that even our chief mechanic Ralph can't find any reason why a plane breaks down, he says the gremlins did it. Doreen and I named him 'The Gremlin'—the commander of gremlins, to keep them out of our engines. I figure if this pup can keep gremlins away from the planes, we'll need fewer repairs, have more fighters in the air, accomplish more missions, save more lives. Good for morale. And, well, we need all the help we can get."

Chennault pointed at George. "And Gremlin needs a good man to raise him. That's where you come in. You're proving yourself, George. Both of you need more experience to help turn the war around." He cleared his throat and coughed, then took a sip of his coffee. "It's been a long day for this young man, Doreen. He'll bunk in Luke's barracks, and I'm sure he'll want to change his shirt. Have Andy get him settled in."

George held me tight and said, "Thank you, General Chennault. I'm—uh—honored, once again."

Chennault said to George, "I'll see you and Gremlin tomorrow in my office, first thing."

Before we left HQ, George held me out to say goodbye to Mom, and I gave her wet puppy kisses on her face. She nuzzled my neck and nudged me back to George.

Doreen attached my leash, saying, "You be good, my little friend." She gave George the leash and a stack of newspapers, saying, "For you-know-who in case of you-know-what. Oh, and a little present for tomorrow—he's outgrowing his old one. And this is for his..." She motioned to her neck as she pressed something into his hand. He looked at it, smiled, and put it in his pocket. As Doreen turned back to her typewriter, tiny trickles of raindrops streaked her cheeks.

Andy walked with us in the chilly evening. George tucked me inside his flight jacket, slipping me into a hidden pocket. I felt warm and cozy, like I belonged with him. As we got closer to a long building, George took me out of his pocket and held me against his chest. A huge tiger smiled at me from over the door, showing its teeth. It wasn't scary like the snarling mouths of the fighter planes.

"Home, sweet home." Andy opened the door. I shook my

The Tiger Den
Kunming, China (WWII)

head in the warm room. The windows and storage areas looked like Doreen's but the air smelled different. A big, black wood-burning stove, too, just like hers. Maybe this one wouldn't make me sneeze.

He led us past the stove into a huge room with bare walls and high ceilings. The space was filled with bunk beds and lockers. Instead of soft furniture to sit on, I saw wooden chairs and small tables with metal lamps scattered around the room.

No one else was in the quiet barracks. Andy pointed to a

bunk and large green bag on a wooden box. "I see your duffle bag and footlocker were delivered."

The last light of the sun peered through the screens on the windows where a few flies buzzed furiously. He set me down on the floor, and I wandered over to the stove. I sniffed one of the legs and squatted to make a puddle.

"Oh, no you don't, buddy." George dropped the newspapers onto the floor and put me over them, picking me up and rushing me outside. Once I piddled, he brought me back in.

"That's a stove," he said. "It's hot, Gremlin. Don't get burned. And don't pee on it. If you have to go, use the newspapers." He put me down next to the pile of papers. I sat down next to the stack and sniffed at it to tell him I understood.

Andy laughed. "Don't let him fool you. He just wants to see what he can get away with." He knocked on a narrow door near the stove. The door opened, and a man taller than George ducked through the doorway—my pilot friend, Luke Williamson.

I wiggled my whole body to greet him, remembering the day he flew onto base as a hero. Luke came into HQ to talk with Andy about meetings in different places around China and what they called flight plans for Luke to take the general on a trip. Sometimes he stopped to say hi to Doreen and give us an occasional treat. He was a good friend, but now I had my best friend.

"Hi there, Andy." Luke smiled at me. "Who's that with Gremlin?"

"This is George. China Air Task Force. He's in Ops. Chennault wants him to bunk here."

"Glad you made it, George. Since most of the AVG

shipped out, we've got plenty of space." Luke motioned to the large room with the with the empty bunks, pillows resting on the folded blankets.

They shook hands. "Good to meet you, Major," George said.

"Let's drop the ranks. At ease and all that," Luke shook his head.

Andy turned toward the door. "Well, I'll let you settle in. See you later, George. Luke." He kneeled to tickle me under my chin. "*Buenas tardes*, Gremlin."

"Thanks, Andy," George said.

Luke chuckled. "Got your choice of bunks and clothes lockers—for now. Expect we'll have more guys here once the other CATF squadrons move into Kunming." He pointed to his room. "I've got the only room on base with a door, such as it is. But I'll probably be the worst roommate you'll ever have."

"Thanks, Luke. I'm sure we'll get along just swell." George moved his duffle bag and foot locker to a bunk. "I'll take this one, closest to the stove. Gets chilly at night."

George moved a table, chair, and lamp next to his bunk, then picked me up and sat on the bunk, rubbing my back. "This is adequate. What d-d-do you d-do for the general?"

Luke sat in the metal chair next to George's bunk. "We go way back—decades. I'll spin some yarns for ya sometime. Anyway, he connived to get me out here. He's got meetings all over unoccupied China, and I'll be his personal pilot."

"Impressive. Hope you d-don't mind the puppy."

"I've known many of Chennault's black dachshunds over the years. He believes in them." Luke scratched his head.

"Something I don't quite go along with since I'm usually in the sky. But these dogs are damned important to him."

Luke rubbed my head and neck. I sniffed his hands for a treat, but he didn't have anything for me, so I put my head down with a sigh. "Anyway, I met Gremlin and the whole family when I first flew in. Mark my words, these dachshunds are good for morale. We'll turn things around here in Kunming and the entire CBI Theater. It'll take some doing, but Gremlin will help us get through the war."

"Yeah, looks like he'll—uh—come along all right. Frankly, I'm d-d-dumbstruck. A puppy in China? In wartime? That's something to write home about." George yawned. "Say, I'm gonna get a little chow and turn in. B-b-been a long day."

"Let's go." Luke put on his jacket.

We walked with Luke down gravel roads through parts of the base I hadn't seen before. When we got to a large building, George picked me up, saying, "Here's the mess hall, Gremlin—we call it *chow*. You'd better stay out from underfoot. People are interested in eating their chow and might not watch where they step."

Crowds of people sat at long tables, talking, and eating. George picked up a tray and stood in a line to get to the food steaming on the tables. I was glad to be perched in the crook of his arm instead of on the floor dodging everyone's feet.

"Extra helping of meat for my little pal, here, if you don't mind," he said to the server. "Do you happen to have a bowl for the pup? He'll need something until I can pick up a dog bowl for him."

"Sure thing, Lieutenant." He filled George's tray and handed him a small silver bowl. For me? I'd never had my own

67

chow bowl before, always having to share with my family. Although Tom nosed me out of his way, and Wench stood guard over the bowl when she took her turn, I would manage to push through and get my fill now and then. Starting that day, though, I had my own best friend and chow all to myself.

George set me on the bench beside him with my bowl of chow. He talked with other people at the table. When my tummy was full, I curled up on his lap. I awoke in the barracks on his bunk. I spun around until the itchy-feeling blanket felt softer, then I lay down with my head on my paws, watching him come and go in and out of the room. Finally, he got under the covers, turned out the light, and fell asleep.

I stretched and sniffed at his blankets. In the quiet of that night, I worried about what life would be like without my mother to guide me.

Mom and Doreen had always taken care of me. Now my job was to protect my own human and guard all the Flying Tigers against gremlins. Mom couldn't help me with my job. I didn't know how to live up to General Chennault's name for me. Didn't know what gremlins were—or what war was. Hoped I could be George's best friend but had no idea about how to do that. Or how to end the war.

During the night, I felt a chill and crawled up to George's head. He made snorting noises as he breathed in and out. Was that because of the bump on his nose?

I burrowed my way under the covers, and my cold nose hit George's shoulder. He sat up in bed, yelling, "*Yingle-yangle!* What is that?" I tumbled into his lap.

Luke burst out of his room and switched on the overhead light. George held me out at arm's length in his huge hands just as I lost control. My pee trickled into a little yellow puddle on the stiff, scratchy blanket.

"Oh, well," Luke laughed. "I guess you two will sort that out. George, you'll find clean towels and blankets in that locker by the door. Goodnight."

Chapter 8: My Good Morning Towel

Good Morning Towel
(WWII)

Choose a job you love, and you will
Never have to work a day in your life.

Lao Tzu

I woke up in the dark, covered by a scratchy blanket, not the
soft towels of the basket where my littermates and I used to
curl up with Mom. *Sniff-sniff.* I missed them. Crawling toward
a dim line of light, I poked out my nose, eyes and ears and
recognized the tall man smiling at me—George, my human,
my new best friend.

I stood and shook myself free from the blanket, blinking
in the bright lamp light. George stood with his hands over the
wood-burning stove. I ran to the end of the bunk, wagging my
whole body and whimpering, *hhhunn-hhhuhn-mmrrrff?*

George sat next to me and stroked my chin and neck with

his warm fingers as I tried to lick them. His smile told me I was his best friend. "Well, good morning, tiger. I was out like a light—after that little incident with your cold nose on my back. You must have conked out, too. Boy, we sure startled Luke, didn't we?" He chuckled, and I wagged my tail, barking in agreement—*aarrarkk-aarraarkk*—and jumped up to kiss his chin. I wanted to make his swollen nose better by licking it, but he pushed me away, saying, "Calm down, buddy. Not my nose. Hey, now—we've got to get to work."

George set me down on the bunk, but I wasn't finished showing him how happy I was. Scrambling next to him, I pawed at his leg, but he pushed me aside with his elbow. Crawling closer, I snuggled under his arm to chew on a button, thinking he'd like that. He picked me up and put me on the floor.

I sniffed at his big feet and nibbled on the white socks covering them. He pulled me away, and I let go, working my tongue in and out of my mouth to get rid of the little threads tickling my throat and gagging me—*ggghhffff*. I sneezed.

He pulled a little towel out of his pocket and took a deep breath. I stood up, breathless, my tail motionless, to see what he would do next. Would he sneeze like I did? He shook the towel, then held it up to his nose, making a loud honking noise. I sat down quickly, startled.

"Sorry there, little tiger." George patted my head. "Just having trouble clearing my sinuses first thing in the morning. Always good to have a handkerchief." He placed his used handkerchief with yesterday's clothes in his footlocker and took out a clean one, and putting it in his pocket along with a little white towel.

He opened the door of the stove and put in more wood.

As smoke escaped, I sneezed to clear the tickle from my mouth and nose. Mom used to wash my face for me, but since she wasn't there and I didn't have a handkerchief, I licked my nose.

George reached under the bunk and picked up his boots. He held them upside down, hitting the bottoms together, making a loud clapping noise. I shied backwards as he dropped them onto the floor.

He put one foot into a boot. "Sorry, Grem—just an old habit I acquired in Karachi to keep the bugs out of my shoes."

Was he telling me bugs attacked him? I knew my job was to protect him, so I growled at the long skinny things coming out of his boots. *Rrgggrrhh.* Did George need help scaring gremlins from his boots? Was he asking me to protect him? *Arrrggkkk?*

Maybe his boots were being attacked by gremlins—I pounced. If I could scare the gremlins away from George's feet, I could help all the Flying Tigers. I growled, biting and pulling on them with all my strength. I braced all four legs to get them away from his feet.

George laughed. I growled louder and pulled harder— *grrrhhggrr.*

George scooped me up in his arms. "Silly puppy. I know you want to play, Gremlin, but I've got to tighten my laces and get to work. Come on." One boot on and one boot off, my best friend carried me to the door and opened it. I looked out at the dark sky and a faint gleam of light in the distance. He sat on the edge of the covered porch and placed me on the cold ground. I shook my head and gave his laces one last sniff, then ran to the bush where I left my mark the night before. Turning

Betsy K. Haydon

around to find the right direction, I squatted to make a little puddle in the dirt.

Tempting scents floated in the cool morning air as the birds twittered in the brightening, cloudy sky. Sniffing and rambling around, I stepped back to the bush, squatted the way Mom did, and pooped. I checked my brown pile, turned around and kicked up the dirt around it with my hind legs. I began my first full day with George panting with joy. Running back to him, I held my head high as my tail wagged circles in the air.

He helped me onto the porch and I saw that both of his boots were on. The things he called laces were wrapped around his boots. Maybe they weren't gremlins after all. It looked like they had a job to do, too, keeping his boots on his feet. No wonder he laughed at me. I yawned to show I wasn't interested in them any longer, but if they ever acted up, I'd pounce on them again.

"Good boy," George said. "Ready to go to work?" I stamped my feet and turned around, hoping for a treat. He took off my collar and held something that smelled like his flight jacket.

"Gremlin, this is your new collar. A present from Doreen." I moved my head to smell it and bite my treat, but he put it over my muzzle and around my neck. I felt it tighten. No matter how low I tucked my chin or how fast I turned my head, I couldn't see it anymore. I shook my head and felt my collar roll around my neck. I liked to roll on our bunk, and maybe my collar liked to roll around my neck.

"Hmmm. It's a little big for you now, but you'll grow into it." My best friend attached the leash to my collar, shivering in

74

the morning sun with a *bbbrrrrr*. He put on his gloves, making his hands look even bigger.

"First, to chow. Let's get breakfast." I chewed on my leash, getting its smell and taste in my nose and mouth. Since it was mine, I wanted to be able to find it again, especially in the dark.

George patted the side of his leg, telling me, "Heel." I didn't know what that meant. Maybe it meant to hang onto my leash, so I tugged on it. My collar came off. He sat on the edge of the porch and took something out of his pocket. "Let's fix that. I'll got a tool on my pocket knife to take care of it." He punched a new hole in my collar. When he put it around my neck, it felt tighter.

"That's better. Heel," he said again. Did that mean I should look out for gremlins on our walk to chow? I walked on both sides of him, watching carefully.

He stopped, stepping over my leash. "Heel." I still didn't understand what he wanted, and practiced going from side to side more quickly, in case he wanted me to speed up. Whenever we stopped, he did a little dance with my leash.

"*Yingle-yangle*, tiger. You've got me so tangled up I almost lost my balance. No wonder Doreen had trouble with the three of you. Heel." He pulled up on my leash, my collar tight around my neck. I stopped and looked up at him.

"Good boy." He patted my side. "You heeled. Now—first to chow, then to work." I wagged my tail, happy to figure out that 'heel' meant I should stop and look at him.

He said, "Heel" and began walking. I stayed where I was. He tugged on my leash, and I went with him, still puzzled.

Along the way, people came up to George. He raised his hand to his eyes, and they did, too. Whenever someone asked about me, George told them my name. Some men knew me already. They knelt and petted me, saying, "Hello, Gremlin," "Have a good day at work, Gremlin," and "You're the mascot of the outfit."

When we got to the mess hall, George stooped to pick me up. A man carrying a flight jacket came out, and George stepped aside, saluting. It was Tex Hill, my friend. "At ease, Lieutenant. We're less formal around here. No need to salute everyone. Just watch for when General Bissell comes to the base. He's a stickler for saluting."

"Good to know, Colonel," George said, lowering his hand.

"Tex Hill. Call me Tex. I know Gremlin. And you are…?"

"George Haydon."

"I'll see ya around, George." He slung his flight jacket over his shoulder as he went down the steps.

Andy joined us in the brightly lit mess hall. "Good morning, George. I see you and Gremlin are getting along well." We walked toward a long table with a line of people standing near it, holding gray metal trays.

"Yes, he should come along fine. Say, Andy, I met Tex Hill—the Ace." George motioned with his thumb over his shoulder.

"Yeah—you'll meet some of the American Volunteer Group Aces on occasion. Just a handful stayed on when the AVG was disbanded. Tex has been here awhile. Let's talk about it over chow."

The large mess hall had more smells than I could breathe in, all interweaving and teasing me. Doreen had never taken me here. She ate with other women in a smaller place. I sniffed the air, enjoying the layers of scents tickling my nose

"Heya there. Good morning, Andy." A large man with a round face stood behind the table with delicious smells streaming from each pan. He wore white clothes and had a dish towel tucked into his belt, like the towels in our basket. "Hi, George. Got a little buddy there today?"

"Morning, Harry. This is my pup, Gremlin. Any scraps you—uh—have for him would be terrific, maybe a b-b-bone at d-dinnertime sometimes, if you can spare something."

"You got it. But just call me Cook. Gremlin, let me see what I can rustle up for you."

"Thanks, Cook. Eggs and toast sound good to me." George smiled as Cook ladled yummy-smelling food onto his shiny tray.

"Sure thing. Grab a mug for your coffee over there." Cook nodded his head toward the end of the table.

George crouched to set me down. I wiggled and turned to grab something off his tray, and his food spilled onto the floor. "Oh no, Gremlin," he said, as I gobbled up the treats that fell on the floor in front of me, all the juicy niblets.

"My crew will take care of that in no time, George. Here's a new tray." Cook shook his finger at me. "And, Gremlin, no more funny business in chow. Don't be a naughty puppy." I sat, not knowing what to do, sorry for my mess in the mess hall. But at least I didn't pee indoors.

"I'll get your coffee. You've got your hands full there." Andy pointed to a corner. "We've got a spot at that table over there. Plenty of room on the bench."

The men sat on a bench that looked like a hard bunk without blankets. They put their trays on a taller bunk they called a table. George told me to "sit" while he sat on my leash.

I slumped on the floor, my round tummy full of George's breakfast, smelling foods Mom and Doreen had never given me. Standing, I stepped away from the bench, wondering if more tasty treats would fall near me. When people walked by in their big boots, I tucked my tail and scurried back under the bench.

Cook came over with a small bowl. "Here you go, Gremlin. That is, if you're still hungry after that stunt." George picked me up and set me next to him, saying, "Appreciate it, Cook. I think he's got a bottomless pit for a stomach."

I sniffed at my bowl of treats and nibbled at it. Cook smiled, whistling as he headed back to work.

"Tex Hill?" George said to Andy. "Heard of him, of course. Fill me in on what I've missed."

Andy set down his fork onto his tray with a clink. "Shipped over with the original AVG group. You know, since the US hadn't entered the war, these guys and gals travelled from the States on ocean liners

"Ah, covert operations. D-Didn't know that b-b-bit."

I licked the last of my breakfast and looked up to see if anyone had something more to share with me. George pushed the tray toward the middle of the table. No luck there.

"Yeah. Secret stuff, until you're working with them. Most Aces left in disgust in July when General Bissell threatened them—either stay on with the China Air Task Force or go back to the States to be drafted as privates. Only Tex Hill and four other pilots stayed."

"Doesn't seem right." George took a sip of coffee. "I saw newsreels of the AVG when they made the headlines."

Andy nodded. "Chennault couldn't change Bissell's

mind, though. Tex said when the pilots left, it was the only time he saw Chennault shed a tear." They sipped their coffee in silence.

George picked me up and stroked my ears. I sniffed at his fingers. "We were stuck in Karachi for months. Heard some things about the transition here on the Fourth of July, from the AVG to the China Air Task Force, but didn't get the whole picture."

I sniffed around the edge of the table for scraps, even with a full stomach. George moved my nose away from the table and scratched under my chin. "The news we got was that Colonel Chennault of the Chinese Air Force became General Chennault under the US Army Air Corps. Good for him — about time for the Old Man to be recognized."

Andy set down his cup with a sigh. "I agree. Chennault's too valuable for his tactics to fight. Being deaf, too, it was too risky for him, but he'd still get up in the air to observe air raids and develop more effective air tactics against the enemy."

"All the more reason for his promotion." George rubbed my big ears.

Andy shifted in his seat. "And Tex Hill is one of the first Flying Tiger Aces, working his way to ten kills so far. Heard of the Salween River?"

"Yep, sure did. Big news, not a lot of details, though." George looked around the table. "Aagh — I didn't get a napkin. Be right back. Hold that thought." He swiveled his feet over the bench.

Andy pulled me toward him. He rocked me in his arms, humming to me and tickling my full belly. When George returned, Andy continued. "Salween River. Japanese were building a pontoon bridge, in a big push from Burma into China to cut off our supply lines. For four long days, Tex and just three other P-40 pilots swarmed them in that deep gorge, effectively stopping an invasion from the west."

George wiped out my little bowl. "My CATF commander, Casey Vincent joined them. Lots of action—can't imagine the nerve and skill. Not to mention the odds. Remarkable that our guys all came back."

"Pretty incredible. Tex deserved the Distinguished Flying Cross. In fact, they all did. A real morale booster after the attacks on Pearl Harbor and Rangoon." Andy picked up his coffee cup and tray. They dropped off the dishes and thanked Cook. "Keep the bowl," he told George.

Andy went to HQ, but George didn't go with him. We climbed the steps to the building next door that George called Operations, where I'd never been before. When he set me down inside the door, I pattered next to him, my nails clicking on the smooth floor. I dodged the feet of the people who rushed from desk to desk and in and out of doorways.

George sat at a desk and held me in his lap. "This is Ops, Gremlin—Operations. We do planning for the missions. Here's my desk. This is where I do my job. You'll hear me using this old Remington typewriter, see? I had to fix it up when I got here. The AVG used to throw it in the back of a Jeep whenever they had to relocate. But a little oil and it works fairly well. Watch how it works."

He rolled a piece of paper into the top of a black machine, punching the round things to make clicking, clacking, and clattering noises. When he pushed a shiny bar on the side, I heard a whirring sound and then a ding. I pushed back against his chest. I'd heard Doreen making these noises all my life, and at last George explained the mystery of the sounds to me.

He rolled his chair back and held me as he kneeled next to the bottom of the desk. "You get to use the bottom drawer, with this old towel for you curl up on. It's a little worn, but it has my scent, so you'll feel right at home. See, it

Remington Typewriter

says 'Good Morning' in English and Chinese. Looks like the words used to be bright red, a lucky color, but now it's been washed so much the lettering's faded. Of course, dogs don't see the color red. It might look gray to you, but, well, that doesn't matter, as long as you're comfortable."

He put my towel in the bottom of the drawer. He motioned to me, making a snapping noise with his fingers. I wanted to find out how he made that noise and nibbled at his fingertips, but he said, "No," and moved his hand into the drawer.

It took me a few tries, but I jumped up, balancing on my hind feet, my front feet on the side of the drawer. He scooped up my bottom and set me down inside the drawer, rumpling up the towel around me so it almost felt like our old basket. Then he sat in his chair and moved things around on his desk. I heard the familiar clacking, rattling, and ringing noises of typewriters, radios and telephones, just like in HQ. Over everything, I heard his voice. And I perked up my ears every time his chair rolled closer to me.

Whenever someone new came into Ops, George took me

81

out of my drawer and said my name. I got lots of rubs and pats from everyone, and they all smelled and looked different from one another.

Casey Vincent breezed into Ops and stopped to talk with George. I thumped my tail against the bottom of the drawer. "What's that noise? It's certainly not a typewriter."

George chuckled. "General Chennault gave me a—uh—puppy."

"He did mention something about that." Vincent peered over the desk at me. "You put him in a drawer?"

"Yes, sir. That'll keep him out of the way."

"Might be good for morale," Vincent said. "But don't let him distract you. We've got plenty to do. I hear you have another meeting with General Chennault today."

"Yes, sir," George said. "Something about getting this sore nose looked at."

"Good idea—about time we all got good medical care."

George nodded, and I moved my head up and down, too.

Vincent took a deep breath. "Well, carry on, George." He walked briskly out the door, and I heard his *tap-tap-tapping* down the stairs.

George lifted me out of the drawer and onto his lap. I could see the top of his desk and a telephone like General Chennault's that looked like a black bone with a leash.

"Gremlin, this is a telephone," he said. "You'll hear it ring sometimes, but I need you to keep quiet so I can hear who's talking on the horn, okay?" He held my muzzle closed. "This means quiet. *Shhhh.* Quiet, understand?" I tried to lick his fingers, but my mouth wouldn't open—*mmmmrrfff*?

After our mid-day meal, I lay in the bottom drawer of his

desk resting my eyes, with my Good Morning towel under me and my head on my paws. I heard George roll his chair away from his desk and popped my head up to check on him. He got up out of his chair and stepped away from the desk. I stood up and whined—*mmrrff-mmrrff*—and looked over the side of my drawer. It was an awfully long way down to the floor. But I couldn't lose him. I had to protect him from gremlins.

I bunched up my hind legs and jumped out of my drawer, sprawling onto the floor. *Oommfff.* I landed on my side but stood quickly to chase after him, through the maze of desks, equipment, tables, rolling chairs, and people's feet. I slid on the floor, my short legs crisscrossing one another—*mmrraarfff.* He turned, picked me up, and put me back in my drawer.

"Stay, Gremlin." His voice was commanding. Doreen talked to Mom that way. Mom didn't follow Doreen when she was told to stay. Finally, I had a human of my own, my best friend, and he didn't want me anymore. I put my head down and crawled under my towel until it covered most of my back. I hadn't done my job. But how would George survive the war without me?

I heard footsteps come closer. George's chair creaked. I heard his voice near my head. "I'm back, Gremlin. Good boy, you stayed." He uncovered me.

Good boy? I remembered how much it hurt when Red gave me a shot in my rump after she called me a good boy. I shrunk into a corner of my drawer, shivering against the cold metal.

"Hey, Buddy, don't be afraid," he cooed to me. "I won't leave you for long. Sometimes you can come with me. I just want you to get used to it here. See—peek-a-boo." He covered his face with his hands and… disappeared. Where did he go?

When he took his fingers away from his face, he reappeared. I wagged my tail and licked his fingers to tell him I missed him. Then he covered his face again and was gone. Would he come back? Yes, he did. Maybe he wanted me to learn that he might disappear but would always come back to me.

Chapter 9: The Acme of All Outfits

"The Tiger Den" Barracks, Kunming
(WWII)

If we live only in peaceful amusement without arousing us to work,
We will, until the end of our days, never make progress.

Chen Pai-Sha

Chennault sat behind his desk, the late morning sunlight streaming in from the window behind him. "Have a seat, airman." He motioned to a chair on the side of his huge desk, and George sat down, his back straight, sunlight bright on his face.

I noticed that when the general talked, everyone did what he said. I sat on the floor next to George's feet, my head up, sitting at attention like George, who wiped his brow with his handkerchief.

Chennault turned and pulled something like a sheet across the window, darkening the office like a raincloud.

"You've been doing a good job in the short time you've been here, son. Leading the staff to sort out that mess of reports and paperwork." Chennault shook his head and lit a cigarette, blowing the smoke toward the window. "Casey Vincent knew what he was doing when he brought you out from Karachi."

"Glad to hear it, sir." George's fingers trembled when he tucked his handkerchief into his pocket. "It's an honor to serve with you."

Chennault placed his cigarette in the ashtray. A long thin line of smoke stretched up to the ceiling and joined the hazy cloud above his head. "How's Joe's pup doing?" The smell of stale ashes drifted down to me and tickled my nose. I scratched at my muzzle with my paw and sneezed.

"Gremlin's d-d-doing swell, General." George smiled and nodded his head. "D-D-Doreen trained him to stay out from underfoot in the office. And he fits right in at the b-barracks."

"Good to hear. Ever think you'd make it to China?" Chennault took another puff and tapped his cigarette over the ashtray.

"Not in my wildest—uh—d-dreams. Glad to b-be here, sir. This is the acme of all outfits," George said.

Chennault called to me, "Here, Gremlin." I trotted around to the other side of the desk and he picked me up. "George, like your young pup here, I want you to grow in this China Air Task Force. We're going through a major transition here, just as China is. Another big change is coming down the pike. We'll step away from the Army Air Corps and become a new, numbered Army Air Force. The Fourteenth Air Force. I want you to play a role."

"Yes, sir," George sat up taller. I shook my head, feeling a tickle in my nostrils, and sneezed, my puppy spit landing on Chennault's hand.

"That's okay, tiger," the general said, wiping my slobber on his pants. "George, you'll set up for the upcoming banquet with your staff in Operations. Talk to Andy and Doreen in Headquarters. I want Ops and HQ to work together. We're inviting Chinese, both Nationalists and Communists. I want everything to go well. All right?"

"Yes, sir. Understood," said George, his face looked pale except for the dark bump on his nose. "How can I be of service?"

"Colonel Vincent will be the toastmaster, a big tradition at these banquets. And you'll give a toast. That's an order. Dismissed." Chennault set me down and I ran to my best friend.

"Sir, yes, sir." George stood and saluted. I danced around his feet, ready for a walk or a visit to Cook. He opened the door.

"Oh—George," Chennault called, tapping his nose. "Get an appointment with my physician—his name's Tom Gentry—to have your nose looked at today. Seems like a painful situation."

"Yes, sir. The medic in Karachi said I might have an infection. D-D-Deep in the—uh—sinuses. Couldn't treat it there, though. Seems to have gotten worse."

"We'll take care of you. Ask Andy to make arrangements. Dismissed."

"Thank you, sir." I followed George to Andy's desk, where they talked, ignoring me. Mom and Doreen weren't in HQ. I pawed at George's boot, but he didn't pay any attention to me. I attacked his laces—*ggggrrrrffff-rrrrrrrrrff*. I rolled on the floor. My front paws grabbed the toe of his boot while I pawed at it with my hind legs.

Andy talked with someone on the phone. He hung up and told George, "You've got an appointment with Dr. Gentry. We'll head out in ten minutes."

"Thanks, Andy. Guess I can't put it off any longer. General's orders." George called to me, "Easy there, tiger."

I growled and chewed on the laces again. Rolling onto my back, I looked up as a young man walked briskly into HQ and stopped at Andy's desk. Tugging on loops and strings. I recognized him as someone who held me when I was little.

"Hi, Andy," he said, extending his hand.

"Well, if it's not Charles Leong." Andy shook Charles' hand and slapped his shoulder. "Back from Chungking. It's been awhile." He turned to George. "Charles, meet George."

"Good to meet you, Lieutenant." Charles tilted his head back to meet my best friend's eyes, since George was much taller than Charles. His hair was straight and dark, and his smile was kind like Doreen's. He had a small nose, like the Chinese people on the airbase.

"Nice to meet you, Charles." George shook his hand. "Sorry, but—uh—you look awfully familiar. I just can't place you."

I wanted greet Charles, but one of my teeth got caught on the laces and I gagged.

"Yeah. Seems we met before." Charles shrugged his shoulders.

"Right... b-b-but I think we met a long time ago. Where're you from?" George disentangled my tooth from his bootlaces and picked me up. He scratched my tummy and rubbed his fingers through the short fur my chest. I drooled, waving my legs in the air.

"Central California," Charles said. "You've probably never heard of the place."

"Huh... that's where I'm from, too." George closed his eyes for a moment. When he opened them, he cocked his head to one side, the same way as Mom when she listened to Doreen. "Any chance you're from Watsonville?"

"Ha—Watsonville High School. I remember now—George Haydon. You were in the class behind me."

"Right—Charles Leong. You were in charge of our—uh—yearbook. Quite a good writer, too. What's your role here?"

"I'm Chennault's interpreter. Mostly public relations. How about you?"

"Operations. Administrative staff for Ops. Colonel Vincent just gave me a—um—field commission. Haven't even had time to pin it on yet."

"That's swell, George." Charles chuckled. "Hey, look at us now. Two boys from Watsonville meeting on the other side of the world. And this little guy sure has grown. When I left his eyes were barely open."

George stroked my forehead. I closed my eyes and sighed, relaxing against his chest.

Charles rubbed a finger along my side. "The Old Man must think highly of you to give you one of Joe and Hedda's puppies. Fine-looking little guy. How old is he now?"

"About two and half months, according to D-Doreen."

"*Nĭ hăo*, Gremlin." Charles wiggled his finger against my chest. "That's the Chinese for *hello*. I bet you'll understand both English and Chinese by the time we win the war. I'll show you two around sometime."

"Yeah? I'm itching to go fishing. Any—uh—place around here?" George asked.

Mom came into HQ with Doreen. I wiggled in George's arms and he let me down to greet her. Mom and I licked noses.

Doreen said, "Welcome back, Charles. How are you doing?"

"Good to be back." Charles shook her hand.

Andy jingled the keys to the Jeep in his hand. "Excuse me, folks, but I've gotta get George to the medic."

Charles pointed at George. "Sunday morning. Crack of dawn. I'll stop by to show you a good fishing hole. Bring Gremlin and whatever fishing gear you have."

"Okay, buddy. D-Doreen, any chance you could—uh—watch Gremlin while I'm out?"

"Sure thing. It looks like he's due for some time with Hedda anyway." She nodded her head toward us as Mom and I peeked out of our old basket.

I wanted to go with George but snuggled with Mom. Whenever I heard footsteps on the porch, I perked up my ears, jumped up, and wagged my tail, but George didn't come back. Disappointed, I lay down sighing. Did he forget about me? Would he ever come back?

When it got dark outside, Doreen took Mom and me outside. I raced around her feet, and Doreen turned around in circles, stepping in and out of our leashes, laughing all the way to her barracks, where she made tea and gave us treats from her plate.

The women's barracks was quiet and cozy, with the wood

stove keeping us warm. The winter wind found its way through the windows and curtains. Doreen bunked in one of the small, chilly rooms but spent most of her time on the couch by the stove with a blanket over her legs, resting her feet on a low table. Mom and I huddled in our basket on the thick rug under the table.

Doreen read a book and sipped her tea. When George finally knocked on the door and Doreen let him in, I wriggled in joy from my muzzle to my hind end, my tail whipping the air. He picked me up, ruffling the fur on my back. I arched my back, glad to feel his fingers again.

"Thanks for watching him, D-Doreen," he said.

"No problem, just like the old days. Hedda liked having her little one all to herself. Tea?" Doreen carried her teacup to the stove.

"Thanks. It's cold out." As sat on a chair, I kissed his chin. I reached for his nose, but he pulled me away. "Sure is quiet here compared to the Tiger Den. Where is everybody?"

"The other women transferred out when the American Volunteer Group left. Nurses stay near the hospital. I imagine more females will be working here soon, once the China Air Task Force is better established." She put water in the tea kettle and put it on the stove. "How did it go at Doc's?"

"Looks like I'll need some work d-d-done on my nose." George rubbed my muzzle gently from my brow to the tip of my nose and back.

"What's going on, if you don't mind me asking?" Doreen's eyes were filled with concern, like Mom's eyes when Wench bit me and I cried. She shook tea leaves into the teapot with little flowers painted on it. The kettle whistled, and

Doreen poured steaming water into the teapot. She put the teapot, cups, and treats on a tray and set it on the low table between the couch and chair.

"Thanks. That looks wonderful. Too bad I can't smell it." George frowned. "Doc says it's an abscess, a cyst in my nasal passages."

"Oh no—sounds painful. What does he need to do?" She poured tea and handed him a cup, taking hers to the couch. "Sorry, I can't offer you sugar or cream. War, you know."

"A short procedure to open it up and let it dry out. I'll be in the hospital a couple of days. Fairly straightforward, compared to what some of our fellows have to go through after combat injuries." As he spoke, I leaned toward to table, sniffing the treats.

"Any surgery is serious. Do they have anything to help with the pain?" Doreen sipped her tea.

"Doesn't sound like it, Doreen. All the anesthesia is needed for the wounded. This is elective surgery." He pulled me away from the table, and bit into something Doreen called a biscuit. I licked the crumbs that tumbled down the front of his shirt.

"I've haven't had a cookie in ages." George popped the rest in his mouth, without giving me any more crumbs. Why did she call it a biscuit and he called it a cookie? People were puzzling. Whatever it was called, I hoped for more.

"Sounds to me like surgery is necessary. For the record, I'd be concerned if I were your mum. Now, just let me know when you'll go to hospital and I'll take care of my little friend Gremlin, okay?"

"I'd appreciate it, D-Doreen. Thanks." George drank the

rest of his tea and put his cup on the tray. He set me down on the floor, and I licked Mom's face to say goodbye. She nuzzled my shoulder and stood next to Doreen.

"Good night, Gremlin. Bye, George." Doreen closed the door behind us. George put me inside his jacket and helped me snuggle into my pocket.

When we got to the bunkhouse, we found Luke sitting in a worn, overstuffed chair. He smelled smoky, like Chennault and the wood-burning stove. He closed his book and greeted us. George lifted his arm to salute.

Luke laughed. "No need to salute me here, buddy. At ease, or we'd be saluting all day and night."

"Hi, Luke." George set me down on our bunk and sat next to me. "Got a new chair?" George put me down, and I ran to Luke's chair, sniffing at the legs, fighting the urge to pee on them.

Luke laughed. "Something I dug up in Ralph's hangar. Lots of stuff in there. Furniture. Office machinery. Pots and pans. Old cases filled with God-knows-what. Stuff left behind by the AVG folks. Say, Old Man Chennault said you saw Doc Gentry. What's up?"

George went to his bunk and brought over his chair. "Got to have some work d-d-done on my nose. After the operation I'll be laid up for a couple d-days." He sat near the stove, warming his hands. I trotted over to him.

"I hear the hospital beds are much better than these old racks." Luke pointed to our bunk. "Too bad you'll have to go through surgery just to get a good night's sleep."

"D-D-Doc says we shouldn't wait, or it'll get worse." George tapped the side of his head. "Says he d-doesn't want the infection to spread to my—uh—b-b-brain."

"Sure." Luke placed his thumb between the pages of his book. "What about the pup?"

They sounded worried. I whimpered —*hhurrfff?*—and looked back and forth between them.

"D-D-Doreen offered to take care of him." George pointed to the book. "What are you reading?"

"*Kim*, by Kipling." Luke closed the book and showed us the cover with little flowers painted on it like Doreen's teapot. "I'll give it to you when I'm done."

"I've read everything by Kipling. In India I saw the places I'd pictured in my mind as a kid." George reached down to stroke my ears and chin. I let out a satisfied *hhhnnnnhh*.

"Thanks, Luke. It's hard to get anything decent to read out here. My *Reader's Digest* subscription hasn't come in yet." George rubbed his hands. "A b-bit cold out. Fire sure feels good."

He didn't sit up as straight as when we talked to the general. He stared at the stove, instead of looking at me. I pawed at his leg, but he didn't respond. I pawed harder and he picked me up. I nuzzled his hand, licking his fingers when he finally petted me.

Luke went into his room and came back holding something. I stood on George's lap to get a better look at it. A stick? A bone? Sniffing the air, I sneezed.

"Guess Gremlin hasn't seen a pipe before, huh?" Luke opened a small bag, pulling out little leaves like Doreen's tea. It smelled like something I would not want to eat. I sat back on George's lap as Luke pushed some of it into the big end of his pipe.

"What kind of pipe tobacco d-d-do you use?" George patted my side.

"Sir Walter Raleigh. Affordable. My brother sends it to

me from the States. Velvet's okay, too, though," said Luke, glancing up at George. "Ever tried a pipe?"

"I guess you could say my family is mostly church folks. Although... my Grandpa Sam and I would usher in the folks to church, then he'd ask if I wanted to d-d-drive his car. So, we'd go out d-driving, then b-be b-back at the end of the service to thank everyone for coming."

"Ha, that's a good one. I thought I'd heard it all." Luke put the small end of the pipe into his mouth, biting it the way I'd bite a stick, but I didn't think the pipe would taste as good as a stick. He took a tiny wooden stick from the box near the stove and dragged it across the side of the box, the way George did to make the room smoky. I backed into his belly, whining—*wwrrrmmm?*

"The trick is to get it going, puff on it, but don't inhale all the way. You want to try it?" Luke held out the pipe. I sneezed—*hhhrrrarrf.*

George shook his head. "Thanks, b-b-but another time. I tried chewing tobacco once and b-boy d-did I turn green. D-Don't think I'll make myself any more miserable than I have to. Anyway, I think I'll write a letter home."

Luke opened Kipling's *Kim* and puffed on his pipe, making little clouds around his head.

George put me down on the bunk and dragged the chair to his little table. He turned on the lamp and made scratching sounds for a long time with what he called his pen. Then he held up a thin white paper under the light. I sniffed at his markings. It didn't smell as interesting as the marks I made outside with my pee and poo, but then people weren't like puppies. He read to me softly.

Dear Folks,

Everything is okay here. Have a new job. More on that later.

I have a dog, a dachshund — they have named him "The Gremlin." A swell pooch. He's dark brown, chocolate with tan eyebrows, short haired, about ten weeks old. Perfectly formed. We've never had a doxie before, but I'm impressed with how quickly he learns. My new buddy, a bright little guy.

I opened my eyes and put my head up, sniffing at the white square he scratched on. I tried to chew the edge closest to me, but he pulled it away.

"Don't chew on the paper, tiger. I'm writing home about you. It's got a long way to go, back to the States." He scratched my back and I lay down again, watching him. He read aloud quietly.

Working on my third six-month stripe, my sixteenth month overseas. And sure appreciate those letters from you.

Thanks for agreeing to send out my camera. I'll be able to get some pictures of China for you. The cost of one here is about one hundred times its true worth, so can see no use in buying even a very cheap camera. Sure wish I'd had one in India. The Taj Mahal is all it's supposed to be, and a lot more. Really a marvelous place.

Good news about my promotion. Would appreciate your sending me a couple of officer's shirts. Make sure they have shoulder straps for my epaulets. I'm out of uniform.

I am naturally elated as I have waited quite a while. But it's still hard to realize people are talking to me when they say "Lieutenant."

Well, time to get some sleep, so had better sign off. Will have some tales to tell later. Keep writing. Love, George.

He caressed my throat and chest, letting out his breath in a long stream of air that I felt on my back. I tapped my tail against the bunk and exposed my belly.

George turned off his desk lamp and sat on the bunk with me. "Well, good night, Luke," he said.

"Just a minute, George. You know, when you read to Gremlin, your speech is quite fluent."

"Oh, is that right?" George scratched my back.

Luke cradled the bowl of his pipe in his hand. "Do you know why you stutter?"

George tilted his head up, like Mom did before she howled. He scratched under his chin. "When I was in first grade, I used my left hand to write. My teacher tied it b-b-behind my b-back to force me into using my right hand. I d-developed a stutter." I nudged his hand to pet me.

Luke asked, "Is there a cure?"

"Not really. But, when I was in high school, some kind

97

older folks at church took me into their vocal choir. We had soprano, alto, and tenor. They put me on the b-bass part because of my low voice. Instead of singing, we spoke the words in rhythms and changed the volume. It was rather musical, and I d-didn't stutter when we—uh—performed."

I licked his hand. He stroked my ears. "That helped me with my speech. I still get nervous sometimes in front of other people. I'm working on my fear of public speaking. Maybe Gremlin can help me. Glad you mentioned it. The old man says I'm giving a toast at the upcoming banquet."

"You'll be fine. Good night, now." Luke took his pipe into his room, followed by the swirl of smoke around his head.

After George got under his blankets, I crawled onto his chest. He stroked each paw as he spoke to me. "I trip over my words." He held up my chin. "Tell you what. I'll read you my letters and practice my toast with you. Then I won't stumble over my words. Okay? Deal? Shake?" He took my tiny paw in his huge hand and moved it up and down. "Just our secret. Okay, tiger?"

I licked his fingers and nuzzled his giant thumb, thinking about the general's order for George to give a toast. Sometimes he had toast and eggs for breakfast. Could I help George make toast for everybody? As he rubbed the top of my head, I heard the crackling of the fire and the whistling of the wind against the barracks window and fell asleep, dreaming of chow.

~   ~   ~   ~   ~

The next morning, George carried a stack of papers into Lieutenant Colonel Casey Vincent's office. They smelled like the newspapers he put on the floor in the barracks in case I peed inside. Why did Vincent need them?

First, George handed Vincent a little paper. "Welcome back from your mission, sir. Urgent news for you."

Vincent looked it over. "Well, I'll be," he said, scratching his chin. "Don't that beat all? I made full bird Colonel. Hot dog—send a cable to my wife Peggy for me, will ya?" Vincent scrawled a message and gave it to George.

"With pleasure, sir," replied George. "Oh, and sir? Tomorrow will be one year since we left the States." He put the newspapers on Vincent's desk. I watched carefully to see what he would do with them.

"A year? Yeah, that's right. I pinned on as a major just before we shipped out of San Francisco. Not bad, huh?" Vincent sorted through the sections and unfolded one with black squiggles that looked like people in squares. The thick smell of the ink made my nose twitch.

Vincent paused, leaning over his desk, holding the big papers with both hands. I held my breath when the rustling, crinkling, and wrinkling sounds stopped. He buried his head in the half-opened paper.

George shifted his weight slowly from one foot to the other. I did, too, waiting to be dismissed.

Vincent rolled his chair backwards and folded the paper with a loud rustling sound. "To top it off, I'm now Milton Caniff's latest World War Two cartoon action hero. I'm in *Terry and the Pirates*." He slid it across the desk. "Well, I'll be. She actually did it."

George picked it up. "What's this? Colonel Vince Casey?"

Vincent laughed. "My wife sent Milton Caniff a set of my military photos. Convinced him to make me a character in his syndicated cartoon strip. My mug is all over the newspapers now."

Later that day, George pinned Vincent's cartoon on the wall near the door where everyone coming into Ops could read it. Colonel Vincent had lots of visitors and phone calls that day. George kept busy sending them to his office, where Vincent thanked people and laughed with them.

One phone call changed Vincent's mood and the kinds of words he said. He called George into his office. "Close the door."

George shut the door and sat down, his pencil and tablet ready. I sat at attention, waiting.

Vincent took a long drag on his cigarette and blew the smoke across the desk, shrouding George in a cloud of smoke. "The word is that the old man will be promoted to major general when we transition to the Air Force."

George coughed, covering his mouth.

"Sorry. Old habit." Vincent took another draw and blew it toward the ceiling.

"That's fine, sir. Would you like me to take notes?"

"Not now." Vincent tapped the ashes into his ashtray. "Did you know Chennault's promotion is being held up?"

"I know there's a delay, but don't know why." George tucked his pencil into his shirt pocket.

"General Bissell is also up for promotion. You know they're always at loggerheads. The word is that General Stilwell wants Bissell to be promoted to Major General first, to maintain his seniority over Chennault." He tapped ashes into his ashtray and puffed again.

Colonel Vincent raised his voice, saying words I'd never heard before. I slunk under George's chair as Vincent continued. "Stilwell holds the key to priorities over what gets shipped into China over the Hump. Our Air Transport Command has a fine record of flying the air route with supplies, but it looks like they won't be able to meet our demand."

George sat up straighter. "What about the Lido Road Stillwell's building to replace the old Burma Road the Japanese destroyed?"

Vincent shook his head. "It'll take months. Meanwhile the Japanese have captured Burma and threaten our limited supply line. Stillwell's decided on a month-long march out of Burma with troops and civilians. Refused Chennault's offer of an airlift. He's so stuck on using ground forces, he refuses to see the value of modern air power."

Colonel Vincent pounded his fist on the desk. "If Chennault could get everything we need, we could smash the enemy and go home." He crushed the stub of his cigarette in the ashtray. "I'll be the first to climb into my fighter and knock them out of the sky. But we don't have enough of anything to make more than a dent in the Japanese war machine."

The stale stench of smoke wafted down to me. A heavy weight in my chest choked my ability to breathe. What was war? Why did it change people? I padded over to Colonel Vincent's feet and whimpered. Maybe he would feel happy again if he could pet me.

He put his head in his hands. "Dismissed."

Chapter 10: The Bamboo Net

George's Censored Letter to His Mother (1943)

Silence is a true friend who never betrays.

Confucius

After a busy morning, Charles and George sat on a bench at chow. Under their bench, my whiskers twitched as I sniffed the warm food Cook gave me. I recalled that General Chennault wanted George to give a toast. For breakfast he'd eaten eggs and toast. But I didn't see him give his toast to anyone. Why did the general want him to give his toast away?

Charles leaned back to look at me. He elbowed George. "What's Gremlin got there, George? Looks like the same as ours."

George set my bowl on the bench next to him. "Cook whomped up something special. Looks pretty good, actually." I sniffed at it, breathing in unusual scents and hesitating to take the first lick.

George coaxed me, "Go on, Gremlin. You're a growing pup. Gotta keep your strength up."

Charles said, turned back to the table. "How about that? I think my spoon can stand up on its own. Is it Soup? Stew? Chowder?"

"Must be Cook's spiced up version of Mongolian goulash. Looks like there's Spam in there."

"Oh, yeah," said Charles. "Looks like it didn't quite pass its physical but worked its way out to our theater of operations anyway."

George chuckled. "This tinned meat still needs basic training, but they passed it along so we could enjoy it. Good old Army meat. How do you like it, Gremlin?" He looked down at me again.

I moved my tongue over the meat and lapped up a little sip. Not too bad. I nibbled at a piece of Spam. My tummy rumbled. Ravenous, I gobbled up everything, swallowing whole bites without chewing. I licked the bowl, and it scooted ahead of me on the bench until it fell to the floor. I licked my lips, watching it roll away.

An airman in a flight suit walked by and kicked it so hard it ended up in the kitchen. "What in the blazes?"

George picked me up and stood. "Sorry, sir—Colonel Hill, sir."

"Oh—at ease, Lieutenant. I'll have to watch my step." The colonel smiled at me, and I licked the air between us. "Just stay out from underfoot, Gremlin, and we'll get along fine." He headed to Cook's table to get a tray.

George and Andy exchanged glances and got up with their trays. George tucked me under his arm and picked up my

104

bowl near the kitchen. "This pup likes your cooking," George told Cook. "Ate every bite. So did I. Say, Cook, if I'm ever going to have a family, I'm gonna make them some of that Hungarian goulash. Tuck a dishtowel into my belt like you do and whomp it up. Any tips?"

"Back home, I'd use ground chuck and a couple cans of tomato paste, then toss in whatever beans and leftover noodles or potatoes I'd have. Salt and pepper and you're about done. Nothing fancy, just a hearty meal."

"I'm gonna remember that," said George. "Just in case my wife is too tired to cook. Something to raise my kids on. Enough to feed an army of kids, in fact. I'd even do the dishes for her. Just gotta find the wife first. Right, Gremlin?" He rubbed his thumb along my snout and I closed my eyes.

Cook slapped him on the back and laughed. "Chief cook and bottle-washer, like me, huh? You do that, George."

"Not bad, Cook," Charles put his tray on the counter. "And I thought I'd tried everything. I've gotta hand it to you."

"Thanks, buddy. Hey, you two going back to work? Got a minute first?" Cook took all our trays and my bowl and put them in the sink, running hot water. He poured something over them and a white foamy thing grew. Was it a gremlin?

I growled at it—*gggrrfff-ggrrrrff*. Cook laughed. "So, you haven't seen soap suds, huh, Gremlin?" He scooped up a handful of the white foam and held it in front of me. I sniffed at it, blinking at the way it crinkled and popped.

George set me down on the slippery floor. Cook chuckled and put his hand in the sink. He made a circle out of his thumb and finger then blew through them. Something as round as the moon floated through the air. I jumped up and snapped at it.

The clear, wobbling circle burst as soon as it touched my nose. A little drop of water landed on my lips, and I shook my head and licked the fur on my chest to get rid of the taste—*ahhwwwkkk*.

"Your pup hasn't played with bubbles before, has he?" Cook made another floating ball—a bubble? I watched the next one more closely. Running and jumping to catch it, I heard a snapping sound and stood still, puzzled about where my toy went. A light mist settled on my face. We played this game over and over, everyone laughing, until I slid across a slick puddle on the floor and panted from exhaustion.

Unable to get up and stay on my feet, George picked me up. "Thanks, Cook. A new experience for Gremlin. I haven't laughed so hard in ages. See you later." He turned to Charles as we walked into the sunshine. "How about stretching our legs?"

"Yeah, sounds good. Gotta get back to HQ in an hour or so. But sure, I'll go with you. And I heard there might be a movie tonight."

"Those movies we get are kind of B-grade, but entertaining. I need to get to the airfield to see what Ralph needs, try to get it on the next shipment. Not that they'll send us much, but we may as well get the Gremlin and his brother together."

Once outside in the drizzling mist, George put me down on the chilly ground. I pulled on my leash, leading them past parked Jeeps and the barracks buildings that all looked the same but had different scents. "Tell me more about Chennault's warning net. I d-d-don't have the full picture."

"Sure. Air raid alerts—called *jin bao* here—become

second nature, so we don't always think about explaining the details to newcomers. What have you picked up so far?" Charles buttoned his flight jacket.

George cleared his throat. "The basics. Intelligence officers set up the plot maps in Ops once they hear of incoming planes. They use wall maps with pins and table maps with movable pieces. Our Kunming air base is in the center. We get warnings about incoming raids and send our fighters up to intercept."

"That's about it." Charles rubbed his hands together and blew on them. A huddle of officers walked past us, and they kept walking as everyone saluted.

George pulled me along when I stopped to sniff at a line of ants at the edge of field. I didn't want to taste them, though. Too many legs. I trotted in front of the men, avoiding puddles. "How do we get the intelligence reports about incoming aircraft in the first place?"

Charles used his hands as he talked. "We also call the early warning network the bamboo net. Local Chinese have field radios and phones in strategic locations. Chennault's set up a system for our friendlies to identify enemy aircraft and call it in to our base."

Feeling a tickle on my ear, I stopped to sit and scratch. Something tickled my gums, probably one of those ants. It bit my tongue—*yyywwwpp*—and it tasted terrible—*bblllekkkk*. I gagged, spit it, out and rubbed my lips with my front paw, afraid it might bite me all the way down to my tummy.

I lagged behind the men on the straight road to the airfield, rubbing my tongue against my teeth and slobbering to get rid of the taste. They didn't seem to notice my troubles.

"Our observers report the types of planes they spot and

107

their direction, speed, and altitude. I'm one of the Chinese interpreters, and I give the information to Andy and your team in Ops that monitors the movements on a plot map, the plots."

"Then what?" George turned to check on me. "Come on, Gremlin." I panted to keep up.

"Andy reports to General Chennault and notifies Ralph to get our planes off the ground. Our fighters scramble to the target area and hover above the enemy. They attack from above, before the Japs can drop their bombs."

"Rumor is that the Flying Tigers have saved hundreds of thousands of Chinese lives so far." We stopped as a roaring squadron of P-40s flew overhead and landed on the nearby runway.

When the noise faded, Charles motioned to his back with his thumb. "Are you familiar with the blood chit?"

Curtiss P-40 Pilot with Blood Chit on Jacket
(WWII)

"The insignia on the back of pilots' flight jackets? I don't read Chinese but understand it says to help our pilots back to the nearest American base."

"Our team did the translation. It's saved the lives of several pilots shot down behind enemy lines. It may take them weeks or months to get back, but friendly Chinese help them out."

"All right, Charles. That makes more sense now." George shifted my leash to his other hand when I leaned over to sniff at a cluster of bushes. "Chennault. A master tactician. Can't believe some of the top brass have a vendetta against him."

Charles shrugged. "I don't either. He rubs some folks the wrong way. He sure gets things done, though—even with outdated equipment and not enough of anything. In the long run, he'll prove his naysayers wrong. Just wait, George. He's going to turn the tide in our favor."

"Yeah," George said. "My boss Casey Vincent—same thing. A born leader."

We strolled toward the rounded Quonset hut where Tom and Ralph lived and worked. I smelled signs of my brother, sniffing the piles he must have left for me so that I could find him. I let out a *bbbrrkkk*. Could he hear me?

Tom called to me with his *yyyipp-yipppp*. George let go of my leash, and I ran to him. We touched noses and sniffed each other all over while the men talked. When we were puppies in Mom's basket, we all smelled the same. Now that Tom and I had humans of our own, we didn't drink Mom's milk anymore. Our humans gave us different foods to show us that they were our best friends. When I smelled Tom's behind, I checked to see if he ate Cook's Mongolian goulash or Spam. No, probably not.

109

My brother bit my leg, just as he had done when we were little. I growled and put my head down and my bottom up, wagging my tail to show him I was ready to play. He lay down and rolled over, showing me his neck. I pounced on him and we rolled over while the men laughed. After growling, tumbling, and scuffing around on the moist ground, I trotted back to George, and he picked up my leash.

Charles told George, "You know, Ralph's a musician."

George's eyes brightened. "What d-do you play?"

Ralph swept his arm toward the airfield. "At the moment, I'm tuning up new arrivals, more Curtiss P-40 Tomahawks, our shark-mouthed beauties. Back in the States, I played violin—concertmaster, tuning up the symphony. Do you play?"

"Put myself through college playing in d-d-dance b-bands. Saxophone," George said.

"Oh, a reed man, huh?"

I lay on my side panting. Tom's tongue hung out of his mouth. George reached down and scratched my head and ears. "Started out on clarinet. Took up d-d-double reeds on the advice of my college professor. Told me if I wanted steady musician's work to get into oboe, English horn, and b-b-bassoon—in fact, his name's Tom, too." My brother looked up when he heard his name.

Charles took a deep breath. "I remember now, George. You were always in the band room in high school. I played French horn—rather poorly, I'm afraid to say."

Ralph pointed at each of us. "You know each other?"

"Yeah." George grinned. "We go way back. Same hometown."

"Don't that beat all?" Ralph rubbed grease off his fingernails with a rag. "And you both end up here." He reached for Tom and rubbed him all over with his oil-stained hands. Tom shook with excitement, darting his tongue out to Ralph's fingers. "Every orchestra needs that oboe for tuning. But wouldn't you have a different embouchure for sax?"

George chuckled. "Right. I'd play a night at the Coconut Grove on the Santa Cruz b-boardwalk with a big band or sweet sixteen, you know, sax section, trombones, trumpets. Great tunes. Like Artie Shaw, the D-D-Dorsey brothers. Nothing in the world like a saxophone section going full b-bore, especially that deep bari-sax. Well, my oboe teacher in San Francisco could always tell—he'd say, 'George, you been playin' that darn saxophone again. Gonna ruin your embouchure.' But I couldn't stay away."

"Can't argue with that. Money pays the bills." Tom wiggled out of Ralph's grip and I squirmed out of George's hands as he said, "Go get 'im, tiger."

I rammed Tom in the chest. We fell over, nipping and yipping. I sat up when Charles laughed. "Okay, how about singers, George? Anyone you particularly like?"

"They're all pretty good, with a big band behind them," George said.

"Aww, come on, man. There's gotta be someone. You know, feminine, husky voice, captivating eyes?" Ralph teased.

"All right. Vera Lynn, that British singer. 'Dah-da-da-dee... Don't know where... Dah-da when...' Sometimes I hear her song 'We'll Meet Again' in my head." I stopped in my tracks. Tom pushed me over, but I shook him off, riveted. I'd never heard George talk that way.

Ralph turned to Charles. "George seems to be quite a singer." I hadn't heard that word before. Singer? When dogs howled—were we singing?

"Oh, yeah. I remember that about you." Charles ran his hand through his hair. "You never stammered when you sang. Maybe you should sing more, George—to Gremlin, that is. Your roommates might not like it too much."

Ralph laughed and patted George on the back. "Serenading a young lady might get you a girlfriend, my man. Anyone you've got your eye on?"

"Well, there was this nurse—Red—from the hospital." George blushed.

Tom nibbled at my rear leg. I didn't want to play anymore and growled at him. He ran away from me, then raced toward me, bowing with his tail whipping the air like a propeller. I barked at him to stop, but he jumped up and ran in circles around me, his big ears flopping and his short legs a blur of motion.

I heard a Jeep coming and barked a warning. Tom charged at me, then side-stepped away. George grabbed me by the scruff of the neck and held me around my tummy. Ralph lunged for Tom, but he danced away, tongue hanging out of his mouth while looking back at his best friend. He ran directly toward the oncoming Jeep. I barked louder, but I don't think Tom heard me above the roaring of the Jeep's motor and the whirring of the propellers of the P-40s under repair.

The Jeep screeched to a halt and sprayed gravel with a loud hissing sound. It stopped inches from Tom. Ralph scooped up my brother, who whined, *hhhnnfff-hhuuunff?*

Four men jumped from the Jeep. George stood in front of the driver, chin-to-chin. "Watch it, buddy. Why in blazes are you in such a screaming rush? Oh—Colonel Hill?"

"Air raid a hundred miles out. Bamboo net is down, just got word. Gotta get into the air, sonny." Tex Hill sprinted after the other pilots.

Ralph handed Tom to Charles and barked orders to his men. "Alert—repeat alert! Let's go, people. Ready the planes. On the double." The mechanics ran from plane to plane, helping the pilots climb into the cockpits. The P-40 engines sputtered to life in clouds of smoke. Propellers turned until they became blurs. Engines roared like tigers warning everyone in the skies over China.

Another Jeep filled with pilots drove up as Tex Hill took his plane to the airstrip, pointed its nose to the sky, and flew away. One after another the fighters took off. The sounds of their engines faded as they grew smaller.

When they had all taken off, Ralph came back and reached out for Tom. "Sorry, little buddy." He stroked his puppy's face with a red handkerchief. "You and I need to come an agreement to keep you safe around here. Right?"

Ralph put his hand under Tom's chin and bobbed his head up and down. "Yes, that's right. When Gremlin comes to play, you get distracted, but we've got to keep you safe. This is a war zone, you know."

George signaled Charles. "We better head back. Glad Tom's okay, Ralph. Close call."

"Sure was." Charles shook his head. "So, what are you doing this afternoon?"

"I've got to get a batch of letters censored." George shook

his head. "Some anxious families back home are going to want to hear from their airmen."

Back at Ops, George held me on his lap and showed me a stinky black stick. "Here's the pen I use to censor letters, Gremlin." He picked up two metal knives held together in a crisscross. "And these are scissors. Careful—they can pinch you."

My best friend picked up a letter from the basket and placed it in the middle of his desk. Using his finger, he scrolled down the writing on the papers. He blocked out some of the words and cut away parts of the paper. Then he put the letter back into the envelope and placed it into a different basket.

I heard the squadron of P-40s return before anyone else and announced their arrival with a whimper. George picked me up, and everyone crowded out the door to see the fighters dart between the clouds in the afternoon sky.

Casey Vincent came outside and looked through what he called field glasses. "Four, five," he counted. "There should be eight. Six… come on, boys, where are you?" He turned to George. "Get Ralph on the horn. Find out what shape they're in."

"Yes, sir." George stepped back into HQ and cranked up the radio. After a few minutes, he reported, "They're A-okay, sir. Confirmed—six so far. Luke is at the airfield debriefing them. I'll keep you posted."

George typed and moved papers around on his desk. The noises in Ops usually lulled me to sleep—the clacking of typewriters, and low voices of the men speaking on phones and radios—but I worried about Tom and the two fighters who hadn't come back.

After a long time, I heard the engines and whined—
hhhnnfff-hunnnfff. I led George to the door, barking. Others
followed us outside, saying, "I don't hear anything. Do you?"
Soon, the last two planes flew overhead, one with its engine
sputtering, smoke trailing behind.

"That's gotta be Tex Hill" Casey Vincent looked through
his field glasses. "I'm picking up Chennault and heading out
to the airfield. George, mind the fort."

George and I stood by the radio. A few minutes later it
hissed and crackled. "Ops—this is the airfield. Over."

George took a deep breath. "Roger, this is Ops. Go ahead.
Over."

"All pilots present and accounted for. Repeat, all pilots
present and okay. Over."

George sighed. "Roger that, airfield. Over and out." He
went back to his desk and filled the basket, then pulled the
letters out and stamped each one with a loud thump. Colonel
Vincent returned, accompanied by General Chennault.

"All right, men," Chennault shouted. "Just a nick in Tex
Hill's P-40, which Ralph's crew will take care of pronto." He
clapped his hands twice. "Everyone out at the airfield. Time
for a good old American game of baseball. Andy, get the bats
and equipment. What position do you play, George? We can
use a shortstop."

"That's me, sir. Be there in a minute. I need to stop by the
base post first." George put the leash on my collar and picked
up the stack of letters. We walked to another building where
he dropped off the letters, then hurried out to the airfield.
What was baseball?

Doreen sat on a chair near Ralph's Quonset hut and

115

reached out for me. "Come here, my little friend. Let me explain this game to you that the Americans are so passionate about."

"Thanks Doreen." George gave her my leash and ran to a group of men who motioned him over.

"Let's see. Two teams. The pitcher throws the baseball at the batter, see—the one holding the stick. If he hits the ball, he runs away. If he swings and misses, he gets strikes. Chennault is the umpire, telling everyone if it's a strike or a ball... Oh, dear, just watch and you'll see. They'll have all kinds of fun, even though they yell at each other."

Chennault (right) as Baseball Umpire (WWII)

I sat up and barked to cheer George on when he hit the ball. I pulled on my leash to run with him, but Doreen said, "Easy, Gremlin. Stay." By the end of the game, everyone seemed tired and happy, slapping each other on the back.

When George and I bedded down for the night, I put my chin on his shoulder and sighed, wanting to hear him sing again. I crawled from his chest to his chin and licked his cheek. When his eyes opened, I licked faster and wriggled, wagging my tail, but he pushed me away, mumbling, "Not now, Gremlin. Go to sleep."

116

I listened to the men in the barracks snoring and the stove popping and sizzling. My thoughts were as jumbled as Cook's Hungarian goulash. I couldn't stop thinking about puppies and people. When Tom and had our play-fight, he was nearly run over. When Tex Hill flew his mission, his plane was hit. Was a gremlin on his plane?

General Chennault told me my mission was to protect the Flying Tigers. But I was too busy playing to do my job. I didn't keep my brother from danger. How could I guard the Flying Tigers from gremlins if I just played around?

Feeling so bewildered I could howl, I gave George one more tiny lick on his hand with the tip of my tongue, curled up next to him, and fell asleep.

Chapter 11: Fishing

The wise man knows that it is better
To sit on the banks of a remote mountain stream
Than to be emperor of the whole world.

Zhuang Zhou

Early one morning, I woke to a click of the lamp and a bright light. George pulled something unusual from his foot locker — a metal box, which he placed next to me on the bunk. I stood up, all nose and ears. My whiskers twitched as I sniffed.

"It's Sunday. Remember, we're going fishing with Charles. Let's see. Tackle box..." His fingers pressed against the side of the box and the lid popped up—*clank*. I backed up in a hurry, falling onto my tail. *Arggrrr*? I whined, struggling to sit up. One of the men in the barracks hissed. *Shhhh*.

I smelled a delicious aroma, better than any treat from Cook. I stood up, tail wagging, and poked my nose toward the shiny things with colorful feathers in little compartments. George picked me up and put me at the foot of the bunk. "Don't put your nose in there, Gremlin. It might hurt. These are fishing flies, hooks and lures." I shook my head and trotted back to the box.

George closed the lid with a *clack* and put it in his duffel bag. He placed a pile of sticks and a basket on the bunk. I wasn't interested in the sticks, which he called a fishing pole, but when he opened the basket, a wonderful aroma seeped into my nostrils. I wanted to climb inside it, but he closed the lid before I could lift a paw. "My wicker creel. After we catch the fish, we'll put them in here." He strapped it onto his belt.

Fish? I still didn't know what that was, only that I couldn't get enough of how it smelled. The fur rose on the back of my neck.

George attached the leash to my collar and put me on the floor. He picked up his duffel bag and something shaped like a spoon but bigger, with shoelaces wrapped around one end.

"Like my net, Gremlin? Smells like fish, huh?" He held it close to my nose. I bit into the net, growling. Then I pounced on it, and he dropped it—*clinkty-clink*. The duffel bag with the tackle box inside fell with a muffled clatter.

Men in the barracks shouted, "Quiet," and someone threw a pillow at us. My paws slipped through the net. George untangled me. I danced to the door and back and grabbed the net in my teeth—*aaarrghhh*.

"Don't tear the net, Grem. We'll need it to bring the fish out of the water." He held onto the duffel bag and net and dragged me to the door. We clunked and clattered onto the porch to a chorus of *ssssshhhhh*! Once outside, he untangled the net from my teeth again and put it in his bag with a sigh.

Charles arrived, carrying a similar load. "*Nǐ hǎo*, Gremlin." He patted his duffel bag. "Morning, George. I've got a thermos of coffee and breakfast from Cook."

"Glad this worked out, Charles. I wouldn't know where to find a fishing hole." I panted to keep up with them, my long ears dangling alongside my neck.

"Once you've been there, you'll know your way around." Their voices seemed as quiet as the last stars in the early morning sky. We walked past HQ and Ops, as their boots crunched on the thick gravel covering the road. Charles pointed to a little building with a single light glowing in the dark. "Military Police. Two Marines. We need to stop at the base gate. Better pick up Gremlin. The MP dog is vicious."

George picked me up and put me inside his flight jacket. I burrowed into the snug pocket and peeked out.

A tall man in uniform came out of the building with a black dog, bigger than Mom and Pop put together. The dog had markings like my dachshund family, with tan eyebrows, chin and feet. Was that a gremlin? He looked like he could eat a Flying Tiger fighter plane. And me.

The dog charged at us, but the man held him back with a leash thicker than both my front paws. I shrunk into my pocket. How could I protect George against a dog growling and barking as loud as a P-40? Each of his teeth looked longer my paw.

Another Marine came out. He raised his hand to his eye.

121

"Morning. Identification, please. Where are you headed?" George and Charles returned the salute.

"Fishing, Sarge," Charles, handing him a small card. "Good fishing holes on the river just over there." He pointed to the sunrise.

Sarge shined a light onto the card and Charles' face. "Oh, right. Charles. Been on temporary duty somewhere?"

"I've had TDY in Chungking for a few months, Sarge. Translating for the Generalissimo's staff on behalf of Chennault."

"Good break, huh?" He handed the card back to Charles and put out his hand. George gave him the card. The light shone on his face and into my eyes. I whimpered.

"What in the Sam hill is that?" Sarge stepped back. Private Rex gave a terrifying growl and snapped his teeth.

My best friend pointed to the snarling dog. "Call off your d-d-dog, will you, Corporal? He's frightening my puppy. Gremlin hasn't d-d-done anything wrong. Can't you see he's scared?"

The Marine grabbed the beast by his collar. "Down, Private Rex. Sorry, Lieutenant. Didn't see any puppy. Rex must have thought it was a rat. Sit, Private Rex." He pushed down on the dog's hind end. "I'm Jimmy, by the way. This is Sergeant John Black, but we just call him Sarge."

Rex sat with his mouth open, drooling. Staring at me like he was hungry. Sarge gave George's card back to him.

"He's a private?" George turned his head to one side. I perked up my ears.

"Marine dogs start their duty with the rank of private." Jimmy nodded.

"Well, I never heard of that. Is this a D-D-Doberman?

Someone's pet from b-back home?" George shifted the duffel bag on his shoulder.

Jimmy patted Rex's side. "Doberman pinscher—that's right. Rex came from a Dobie club in the States. Jimmy trained with him in North Carolina. Camp LeJeune."

Sarge reached into the guard house and showed George and Charles a paper. "Here's a picture."

"Proudest day of my life when I got my dog." Jimmy rubbed Rex's huge head with both hands. George could hold me in one hand. The dog stood still and quiet, leaning into him. Sunlight poured over the hills, and we saw Rex's eyes close as Jimmy patted him.

Camp LeJeune U.S. Marines War Dog Detachment (WWII)

George held me firmly in both hands and placed me next to his chest. "Well, this is Gremlin, one of Joe Dash's pups." I sat up straighter in his arms when I heard my name. "Not quite three months old. Not even a mouthful for Private Rex. So, don't get any ideas, buddy."

Sarge laughed. "Quite a difference between them. Rex could eat your pup for breakfast. We'll keep 'em apart for now. See if they get along when Gremlin's a bit bigger. You're all clear. Catch a few for us, huh?"

George and Charles put their hands up again. I put one

paw up to scratch above my eyes. The MPs saluted us, then smiled.

"Aww, look, Rex. Gremlin's saluting us." Jimmy kissed the top of Rex's head.

"Yeah, did you see that? Never saw the like before." Sarge smiled. "Heh, something new to write home about. Finally." Rex barked as a convoy of trucks and Jeeps stopped at the gate.

~   ~   ~   ~   ~

Soon we were far away from the rumble of the planes and vehicles. George whistled into the cool morning air as we hiked into the countryside.

"I haven't been fishing in ages," said Charles. "I've got a special spot where I had some luck last spring. We take this old dirt road."

"How'd you find it?" George tripped on a tree root and caught his balance.

"A buddy of mine showed me around before he left for the States. R. T. Smith. One of the original pilots in the American Volunteer Group. Took me under his wing. Great fisherman, as well as an Ace, eight kills. Nine depending on who you talk to." He pointed to a narrower road. "Here's the trail to the River."

George took my leash off, saying, "Stay with me, Grem." I sniffed every new scent I found along our path, but always looked for him so I could protect him in case of gremlins. I wouldn't know what a gremlin looked like, but I was on guard, just in case.

I stopped when I heard a rustling sound in the grass. *Brrrkkk?* Something slithered. I pointed at it with my front paw. What was it? *Sniff-sniff.* No scent. It kept gliding along, without legs. *Brrrkkk?*

George pulled me away by the scruff of my neck. "Good boy, Gremlin. That's a snake, buddy. Could be poisonous."

"That's right, Gremlin," said Charles, pointing at it. "Better to stay away, but good job alerting us to a danger." I licked their fingers when they petted me, feeling glad that I could do the right thing to protect them, at least from snakes.

The sun warmed us on the climb up a hill. Charles stopped. George and I caught up with him. A long green snake shimmered in the morning light. *Brrrkkk?* A snake? A really big snake? Puzzled, I blinked my eyes, shook my head, sat down and scratched my neck, jingling my collar.

"Ah," said George, breathing in deeply. I lifted my nose, filling my nostrils with delicious, wet smells. *Brrrkk-brrkkkk.* I pranced around him, anxious to explore. Charles headed down the steep riverbank, half-walking and half-sliding. George picked me up, and we slid down the moist trail. Somehow, he balanced me and his duffel bag against his hip, running a few steps at the bottom of the hill.

"Here we are," Charles announced, setting down his gear. "Let's give this spot a try. The river changes over the seasons with different water flows. There are promising rocks and holes upstream under the trees."

The water smelled luscious and rich with all kinds of scents. The ground felt squishy between my tender toes. I lifted each paw one at a time to shake off sticky, tiny rocks. I licked my front paws, then spit out tiny grains of something that caught on my tongue. *Aawwkkkk.*

"Gremlin's first encounter with sand." George and Charles laughed and patted the backsides of their pants to brush off the sand.

Arrchooo... ggwwrrff. I sneezed sand out of my nose and mouth.

George took his gear out of the duffel bag and put the sticks together. "Just got a new spinning reel for my pole from my Dad. Let's try it out." He put string on the pole and unlatched his metal tackle box, laughing when he swung up the lid.

Charles looked up. "What is it?"

"My father sent me these hooks after I wrote him a letter that I'd heard the fishing is pretty good here. He sent me this." He held up something shiny.

Charles chuckled. "That's a big hook. We don't have fish that size here."

"He included another, bigger than this one. I gave it to General Chennault. He tells me he's actually had a few chances to use it, that it comes in handy." He put the hook back in the box and picked up a smaller one. "This one looks more like the right size for today."

"That's it," nodded Charles. "We'll need to find some worms."

I trotted over to George and leaned forward to see what he was doing. He elbowed me away. "Sit, Grem. I'm tying this hook onto the line of my fishing pole. Not for a puppy." The tone of his voice warned me I shouldn't get closer.

He used his hands to dig into the soft, moist sand on the river's edge. I tested the sand with one paw. Then two paws, alternating slowly. Faster, back and forth, digging. Crumbles of dirt and sand landed on my muzzle. I shook my head, ears flopping. Coughed and sneezed and barked, tasting flavors unlike anything I'd known. I dug deeper, yipping until so much sand ended up under my belly that I fell over.

126

I climbed on top of my little hill and used my hind legs to scoot it away from the hole. Dig, scrape, push. Dig, scrape, push. I dug faster. Small black bugs and long, squirmy, stringy things flew out of China's fragrant soil. What else was in there?

I heard George's laugh, a hearty, relaxed chuckle. I sat on my haunches, wheezing and panting so hard my tongue fell out of my mouth almost down to my chest. He smiled at me, blue eyes twinkling, with the sunny sky above us. He held a handful of skinny, squirmy things. I sniffed them.

"Good boy, Gremlin," he said, stroking the dirt off my chest and legs. "You found some beautiful worms—nightcrawlers. Hey, Charles, here's our bait." Worms? They wanted worms?

"Thank you, Gremlin. I won't forget this," Charles picked up a few.

George petted my head. "Good boy. Good dog."

I eased my nose closer to George as I watched him thread a worm onto his hook, but he pushed me back with his elbow. "Not too close—this is sharp. Find more worms. Dig, Gremlin. Dig."

He took his gear onto a large, flat stone at the edge of the river. He threw his arm back as he held the pole, and I watched the worm fly back and forth in the air. Toward the river, and away from the river. The reel made a singing sound as the worm flew high in the air. The hook and bait landed into the water with a loud plop.

George moved the pole slowly up and down, side to side. He sat on the edge of the rock, dangling his feet and gazing around the river. "Ah, nothing like dropping a line in the water."

Since George called me a good boy, I returned to the shore and made a hole big enough for my head and shoulders. I took my head out to breathe, then burrowed even deeper. I made the opening bigger, whimpering with delight. My tail waved in every direction.

George shouted, "I got one! A big one, Charles. Hope my reel holds." The tip of the rod bent toward the water. He cranked the handle around on his spinning reel.

"Hold on, George. I'll get your net." Charles ran across the rock to George. I sprinted to him as fast as I could. *Bbrrkk—bbrrkk—bbrrkk.*

Something on the line swam back and forth in the river. Maybe it was what he called a fish. Or was it a gremlin? I perked my ears up and snorted the dirt out of my nostrils to smell better. I watched the line, the fish, and my hero and snorted again. *Wwwwffft.*

The tip of the pole went underwater as the fish came closer. George kneeled on the rock, and Charles picked up the net and captured a shiny, wriggling, silvery fish just about my size.

Charles smiled. "Catfish. Good sized one. First catch of the day."

It looked wet and shimmery, smooth and slippery. I couldn't tell if its eyes were looking at me, or not, but its smell was heavenly. I got closer for a better whiff.

"What a beauty—Cook'll make a purty good meal out of this one," he said. "But not for you, Gremlin. Too many bones."

Brrkk-brrrrkk. I watched the fish flop around, its mouth opening and closing. George put his thumb and finger into the fish's mouth. I darted toward the fish, opening my jaws to grab the thing before it could hurt George. Biting into its tail, I braced my back legs and pulled.

"Ow!" George yelped like Tom when he got a sticker in his paw.

Grrrrr. That dangerous fish bit George. I pulled on it to protect my best friend.

"Stop it, Gremlin! Let go of the fish." He held onto it, while I pulled on the tail, my teeth scraping against the slimy scales until the tail slipped out from between my teeth. I fell onto my bottom. The fish fell with a plop into the water.

Brrkk—bbrrkk—bbrrkk. I scolded the fish for hurting George.

"I've got it." Charles knelt and netted the fish again. He pulled out the hook and tossed the fish into George's creel. "Is your finger okay?"

"Sure, it's fine. Gotta keep Gremlin away from the fish." He threaded another worm onto his hook and pointed to the shore. "Gremlin—find more worms. Dig, Gremlin, dig."

I scampered to the shore and dug with renewed effort, pouncing on the beach as I would a good bone. I wriggled into my hole in the sand, like a comforting hug all around my body, almost as if I were back in the basket with Mom, Wench, and Tom.

All morning, Charles and George fished along the river. I dug for worms wherever they went. When the sun was high in the sky, Charles gave George breakfast. George passed me bits of ham and eggs. He poured steaming hot, black liquid into metal cups. I smelled it and turned away, wading into the river until it was up to my belly. I lapped up the fishy-tasting river water.

129

"*Mmmm.* Coffee. Glad you don't like it, Gremlin. More for us." The men held their cups, breathing in the strong aroma. They sipped it, closing their eyes as they rested on the beach.

I wandered around the beach and spied a long line of little black bugs crawling toward George's plate. Ants? I wandered over to the plate and licked it. Yummy left-overs coated my mouth—until I felt a prickle on the tip of my tongue, then searing pain on my lips. *Yyiipppp—arrrrggwww!* The awful taste of ants filled my mouth. I couldn't spit out George's breakfast fast enough.

"What is it, Grem?" George pulled me away from the plate and brushed his fingers around my mouth. He shook off the ants and put me on his lap, stroking my chin and neck. "When I was in India, I saw people sweeping pathways with brooms."

"Who were they?" Charles picked up the plates and crouched on a rock, swirling sand in the plates and rinsing them in the river.

"Jains. An ancient religion. They protect insects, like these ants, by moving them out of harm's way."

"Well, Gremlin. Live and learn, huh?" Charles stroked my ears. "Now that you know about Jainism, you'll be more careful around ants."

George put down his net and fishing pole and pulled the fish out of his basket. He laid out several fish, most of them bigger than me, on the rock. *Mmmm.* Before today, I'd never smelled freshly caught fish before and oh—they smelled good.

I crept toward him slowly and sat next to him, but not right next to him. I knew he'd elbow me away again if I got too close. But I leaned my head forward as far as I could, smelling the fish, until I was lying down with my nose near his knee.

George dug a hole. He and Charles took out knives and cut off the fish's heads, then dropped them into the hole. They cut open their bellies and pulled out white, stringy guts with dark blood and threw them in with the heads and covered it all with sand.

I followed George to the rock. He held each fish by the tail and swished it in the river, then put them back into his basket and closed the lid. He splashed his hands in the water and washed the blood off his knife. Ah, the wonderful smells of dead fish guts. Maybe George meant to come back for them, the way I dug up my buried bones. George washed his hands, and I thought that I should wash myself, too.

I uncovered our treasure and put my nose into the leftover fish heads and guts. I took long sniffs of their tangy aroma. Unable to resist a strong urge, I pushed off with my short stubby legs, bent my neck and put my shoulders into the gooey mess. Soon my back was coated with slimy blood and guts as I wiggled and wrestled with them. Once I started, I just couldn't seem to get enough of these fishy smells.

Uh oh! George returned and stood high over me with wide eyes. I thought he'd be pleased that I found a way to clean myself. He laughed and called me a naughty puppy. He picked me up by the scruff of my neck the way Mom used to carry me when I was little. Putting one hand under my belly, he held me far away from his face and carried me to back to the rock.

"No, boy. You stink." His hands held me tight as he dipped me in the cold water of the river to scrub off my wonderful perfume. He moved me back and forth in the river water like I was a fish. He inhaled quickly and said a word that

I thought I'd remember for the rest of my life: "*Pee-uuu*—it's time for you to have a BA-A-A-TH."

I didn't really like having the cold water on my fur and dog-paddled in the river. I didn't like that BA-A-A-TH. I'd much rather roll in fish guts again. After he pulled me out and set me down, I shook off the waterdrops and ran toward the fish guts to get warm again. George whistled for me and shouted, "No, Gremlin, come on, be a good boy."

He and Charles packed up their fishing gear in the warm sunshine and walked up the hill. I didn't want to be left behind at the river. I wanted to be called a good dog. Sniffing the fishy air one more time, I trotted along beside George, heading back to the airbase.

I promised myself I would roll in whatever smelly stuff I found whenever I got a chance, just as easily as George washed his hands.

He dropped off his duffel bag in the barracks before heading to chow. On his bunk was a book with a note. "Gremlin, Luke left us *Rikki Tikki Tavi* by Kipling. Hopes I'll read it to you to help me talk. Good idea. We'll get started tonight."

We dropped off the fish for Cook, who gave me the biggest bone ever. After a warm, soapy BA-A-A-TH, George put me on the foot of his bunk and lay down to write a letter home. I chewed on my bone. Gradually, I crept up to his tummy, dragging my treat with me.

He laughed and read to me.

> Dear Folks,
>   Today's Sunday, a good day for

> fishing. Took Gremlin. He needed a bath
> after getting into the fish guts.
>
> He's on my bunk wrestling with a
> bone that's bigger than he is. That's why
> my handwriting is shaky, hard to read.
>
> I found an embroidered scene of people
> fishing at the base store. The scenery here is
> so different I want to remember it. I wish I
> was the one in the boat.

My best friend chuckled as he got up and crumpled a
newspaper. He opened the stove and tossed it in with a few
pieces of firewood. I sneezed when the smoke hit my nose. He
sat and wrote some more, reading to me.

> In this job I have now I meet all the
> "big-shots." Rank doesn't awe me
> anymore—consequentially I'm never ill at
> ease. In fact—I think I've grown up.
>
> This letter may sound as if I'm pretty
> well pleased with myself. I am. And I
> realize I was lucky—and know the right
> people. But in knowing the right people in
> the Army—you have to produce or else
> they cease to know you.
>
> Love, George

"All right, Gremlin." He stroked my ears. "Let's give
Rikki Tikki Tavi a try." I snuggled under the covers and
turned around to pop my head out, licking his chin. The
more he read, the more he talked like Luke, without the

extra sounds and pauses he used to say when he first became my best friend.

I rested on his chest, feeling his heartbeat and the deep rumbling of his voice as he read to me about the mongoose and the snake.

Chapter 12: Operations

The "Blood Chit" (WWII)

A leader is slow to speak but prompt in action.

Confucius

"Stop by my barracks tonight, George," said Andy. "Bring Gremlin, *mi hijito*, with you. I have someone I want him to meet."

After chow, George carried me up the steps to visit Andy. Who was this mystery person he wanted me to meet? Andy greeted us at the door. He gave George a cup of coffee and invited him to sit down. I stood next to his feet. What was my surprise?

"*Un momento*—just a minute." Andy disappeared into the darkness of the barracks. The lights were off and the room was dark. Sparkles of dust danced in the little streaks of sunshine streaming through the blinds on the warm spring day, spotlighting Andy's bunk. The barracks was cluttered with bunks and a hodgepodge of footlockers, tables, and chairs.

Andy brought a cardboard box and placed it on his bunk. He put me on his lap and I sniffed the box, smelling something like a dog, but different. George stepped closer as Andy took the blanket off the top of the box and pulled out a puffy gray ball of fur with legs shorter than mine.

"Found a kitten near Mac's canteen. She was mewing so loudly." He held the little thing against his chest and stroked her long fur. "Must have gotten lost from her mama. I call her Sadie, my little lady."

The thing Andy called a kitten made a loud grumbling noise in her throat, almost a growl but different, like a long chuckling sound. I put my paws on his knee and sniffed again, my ears perked. A new puppy?

Sadie the kitten growled at me. Surprised, I poked my nose toward her to take a closer look. Her bluish-green eyes reminded me of the color of the river where we fished. She shrank into Andy's hands, flattened her ears, and growled again—sounding like Mom when she wanted me to stop my naughty behavior.

But I wasn't doing anything wrong. Just being friendly. I whined—*hhnnnnn*? Wagging my tail, I moved my head along the top of Andy's knee. She lashed out, tiny claws extending from her short, fuzzy paw. I jumped backward, feeling a quick brush of danger along my whiskers.

"Oh, no, *mi hijito*—are you all right?" Andy put Sadie back into the box and leaned toward me.

"He's fine," George said, putting me into his lap. "Just a

little shook up. Didn't expect that kind of greeting, did you, tiger? We need to have a talk about dogs and cats."

~   ~   ~   ~   ~

When George had his operation, I stayed with Doreen and my mom. The next day, Andy took Doreen and me to the hospital in the Jeep. She held me close. I kept her warm from the wind, even though I shivered.

Red showed us where to find George. "Dogs really aren't allowed here, but I know how sweet Gremlin is. This puppy will cheer up everyone. Aren't you a good boy?"

Uh oh. Red called me a good boy, like when she gave me a shot. I didn't want her to touch me and squirmed backwards in Doreen's arms to stay away from her. I wanted to growl at her, but she was a friend of Doreen's, so I made a big smile for her, showing her my tongue and teeth like humans do when they meet someone they like. I hope she hadn't hurt George or I would growl at her.

We walked along a hallway, as long as our walk from Ops to the mess hall. Red opened the doors to a long, narrow room lined with beds. People in white uniforms pushed squeaky carts down the long center aisle. The whole place smelled like Red's hands and made my nose tingle and burn.

Curtains hung between the bunks instead of in the windows, where bright sunlight streamed into the room. I sensed George was there somewhere. Wiggling out of Doreen's hands, I dropped to the floor, landing on all four paws.

"Oh, no, Gremlin—come back," Doreen said.

Running through the room, my nails slipped on the smooth floor. I fell onto my side with an *oooowwfff* but picked myself up and scampered through the room. I looked from one bunk to another. Where was he? The clip-clopping sounds of Doreen's shoes followed me.

Finally, I found him. I slid to a stop and yowled, "Where have you been? How are you?" — that came out as *Woorrrwyl? Arrrwowl?*

George laughed and leaned over to pick me up. "Fortunately, the orderlies didn't see you race through the room or both you and I would be escorted out. Not that it would be a bad thing."

Doreen rushed to George's bunk. "He's a slippery one, George. Naughty puppy. He's just glad to find you."

"Thanks for b-b-bringing him, D-Doreen. What a b-breath of fresh air."

I smelled my breath as he rubbed my head with his huge hands. Not as fresh as the air outside but had a much better scent than the hospital smells. I shook my head and licked George's fingers, my tail wagging as fast as I could shake my hindquarters.

Doreen put me on George's bunk. "My little friend here has been waiting impatiently for you to come back to HQ," Doreen said, "We're pretty busy without you, but getting by. How did the operation go? Your nose is all bandaged up."

"D-Doc said it went fine." I curled up on his chest, and he stroked my back.

Red caught up with us. "Doc had to open and drain the abscess and pack the area with gauze. Now we need to let it dry out for a few more days. How are you feeling?"

"Still a bit tender." He chuckled. "The good news is—I'm not... pregnant."

Doreen held her hand up to her mouth. "Oh, I shouldn't

laugh, but your humor under these circumstances is so peculiar. You poor dear."

I crawled up to George's neck and looked for his nose. It was hidden under a small white blanket. He pushed me back to his chest. "Good dog, Gremlin." I could breathe again, now that we were together again.

Doreen and Red pulled up chairs and sat next to us. I burrowed into the blankets, turned around, and stuck my head out.

"Your friend George here is a real trooper." Red felt his wrist and forehead. "He was conscious the whole time. Through every step of the procedure."

"What?" Doreen raised her eyebrows.

"Right. Elective surgery. No anesthetic. The doc can only use painkillers for those injured in the war effort."

I lay down on George's chest while he stroked my ears.

"What on earth happened?" Doreen leaned toward Red.

"He sat in Doc's metal operating chair. Doc cut his nose from the bridge all the way down to the tip. Never said a word, never flinched. But Doreen, George pulled up so hard on the arms of the chair he bent those arms up a couple inches."

George grunted. "Sorry about that."

The hair on the back of my neck started to rise. But the way she looked at George, it seemed like she cared about him and didn't want him to be hurt. "It's understandable. The thing is—two orderlies couldn't get those armrests down again. I guess we'll have to call it the Haydon chair from now on."

Red patted his arm. "Can I get you some water, George?"

"Maybe something a little stronger, b-but I d-doubt you

have it here." He blushed, like the blood suddenly rushed into his cheeks. His chest became warm, too.

"Maybe we can find a strong man to bend them back." Doreen laughed.

George chuckled. "Or use one of Ralph's cranes to get it b-back into shape,"

Red patted George's hand. "I can't get over your sense of humor. After all that and you still can make jokes."

George's face blushed deeper.

"Well, I'm off to check on my other patients," said Red. "See you around campus, Hercules." She walked away, her shoes squeaking on the smooth floor.

"I'll be back to pick up Gremlin after chow. Have a good visit, you two." Doreen clip-clopped away.

"That Red's sure a cutie, isn't she, Gremlin?" said George. "What do you think, Sam?" He looked at the man in the bunk next to us. I sat up and wagged my tail. He had a big blanket on his head.

Sam smiled back at George. "She's a mighty fine lady, Nurse Red. Could be a pin-up girl. I'd paint her picture on my plane for sure, if I had one."

"Same here," said George, reaching toward the table between them. "Well, Sam, I think I'll write a letter home to the folks. Tell them who I'm gonna to bring home as a bride."

"Sounds like you have a crush, you old dog," Sam said.

~   ~   ~   ~   ~

George read his letter to me.

    Dear Folks,
        Just received your letter. Thanks.

I'm off base in the Hospital. Been here a couple of days and everything is fine. Good chow, good bed, service. Only thing is, I can't see very well around this bandage on my nose. Guess the operation was a success. The doctor seems happy about it.

I looked up at his face. So, it wasn't a blanket on his nose. It was a bandage. I rubbed my nose with my front paw. So many human words to learn. Communication in my family was much simpler.

George continued reading to me. I sat up to pay attention.

What would you think about having a nurse as a daughter-in-law? I think my nurse is the gal for me—but don't worry about me getting married yet. Maw, I'll give you at least two hours' notice. Probably.

It's getting kind of hard to write in bed, so guess I'd better knock off. Everything is OK. Nothing to worry about. Will write again soon.

Love, George

Doreen came back, her heels clicking on the hard floor.

"Come along, Gremlin, my dear little friend. George, you'll be fine, especially with Red taking care of you."

George blushed again. "Is she available?"

141

"Hate to say it, George, but she's not." Doreen shook her head, her brow wrinkled. "See, Red came over on one of the ships bringing the very secret AVG here. Only two women and all those men." She rolled her eyes. "Oh, but none of them were good enough for Red. She thought they were just boys, too full of themselves."

George sat up. "How did you find this out, Doreen?"

"Well, we have tea now and then." She shrugged her shoulders. "No one measured up—until she got to know one of the pilots. He was a gentleman, genuinely cared about her. They got married in secret when they were in Burma."

"Oh." George sighed. "She doesn't wear a ring."

"Not practical in her line of work. Besides, it's not so important to her. They're apart so much, it's best for her to stay busy here at the hospital."

"So much for my dream girl," said George. "Do me a favor, Doreen? Mail this one for me? Although my news is now null and void."

"Sure enough." She plucked the letter from his hand and tried to pick me up. I whimpered when it was time to leave George. When he picked me up and said goodbye, I went limp in his hands and whined the whole way back to Doreen's barracks.

~   ~   ~   ~   ~

The next day at lunch, Doreen left Mom with Andy and drove me in the Jeep to see George. Waiting for her to stop the Jeep, I shook all over, excited to see my best friend. Dancing in the passenger seat, I chewed on my leash to hurry Doreen along.

She stopped the Jeep and climbed out the door. Walking to the hospital, we were stopped by the Military Police, Sarge and Jimmy. Private Rex towered over me. I scrambled behind Doreen's shoes, my tail between my legs.

"Hello, gentlemen. Hi, Rex." Doreen greeted them. "Anything unusual? Usually. you're at the base gate."

Sarge and Jimmy nodded their heads. "Just out on patrols, ma'am. Stretching our legs."

Grr-rarrff-gggrrrrrff—Rex lunged at me. Jimmy stepped back, holding tightly to Rex's leash with both hands.

Brrarrk—bbrrarrk—I ran in front of Doreen and making myself as tall and puffed up as I could, telling him not to hurt her.

"Heel, Private Rex—heel! At ease, Private Rex." Jimmy stepped back, wrapping Rex's leash around his hand.

Rex strained against his leash, barking loudly at us— *rrkkk-ahrhkk—rrkkk-ahhrkk*—snapping his huge teeth, as scary as the shark's mouth on the P-40 fighters.

Sarge stood between Rex and me. "Sorry, ma'am. Rex's usually not this edgy." He lowered his voice. "Seems like something's about to happen. That's why we're making rounds. Rex can sense these things better than we can."

"You okay, little fella?" Jimmy poked his head around Sarge, while Rex continued a low growl. "Quiet, Rex."

I shook all over when Doreen picked me up. "We're all right. Better keep Rex away from Gremlin."

Sarge shrugged. "Don't know what happened, ma'am. He's usually good around other dogs. We'll keep him in check."

Jimmy shook his head. "Something's up, so we'll be on special alert tonight."

~   ~   ~   ~   ~

143

"I tell you, George, something's not right. That Military Police dog, Private Rex nearly bit Gremlin's head off." Doreen leaned forward in her chair next to George's hospital bed.

Arrrkkk? If I didn't have a head, how could I eat bones?

"There must b-be some explanation. Just a b-bad day, maybe, or a b-burr under his ear or a sticker in his paw. Take it from one who knows—pain can make anyone grumpy, even a D-D-Doberman pinscher."

"I've known Rex for months now. It's just not like him. And what dog would harm a helpless puppy? I was scared half out of my wits when couldn't protect him."

"He'll be all right. More likely, he wanted to protect you. Let him stay with me this afternoon. After work, have Mac at the Canteen make you a hot toddy."

"What's that?" Doreen's eyes softened.

"Hot water, honey, lemon, and whatever b-booze he has."

"Come on, now. You're such a youngster. How would you know about something like that?"

"My Aunt Hazel. Always sat on the porch at sunset. Overlooked Klamath Lake in Oregon. She'd look out over the fields and orchards. With her hot toddy for the b-body, as she called it. Probably doing that tonight, or whatever time it is there now."

"Makes you a little homesick, huh?" Doreen sat back in her chair.

"Sure, b-but we've got a war to finish here. Can't wait to get back to HQ. Thanks for b-bringing Gremlin. Sorry about that incident with the MP's d-dog."

"Not a big deal. I'll be back later to pick up my little friend."

After Doreen left, George wrote another letter. I lay on his chest, listening to his steady heartbeat. Feeling his warmth, I curled up with my muzzle on my paws. My eyes drooped. When he read to me, I watched his lips move, wagging my tail just long enough to let him know I was listening.

> Dear Folks,
>
> Well, the doctor says I can leave tomorrow. He's going to pull the stitches & let me go back to work, and will I be glad.
>
> My nose is just a little sore, but it was a good thing I had it taken care of. In another six months that infection would have caused a lot of trouble.
>
> It would be swell to go back to see you but doesn't look like it'll happen any time soon.
>
> It's close to lights out, so guess I'd better get all the good rest I can out of this soft hospital bed. This is the best bed I've slept on since I last was home.
>
> Will write more later.
>
> Love, George

He folded up his letter and put it in his pocket. I burrowed under the covers. The air raid sirens sounded. I heard a singing noise and a sound louder than all the P-40 engines on base. An explosion hit the back wall of our hospital room. George and I were thrown out of the bunk onto the floor.

~   ~   ~   ~   ~

I woke up to a loud *kaboom* and a ringing sound, like the phone on George's desk. It wouldn't stop, and my ears hurt. I shook my head and opened my eyes. The bed was on its side and George was on the floor. I crawled over to him and licked his face. I whimpered and barked to wake him up. Was he breathing? I sniffed at his face and barked again.

Finally, George took a deep breath, shuddering. He put his hands on his head and face, then looked at his hands, shaking as hard as my whole body. The bandage over his nose darkened with red.

"What happened? Must be a bombing raid—Gremlin, are you okay?" He turned me around in his hands. "Hold still, buddy, you've got glass in your neck."

Aarrkk! I screamed at the pain when he pulled it out, then I whined. *Mrrrmmff*?

"You'll be okay." George wrapped me in his blanket and set me against the head of the bed.

"I've gotta help. Stay, Gremlin. You know what that means. Stay." George pointed at me. He found his boots and knocked them together, shaking out sparkling pieces of glass. Pushing them onto his bare feet, George didn't tie his shoelaces like he usually did.

He shook Sam's shoulder. His bed was turned over, too. "Quite a blast, Sam, but the bombing raid's over. You're a little bloody, but you're okay. Here's your boots. Put 'em on— there's glass everywhere. Let's check on the others."

George's legs trembled, and he nearly fell, but held onto bedframe and stood up slowly. The lights flickered and died, but the fires lit up the shapes of George and Sam as they

146

scrambled around beds, trays, and carts toward the area of the room where other patients and hospital workers were crying and screaming "Help—over here!" and "Doctor, this one needs immediate attention."

I smelled fear and panic, blood and pee and smoke. Nurses and doctors in white coats ran past me. George and Sam turned beds upright and helped people back into bed.

I didn't feel brave like George. I burrowed into my blankets, leaving my ears and ears out and tucking my sensitive nose under the blankets. I kept my head up, watching George as I shivered and shook.

The back wall of our room was gone. People slapped blankets against the fires. I whined as my head spun. *Mmmrrff? Mmrrff?* I closed my eyes and buried myself deep in George's blanket. Who did this? Dragons from the village? Gremlins? Or did the enemy cause destruction in the quiet place where people were healing from their wounds?

~   ~   ~   ~   ~

At last, the screaming and crying stopped. I heard Doreen's voice calling, "George? Gremlin? Where are you? Here, Gremlin. I know you're around somewhere."

"Corporal Jimmy, can Private Rex help me find Gremlin?" Doreen's voice sounded far away.

"Sure, ma'am, he'll remember that dachshund pup. Let him smell your hands. Smell, Private Rex—find, Private Rex."

The voices became louder. "I think George's bunk was over here. Here, Gremlin!"

Wagging my tail, I inched my way to the surface. Smoke stung my eyes and I sneezed several times. I emerged to look into the eyes of the dog I hoped to never see again—Private Rex.

147

His long tongue dripped with saliva as he panted loudly. His bright eyes looked right at me. Was he going to bite me and eat me?

"There you are, sweet puppy." Doreen picked me up as tinkling glass fell onto the floor. I licked her cheeks and ears, whining and whimpering. Was George all right? *Oooahrwrll?* Where was he?

"Thank you, Private Rex. Good job. Now, let's find George and get out of here. Don't worry, Gremlin. You and George will be good as new." I fell asleep on her shoulder, my muzzle pressed against her neck. I barely remembered feeling George's big hands around my middle. I licked his neck and fell asleep again.

Chapter 13: Humming in the Hangar

Triple Ace David Lee "Tex" Hill (right) and Officers on
the Kunming Airfield (WWII)

Seize every minute of your time.
The days fly by; ere long you too will grow old.
See there, in the courtyard, how the frost glitters
White and cold and cruel
On the grass that once was green.

Tzu Yeh

"Welcome back, airman," Andy said when George and I
walked into Headquarters. "Feeling okay after that air strike?
Looks like you've been through the ringer."

"Yeah, I'm better now. So's Gremlin." George fingered the
bandage on his nose. The cuts on his hand looked like brown
lines. "But glad to be out of the hospital. All the patients who
could walk were discharged—I limped out—and the Chinese crews
got to work on repairs. I tell ya though, best bed I ever slept in."

149

Andy shook his head. "Those bombs fell awfully close, huh? But no casualties."

"Seems like everyone'll be fine. If only I could get my ears to stop ringing." George wiggled his finger in his ear. "Just my luck."

The men laughed, but their voices sounded muffled, as if a towel was wrapped around my head. I sat on the floor and scratched behind my ear. Maybe the exploding bombs that hit the hospital hurt my ears, too. Now I understood why people shouted at Chennault, so he could hear them.

George sat in his rolling chair and helped me into my drawer. Yawning, I settled down onto my Good Morning Towel for a nap, lulled by the rustling of papers on his desk, the clatter of the typewriter keys and ringing and zipping sounds as he worked.

After work and chow, George said, "Let's get out and stretch our legs, Gremlin." We took a slow walk to the airfield, watching the noisy airplanes take off and land. Colonel Tex Hill zipped by in a Jeep with two other officers.

Tex stopped and backed up, idling the Jeep next to us. "How are ya doing now, George? Heard about your encounter with explosives."

"Just fine, Tex, thanks." George nodded his head and saluted the officers.

"Okay, just checking." Tex put the Jeep in gear and left a cloud of dust on his way to the airfield.

I trotted with George to Ralph's hangar and the Quonset hut, which looked like half of a giant can among the gravel roads. A few trees nearby shaded the mechanics working on the planes in the early evening sun.

We found Ralph inspecting the nose of a P-40 fighter as three mechanics climbed ladders to work on the engine and propeller. Two more mechanics worked under the plane. Tom charged toward me from the Quonset hut where he and Ralph and the other mechanics worked and bunked. I met him with a *gggrrrrrfff* and we tumbled and wrestled among the oil-stained rags. Ralph smiled as he walked toward us.

"Well, look who's back." Ralph wiped his hands on his coveralls. "Tom always seems to know before I do when his brother's coming around for a visit."

"Hi, Ralph." George smiled. "Thought we'd take a walk and see how things are going."

Ralph pointed to the plane, surrounded by a crew, who reminded me of an army of ants attacking a buried bone.

"I'll tell ya George, not many people would understand why a mechanic would be interested in music. It's really the other way around. I got called up, like every other Joe. Left my wife and two kids, everything I knew. Boot camp wasn't too bad since I grew up on a farm. My dad raised me on fixing farm equipment. That is, when my mother wasn't teaching me violin. So—mechanics and sound—vibrations—became my specialty."

George nodded and said, "Sure, I can see that. Unfortunately, for all the work you and your crews do, repairing the few fighters we have, the enemy's shot down two more planes."

"Tough to hear, especially when we wait on the airfield, and they don't come back. We lost two pilots yesterday." Ralph scraped the toe of his boot in the rocky soil, rolling a small rock back and forth. He looked sad, so I pounced on his shoelaces to cheer him up. Tom joined me, and we growled and clawed at his boots.

"I notified their families on behalf of General Chennault." George said. "Telegrams, letters. Can't imagine what it would be like for my folks to get a message like that. I try to write if they were my own family."

"Rough, all the way around," said Ralph. "You know, we're up against terrible odds, and we're outnumbered in the skies. It's amazing we haven't lost more men and planes."

George rubbed the scar on his nose. "It really is miraculous how effective they are, so few against the enemy's leagues of bombers and fighters."

"Well, our boys use the aerial tactics the Old Man developed, flying down on the enemy, out of the sun. He's the Beethoven of aerial pursuit." Ralph rubbed his greasy fingers with the rag he kept in his back pocket. "And my crews and I keep the P-40s up and running so they're ready to go on short notice. We could do even better with replacement parts, fuel, and equipment, but we're not getting it over the Hump." He jammed the rag into his pocket. "You're in Operations. What's the hold up?"

George sighed. "We have an army general in India thinking about land wars, while we're protecting this huge Chinese territory by air. He just can't seem to think in three dimensions and approve our supplies. Plus, since the Japanese hold all the seaports, there's a backlog of material to go over the Hump, plane by plane, especially now the Burma Road's been taken over by the Japanese."

A plane roared in over the field and landed with a whirr. It taxied near us, and Ralph called Tom and me over. "Keep away from those wheels, boys."

Ralph gave us a clean rag, and we both grabbed it, growling and tugging on it. We trotted to a nearby tree, snorting at each other.

George nodded toward the planes. "Those Hump pilots have their work cut out for them, and they're playing their part. Dangerous business, flying The Hump. So cold getting over those mountain passes. No heat on my trip here. Why was that?"

"Heaters run the risk of blowing up the plane. Gasoline can leak from the tanks. If it does, it drains to the base of the wings, but there's no way to eject it. We're learning that when the pilots fire up the heater at a certain altitude, the heater can spark and ignite the gasoline. Blows up the plane. Most pilots prefer the cold to chancing a mid-air explosion."

George shuddered. "I'd prefer the cold to the alternative."

Tom and I growled and nipped at each other, racing around a tree where a crew worked on a P-40 in the shade.

Ralph sighed. "Seems like no matter what we request, we never get enough of

P-40 Tomahawk &
Maintenance Crew
Kunming, China (WWII)

what we need. But I'll keep tuning, picking and grinning. Between my crew and Gremlin's good luck, we'll keep the tigers flying."

"By the way." George scratched his upper lip where short

hairs were growing. "Speaking of picking, do you have your instrument here? I'd like to play a few tunes. Maybe we can get an ensemble going."

"I found a violin in Kunming. Worked it over, reset the sound post inside, bought new strings. Hard to find a good bow but got a decent one and re-haired it myself. Managed to concoct some resin for the bow." Ralph shrugged. "So, yeah. I'm in. What did you have in mind?"

George wiggled his fingers. "I'd like to acquire a clarinet or saxophone. Not likely to find a double reed here, except for Chinese instruments, a different set up. And I'd like to find other musicians on base."

"Do you mean someone who plays bass or lives on base?" Ralph chuckled. "Come with me, George." He whistled. "Tom, Gremlin—heel." We ran to our friends. They attached leashes to our collars and we followed Ralph to the largest building on the Kunming Air Base—the hangar at the end of the airfield.

"We've had a lot of traffic in and out as the China Air Task Force got up and running." Ralph opened a huge, squeaky door that rattled and shimmied. George helped to push it along a track high on the outside wall. "People leave stuff on the planes all the time. No identification, no one asks about it. Kind of a lost and found."

"Oh, yeah." George wiped his hands on his pants. "Luke has an old chair from here."

"I think there's something you might be interested in." We walked through the wide door and stepped into the hot, humid space with planes and equipment and all kinds of smells. The crews climbed ladders, clanged on metal, and spoke in loud voices, more men than I'd ever seen outside. I let out a *wwooffff* in surprise—and heard the response of many other dogs. Where were they hiding? Tom and I *wwwooffffed* again and heard even more dogs.

George and Ralph laughed as I perked my ears, tilting my head one way and another. "Looking for someone, Gremlin?" George said in a teasing voice. "It's just you and Tom and your echoes." Echoes?

"Pretty lousy acoustics in here, but we've got a place to practice." Ralph rummaged through a shelving unit against one of the walls. "Here you go. Looks like a B-flat clarinet, if I recall correctly." Ralph pulled the case off the shelf and set it on a nearby tool bench.

George opened the case and took out the instrument. He fitted the pieces together. "I see a couple reeds there. All the pieces. Tell you what? I'll take it back to my barracks and work it over." He held the instrument and wiggled his fingers on the keys, making clacking sounds as his fingers went up and down. "Seems to be in decent shape. You sure no one claims it?"

"It's been here for several weeks. Anyone would've let us know by now." Ralph bowed and gestured to the instrument. "So, you, my friend, have just acquired one clarinet."

The men chuckled as George took the instrument apart and put it back into the case.

Ralph said. "How about coming back tomorrow night? I'll ask around to see who else is interested. We'll see what we can put together."

"All right." George put the instrument back in the case.

"See you then, George." Ralph rubbed my head, and George and I headed back to the barracks in the twilight.

~   ~   ~   ~   ~

That night after chow, I lay on our bunk watching George work on the clarinet. Once he finished rubbing the outside of the black instrument with a cloth, he pointed to the light brown places at the ends of the round tubes. "Corks look good."

He peered under the silver keys, almost like the keys of his Remington typewriter, but without the squiggles. "The corks under the keys are good. Hey, there's even cork grease here," he said as he rummaged around in the case. I sniffed the lining and sneezed. Licking my nose, I decided to keep away from the instrument and sat in the case.

George laughed. "Out. That's not a doghouse." I jumped out, and he opened the lid to a small compartment inside the case. "Now let's check for reeds. Yep, there are a few." He put little tan squares of something in a glass of water on his table. "They need to soak." After a few minutes, he put one into his mouth. Was it a bone for people? Would he chew on it?

George put the instrument together and tightened the reed onto the top of the instrument with a peaceful, intent look on his face. He blew into the clarinet and made noises I'd never heard before. I stood up and howled.

He stopped and closed his eyes, smiling. He chuckled softly. "You're singing with me, huh, Gremlin? It's okay, buddy. This is music. You'll have time to sing later. Right now, it's my turn to play." He touched my muzzle softly, pressing my mouth closed, like being quiet in HQ.

I got the message and lay down on the bunk but couldn't stop my tail from wagging in time with the music he played, with the movement of his fingers on the keys. I breathed in

156

when he did, fascinated by the beautiful melodies that poured out of his instrument.

When George played high notes, I sat up as tall as Pop could, but I fell over because I couldn't sit all the way up. When he played low notes, I lay down on my back to feel the vibrations through the bunk. As he played faster, I rolled and tossed and turned, and when he played slowly, I gradually sunk down into the mattress, my chin on my paws, listening in awe of his music.

"Here's one for you, Gremlin. It's called 'My Buddy.' Popular when I was a teenager." George stood in front of me and sang phrases of words and da-da-dees, humming in between. He held the clarinet up to his mouth and played the tune, swaying. I'd never seen him dance the way he did with his clarinet.

What was it about music that made me feel so loved? My buddy had a special way of letting me know he cared about me.

~   ~   ~   ~   ~

Two or three times a week George took me to the hangar, his clarinet tucked carefully into its case. Ralph found a few more musicians on base and located instruments for them that had been left behind on planes or were discarded as broken. George, Ralph, and the aircraft maintenance crew fixed up each instrument, sometimes with tape and chewing gum.

Whenever they started working on an instrument, they played it—with all kinds of shrill, groaning, moaning and shrieking sounds. I hid in Tom's bed then, burrowing under his towels and blankets, until I heard them work on it, banging and scraping until it sounded better. By the time they gave the instrument to a player, it blended in harmoniously with the rest of the band.

The musicians played styles they called swing, big band, and oldies. Sometimes someone stood up and sang with them. Ralph or George called out the name of a tune and the key and counted out one, two, three, four and everyone played at the same time. Tom and I danced, running and spinning in time to the music.

At the end of one session, George told the group, "Let's take this show on the road. Mac has a spot just made for a band at the canteen. Let's build a stage give it a whirl. Just like the Coconut Grove at the Santa Cruz Boardwalk."

The band played on Friday and Saturday nights after chow. Every time, the canteen was filled with people who laughed and sang and danced. Wench, Tom, and I danced together, barking as we ran from one end of the canteen to the other. And sometimes we howled with joy.

Chapter 14: Chinese New Year

Sara Haydon in Mandarin Jacket from China
(2015)

I hear and I forget,
I see and I remember,
I do and I understand.

Confucius

One morning I heard a low whisper in my ear, "Wake up, little dachshund. Come out from under the covers, Gremlin. Today we're going to a festival in Kunming. No work today." I burrowed out from under the warm blankets and wriggled on top of the heap while George attempted to straighten the covers underneath me. I nipped at his fingers, ran away from him, then rolled on my back, excited to wake up with him.

He picked up my collar and leash from the floor. As he brought them close to me, I sniffed the spot on my collar where I had chewed on them the night before. I backed up, snarling at it. *Rrrrgrr.* He laughed and I barked at him—*arbbrrkk-brrkk.* I stamped my tiny feet, raised my short tail in the air and pounced on my collar.

"Steady there, Gremlin." He put my collar around my neck while telling me about the festival. His voice calmed me down. I stood still on my short legs and listened, feeling the blankets under my belly. Without the collar and leash, we wouldn't go anywhere.

Luke came into the bunkroom. "I hear Gremlin's making his first trip into Kunming."

"He's ready for a longer walk today. We're heading in for a festival. Huh, Gremlin?" I looked up at George's face as he said my name and licked his chin. He laughed and held my head in his hands.

Luke said, "We lost a dog back home during the Fourth of July fireworks one year. Sure spooked him. He came straggling back a few days later."

George held my chin and looked into my eyes. "The Chinese people invented fireworks a long time ago, Gremlin. They make loud popping noises that might be scary for a little puppy. They'll set off firecrackers at the festival and I don't want to lose you in the crowds, so we'll use your leash."

George lifted me off the bed and onto the worn wooden floor.

"Catch you later," George told Luke.

"Stay with George, Gremlin. We need you here, understand?" I sent licks in the air to Luke.

The door opened with its magical smells of outside filling my nostrils. I danced on the tiptoes of my nails. But first, I wouldn't let George go anywhere until I had my morning ritual in the bushes, finding just the right spot after sniffing around to discover who had been there during the night. We went to chow for a quick breakfast, then set off for the day. So many odors, each with a story I wanted to explore, but we kept on walking. George had his head up and I had my head down, searching for new scents.

George picked me up as we met Rex. All the men held their hands up to their eyes. This time he didn't bark as loud, but George didn't put me down near him—and his big teeth.

We walked down the busy road toward Kunming. George put me down, saying, "Good job, Gremlin." I explored China with my eyes, nose and ears. I lifted my face into the warming morning sun as George pulled the collar of his flight jacket up around his neck.

Soon someone walked beside us. "Hi, George. Gremlin. Going into Kunming for the festival? That's where I'm headed."

"Quite an event, I hear." George said. "This is our first trip into Kunming. We'll see how the pup does with all the commotion." He set me down, holding onto my leash.

The three of us walked toward the gates of Kunming, the two of them talking as I sniffed and snorted, sneezed and trotted along. More people walked and talked around us. Jeeps made loud noises sounding like big dog growls as they whizzed by us. Huge animals that George called horses or oxen or buffalo pulled people and animals. I heard squawking chickens and quacking ducks.

I looked all around as we were funneled into a narrow place like the gate on base. George picked me up when crowds of people came close to us. Once I was up off the ground, I saw the brightly painted arched city gate with animals that looked like they'd eat me. Although I couldn't smell them, they looked real to me and I snuggled into George's chest.

"Just carvings, Gremlin. Don't be afraid. They're carvings of lions, dragons, and phoenixes." He held onto me and I felt safe, with his big fingers cupped around my middle and my feet hanging over his wrist.

Charles smiled. "Traditionally, the dragon represents the emperor and the phoenix is the empress. I've always admired the carved city gates of a Chinese city." His eyes were open wide as he looked up at the gate, then he looked toward the city. "Oh, there's the square. We're just in time for the parade."

People were crowded everywhere. We must have been special, because as we came into the square the people moved aside for us. Maybe I was more important that I thought, being The Gremlin. We moved onto the sidewalk, surrounded by other Air Force people and local Chinese people. I saw dancers in flowing clothes, waving bright red, orange, and yellow ribbons as they jumped up and twirled. Girls in long dresses spun their parasols and created giant flowers, opening and closing them quickly. Young men leaped and danced with long colorful streamers as everyone watched breathlessly.

"The dragon dance." Charles nudged George with his elbow and we looked over at a tall scary creature. Even though I could see men in costumes under the fabric, when the long red dragon shook its head and ran around the square, I became frightened and tried to climb higher onto George's shoulder.

He held onto me firmly. Two big white and yellow dogs jumped and reared up. Although I was shaking, I couldn't take my eyes off the dragon and dogs. I barked at them to protect George and Charles. I stood up in his arms to defend my territory against the big dogs. He laughed, and I relaxed my grip on him, knowing that I was there to save him from these threats and that he really was all right.

Once I scared them away, we followed Charles to a less crowded street with more to see and smell. George set me down on the street and my toenails clickety-clacked along the uneven cobblestones.

"Candy makers pound caramelized sugar and peanuts together on that ancient stump. They still carry on traditions from long ago," Charles said. "And this booth cooks up braised pig's feet. I heard from my grandparents that they're a real delicacy. And good for your skin."

"Sure smells good. What do you think, Gremlin—smoked duck, roasted pork, long white noodles, spices?" George tickled my nose as I breathed in many new scents. Every time we moved to a different booth, I was fascinated. I kept my muzzle in the air and sniffed everything I could. Something with a peppery smell made my nose itch. I sneezed. They laughed.

"Cedar and cloth fans. Necklaces of precious gems, tapered calligraphy brushes of all sizes, combs made from ox bones in the shapes of birds and animals. Never thought I'd ever have a chance to see such things." George shook his head.

"Let me know if you want to buy something to send back home. I've gotten pretty good at bargaining. They don't expect it from a U.S. serviceman, let alone a Chinese American, but it's always a good time and the seller and I both come away happy." I got close enough to taste a comb—was it as tasty as the bones from Cook? Before I could check it, my leash got a tug and I followed George.

Women with cloth bags pushed through the crowd to get to the front of the lines at the booths. George picked me up, saying, "It's getting even more crowded now." Two small ladies with wrinkled skin and gray hair looked at us and pointed to the tigers on George and Charles' shoulders.

"*Fēi Hǔ! Fēi Hǔ shì yīngxióng! Xièxiè!*" Charles smiled at them and spoke in Chinese. The women giggled and covered their mouths. He smiled back at them.

"What was that all about?" George looked between Charles and the women; his eyebrows raised. I opened my eyes and raised my eyebrows, too, cocking my head to one side. "I heard something about thank you and Flying Tigers but didn't understand the rest."

"They just told us that all the Flying Tigers—*Fēi Hǔ*—are heroes."

"What did you tell them? You really got a reaction."

"I said—*Nǐmen dōu hǎo piàoliang*—you are all so beautiful. That always gets a positive response, especially with the older ladies. My grandmother laughed shyly like them when I used to tell her that. Seems to be universal." Charles smiled.

"They sure seem to be good at haggling with the vendors." George nodded toward the women's feet. "I see some of the older women have such tiny feet."

"They grew up in time when their feet were bound from infancy," Charles said. "If they didn't have small feet, they didn't feel beautiful. They thought that they would not have the advantages of women with bound feet. Things are changing now — their men are gone, and they have to fend for themselves."

Charles sighed. "Something to remember. I'm keeping a journal of my time in China. Kunming marketplace. Crates overflowing with neatly arranged dried noodles of different colors and thicknesses. Beans, spices, fruits, and teas weighed using a stick and counterweight. I'll be writing this down as soon as I get back to base."

My whiskers twitched up and down as I squirmed in George's arms to get closer to the things that smelled delicious. To my disappointment, George moved down the street and I had no choice but to go along. I looked longingly over his shoulder, with my ears perked up and my nostrils opened wide to catch a last scent of the fascinating things in that marketplace.

"This is it." Charles paused before a store window crowded with antiques and art. George set me down on the stones in front of the door.

"I heard from Andy that the owner is honest and will give you a good deal. If you're looking for something special to send to home, this fellow can help you."

I could not jump over the board blocking the doorway.

Charles knelt beside me. "Gremlin, you might want to know that this board in the bottom of the doorway is designed to keep ghosts from entering through the door." He stood up. "Remember, George, men cross the threshold with the left foot first."

George picked me up. He stepped over the tall board at the bottom of the door and I felt his body sway as each foot was raised up and down, first the left and then the right. He set me down on the old wooden floor. "Stay in the shop, Gremlin." I thought to myself that there was no way I could get over that threshold by myself, no matter which leg goes first. While they looked around the shop, I sniffed up and down, throughout the store, trailing my leash behind me.

I smelled teas and incense and old dusty things that made me sneeze. I circled around a table leg that smelled curious and resisted the urge to pee on it because I knew I shouldn't relieve myself inside.

Once George made his choices, he untangled my leash from around the table leg. "We'll just let Charles bargain with the shopkeeper to get the best deal," he whispered to me. Charles helped George find little papers and jingling coins to put on the shopkeeper's counter.

George picked me up and showed me the embroidered black jacket on the counter with tiny birds on the white cuffs and puffy rainbow clouds on the shoulders and back.

He smiled and turned to Charles. "Thanks, old friend. This antique Mandarin jacket is absolutely beautiful, like the older women we met. I'll treasure it when I get back home as a reminder of my service to two countries, the U.S. and China. And if I ever find a gal and get married, I'll tell her about all it."

The shopkeeper beamed and thanked George—xièxiè—as he wrapped it in brown paper. George carried me and the precious package outside the shop into the street. By then it was dark and hundreds of red Chinese lanterns were lit above the sidewalks. I was getting sleepy after a long day and dozed in his warm, comfortable arms, knowing that I was a precious package, too.

Whiz! Crack! Pop! Pop! Crack! I whipped my head around as the loud sounds terrified me. I clawed the air to get away from them. I saw bright lights flash on the ground and a giant golden dragon roaring and rearing in the crowded street as musicians clanged bells and drums. Huge, loud sparkling fires lit up the sky. My thoughts flew like a P-40 kicking into action—thinking that this must be a bombing raid. Or maybe this was a gremlin! Whatever it was, I knew I had to protect George.

My plan was to run away from the danger so that he would come with me and we could escape the dangerous dragon and ferocious gremlins. I got ready to jump down from his arms and run away from the noises. And then I thought a little more—but what if I lose him? Too late—I had wriggled away from his grip and landed in a flowerbed.

Tumbling to the ground, I landed on all four paws and found myself swimming in a river of unfamiliar feet. People were shouting at the fire and everyone was looking up into the sky. I shook my head and ran away as fast as my short little legs could go, while my leash lashed around behind me. I was blocked by someone's feet and two hands reached down for me, but I found a way around them, determined to lead George to safety. I heard him call my name. Good—he understood he should follow me and take cover.

Toward the edge of the crowd, there were fewer people and I slowed down. My heart was beating quickly. My legs and paws were sore from running on the uneven rocky streets. I could hardly breathe because of the thick smoke and shook so hard that it was difficult for me to stand up. I felt two small hands around my middle, raising me up into the air. My feet pawed the air and I whined for George, but then I relaxed and gave in to the strong fingers holding onto me.

Charles smiled at me. "Here you are, brave little Gremlin." He handed me to George, who came running up behind him. I licked their faces, glad that I could save both of them from the fire-breathing dragon and a thousand gremlins.

What would they have done without me? I shuddered and settled into his warm arms. My heart felt full of pride for fulfilling my role as protector that day.

As we walked back to the airbase, George held me tightly as I nuzzled and licked the buttons on his shirt. "Charles, d-d-do you know of anyone who teaches Chinese? After mingling with the local people here, I'd like to b-be able to speak for myself."

Charles was silent for a moment. I listened to the soft crunching of their boots on the road. The evening breeze blew into my face and I burrowed into George's flight jacket. He helped me find the way into his inner pocket, and I rolled around to peek out at them.

"Yes, I do," said Charles. "I spoke with a gracious woman in one of the embroidery booths this afternoon. Beautiful handiwork that she makes for the Americans and Brits as souvenirs of their time in China. She spoke only pidgin English, so I switched to Chinese—Mandarin, that's the universal language in China since there are so many dialects—and found out her husband used to be a Chinese teacher in Shanghai. They escaped during the bombing of the city—just in time. Came back to her family's village, not far from the airbase."

"That's encouraging. Do you think you might have a

chance to talk with her again and set up Chinese lessons for me?" George stroked my neck as we made our way through the evening chill.

Charles nodded. "Sure, George. I have a meeting for public relations in Kunming next week and I'll see if I can find her."

I had heard a different language all day and wondered what it was called. It made sense that people in China would speak Chinese. I licked George's fingers to let him know I wanted to go with him to his Chinese lessons. Maybe I could learn more about China, too. Maybe the teacher would know about gremlins. Anything that would help me be the guardian of the Flying Tigers and the Chinese people.

I hoped with all my heart that I could continue to protect George. Saving him from the dragons felt like a good start. I rested against his chest, listening to his steady heartbeat, and fell asleep.

Chapter 15: Mandarin Lessons

Embroidery of Phoenix and Flowers on Silk (WWII)

Discard your petty wisdom and great wisdom will come into being;
Discard your pretentious goodness and natural
Goodness will come into being.

Chuang Tzu

The phone jangled on George's desk. Waking from a dream of running on the sand by the river toward a pile of fish innards, I shook my head and recognized the familiar aromas of typewriter ribbons, smelly socks, and stale cigarette smoke. Shaking myself awake and rumpling my good morning towel in the drawer, I sat up to listen.

George picked up the black bone on his desk and spoke into it. Would that bone taste as good as the bones from Cook? I licked my lips. I cocked my head to one side, trying to recognize the tinny voice talking through the bone.

"Yes, Charles." George wrote something on his pad of paper. "Monday, Wednesday, Friday. Yep, I'll be there this evening, just after chow, around six—if nothing comes up."

He paused for a moment, and I heard Charles' voice, as thin as the wire on George's telephone. "Okay, we'll be ready to go into town with you at oh-thirteen hundred this afternoon to meet her. Thanks for making the arrangements, Charles." George hung up the phone.

The sunshine streamed through the windows, telling me it was close to noon. The growling in my tummy reminded me it was time to eat. After Cook's meal in the mess hall, we walked to HQ and took a Jeep ride with Charles into Kunming. When we drove under the gate with the scary animals, I growled at them, but they probably couldn't hear me over the roaring, sputtering engine and the bumping sound of the tires. We bounced up and down along the uneven road to enter the city. My warning must have worked, though, because the lions and dragons stayed in their places, unlike the time they danced in the streets with smoke and fire during the New Year's festival.

Charles stopped the Jeep with a lurch. We walked down a crowded road filled with Chinese and Americans pushing past one another. I peered over George's shoulder as he carried me down the busy streets. People shouted at us from their stalls, pointing to boxes and baskets of yummy-smelling foods and spices.

We stopped in front of a shady stall where several women sat with cloth on their laps. They held sharp-looking needles, like the ones Red used to hurt my littermates and me. I whimpered and struggled in George's arms, thinking that he might have brought me there to get more shots.

His shushing calmed me, and we waited while Charles spoke with one of the women. George touched the fringe of a cloth and traced leaves and flowers with his fingertips. A large bird in the center curled around the blossoms. I sniffed at it, but the flowers didn't smell anything like the bushes I visited every day. And I'd never seen a bird like that one.

Charles spoke in the way he spoke sometimes and motioned to us. The woman stood and set her fabric on the chair.

"How-you do, *Lu-ten-dant* Haydon?" She looked up at George. From where I was in his arms, I could reach my tongue out to lick her cheek, but I didn't know her, so I licked the air.

"I'm glad to—uh—meet you, Mrs. Liu," George stammered. His face blushed.

She smiled. "You want take lessons Chinese? Why?"

George stroked my back. "Well, ma'am, I—uh—find myself in China after a long journey from the States. We're in this war together, allied countries. My father taught me a little Chinese he—uh—picked up as a kid. I've always been fascinated to learn more."

Mrs. Liu nodded then spoke with Charles, using words I didn't know. "Okay, *Lu-ten-dant*. You meet Dr. Liu. We start tonight."

"Thank you, ma'am." George pointed to the fabric with the bird. "I'd like to purchase this piece for my mother."

173

Charles spoke with Mrs. Liu, and they settled on a price, which George paid. She wrapped it up in brown paper.

George asked Charles, "How do I say thank you in Chinese?"

"*Xièxiè*," Charles coached him.

"She-she," George said.

Mrs. Liu giggled as she handed him the package. We headed back to the air base to finish the work day. I didn't understand George's plans after dinner, but whenever he put my leash on my collar, I was eager to go.

In the mess hall, George told Cook where we were going. After we ate, Cook knelt by me and opened something wrapped in white paper. For me? I wagged my tail and sniffed two small round bones with holes in the center with a delicate, moist and heavenly-smelling treat inside those holes. I drooled and licked my lips.

"For later, Gremlin. Beef bones, with marrow. Something to keep you occupied," said Cook. "Good for a growing pup." I raised my front paw to thank him and he shook it. Then I fell over, embarrassed that I couldn't stay upright yet. He chuckled and rubbed my belly. My hind leg automatically scratched the air in delight.

Cook handed George a small brown paper bag. "You need to take a gift. Tea from Formosa. We got a big shipment last month. They'll appreciate that."

George thanked Cook and placed the brown bag inside his jacket pocket, where I used to fit when I first went home with him as a puppy. George put the bones back into the white paper, holding my parcel in one hand and my leash in the other.

"Say, Cook, I know you don't get out much, so I'm taking my camera." George held up the brown box that hung it over his shoulder. "When I get these photos developed, I'll show you scenes from the countryside."

Cook slapped George on the shoulder, saying, "Thanks, buddy. I've got to live vicariously through you and everyone else here." He shook his head, then yelled over his shoulder. "All right, men. Let's get those pots and pans soaking. Gotta get ready for breakfast. Oh-three-hundred comes early, so let's get a move-on."

George smiled. "Never lets up, does it, Cook? Thanks a million," he said, patting our treats wrapped in white paper.

We walked out through the main gate and saluted the guards in the late afternoon sunlight. Private Rex sniffed in our direction. Was he trying to find my package of bones? I growled at the giant black dog in warning—*mrrrgggrrh*—and he backed away in surprise. Keeping my tail up and ears forward, I held my ground, thinking we might become friends someday, if he didn't bite my head off. I decided to teach him how to treat me with respect.

We took the main road to Kunming, where I'd saved George from the dragons. When he said, "Heel," I trotted on one side of his legs, then the other, to get a better whiff of my promised treat. My leash caught around George's ankles. As he stepped over it, nearly losing his balance, he said, "*Yingle-yangle*, Gremlin. All in a tangle. Heel." We kept going—not time for bones yet.

We left the paved road and walked down a wide dirt path, wet with puddles. As clouds passed overhead, the temperature changed from sunny and warm to dark and

175

chilly, and then back to the warmth of the sunlight. I chased noisy little insects jumping in the tall grass. What did they taste like?

"Hear that, Gremlin? Crickets chirping," said George. Their chirping stopped, and I held a pose, listening, one paw lifted… One chirp, then another, then more. I lowered my head to search for them. The insects made their music, but they disappeared into little holes in the ground. As I dug into the wet earth after them, George tugged on my leash, saying, "Gotta go, buddy. Heel." No bones, though.

Soon we reached a village of small houses. George held up his camera. "Cook will want to see this." He took pictures with a *click-click*. "Stone and brick houses with gardens. Rice paddies in the back stretching far into the distant hills." *Click.*

Large animals were led by young children from the rice paddies toward a house with grass and leaves on top. Whatever they were, I didn't want to get near their huge hooves.

George murmured, "Water buffalo, coming back from plowing the rice fields. Must be time for their dinner. Ah, here we are. Charles told me it's the third house."

A gust of wind picked up dust from the road, stinging my eyes. I blinked and shook my head then listened to high-pitched, tinkling bells.

We walked up to a house, red paper banners on either side of the doorway. Several strings of silver bells hung from the roof over the porch, sounding like Doreen's laughter. He checked his watch. "Right on time, in spite of our tangles." He knocked on the door.

A Chinese man opened it with a slight creaking noise.

"Welcome, Lieutenant Haydon." He looked like Charles but was taller and thinner. His hair was black as Private Rex's fur, shiny and short, with gray around his ears. As I peeked from behind George's legs, I noticed his loose black pants and long brown robe with colorful bird designs on his sleeves. He wore soft-looking black shoes, not boots like George.

"I understand, from your friend Charles you wish to learn Chinese. Please come in. My name is Dr. Liu Bing-wen, but as my student, you may call me teacher, or *Lǎoshī*, in Mandarin."

I cocked my ears, wondering if I heard him correctly. Did he say *loud* and *shhh*? Maybe he meant that George should speak with him loudly sometimes and be quiet and listen at other times.

"Thank you, *Lǎoshī*. I b-b-brought you this small gift." George gave the bag of tea to him and bowed slightly, then asked if I could come in, too.

"That's fine, fine. May I ask what kind of dog this is?"

"This is Gremlin, my d-d-dachshund puppy, b-bred to hunt b-badgers in Europe."

Lǎoshī smiled at me. "Short legs, good coat, strong whiskers, bright eyes. I'm sure he'll listen to everything we say. Maybe you will learn to understand Chinese, too, Gremlin, hmm?" He motioned George to a chair. "Please, sit here."

George stopped in the doorway, looking down at a row of shoes. "Oh, sir, ma'am—should I take off my boots?"

"Not at all," said *Lǎoshī*. "Make yourself comfortable."

"The road here was pretty muddy. I'll just leave them outside." Balancing against the door frame, he untied each boot and set them on the porch. As he sat in the low wooden chair, he wiggled his toes inside his socks, and I pounced on his foot. "Shoo, Gremlin. Sit."

I sniffed at his sock and sat, watching *Lǎoshī* sit on a taller chair. He set the bag of tea on a small table and reached down for me to smell his hand. I glanced at George, who nodded, and went to *Lǎoshī*, nuzzling his hand from fingertips to wrist, which smelled of spices and fish. He patted my head and stroked my back. I smiled up at him, panting, my tail swishing across the floor.

"What a b-b-beautiful, carved chair," George said. "I've never seen anything like it."

Lǎoshī put his hands on the armrests and stroked them. "This chair has been in my wife's family for eleven generations. This is the family treasure traditionally used only by the patriarch." He leaned toward George. "Just between us, my wife is the true head of the household, and as such, really should take this place." He shrugged his shoulders. "But she insists."

George leaned forward to look out the windows. "You have b-beautiful gardens and rice terraces." He turned back to *Lǎoshī* and me. "I've never b-been in a Chinese home b-before. I'm so honored—actually, I'm fascinated with the Chinese culture and appreciate being your student."

Peering around the room, I noticed the high ceilings and saw a long wooden seat, like George's bunk but with a back and arm rests, that looked like ten people could sit on it. I thought it didn't look very comfortable without a mattress like ours. Large photographs of people hung on the wall behind it.

Lǎoshī sat back in the tall chair. "You are very welcome

here. Aside from Charles, we don't have many visitors from the base. My wife and I are interested in learning about your customs and cultures, as well as sharing ours. Now, what would you like to learn, George?"

George rubbed his hands over his face. "I'd like to be able to get around China, ask for noodles, how to get to the American air bases if I get lost. Things like that."

The teacher nodded. "How about learning to write characters? Are you interested in reading and writing Chinese?"

George shook his head slightly. "No, sir. Respectfully, I'm interested mostly in speaking. Since I'm on duty, my time is limited. I don't think I'd have any chance to practice writing."

Lǎoshī leaned forward, his head held high. "Let me see what you know. Repeat after me. *Nǐ hǎo.*" It sounded like *knee how* and his voice sounded like he was singing.

"*Nǐ hǎo,*" George sang back. "Charles taught me how to say hello when we went into Kunming for the New Year's festival."

"That's pretty good. You've listened for the inflections. In Mandarin, we have different tones, to change the pronunciation and thus the meanings of words. When we add *ma* at the end of a sentence, we ask a question. Try this: *Nǐ hǎo ma?* This is our greeting to ask if you're all right."

"*Nǐ hǎo ma?*" George repeated. I shook my head, my ears flapping against the side of my head. When he read his letters to me, sometimes he called his mother 'Ma.' I wondered if asking a question meant saying your mother's name, but that didn't seem right.

Lǎoshī smiled. "*Hǎo*—very good. You must be a singer

because you pronounced the tones correctly. The response to *Nǐ hǎo ma?* is *Wǒ hěn hǎo*, meaning 'I am good.' You try it."

As *Lǎoshī* and George practiced back and forth, I lay down, looking from one to the other until my eyelids closed. My long body slumped to one side. As I breathed in the unusual smells in *Lǎoshī*'s home, I heard the new sounds George picked up, without stuttering. I thumped my tail against the floor to tell him he did a good job and listened to hear more of *Lǎoshī*'s songs in Mandarin.

I heard a door creak and opened my eyes. The tiny woman from the market stepped into the room, carrying a tray. Something for me? I sat up.

"Ah, Mrs. Liu, please come in." *Lǎoshī* motioned to us. "George, you've already met my wife, Liu Li-jing. Her name means beautiful spirit, but it is polite in our culture for you to call her Mrs. Liu."

George stood up, and so did I, wagging my tail and sniffing the air. "Pleased to see you again, Mrs. Liu." George bowed slightly. I wondered what she had for me.

"It is my honor." Mrs. Liu put the tray on a long, low table and sat on the bench next to it. "Would you like tea? Biscuits?"

Biscuits? Cook made huge doughy biscuits that stuck in my throat. Were Mrs. Liu's biscuits like Cook's?

"Thank you, Mrs. Liu," said *Lǎoshī*. "But before we indulge in the English pastime, George must learn to say tea in Chinese. *Chá*."

"*Chá*." George held took the cup she filled. "Mrs. Liu, I d-d-don't think I've pronounced the Chinese word for 'thank you' correctly, b-based on your earlier response. Can you help me with that?"

"*Xièxiè.*" Mrs. Liu pronounced the word slowly, like part of a song. George repeated the sounds, like two little sneezes.

Mrs. Liu giggled. "Mind that you don't say *she-she*, which translates to *pee-pee*." She poured tea for *Lǎoshī* and gave it to him. They smiled and nodded at one another. She poured herself a cup and sat on the long bench as gracefully as a butterfly landing on a leaf.

George's tummy shook as he chuckled. "Okay. Mrs. Liu, I think you played a joke on me earlier in the market when you spoke pidgin English. Please tell me about yourselves. How did you come to speak English so fluently?"

Lǎoshī smiled. He held out his arms. "You mean, how did two old folks living in a tiny village in southwestern China become educated in American ways? In a moment. Please, we've saved a tin of these biscuits—sorry, what Americans call cookies—for a special occasion. Having a Flying Tiger in our home is a great honor." Cookies? I wagged my whole body as I stepped around the low table to sit in front of Mrs. Liu.

He shook his head. "*Lǎoshī*, Mrs. Liu, I'm not a fighter pilot. They're our true heroes. The marines fighting in the Pacific. Soldiers and sailors stationed at the front, but not me. I'm just a clerk. I do paperwork, not flying."

Lǎoshī leaned forward. "Nonsense. All the Flying Tigers are heroes. Whether the eagle diving from the sky or the cobra striking from the ground, you are a hero, protecting us in this war of resistance against Japanese aggression."

George sat up straighter, and *Lǎoshī* pointed at him, nodding his head. "It's true. The Flying Tigers together have saved hundreds of thousands of Chinese lives already. And not just the Aces."

Mrs. Liu held out a tray to George. "Please, have a ginger cookie." I lifted my muzzle to take a deep breath, smelling the rich aromas of tea and cookies.

He took a biscuit from the tray and set it on the little plate under his teacup. I smelled something else. Ah—my bones slipped out of George's pocket and waited for me on the edge of his chair.

I lay down and crept under the table to George's feet. Sitting at attention, I begged for my bones with a soft whimper—*hhhnnnnff?* He ignored me and took another bite of his cookie. I wagged my tail and licked my lips. No treats.

Mrs. Liu looked at George. "Imagine—if your Army Air Corps had not arrived in China, stopping the attacking planes, countless bombing raids would have destroyed even more villages and cities—and their inhabitants." She smiled at me. "We are grateful for everyone who keeps the *Fēi Hǔ* planes flying." I sat up taller, feeling included in my role of scaring gremlins away from the planes.

"We wouldn't have survived as a nation," *Lǎoshī* added. "And it takes every one of the Flying Tigers to make the difference between life and death."

"You are very kind. Thank you—*xièxiè.*" George ate the rest of his ginger cookie in one bite, then rattled the teacup against the plate as his big fingers picked it up. He took a few sips of chá, then set his cup on the table and sat back in the chair. "It is an honor to be with you. Now, please tell me about yourselves."

I placed my front paws on the chair leg and inched up as high as I could, nibbling at the paper holding my bones. Gently, my teeth grabbed a wrinkled corner, and I pulled on it until it slid down the leg of the chair. As Cook's package hit the floor, one bone popped out and rolled along the floor. I chased that bone, opened my mouth wide, and grabbed it—mine!

"Gremlin?" George spoke my name, using rising tones. I peeked up at him, protecting my reward under my chin. His look told me I was in trouble and not to take a bite until he gave me permission.

"So sorry, Dr. and Mrs. Liu. Please forgive his manners." George put his fingers around the bone and pulled. I wrestled him for it—*ggggrrrrrff*.

"Gremlin has a treat." *Lǎoshī* laughed. "Who are we to get between a pup and his need for gnawing on a bone? Enjoy, Gremlin. Get at the marrow of life. Growl at it."

George nodded to me. "Okay, Gremlin." He let go, and I fell backwards onto my bottom. Seeking my new friend, I settled down near our teacher's slipper to lick, chew, and growl at my bone.

"Well, George, when I was a small boy in Shanghai, American missionaries came to our neighborhood. They started a school to teach children English. Upon graduation, these mentors asked my parents for permission for me to attend St. John's University in Shanghai, and then to earn a higher degree in America—Teachers College at Columbia University, New York. Have you heard of it?"

"I've heard of it, never been there. I'd love to get to New York sometime."

My bone popped out from between my legs and rolled a short distance away. Pouncing, I recaptured my treat and dragged it back to *Lǎoshī*'s chair. I heard laughter above me as my tongue worked at the marrow again.

George grinned. "Sorry about that. Our cook gave Gremlin those bones. But they'll keep him busy." He tipped his head to one side. "Speaking of cooks, my father went to a private high school in San Francisco, and a Chinese cook fixed their meals. My dad didn't understand his language, but he learned enough and taught me how to count to ten."

George said some words I didn't recognize. Mrs. Liu smiled. "George, you're counting in Cantonese. This cook was probably from the province of Guangdong, in the south of China, near the Pearl River."

"Pearl—my mother's name." George's voice sounded softer than usual.

"Ah, a beautiful name in English and Chinese—*Zhēnzhū.*" It sounded like *Lǎoshī* said *ginger.* "Well, I came back from America to teach English at a college in Shanghai, where I met my future wife, my brightest student. Together we heard the great American educator John Dewey. Did you know he was here in China for two years? His lectures changed the way we teach."

"Oh? How's that?" George shifted in his chair.

Lǎoshī tapped his forehead. "Some held fast to the notion that academics were only for the rich and powerful. Dewey's ideas suggested students learn through experience, very progressive. Dr. Sun Yat-sen, the esteemed revolutionary, father of modern China, broke the hold of the dynasties and their traditions. He listened to John Dewey and sought to provide education for all, regardless of status."

"I'm not familiar with his name." George ate another cookie.

"Perhaps we'll discuss Dr. Sun's role in modernizing China later. All in good time." *Lǎoshī* sat back in his chair.

Mrs. Liu stood and picked up the teacups and saucers, placing them on her tray. "You might need to know, George, that Mandarin is our formal, common language, so it will be useful to you when you travel around China. But remember that in remote villages where they don't know Mandarin, you might not be able to understand their dialects. Use your gestures."

"I'll remember that. And my pocket-sized war diary has some phrases I can point to." George turned to Mrs. Liu. "If I may ask, ma'am, how did you learn English?"

She sat down again. "I was the only girl here in my hometown sent to Shanghai to study. Dr. Liu was my teacher, very encouraging of my studies. We fell in love, but I was already in an arranged marriage. However, once my family traveled to Shanghai and met Dr. Liu, they canceled our marriage contract with the local boy. *Lǎoshī* and I started our own school in Shanghai and taught English together for years."

Lǎoshī said, "After we married, the Japanese began their attacks on China. In the summer of 1937, a fellow teacher told us of rumors he heard of an upcoming attack by the Japanese and where to go for safety. All entrances to the International Settlement were blocked by high gates and barbed wire, except one. We were the first of thousands of refugees to cross over the camelback *Wàibáidùqiáo*, the Garden Bridge and through that one gate. Disastrous times."

Mrs. Liu picked up the story, and I stopped chewing on my bone to listen. "The streets were crowded with families. The gate closed as the bombing intensified, with nowhere for all those unfortunate people to go. Bombing raids on Shanghai killed thousands in the streets, and many more perished under the buildings that collapsed."

"Between the bombing raids, we fled Shanghai and finally arrived here to live with my wife's family." *Lǎoshī* looked out the window and pointed. "The elders of her family are all gone now, buried in that cemetery. The younger relatives fled to Chungking, but we stay to keep the ancestral home and tend the graves in the final stage of our lives."

"We intend to make a difference in saving Chinese lives," George said softly. "I believe Charles introduced us for a reason beyond my learning Chinese. Learning from one another and our leaders' international relations are the keys to our success."

Lǎoshī leaned forward and poked George in the shoulder. "Yes, indeed—and certainly Americans are making a difference, with the British, Koreans, and Russians." George's teacher sighed. I put my head down on my paws and let out a groan—*gghrrrwwwmm*.

He took a deep breath. "We thought we would be safe here, but it's not without sacrifices on Mrs. Liu's part. In this village where she was raised, as well as all through China, the man is the head of the family. We decided that I would teach English and Mrs. Liu would take the role of a traditional rural housewife. But she is quite learned, as you can see."

"Oh, now. Stop it, Dr. Liu." She shook her head, peering up at him with flushed cheeks.

He shrugged. "My mentors encouraged me through many years of study, and I have been rewarded with multiple degrees. My wife has overcome many hardships as a Chinese woman earning her place in academia. And… she is my heart and soul."

Mrs. Liu looked down at her hands, closing her brown eyes for a moment, then raised her head with little raindrops on her cheeks. I left my bone and crawled closer to her. Sitting next to her feet, I rubbed my head against her leg.

"Even with my big feet," she lamented. "We were too poor for my feet to be bound, like the beautiful women in the city. The family needed me to work on the farm. I always felt I was ugly because of them, but Dr. Liu assures me beauty comes in many forms."

Lǎoshī smiled back at her. "Now, instead of teaching, she creates embroidered tapestries on Chinese silks. As you've seen, she sells them in the Kunming marketplace. Americans like you and Charles buy them to send home. We use her earnings to feed the less fortunate."

"When I'm there, I speak Pidgin English," she said. "That way, no one knows that I understand what the Americans and the British are saying. Besides, I don't want to stand out in our village. It's easier for me to get along with the other women."

Lǎoshī looked at George. "So, you see, George, we keep a simple life. Who knows what the future will bring? We have seen war, destruction, terror. But we will do our part to win the war, just as you have a role with the Flying Tigers."

Mrs. Liu leaned over to scratch my neck. "And I'm certain you have a role to play, too. Don't you, little Gremlin?"

How did they know about the mission General Chennault gave me? She rubbed my neck and back. I panted and made a big puppy smile as I looked into her kind face.

Lǎoshī sat up and opened a small box on the table, holding it out to George. The lid had birds and leaves carved on it. "Take a coin, George."

George picked up a round coin, holding it between his thumb and finger. "I picked up coins like these in Kunming during the festival. Why is there a hole in the middle?"

"We string coins together through those holes." *Lǎoshī* placed the box on his lap. "When the coins are made, their edges can be rounded. It's easier to count out money that way, too. Mrs. Liu and I brought these from Shanghai."

"We want you to take two," Mrs. Liu said, pointing to the box. "One for protection and one for good luck. You'll need both here in China... and for when you go back home, which I'm sure will happen eventually. Of course, you have Gremlin to protect you, but a little more assistance is always welcome, don't you think?" I wagged my tail to thank her.

Lǎoshī held the box out again, and George took a second coin from the box. "Rub them together for prosperity. When you do, remember our best wishes for a long life." He covered the box with the lid and placed it back on the table, sitting back with a sigh.

"*Xièxiè*, Mrs. Liu. *Xièxiè, Lǎoshī.*" After saying goodbye, "*Zàijiàn,*" we walked back to base. I heard George jingling the coins in his pocket. He whistled a tune and sang parts of it, "Daa-da-dee-dee... Da-dat-da-dee-dee... ain't we got fun?"

~   ~   ~   ~   ~

After our first visit, George and I took the long walk out to the Liu's home three times a week to learn Mandarin and become familiar with their world. Cook gave me a treat each time. The sun set later in the evenings and the days became warmer. George spoke Mandarin more often in his conversations with Dr. and Mrs. Liu.

I was proud of him and wagged my tail when he learned

188

how to say important things like *"Wǒ shì měiguó rén,"* *"Zuìjìn de kōngjūn jīdì zài nǎlǐ?"* and *"Yī wǎn miàn duōshǎo qián?"* He would be able to tell people he was American, ask where the nearest air base was, and find out how much a bowl of noodles cost.

I tapped my tail on the floor whenever *Lǎoshī* or Mrs. Liu said, *"Zuò dé hǎo"* in the same tone of voice George used to tell me I did a good job.

One evening after they taught George to read a few characters he might need to know, they talked about what might happen once they won the war. Mrs. Liu asked about George's plans. "Do you think you'll settle down and raise a family?"

"Just need to find the right girl." He blushed. "Hope I'm as lucky as *Lǎoshī*."

Mrs. Liu giggled. Her husband smiled and lowered his voice. "We'll see about China once the war ends, George. Instead of a marriage between our two major parties—the Kuomintang and the Communists—we might be looking at the continuation of our civil war. But let's save that for another day in the far distant future. You have important work to do with the Flying Tigers tomorrow."

After everyone said, *"Zàijiàn,"* George and I stepped outside. Mrs. Liu closed the door behind us. George sat on the steps of the porch and tied his bootlaces. The wind chimes above his head swayed in the soft summer breeze with a bell-like sound—*tink-tinkle-ting*.

We walked back to base in the setting sun, to the accompaniment of crickets, buzzing insects and the chorus of what George called frogs. A squadron of Curtiss P-40 fighters returned for a landing at the Kunming airfield. Their silver sides glinted in the last rays of the sun peering over the mountain range. The engines drowned out the moaning and groaning and chirping of the countryside.

After the planes passed overhead, the croaking sound began again, and soon others joined in. The crickets resumed humming. The air pulsed with the warmth of summer, like the purring of Sadie the cat curled up on Andy's lap.

Too sleepy to search for crickets, I stumbled on the gravel road. George picked me up. "Here you go, buddy. I've gotcha," he said. Draped across his arm, I relaxed into the twilight. Stars began to twinkle in the darkening sky. My eyes closed slowly, and the smells of China faded away as I fell asleep to his words in Mandarin and the rocking of his steps.

Chapter 16: An Air Force of Our Own

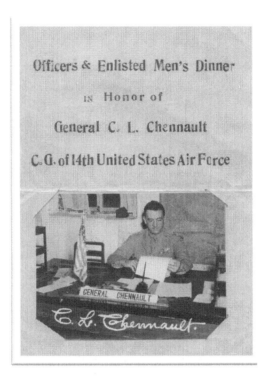

Officers & Enlisted Men's Dinner

in Honor of

General C. L. Chennault

C. G. of 14th United States Air Force

Banquet Program for March 25, 1943

The best fighters display no anger.
The best conqueror seeks no revenge.

Lao Tzu

"Come on, Gremlin. Out of your drawer. We've got a meeting in Headquarters." George put on his flight jacket and we dashed out the door. At HQ, I greeted Mom and Doreen, Andy, Charles, and the other staff members.

They gathered around Doreen's desk, rolling chairs into

a circle. I sat on George's lap, and he held his notepad above me. Andy started the meeting. "At our last meeting we set the date for the banquet. The fifth of March. We've got six weeks to plan."

Charles smiled. "I wonder if the Chinese think it's an auspicious date. We're in the year of the sheep, according to tradition."

Doreen lifted her pencil and looked up from her small yellow notebook. "What does that mean, Charles?"

"It's one of the twelve signs of the Chinese zodiac. Each describes certain life responsibilities. The banquet is an opportunity to build lasting friendships with the Chinese people."

George nodded. "The new Fourteenth Air Force and Chennault's promotion to two stars renews our commitment to protecting and d-defending our allies." He rubbed one of my long, floppy ears absentmindedly between his thumb and finger. I shook my head to make him stop so I could hear better.

Andy leaned forward in his chair. "Okay, people. These are the duties."

Restless, I looked over the side of the chair and wriggled to get down. He lowered me to the floor. When I nibbled at his bootlaces, he scolded me saying, "Shoo." I wandered over to the basket under Doreen's desk and sniffed Mom's face, but she was asleep. I sprawled onto the floor with a sigh.

As the voices droned on, I dozed until a fly tickled my nose. Sitting up, I batted at my nose with my paw and watched it buzz away.

"Is Stillwell planning to attend?" Andy raised his eyebrows.

Charles's chair creaked. "According to his staff, he'll be there. After all, it's not every day a numbered Air Force is established."

"Let's plan on it." Doreen tapped her notepad with her pencil. "But better keep the MPs close, in case Chennault and Stillwell get into it."

"Aww." Charles rubbed the back of his neck. "I'm sure they'll be civil for this occasion. Or else who would pin that second star on Chennault? Major General—isn't that something for the Old Man?"

Andy sat back in his chair. "Certainly, for Chennault, who quit the Army Air Corps back in the thirties. They ridiculed his flight tactics for teams in aerial combat, calling them throwbacks to the first World War, dog fights."

"He's proving them wrong here." When Charles raised his voice, I sat up, ears perked. "Our pilots are consistently outnumbered, but the way he taught them, Chennault's record will end up being the most outstanding in the world once the war is over. His commanders better thank him then."

Doreen tapped her pencil on the desk. "I still don't know about getting our general and the theater commander together. 'Uncle Joe,' as you Yanks call him—"

"Vinegar Joe," someone called out.

She rubbed her forehead. "Okay—anyway, Stilwell's been in and out of China since their revolution in 1911. He speaks the language, walks the front lines. Roosevelt put him in command of the China-Burma-India Theater of Operations for a reason."

"I'll give you that," Charles said. "But the last time he was here, you and I heard the racket coming from Chennault's office. I can't believe what he called Generalissimo Chiang Kai-shek."

"Right." Andy rolled his eyes. "Peanut."

"What does that mean?" George wrinkled his forehead. I did, too.

Andy put his chin in his hand, resting his elbow on Doreen's desk. "You've seen the photos of the Generalissimo in your War Diary, right? Well, Stillwell looks at his bald head, brown skin, and comes up with that insult—to his face. We've got a name for Stillwell, you know."

"Oh, yeah." George smirked. "Old Vinegar Joe."

"Right." Andy motioned in the air with his hands. "Chennault argues with him. 'You can't win on the ground.

Generalissimo Chiang Kai-shek
(War Area Service Corps Diary for
1944—China)

We've got to use air power. We need more fuel and airplane parts. When are you going to ship them to us?'"

Doreen wrote in her notepad again, saying in a louder voice, "Okay, let's get back on topic here. Casey Vincent will serve as Toastmaster. A big part of the evening. We have a list of the dignitaries and who will make the toasts."

Charles poked George in the shoulder. "The Old Man called on you for a few words. Are you ready?"

"I'm always nervous with public speaking but will give it my b-best shot."

Doreen looked George in the eye. "Practice with Gremlin. Your speech is fluent when you talk with him." I sat up when I heard my name.

My best friend gave her a half smile. "You're right. We'll give it a shot, huh, Gremlin?" My tail whisked the floor in agreement. George's eyes twinkled. "Ralph and I are putting together some music, so we'll have entertainment afterwards."

"Excellent. We'll meet again next week with a bigger crew to work out the details." Andy stood. "By the way—just heard we're getting an influx of Air Force personnel. Meaning that all barracks will be full. We'll be moving in more racks and lockers."

George patted my back. "Maybe we'll get more band members."

~   ~   ~   ~   ~

We took long walks every day. George pulled his flight jacket collar up over his neck on cold and windy days. He rolled up his shirt sleeves when it was warm and sunny, practicing the same words over and over, gesturing as he spoke, while I pranced next to him.

When we visited Ralph and Tom, the men sat on tall stools next to a work bench in the Quonset hut. Tom and I sat in their laps as they planned the music for the banquet. Pieces of greasy-smelling engines and tools made me sneeze, and I licked my nose.

Ralph moved the tools to the back of the work bench and rubbed Tom's chin and neck. "Let's keep it uplifting. Tunes like 'Hail, Hail, The Gang's All Here' and 'For He's a Jolly

Good Fellow.' Everyone knows those, and the Chinese dignitaries can easily pick them up."

George set his notepad on the bench and jotted down notes one-handed, keeping the other hand on my back. "How about 'Side by Side' and 'On the Sunny Side of the Street?'"

"Good possibilities." Ralph nodded.

"We should include some patriotic pieces. What's the name of that one... dee-dee-daah-daah-daah? Uh..." George snapped his fingers. "'You're a Grand Old Flag.'"

"Okay. Those will be good after the banquet." Ralph tapped his fingernails on the work bench. "We should open with the Pledge of Allegiance. Cook has someone in the mess hall who can sing 'The Star Spangled Banner'—sounds like he's a trained singer from Los Angeles."

"George said, "I found the National Anthem of the Republic of China printed in my flight log. It's in English and Chinese. Maybe Mrs. Liu can teach me how it goes. I'll arrange it for the band and ask Charles to check with the Chinese group for someone to lead the singing."

Tom sniffed my muzzle. I growled quietly and pretended to snarl. We both wiggled, and the men put us on the floor. We nipped and barked at each other. When they walked to the door, Tom and I chased each other outside. Tom picked up a big rag, and we played keep away from each other. George called to me, and I gave the rag one last tug against Tom.

I heard a Jeep approach and barked a warning, running as fast as a tiger to George's heel. The Jeep sped around the corner and skidded in the gravel, barely missing me. It stopped with a jerk. The engine died, and George picked me up, both of us shaking.

I couldn't find Tom, but I heard him yelping. Barking, I struggled in George's arms, trying to dash to my brother. George held me. "Stay, Gremlin."

A young man stepped out of the Jeep, pale. "Just learning how to drive a clutch. So sorry, sir. Is everyone okay?"

Ralph ran to the other side of the Jeep. "Oh no–it's Tom. He's hurt bad." When George looked up, I slipped out of his grip and crawled next to my brother to lick his face, whining. Ralph elbowed me away. He pulled out his handkerchief and pressed it against Tom's hind end. It turned quickly from white to the color of Ralph's rags.

George shouted at the driver of the Jeep. "You—out of the way—now." He grabbed me and climbed into the driver's seat, turning the key as Ralph jumped in, huddling over Tom in the passenger's seat. Tom whined and yelped. George's hand trembled as he shifted gears, speeding away from the airfield. "How is he?"

"Looks bad, but he's still with us." Ralph's voice shook. I whimpered, smelling Tom's fear and an unusual salty scent mixed with the familiar smell of his fur.

Red, the nurse, met us at the front steps of the hospital. "Someone called from the airfield. What happened?"

"Jeep accident. Tom's hurt bad. Is Doc in?" George had his hand on Ralph's shoulder. Red led us into a small room and motioned for Ralph to put Tom on a bunk. She pulled towels and bottles from a shelf.

"Doc's out. Let's take care of him." Red and Ralph bent over Tom, speaking in low voices. I whined as I heard her say, "Good boy." Would she give him a shot? George took me away from my brother as I looked back at him, whimpering—*hhhnnnn-hhhhnn.*

~   ~   ~   ~   ~

The next day, we took a Jeep to the hospital before breakfast. Red told us, "Ralph stayed up all night with Tom. Doc Gentry got in after midnight. Saved his life but couldn't save his hind leg. He tried everything." She looked into my eyes and caressed my face. "I'm so sorry, Gremlin." I closed my eyes halfway. My whiskers felt like they would fall to the floor.

She led us to Tom, curled up next to Ralph on the cot. Ralph's eyes were red, and his mouth drooped. "He lost his leg. I should've kept him on a leash. This shouldn't have happened." His voice quavered and his shoulders shook.

George picked me up and placed me next to my brother. I nuzzled Tom's ear, smelling a strong whiff of medicine that hurt my nose. I nestled next to him and licked his snout to soothe him. Maybe my scent would mask the hospital smells.

George said, "Accidents happen, Ralph. I'm sure he'll pull through. He's got Joe and Hedda's blood in him." He looked up when someone entered the room. "Doc Gentry, any updates about Tom?"

The doctor wore white, like Red the nurse. He wasn't as tall as George, but he stroked Tom's back and put his big fingers under my brother's chin. "He's getting better. Ralph can take him home soon." He patted me on my shoulder. "You must be Gremlin. You'll be able to play with Tom again soon, little fella."

"Thanks, Doc." Ralph shook Doc's hand. "Say, George, will you get the band together next week? We'll practice in the hangar. It'll be good for Tom—and me."

A few days later after chow, the band met in the hangar

for their practice. When we arrived at the hangar, I found Tom lying on towels in his wooden crate. It was turned on its side, open on one end. I nuzzled his chest and sniffed at the white bandage on his hindquarters where his leg had been. I cuddled with him and licked his forehead, slowly, the way Mom licked us when we were little.

Tom snorted and stood on his three legs. Ralph and George clapped, saying, "Atta boy, Tom." I gave him an encouraging *wwwffff* when he fell onto his towels.

My brother stood again, a little wobbly. I got to my feet and walked in a circle around him. Nuzzling his neck, I nosed him toward the opening. He hopped out, growling at me. When he nipped at my shoulders, I pretended to charge at him, pulling back at the last instant—my head down, tail raised and wagging, waiting for his next attack. Just like old times when we were puppies with Wench and Mom. He stepped closer to me.

"Look at him, back at it already. It's been about two weeks. Doc thought Gremlin would be good therapy for Tom. Looks like he's right" The wrinkles on Ralph's face disappeared when he smiled. "Okay, that's it, boys. Enough exercise for you for now, Tommy. Back in the box for a little more rest." Ralph put a piece of wood across the opening of the box, too high for my brother to jump over. Tom whined, then lay down and closed his eyes. I hopped in to lay next to him.

George and Ralph greeted the other musicians when they arrived. They took out the instruments they called saxophone, guitar, trumpet, and trombone. When they tuned up, their instruments echoed through the hangar. Tom and I buried our heads in the towels when they played. I howled through half of their rehearsal, adding to the din in the hangar.

In the middle of the session, Ralph announced, "Okay, boys, we're moving to Mac's canteen. Acoustics are just awful in here. Can't hear myself think."

For the next practice, we met in the canteen. Ralph motioned to a group of men. "Bring it in, boys." Four men pushed a tall desk-like box through the door of the canteen, across the floor, and onto the stage.

Ralph clapped his hands to get everyone's attention. "Listen up, Tigers. I want you to meet David Knight, mechanic. Just transferred in from Chungking. A piano man from New Orleans. Met him in Chicago when he was the guest performer with my symphony. Charles and I arranged for one of the hotels in Kunming to donate an old upright piano to our base."

As the men took the instruments out of their cases, Ralph called to the pianist, "Play something for us, Dave. We haven't heard a keyboard in ages."

David sat on a round stool that creaked like a cricket. "Hello, gentlemen. In honor of our Old Man, Claire Chennault, here's my rendition of 'Claire de Lune' by Debussy."

Tom and I sat side-by-side as David ran his fingers over the keys, the way George typed, but without the rings and clicks. The men put their instruments back in the cases and stood around the piano with their mouths half-open The music flowed like the river where we fished, soft and melodic. When he finished, the men were silent, then broke into cheers and applause, slapping him on the back.

"Okay, Davey," Mac's cigar hung from his mouth as he

shouted from behind the bar, rubbing a glass with a towel. "That's fine, but can you play boogie-woogie? After all, this is a canteen, not a concert hall."

David rolled his shoulders back and sat up with a grin. He wiggled his fingers and attacked the keyboard with his lively music. I jumped on Tom's shoulder and gnawed at his ears. He pressed me down on the floor, and we wrestled until Ralph separated us. The men cheered again. Dave and the band and played into the night.

One evening, Ralph told the musicians at their practice, "Just got ahold of the sheet music for the 'Army Air Corps,' the song by Robert Crawford. Let's surprise everyone."

Slim, the trombone player, cleared his throat. "Ralph, I heard our own General Hap Arnold announced that Crawford's song won the competition, back in nineteen thirty-nine."

"Right. Last minute entry. Good tune, by a pilot with the pulse of flying in his blood." Ralph scratched his head. "Maybe someday they'll change the lyrics to the U.S. Air Force, but for now, we'll play it as written."

"What's the order of the tunes?" Slim asked.

Ralph cleared his throat. Well, we'll start with the national anthem after the Pledge of Allegiance. Then the Chinese national anthem. We'll start a new tradition and end with the Army Air Corps tune. As for the rest, we've got all the tunes memorized. I prefer to read the audience and find out when they want to dance and when they're ready to talk. George and I'll call out the titles of the tunes and the keys when we think it's right—you know, ad lib."

~   ~   ~   ~   ~

After setting up their instruments in Mac's canteen, Tom and I played under the round tables in the big room. Tom hopped on three legs, nipping and growling at me until Ralph stopped us. He told George, "Good luck with your toast tonight, buddy. Gremlin's a good coach. Just pretend you're holding your oboe and tuning up the orchestra. You'll do fine. Not so sure about these two naughty puppies, though."

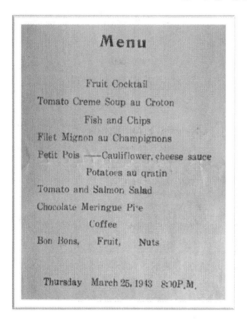

Banquet Program
March 25, 1943

George snapped my leash onto my collar. "Hope it goes okay. Doreen offered to watch Gremlin. Maybe Andy can take care of Tom. See you later." We walked to our barracks as George practiced his words. He changed into a different uniform and hat. He mumbled while he buffed his shoes and polished my collar.

When we returned, the canteen was brightly lit. People began to arrive in stiffly starched uniforms and shiny medals. I heard conversations in Mandarin as well as in English. Mac's tables were decorated with flowers, and the air felt warm and stuffy with the candles lit on the tables. The musical instruments were ready on the stage, and Dave's piano had a white cloth and a vase of flowers on top.

Once everyone sat down and began to eat, several of my

friends called to me and passed me bites of steak and carrots under the table from their fingertips. I grew full and drowsy, and my tummy nearly touched the floor.

I was startled by the ping-pinging of metal on glass. Everyone stood and held their glasses in the air as Casey Vincent spoke, then everyone took a sip from their glass and sat down.

Doreen pulled me onto her lap just before Colonel Vincent called on George. My best friend made his way in front of the crowd to the head table, decorated with shining silver and colorful arrangements of flowers. He stood at the podium next to General Chennault, took a deep breath, and raised his glass.

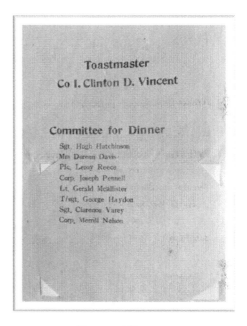

Banquet Program
March 25, 1943

"General Chennault, honored guests, officers, and enlisted airmen, welcome to this gathering to celebrate the promotion of Claire Lee Chennault to the rank of Major General." My best friend's forehead glistened with sweat, but he spoke the way he'd practiced with me. "Let us raise a toast together, to Major General Chennault, to the new Fourteenth Air Force, and to our esteemed Chinese friends."

Just as I'd heard so many times, but better. He raised his glass, and everyone did exactly what he did. I jumped from Doreen's lap and ran to him, barking all the way to the front of the room. George set down his glass next to General Chennault and held me so high I could see everyone as they clapped. "Thank you, Gremlin," he whispered in my ear. I licked his cheek and chin, my tail waving like a flag as our friends smiled at us.

After George's toast, the other officers patted him on the back and congratulated him as he walked back to his seat, holding me in his arms and tickling my tummy.

The band played all the songs they'd practiced for weeks. Ralph and George waited a few minutes between pieces, talking over which tune to play next as people talked and danced. I stayed by George's feet until Doreen picked me up and danced with me. She passed me to others when she was asked to dance. Everyone stood to sing the final song about the Army Air Corps, putting their fists in the air toward the end of the song, shouting, "Hey!" Everyone cheered the band, their eyes glistening, including Chennault.

Doreen took me outside for a moment for me to relieve myself when the musicians began to clean their instruments and put them into their cases. She brought me to the stage as Ralph told the group, "Everyone had a good time. Good arrangement of that Air Corps tune, George. Thanks, buddy." All the band members shook hands and slapped each other on the back.

Doreen gave me to George. My eyes drooped, until General Chennault came to the stage. "Good work, boys. I appreciate the musical tributes for my promotion dinner. And

George, you sure surprised me with your toast."

"I surprised myself, sir. Gremlin's a good listener." George stroked my ears and scratched me under my chin.

The general rubbed my head with his smoky-smelling fingers. "You, too, Gremlin. Good job, tiger." I panted in joy, and a warm feeling spread in my chest and tummy, almost as good as slurping a big bowl of Cook's Hungarian goulash. With Spam.

Chapter 17: Our Enemies

Flying Tiger Shoulder Patch on George's
Flight Jacket (WWII)

Our enemies are not demons, but human beings like ourselves.

Lao Tzu

George and I walked from Operations to Headquarters for a
late afternoon meeting with Doreen. My tummy rumbled as I
snuggled with Mom in our basket under her best friend's desk.
She licked the top of my head as I relaxed.

Andy's chair flew backwards, and we jumped to our feet.
He stood and shouted, "Bamboo net reports a squadron of ten
Jap Zeros on their way from the southeast. Five minutes."

He yelled into the radio, "Attention, airfield. Air raid—
repeat—air raid! Heads up, pilots and crews—Zeros in five
minutes!"

The buzzing, crackling radio responded, "Roger that—airfield has six pilots ready to go."

"Roger. Eight pilots on their way from HQ." Andy flipped a switch, and a loud sound pierced my ears. He tossed a set of keys to Charles and motioned to the door. They ran out and clattered down the steps. I heard the Jeeps' engines outside as Colonel Casey Vincent and other pilots rushed from Chennault's office and ran outside, pulling on their flight jackets. The Jeeps rumbled away.

George sat at Andy's desk, talking on the radio and answering the phone. Should I follow the fighter pilots to scare gremlins? No, I should stay with George. Jump into his lap? No, he'd push me away. Hide with Mom in her basket? No, I was George's puppy now. I stood at attention next to him, holding my breath. Waiting for orders.

General Chennault burst from his office, followed by Pop, head held high. "To the bunker, Doreen. Take the staff and Hedda. Evacuation—this is not a drill."

"Heel, Hedda." Doreen and the rest of the HQ staff left everything on their desks and hustled out the door.

"George—" Chennault turned to us. "Turn that damn alarm off. Notify Ops that you're staying with me to watch our boys in action. Bring the pup. Joe will train him to get used to the racket." He handed George something like a camera. "Use this set of field glasses. You won't see a sight like this when you get back to the States."

George made a quick phone call then took me on my leash to the steps of HQ. I trembled at the commotion. Airmen running past. Jeeps zipping by. Planes filling the sky. Pop sat calmly on the top step near Chennault's feet. The general saluted the setting sun, shading his face. "There go my boys."

George held the field glasses up to his eyes. "What a sight..." Fighters with their shark's mouths shot into the sky and circled above the Kunming air base.

The Flying Tigers—I needed to guard them from gremlins. Bracing my feet and taking a deep breath, I opened my mouth and barked as loudly as I could. I had to help Ralph, his crews, and our pilots, scaring any gremlins hiding in our planes' engines.

"That's it, Gremlin," Chennault told me. "Give 'em the gun!" Pop barked, too—from deep in his chest. I sounded like a chirping bird compared to his tiger's roar.

Shiny planes with dark circles painted under their wings flew over the river where we fished, humming toward the airfield. Our planes dove together from the sun, like a team of tigers, and the Zeros scattered like a startled flock of birds.

Bursts of light and smoke shot from our fighters. Were gremlins playing tricks on our pilots? I barked louder, twisting my body and stamping my feet. I heard a faint *rat-a-tat-tat-tat*! Two distant planes slowly glided to the ground, clouds of smoke following them.

"We got a couple hits on those Zeros." George put down his field glasses to glance at Chennault. Our fighters spun and wheeled in the sky, spitting fire.

"Our men are staying in formation, following training, pursuit tactics." Chennault kept his voice low voice. "This old schoolteacher's drilled it into them."

As the air battle continued, larger planes flew overhead, dropping little black flies. I heard high whining sounds. Chennault frowned. "Bombs away—we're under attack. Time

209

to head inside. Back to work." He and Pop strode into his office. George sat in Andy's chair, rolling between Andy and Doreen's desks, answering phones and the radio.

I crawled into the empty basket under Doreen's desk, trembling, confused and frightened by the awful noises hurting my ears—*hhhnnnfff-hhhnnnnnff*. I burrowed under our worn towels and curled into a ball. Shrill, shrieking noises became louder. The whole building shook with explosions, like the ones at the hospital. I wanted to run away, but I stayed to help George.

The bombings stopped, and he lifted the towels. I licked his hand. "Steady, Gremlin," he said in a calm voice. "If it's my time, there's nothing I can do about it. If it isn't, I can complete my mission. Our commanding general's at his desk, and I'm manning this station." He covered the basket with his familiar-smelling flight jacket, leaving an opening so I could see him.

I shivered and shuddered when the bombing started again—first the whining noise and then the explosions. Nosing through the opening, I saw chunks of the ceiling fall onto George's head and shoulders. He brushed them away. Pictures of our commanders danced on the walls whenever the building shook. Clouds of cigarette smoke poured out of General Chennault's office.

Gradually the explosions stopped and the low engine sounds of the bombers faded away. George pushed his jacket aside and lifted me into his arms. I licked his face and neck, wriggling with relief. Picking me up, he staggered to Chennault's office and poked his head through the door. "All right, sir?"

"Hmph. Fine. You?" The general puffed on a very short cigarette and lit a second one with its glowing tip.

"We're all right." George took me outside to walk around the building. The smoke in the air made me gag. I relieved myself in every way possible, shook all over, and scratched at the dirt and pebbles with my hind legs. I ran to George and jumped up, growling at his boots. I ran away for him to chase me, but he didn't seem to want to play, so I pranced in circles around him, lifting each paw above the grass. We joined General Chennault and Pop on the steps of HQ.

In the setting sun, the Flying Tigers spit fire at the remaining Zeros. *Rat-a-tat-tat — rat-tat-a-tat-tat!* The planes shot at each other high above the air base. A Zero dove toward the ground, flames streaming from the engine. I heard a loud crash in the direction of the airfield and stood at attention. Were Tom and Ralph all right?

"Another Japanese Zero." Chennault looked through his binoculars. "Looks like we're knocking 'em out of China's skies." A black cloud, like smoke from our wood stove, billowed into the darkening sky.

The men watched quietly as the last Zeros flew over the distant hills. George took a quick breath and shouted to Chennault. "With your permission, sir, I'll sound the all clear and get on the horn. Check in with Ops, the military police, airfield, and hospital. See how the staff is doing."

Chennault gave him a pat on the back. "Good man." He went into his office.

George made announcements over the loudspeaker, talked on the phones, took notes, and relayed messages to Chennault, who leaned against the doorway of his office and chatted with returning personnel. "Airfield reports all pilots have returned, sir. No casualties. Minor injuries. A few holes in the planes, all still usable." The general nodded in response.

George cleared his throat. "Ralph reports his crew extinguished the fire in the downed Zero. They'll salvage what they can of the plane to determine the current model and any innovations. No remains in the plane. Pilot at large, likely wounded. The MPs are searching with Private Rex."

Chennault flicked ashes from his cigarette. "How about administrative personnel?"

George checked his notes. "Staff is okay. Hospital has seven wounded from shrapnel and rubble. No casualties."

Charles returned to Headquarters with Casey Vincent and two other pilots, who trooped into Chennault's office and closed the door. Charles sat at his desk. "Looks like you got all our work done. Don't do so well, or you'll replace all of us."

George blushed. "Chennault asked me to stay with him. Personnel in Ops followed procedures. Don't worry, I'll get out of your hair once Andy gets back, maybe get some chow. How about you?"

I pattered up to Charles, and he put me in his lap. "I had something at the airfield." When he scratched my neck, I sensed something tasty on his fingers and licked them.

"Here, Gremlin." He opened a napkin and gave me pieces of cheese and Spam. "I picked up a little something for you, just in case."

Charles took a deep breath. "Pretty hairy at the airfield. I spoke with the Chinese construction crew chiefs. They're already repairing the holes in the runways and pulling those big rollers to smooth out the surface."

George stood and straightened the pictures on the wall.

"Lots to take care of." He took a broom from the corner and swept the crumbles from the ceiling into a dust pan, emptying them into a waste basket.

"It'll be a long night for me if they capture the pilot." Charles stroked my back as I licked my lips. "I'll serve as the Japanese interpreter. I'd better check in with the MPs now."

"You speak Japanese, too?" George turned to Charles, his mouth open, eyes wide.

Charles nodded. "Long story—I'll tell ya later. Gotta head out."

I heard the Jeep whiz away, and another arrived. Andy, Doreen, and the rest of the staff returned to the office. Mom and I nuzzled and licked each other as George put the broom away, coughing.

Doreen put her jacket on the back of her chair. "George, have you been here the whole time?"

"Sure, the Old Man and I held down the fort. Better get back to Ops." People crowded around him on our way out of Headquarters, patting him on the back, the way he patted me when I did a good job. We walked to Operations, where George checked in with each person before we walked to the mess hall in the dark. Charles joined us at the table. I didn't look up from my bowl of chow under the bench.

I heard George say, "Back already?" I wolfed down my food and licked the bowl, pushing it around on the hard floor. George spun around to pick me up. He nudged my bowl under the bench with his foot and set me down on the bench between him and Charles. I waited for crumbs and treats.

"It's nearly midnight." Charles dug into his food. "Military Police spent hours looking and didn't find the pilot."

"Must have skedaddled." George sipped his coffee. "Listen, wherever he is, they'll pick him up."

"Most likely any Jap would avoid our base and head across the river. But what chance would he have if the Chinese caught him?" Charles stared at something far away. "If we capture him, we'll interrogate him. They're trained to commit suicide rather than endure the shame of being held prisoner. He's in a real pickle."

George took a few sips of coffee. "Say, Charles, what's this about you learning Japanese?"

"Huh?" Charles turned to George. "Oh, yeah. Always found languages easy to pick up. The Japanese boys in Watsonville taught me—they call themselves the *Nisei*. Parents were from Japan, and their kids were born in the U.S. Sometimes they tricked me into saying bad words, but eventually I caught on to their sense of humor."

George moved his legs to the other side of the bench, leaning his back against the table, shifting to face Charles. "How'd you become an interpreter?" He crossed his legs and picked me up.

Charles folded his hands on the table. "I joined the Army Air Corps in summer of forty-one. They needed military linguists, for German, French, Japanese. I heard about the Army Intelligence School language school opening in San Francisco. November, good timing. Some of my Nisei buddies were recruited. I heard about the language program from them and joined up."

Cook came to the table with a pot of coffee. "Refills?" He scratched my chest, and I licked his thumb.

"Sure, Cook. Thanks." George smiled. "Glad you're still open."

"Maybe later." Charles covered his cup with his hand. Cook set the coffee pot on the table and wiped down nearby tables.

"When Pearl Harbor was attacked, the Nisei were looked at differently, like traitors. They were excellent translators but they were distrusted. A real conflict."

"What happened to your friends?"

"The school could have expelled them—and they would've been interned with their families at Manzanar, in one of those god-awful camps. People were treated like livestock in horse barns."

George twisted around on the bench and picked up the coffee pot. Charles nodded, and George filled both cups. Charles swallowed his coffee and held the cup in his hands. "Well, the leaders wouldn't let that happen to their students, so they moved the whole program to Minnesota—Camp Savage. We all finished and became military translators. My Nisei friends are scattered across the Pacific now, and here I sit with you, enjoying Cook's coffee."

Cook smiled from the next table. "I'm here for you, buddy."

"I had no idea." George raised his eyebrows. "You go to school with someone, end up on the other side of the world together. Incredible."

Charles said, "It'll take a while for the MPs to shake out that pilot, if he's still alive. You should head back to the barracks."

George smiled. His eyes looked tired, ready for sleep. "Thanks, buddy. I'll be tied to the desk awhile longer. Gremlin can take a catnap in my desk drawer." Catnap? Wasn't that something Sadie did?

Cook collected the trays, mugs, coffeepot, and my bowl, refusing help. I hoped for more treats—but no luck.

We walked through the quiet base, leaving Charles at Headquarters. I wagged my tail as I sniffed the trails of mice and rats, boots, and Jeep oil between HQ and Operations. Finding a good spot, I squatted to pee.

George pulled gently on my leash. "Let's go, tiger. Heel." We walked around the corner of the building into the dim light outside Ops. George put his foot on the first step. I stopped, sensing something—or someone—breathing hard under the staircase. *Sniff—sniff.* A new scent–full of oil and smoke and sweat. I pawed at the ground and pointed, whining, straining on my leash.

Hearing George cock his sidearm, I darted under the stairs, yowling and barking. Was this a gremlin? I had to protect George. Could I be as brave as he was during the bombings?

I heard rustling and a muffled cry from under the stairs. I backed out, standing as tall as I could, grounding my four feet into the soil. I barked louder than I ever had before, hackles rising along my neck and back.

"Come out of there!" George jumped off the step and stood with his feet apart, holding his weapon with both hands.

Charles dashed from HQ, shouting, "What is it? I've never heard Gremlin sound like that." Other people came running.

"Over here!" George shouted. "Enemy alert! Call the MPs!" Enemy? It must be a gremlin. I was born to take out gremlins. I crawled under the steps and grabbed hold of whatever I could. The gremlin cried and shook his leg.

216

Charles yelled at the gremlin in a different language. I held on, even though I could taste blood through the cloth. My head ached from his kicking and screaming.

"Military police—let us through," shouted Sarge. "Watch, Private Rex." The huge Doberman pushed against my behind, snarling and growling louder than I'd ever heard him. Was he going to eat me? I didn't care if he did. Wouldn't let go. I acted meaner than my sister Wench, growling at Rex— and the gremlin.

George tugged on my leash and ordered me away. "Heel, Gremlin!" Maybe Rex was there to help me, but he was too big to get under the stairs. Determined not to let go, I pulled the gremlin with me as I backed out, even though he trembled and twisted.

"Attack, Private Rex," Jimmy commanded. Rex grabbed onto the gremlin's leg with his huge jaws. Sarge bent down and pulled him all the way out.

"Release, Private Rex," Jimmy commanded. "Release. Sit, Rex." The huge dog with the pointed ears stepped back and sat next to me. His tongue seemed longer than my body, panting and slobbering as he kept his eyes on the gremlin. We growled as the MPs held the gremlin, who shouted, but not in English or Mandarin or Cantonese. Gremlin language?

Charles shouted orders, using words I didn't know. The gremlin put his hands on his head. Sarge pulled the gremlin's hands behind his back and clicked them together.

The gremlin was half the size of Sarge. He had blood on his face and hands and wore a pilot's hat like Luke's, with goggles and a thick flight jacket. I bared my teeth and snarled at him, darting at his feet. The gremlin jumped back. I grabbed hold of whatever I could—his shoelaces—and pulled. Sarge ordered me to release.

I didn't know what that meant, but George kneeled and gathered me into his chest, taking the stringy shoelaces out of my mouth. "Steady, Gremlin. You did a good job, boy. Good dog. Let go." He held me tight and I felt as important as Private Rex, who seemed to smile at me. Maybe we could be friends someday—if he didn't eat me.

Charles knelt next to us, petting my head. "You saved the day, Gremlin," he said. "You found the missing Japanese pilot."

Japanese pilot? Not a gremlin? I put my head down and whined. I couldn't tell a person from a gremlin. Charles stood and extended his hand, helping George to his feet. I felt his knees buckle for a moment. He nodded and stood up straight. "I'm all right."

Sarge kept his gun trained on the pilot as he climbed into the driver's side of the Jeep. "Charles, come with us to the base jail. We need to have a talk with this gentleman." Charles sat in the passenger seat while Jimmy and Private Rex guarded the pilot in the back seat, Rex slobbering on the pilot's knee.

"Good job, Gremlin." George carried me into Ops and turned on his desk lamp. He turned me over, checked my head and body, and felt each of my paws. "You're fine. Quite a day, huh?" I shivered all over. His arms warmed me and calmed me, even though he was shaking. I felt so tired I fell asleep next to his chest, awakening for a moment when he placed me in my drawer and tucked my Good Morning towel around me.

~   ~   ~   ~   ~

In the morning, Cook gave me the biggest bone ever. I hid

under George's desk in Operations, gnawing on the bone and slurping out the marrow. I felt silly for thinking I'd found a gremlin but I felt like a hero for alerting George and capturing the missing pilot. Why did the Japanese pilot use his plane to hurt the Chinese people and the Flying Tigers? I worried my bone as many thoughts spun around in my head.

Charles visited, dark circles under his eyes. "Come here, Gremlin. You're the hero of the day." He picked me up and leaned against George's desk.

My best friend sat back in his chair. "Who was he? What did you find out?"

"A farmer. He wanted to stay on the family farm. Didn't want to enlist, hated being recruited. Reluctant to give up his life for his country." Charles blinked, his eyes glistening.

A farmer? Dr. and Mrs. Liu lived on a farm—and they were kind people who gave me treats. George leaned forward. "Like the Japanese families back home. Hard-working people."

"Sure, I think so, too." Charles scratched his head. "He didn't have much information. He was taught to fly and fight. Ordered to kill himself if captured. Die rather than surrender."

"Why is that?" George raised his eyebrows.

Charles became very still, looking out the window into the cloudy sky as he rubbed my neck and shoulders. "Better to commit hari-kari than to be killed by an enemy. They don't want to lose face—show themselves as cowards."

"Tough spot. I'd hate to be in that position."

Charles sighed. "After our interrogation, the MPs turned him over to the local Chinese."

"What'll they do to him?" George's voice was soft and low.

Charles held his lips together. He held me so close to his chest I could hear his heartbeat. "Japanese soldiers have brutalized and murdered hundreds of thousands, if not millions of Chinese—so far."

George nodded. "The Chinese have gone through years of oppression. What they call the war against Japanese aggression. Invasion of Manchuria, 1931. Marco Polo Bridge in 1937. And then the rape of Nanking. They've got a stranglehold on China."

Charles shook his head slowly as I licked his fingers. "I'll tell you what, though, George. When they walked him off base... it was... it was the quietest procession I ever heard. No one talked. His hands behind his back, head down. Don't know what'll happen to him... but I don't want to know, either."

Charles handed me to George and pulled up a chair. He sat next to us, showing George a newspaper, like the ones George put on the floor before I could make my water and piles outside. I sniffed it. Yep, the same newspaper, only not used yet.

Charles pointed to squiggly lines on the paper. "News from San Francisco is that they're releasing some of the West Coast Japanese Americans from the internment camps. They can go back to farming."

"About time," George took in a deep breath. "All the kids we knew—interned in those blasted camps. Dastardly to think of what their families lost because of their countrymen. Their freedom, homes, stores, farms."

Charles opened his hands, elbows on his knees. "Fortunately, some towns rallied around local Japanese, holding their lands in trust, keeping the businesses going, crops in."

That night, George wrote a letter to his folks and read it to me, which he didn't do very often after making his toast at the banquet for General Chennault.

> Dear Folks,
>
> We've been a little busy here, so I'll get caught up on writing. You might remember Charles Leong from Watsonville. He set me up with a Mandarin teacher here—too busy to teach me himself.
>
> I take lessons near a local village about three times a week. I'm not even attempting to learn to read characters. Too much work.
>
> I read they're releasing some of the West Coast Japanese to go back to farming. That's a good idea, as I understand labor is hard to get. Have you heard of any of the Japanese Americans around Watsonville? Hope they'll all be released soon.
>
> Love, George

Chapter 18: A Jade Necklace

Dragon's Backbone (WWII)

The man of wisdom is never of two minds;
The man of benevolence never worries;
The man of courage is never afraid.

Confucius

I rode in the passenger's seat of the Jeep, pacing back and forth, sniffing the country air while the wind flopped my ears in different directions. Our open Jeep bounced along the road to the Kunming air base as we returned from a mission for General Chennault.

After driving along under the warm summer sun, George stopped the Jeep and pointed his camera to a man by a stream pushing the sticks on a wooden machine He took a picture— *click*. The water moved uphill as the man pushed back and

223

forth on the sticks. The water at the top of the dragon backbone flowed gently toward the fields.

George scratched my chest. "Fascinating, tiger. Looks like an Archimedes screw from a distance. Here in China, Gremlin, they call it a dragon backbone. So that's how it works. Read about it ages ago, always wanted to see one in motion."

As we drove away, George waved and the man raised his chin in reply

We drove along, and my tummy began to rumble with hunger. Ahead, I saw something odd, moving slowly toward the road. We got closer, and I stood at attention on the seat, ears cocked, ready to protect George. *Bbbbrrkk-brrrrkkkkk*—two huge gremlins and a man waded in a flooded field. *Grrrfff-bbbrrkk-brrrrkkkkk.*

"Hush, Gremlin." My best friend pointed to my nose, a reminder to be quiet. "That's a farmer plowing the fields to grow rice." He skidded the Jeep to a stop and stepped out, calling, "*Nǐ hǎo,*" to the man walking behind the two huge beasts. I growled deep in  my throat. George motioned to the camera slung around his neck as if to ask the farmer a question. The man smiled and nodded, and George clicked his camera. They waved at each other. George got into the Jeep but didn't start it.

"Nice soil, Gremlin. Reminds me of my dad's old ranch

in Oregon. We used to fish all over the Klamath Basin." He folded his hands on top of the steering wheel, peering over the Jeep's hood, his chest leaning against the steering wheel. "Sure wish I could go fishing with him now." He took a deep breath and waved again, saying, "*Xièxiè,*" to thank the farmer.

Fishing? Were there fish in the farmer's field? I gathered my stubby legs under my long body to jump down and find out, but George sat back in his seat and started the engine. No

luck. As much as I enjoyed riding in the Jeep, I wished we were fishing, too, so I could roll in something delicious. Like fish guts.

We drove on, passing fields and farmers and a man carrying a heavy load on a pole over his shoulders.

"He must have enough in his garden to sell in the village. Hard work. There's gotta be a better way to earn a living."

Farther on our way, we saw a family irrigating their field. They pulled on a dragon backbone, just as the man had done. They

225

smiled at George as he took their picture—*click*. An old woman and a little child sat near a hill with a door. "This is a smart family," George said. "They have everything they need for survival. Water, garden, irrigation system. See that hill? My guess is they shelter underground to protect themselves during bombings."

The Chinese people worked hard in the countryside, just as they built and rebuilt the Kunming airfields after they were bombed. They rebuilt the hospital. In China's countryside, they plowed, planted, and irrigated.

We drove through a village and stopped on a bridge made of rocks. George took a picture of the women washing clothes in the river, who waved. Young children played on blankets spread out on the ground, bundled in hats and thick clothes. I ran up to the children and rolled on their blanket. They giggled and cuddled me, scratching me behind my ears and on my belly. George sat on the ground and held the kids on his lap, tickling their bellies and laughing with the children as they felt his face and the patches on his flight jacket.

He stood, saying, "*Zàijiàn. Nǐmen dōu hǎo piàoliang.* Gremlin. Heel." I thought they were beautiful, too, and licked my new little friends goodbye on their cheeks before following my best friend.

"Here's water for you to drink." George filled my water bowl with water from his canteen and placed them on the top of a rock wall on the bridge. He tore up a sandwich and passed treats to me as he munched.

As I finished my nibbles, heard an airplane behind us. *Ggggrrrrarkk-ggggrrrawwrkkk.* It didn't sound like any of the planes on our air base. George turned and squinted into the sun, cupping his ear.

"That's not one of ours." He ran to the children, scooped them up in his arms, and passed them to the women at the top of the stairs, who ran into a building, crying.

I looked down at the road. Too high for me to jump down. I ran along the wall to the Jeep, bunched my muscles and jumped farther than I ever had before—into the passenger's seat—as George ran back, jumped in, and cranked the engine.

"Hang on, Gremlin. They'll want us for target practice." He raced down the road and skidded to a stop. "Come here, buddy. That big tombstone in the cemetery might give us cover from strafing." Carrying me behind a big rock, he crouched, panting, as the engine noise grew louder.

Strafing bullets from the plane zinged around us, cutting into the top of the tombstone, chips falling onto us. I felt stunned, cradled between his arm and chest, and shivered from muzzle to hind paws, my tail tucked between my legs.

The plane passed over us, so close I thought George could reach out and touch its belly. He unholstered his sidearm and shot toward the belly of the plane when it passed overhead. I yelped when I heard the loud shot. It flew into the distance, and we sighed. The plane turned, making a big circle in the sky, and came back. I yelped—*yyyyiiippp*—and George sprung up, half-crouching as he carried me around the tombstone to the other side. Bullets pinged around us, until the plane flew up into the sky. Again, it turned and flew toward us, and George dodged to the other side. Was the pilot playing with us—the way Sadie played with a mouse?

We ran around the tombstone many times before the plane finally flew into the far horizon. "He must be running out of fuel." George slumped to the ground. We trembled like the last two leaves clinging to their tree in a winter storm. George held me in both hands, and we looked into each other's eyes. "You okay, buddy?" I licked his chin, but my tongue was dry. I wiggled to the ground and relieved myself on a corner of the tombstone. The Chinese women ran into the cemetery, holding the children. They bowed to George, crying, "*Xièxiè, xièxiè!*"

A woman with white hair held something in her hands, tears streaming down her cheeks. George smiled, shook his head, and motioned with his hands. "A jade necklace? *Yù?* Priceless...uh...*Wú jià.* Thank you, but no—that's too much. *Bù, xièxiè.* Family heirloom—keep it for the children—um—*gěi háizimen.*"

The mother snapped a small jade piece from the necklace and pressed it into his palm. George's eyes widened, and he folded his fingers over it. Clasping his hands under his chin, he slowly recited what I'd heard Dr. Liu teach him. "Thank you. *Xièxiè.* I am honored to accept your gift—um—*Wǒ hěn róngxìng jiēshòu nín de lǐwù.*" He closed his eyes. "My family and I will treasure your kindness for many generations." He opened them and smiled. "*Wǒ hé wǒ de jiārén jiāng shì shìdài dài zhēnxī nǐ de hǎoyì.*"

The family smiled, nodded, and bowed, saying "*Xièxiè*" and "*Zàijiàn.*" The children shouted, "*Fēi Hǔ*" and "*Yīngxióng.*" They smiled at me, their hands behind their backs. George set me down, and I ran to them. They held out their hands, holding the canteen and my water bowl. They laughed when they gave them to George, and I jumped up to kiss their cheeks. As

George drove away, I stood on the back seat and barked goodbye to the families who lived in China's countryside— *Zàijiàn.*

On our way back to base, we stopped at a noodle stand in a village, our bellies growling. George asked how much the noodles cost. "*Yī wǎn miàntiáo duōshǎo qián?*" He dropped jingling coins into the cook's hand, and I ate all the warm noodles my best friend put in my bowl.

From a shelf in the little booth, George added smelly garlic and onions to his bowl. He let out a deep breath as he picked up his chopsticks. After his first bite, he wiped his chin, saying, "Ah, Gremlin. Nothing like a bowl of hot noodles when you've been out driving a Jeep all day—other than having your best friend with you." He smiled as he rubbed my head, then we both slurped our noodles until we cleaned the last ones out of our bowls.

Chapter 19: Old Shanghai

Embroidery of Hawk
Silk on Parchment (WWII)

To put the world in order, we must first put the nation in order;
To put the nation in order, we must put the family in order;
To put the family in order, we must cultivate our personal life.

Confucius

Mrs. Liu greeted us at the door, the silver bells on the porch creating a musical accompaniment to her low, rich voice. "Good afternoon, Lieutenant and Gremlin." The colors of the banners on either side of their doorway had faded over time since our first visit and their edges crinkled in the warm breeze.

We took our places in the large room with its high ceilings and dim light from the windows overlooking their garden. I caught glimpses of birds darting under the eaves of the house to feed babies in their mud nests attached to the side of the outside walls.

Mrs. Liu motioned to her husband, who sat in the ancestral chair, as usual. "Dr. Liu has a sore throat today. He'll be in the room with us, sipping tea, but I'll conduct your lessons." She held a big book, which she set on the table.

"Thank you, Mrs. Liu," replied George, taking off his hat and boots before entering. He handed her a package from Cook, saying, "Ma'am, please accept this small token of my gratitude." She bowed slightly and took the package through a door in the back of the room.

George greeted his teacher. "Hello, *Lǎoshī*—please don't get up. Maybe we'll make this a short session today to avoid tiring my teacher."

Lǎoshī nodded, tapping his throat, which I guessed meant he couldn't talk. He raised his teacup, smiling, and took a long sip.

George turned to Mrs. Liu, returning to sit on the long, low bench. "Should I call you '*Lǎoshī*' now?"

She giggled, holding her hands in front of her mouth. "Not at all, my dear. Just Mrs. Liu." She motioned to George's usual seat. As he sat down, so did I, staring at him and hoping he'd remember to give me a treat for being a good puppy. I licked my lips in anticipation, but he didn't notice me. I waited, looking at each person in the room, knowing that at some point in time George would figure out what I wanted.

"Today, I'd like to share with you about our cultural past," Mrs. Liu said. I noticed the carved wooden back and armrests had designs of flowers rather than scary animals like the ones on the old Kunming gate. For a moment, I wondered why Doreen's furniture had soft cushions and theirs didn't.

George's bunk had a mattress we slept on. I couldn't imagine sleeping on a such a hard surface. It looked as hard as the wooden desk chairs George sat in at HQ. I pawed at George's stockinged foot to catch his attention.

He moved his feet away from me. "I'd like that. But first, I brought something that I just acquired. I'd like to ask you about it." Oh, good—he'll show them my bone. I sat up, ready to grab it.

She motioned to the low table in front of her and pushed the tea tray toward George. "Yes, of course. Please help yourself to tea and sugar cookies first. And maybe you brought a little something for our precious Gremlin?"

My mouth watered as I wagged my tail, thankful that Mrs. Liu remembered me, even if George didn't. He opened the package and set it on the floor. I pounced with a muffled *gggrrrrrowwff*, and everyone laughed.

George scooted his chair closer to Mrs. Liu's table. He stuck his fingers into his front shirt pocket and fished around, pulling out a small cloth bag. He held it out to her and dropped it into her open palm. I gnawed on a bumpy edge of the bone, and it broke away easily. *Crunch-crunch.*

Mrs. Liu's expression changed when she saw the jade piece. She took a sharp breath. "George, this is exquisite. How did you acquire it?"

"Gremlin and I were on business for General Chennault. As we returned to base, we happened to be in a rural village when a Japanese plane attacked. I made sure the children were safe with their parents and distracted the pilot so that they could run to safety."

She made a *tsk-tsk* sound with her tongue, shaking her head. "You brave soul. You saved those families, didn't you?

Protected their little ones. And they wanted to show their gratitude, didn't they?"

"At first they offered me an entire jade necklace. 'That's too much—no, thank you,' I told them—in Chinese, like you taught me, 'Bù, xièxiè.' So, they gave me this one piece of jade from the clasp."

"You gave them back their lives and their children's inheritance. This green jade is high quality, with a beautiful hand-crafted gold leaf in the center. I know you will treasure it, a memento of the good thing you did for that family."

George's eyes misted as he showed the jade to Dr. Liu, who nodded his approval. He tucked it away in his pocket. "Thank you for telling me, Mrs. Liu. I knew you would understand. Someday, when I get married, I want my bride to wear that jade piece. And I hope all the brides in our family will wear this beautiful memento from China."

I wondered if my mom and pop were married. Was Mom a bride? I closed my eyes and licked the marrow from the center of the bone, trying to picture what marriage meant.

George patted the pocket where the jade was hidden. "By the way, the children told me something I'd never heard before. What does, 'yīngxióng' mean?"

She smiled. "You are and always will be their hero, throughout the generations."

George blushed. "I'm a clerk, not a uh—um… hero. Anyone would have protected those kids." He cleared his throat. "What d-d-did you have in mind for today's lesson?"

Mrs. Liu picked up the large book from the table. "My memories of Old Shanghai. Did you know it was a walled city? Built in the Ming dynasty, back in the fifteen hundreds. Of,

course, that was before my time... and even before *Lǎoshī's*."
They smiled at each other. He started to laugh but coughed
instead. I carried my treat to his big chair and lay down, with
my side against his foot to comfort him.

Mrs. Liu continued, "Not much of that old wall remains,
but I have touched the last remaining wall of the Old City of
Shanghai."

"Quite a history," murmured George, blowing on the tea
and munching a cookie as I scraped my teeth against the bone.
He took a sip and swallowed. "Tell me about your family, Mrs.
Liu. I'm all ears." I lifted my ears and cocked my head to one
side. George's face hadn't changed. He had only two ears.
Maybe he meant he was ready to learn, the way I listened
when he taught me a new trick.

"My family was in the working class under the Qing
dynasty. Honest tenant farmers. My grandparents migrated
from our village to Shanghai after the Treaty of Nanking
opened Chinese ports for trade with westerners. In the mid-
eighteen hundreds, the *wàiguó rén* — the foreigners — built their
neighborhoods with wide streets and thick walls, and we
created our alleyways, our *lòngtáng*."

George scratched his head. "I haven't heard of those."

"They're neighborhoods with shared roofs. Families
crowded into the small living spaces, usually two or three
stories high. You learned at a young age how to find the single
gate to get in and out of the *lòngtáng*."

George leaned forward. "Wasn't that a fire hazard? After
the 1906 earthquake in San Francisco, whole blocks of homes
and businesses were destroyed in fires. It was devastating.
Hundreds, thousands were homeless, living in the city parks."

"A similar situation, George. There were thousands in Shanghai in the 1860s, made primarily of wood. Most burned down."

"Were they rebuilt?" George sat back in his chair.

"Yes. In a new style, made with stone. Courtyards and skylights let in more sunshine. Generations of families created neighborhoods where everybody was known, and everything was shared. Almost like our small village here, but in the bustling city." She chuckled. "In fact, every morning, the women cleaned out their bedpans and chamber pots in the streets, with stiff brushes, so musical that the Shanghainese called this ritual the morning symphony."

They laughed, except *Lǎoshī*, who smiled, nodding his head and closing his eyes.

"But look here, George. This is the Bund." Mrs. Lui turned the page.

George leaned over the book. "What's the Bund?"

"That's the main port of Shanghai on the Huangpu River. On weekends, *Lǎoshī* and I would go to the museums." She pointed to the framed picture of a bird that looked big enough pick me up and eat me if it was real. "And I loved the embroidered silks on display. My dear husband saved for months and bought this piece with the hawk, exquisite embroidery on parchment, with tiny stitches I could never hope to replicate. Anyway, we'd walk the Bund to see the rich westerners, streetcars and shops, the docks extending into the river, and all types of boats on the water."

"I've never seen such a busy port," said George. "From these old photos, it's even busier than when I left San Francisco during wartime. Look at all the watercraft."

She nodded, turning the page. "No doubt you have seen rickshaws in this part of China, perhaps ridden in one, but have you seen these wheelbarrows? Rickshaws are much more comfortable, with an actual seat. The wheelbarrow on a farm would have a small wheel in the front, two handles to lift and push it, plus a kind of box for carrying things."

George nodded. "I'm following you. We used them in our yard back home."

Mrs. Liu smiled, then tapped on a black and white picture. "Notice this wheelbarrow has two handles for the workman, and a huge wheel in the center. The passengers ride on either side of the wheel, each half-sitting on a little shelf, with one foot on a rope to keep their balance and a place for their elbows over the wheel, for extra safety."

Mrs. Liu winked at *Lǎoshī*. "Well, once we were married and I started teaching, we were good about saving our money, but one special day we splurged and took a ride on a wheelbarrow. Quite the adventurous youngsters, way back when the twentieth century was new."

George's teacher set down his teacup and folded his hands. Mrs. Liu smiled and turned the page. "And here—the *Yú yuán* gardens, zigzag bridges across the waterways, the City God Temple. We would walk over the *Jiǔ Qù*—the Nine-Turn Bridge—for good luck, buying treats at the old teahouse, just as Gremlin here enjoys his treats." I set my bone down and licked my lips, yawning as they beamed at me.

"I can just smell the roasting ducks filling the air. And the *xiǎolóng bǎo*, remember, my dear? The delicious steamed dumplings? Still makes my mouth water." Mr. and Mrs. Liu smiled at each other.

"Show-long-bough? I'm not familiar with those. How do you eat them?" George scratched his head.

"You can get six or eight in a traditional steaming basket for little money. Pick one up with chopsticks. Nibble a little bite and suck out the juice. They're hot at first—so be careful. Then dip it in vinegar—Shanghai has the best vinegar—and savor the pork and dumpling." Her eyes gleamed as she described what must be her favorite treat. I could almost taste the food I remembered from the booths at the Kunming festival and sighed and rolled onto my side, feeling too full to gnaw on my bone any more.

Mrs. Liu slammed the book shut, startling me. I sat up and whined, looking at her with my head cocked to one side. *Mmmrrrff?* "Sorry, my boy. But… my memories of Shanghai have been darkened by this enemy invasion. Just think of it, George."

She opened the album to another page, tapping a picture. "The Peace Monument on the Bund, commemorating the deaths from the first World War. Toppled by the enemy occupying Shanghai." She blew her nose into her handkerchief, shaking her head slowly as her eyes filled with tears. I sat next to her feet, leaning against her leg to comfort her.

Lǎoshī nodded his head, frowning. George leaned forward, his face troubled, chin in his hand.

Mrs. Liu told us, "Sometimes, this war against the aggression of our enemy is just too much to comprehend." She sobbed into her handkerchief. Drawing a ragged breath, she picked me up. I licked her hands as she rubbed my neck and stroked my back.

"Everything has changed for us. The escape from Shanghai with the stench of death and destruction all around us." Her shoulders shuddered as she closed her eyes and held me close. I held still, feeling her heart pounding in her chest.

"We barely navigated through the frantic crowds heading west. Most people headed to Chungking, the capital after Nanking fell. We had a hard time scrounging for food along the way, weary with travel. Fortunately, we brought a few provisions and our savings. More than most families had, but still...." Her breathing slowed, but her hands trembled when she touched her handkerchief to her eyes, unable to continue.

I nuzzled her hand for her to pet me. She sat up and sniffed, stroking my paws with her long fingers. Nodding her head and taking a deep breath, she said, "Thank you, dear Gremlin. So, we are here now. We are alive. And you, George, you have sought us out and, in a way, we needed you."

"What?" said George, an expression of surprise on his face. "I—uh—" He opened his hands and cocked his head to one side.

"Yes, we wish to give you the lessons we have learned over our lifetimes. A gift needs a recipient. You have been given jade, a precious gem from a family who did not know you. You are giving us the gift of your presence. And now we share with you so that our memories will continue. It is a great gift you give us, as well."

Dr. and Mrs. Liu beamed as George clasped his hands in front of his chest, bowing his head and saying, "I will always remember your kindness. It is my honor."

"One moment, George." Mrs. Liu set me down and

239

stepped out of the room. I wagged my tail and pawed at my bone. I sat next to George, no longer hungry.

A moment later she returned with a long stick attached to something round, like one of Cook's cans. "You seem to be very musical in your speaking tone. I'd like you to have my mother's *húqín*."

"*Whoo-ching*?" repeated George, looking puzzled. "What is this?"

"Hoo-chin, spelled h-u-q-i-n," she said, correcting him. "It's a Chinese melody instrument, perhaps like your western violin. But listen, I'll play a little for you." Holding the instrument on her lap, she moved her fingers up and down the stick, singing without her voice.

I stood next to her on the bench, wondering how she could sing so beautifully through her fingers. All the things she said about Shanghai… and the feelings behind all the tears she shed were expressed in the song she played on the huqin.

Lǎoshī had a smile on his lips. He kept his eyes closed, a tiny trickle coursing down his cheek.

George sat silently as the final notes tingled in the air. After a pause, his low voiced seemed to echo in the room. "Mrs. Liu… Such hauntingly beautiful and touching music. Thank you for playing. And for offering this incredible instrument to me. I'm sorry, but I could never do it justice as you just did. And I imagine you learned from your mother, who must have been an amazing person and very accomplished musician."

Mrs. Liu held the delicate instrument out to him, her brow furrowed. "I have no one else."

George leaned toward her, his eyes moist. "With your

permission, I ask to care for the huqin until I can pass it along to someone who has a deep understanding and appreciation for stringed instruments." I sat up, panting. Could he mean Ralph?

"*Xièxiè*, George. *Xièxiè*," said Mrs. Liu, clasping her hands and smiling.

~   ~   ~   ~   ~

George carried my bone home from our lesson that night. I sprawled under the desk in the Tiger Den, chewing on it while he read the letter he wrote to his folks.

His chair screeched against the floor when he twisted to check on me. "Making progress on that bone, buddy?" He chuckled. "Same with me making progress on public speaking. So, listen while you chew, Grem. I still need more practice. Here goes."

> Dear Folks,
>
> I shall probably get this letter written – then tumble into bed. Five-thirty comes plenty early with calisthenics, a shower, and chow. We start work at seven am and go 'til we finish, without more than a few minutes out for meals sometimes.
>
> Chinese lessons are coming along fine. I'm studying Mandarin with a local couple and have gotten so far as to count and know a few simple phrases. They're fine people, teaching me about China's history and fine arts.
>
> I have acquired a huqin from my

241

teacher's wife. It's something like a violin, but only two strings. Played with a bow between the strings, if you can imagine that, but held like a banjo, and sounds ethereal—in the right hands. Will pass it along to a concert violinist.

He paused and scratched behind his ear. I scratched behind my ear, too, to show him I paid attention. I smacked my lips and set aside my bone. Sitting up and listening, I watched his lips move as he continued reading.

He paused, pen in the air. Then he scratched his pen on the paper again and read aloud.

Have been gone over two years—hope it's not another two before I get home again. Also hope to hear from you— nothing for several weeks.

Love, George.

He set down his pen, picked me up and held me on his lap, his big thumbs gently rubbing my ears and the top of my head.

"Well, Gremlin. Some things you are hard to say, right?" He peered into my face. I gave him a smile, panting with my tongue between my teeth.

"You're a big help, tiger." I snuggled into his chest, resting against his beating heart, hoping he knew I cared.

Chapter 20: The Forward Echelon

Gremlin and Master Sergeant Robert
Landgraf in Kweilin (WWII)

Put the nation's worries before your own;
Put the country's happiness after your own.
War Area Service Corps Diary for 1944 — China

Colonel Vincent's footsteps rang out from the staircase leading
into Operations. The door burst open like a small explosion.
Everyone's head snapped up, including George's and mine.
He threaded his way through the desks of the administrative
staff. The clerks' backs straightened as Vincent passed through
the crowded office. Their fingers clattered on an army of
typewriters, as if a hundred tiny drummers marched on the
keys. Vincent stopped in front of George's desk.

"Pack up, Lieutenant Haydon," he said, as loudly as he

usually addressed General Chennault. "We're heading out to Kweilin."

George pushed his chair back and stood at attention. "Sir?" I jumped out of my drawer and ran to the side of the desk to see the colonel more clearly. The room went silent.

"It's confirmed. I'm to establish and command the base at Yang Tang Airfield. The Forward Echelon." Vincent stood taller than I'd ever seen him. Everyone's eyes were on the colonel.

He smiled, showing his teeth. A dimple appeared on his cheek. "Lieutenant, you're coming with me. For now, Kweilin is a small outfit—you're to be my chief clerk... well, you're the only clerk. Put in your flight orders for today, May seventeenth, nineteen hundred forty-three." His eyes twinkled. "You and the pup are on the transport plane. We depart at fifteen hundred hours."

"Yes, sir." George opened the drawers of his desk and gathered pads of paper, pencils, and files, stuffing them into his briefcase. He knelt and rubbed my head briskly. Picking up my good morning towel that kept me warm and cozy in his desk drawer, George wiped my water dish and chow bowl and said, "Can't forget these." I licked his hand and wagged my tail, dancing on my nails with an excited *tap-tappity-tap*.

Our friends in Ops said goodbye to us as we headed out the door. George bounded down the stairs and took off at a pace like Casey Vincent's, indicating I wouldn't be stopping for a break in the bushes. I ran to keep up, sniffing the warm air along the short walkway to Headquarters. We made a beeline to Doreen's desk, where I greeted her and Mom.

"Doreen, Andy, Charles—maybe you already know—

just g-g-got orders for—uh—Kweilin. Not sure how long my d-d-duty there will be." George sounded out of breath.

"Wrote up your orders myself." Andy shook hands with George, then knelt to pat me goodbye, saying, "*Adiós* for now, *mi hijito*. And good luck to you, Jorge, *mi amigo*."

Charles held out his hand. "Hey, buddy. Well, it's been good to catch up with you. We did a little fishing, saw the town. Gremlin, you rescued us from that dragon, huh? I've seen how you protect George. Keep it up, okay?"

I wagged my tail and barked in agreement—*bbrrrk-bbrrrrkk*. I hopped into the old basket under Doreen's desk to snuggle with Mom, who nuzzled my neck. The two of us barely fit against its rickety sides. It squeaked in protest as I made myself comfortable.

"Right. Charles, would you d-d-do me one more favor?" George stood with his hands in his pockets, jingling coins.

"Sure. You name it." I heard Charles' soft voice as Mom held me firmly between her paws. I closed my eyes while her tongue cleaned my face.

"Would you get a chance to tell D-D-Dr. and Mrs. Liu goodbye for me? Wish I could, b-but we're on a short timeline here."

"Not a problem. I'll drop by the embroidery booth in Kunming next time I'm in town and let Mrs. Liu know."

"Hope to see you again sometime. When we get back in the States, I'll be watching for your name in the papers, buddy." George picked up my leash and I jumped out of the basket, giving Mom two licks on her cheek.

He said goodbye to Doreen as he picked up my leash. "Thanks for everything, Doreen." When he shook her delicate hand, her slender fingers disappeared into his, which was like a big baseball mitt. "Hope to see you before the war's over."

She laughed, sounding like the tiny, tinkling bells on the Liu's front porch. "I'm sure we'll have more to suffer through, my friend. Take care of George, Gremlin. Keep him out of trouble."

We left HQ, and I sneezed and pranced down the stairs beside my best friend's feet. When we reached the barracks, George dropped my leash and jumped up the steps. I scouted the bushes and relieved myself quickly, then climbed the steps. Inside the barracks, he moved quickly back and forth between his footlocker and the bunk to stuff things in the duffle bag. While he rummaged around, I crawled under the bunk to stay out of his way.

Luke came into the barracks, and George said, "Heading out, Luke. Off to Kweilin for duty with Colonel Vincent."

They shook hands, and Luke said, "Good luck, George. Most likely I'll be flying General Chennault out to the Eastern Echelon, so I'll see you now and then."

Luke peered under the bunk and pulled on my leash. "Come on out, you little sausage dog. Atta boy." He picked me up and stroked my ears. "I'll see you later, too."

George folded the end of the duffle bag and buckled its strap into place with a snap. He slung it over his shoulder and picked up his satchel. "See you in Kweilin sometime, Luke."

Luke set me down on the floor and handed my leash to George, who grabbed his flight jacket from its hook by the door. We set out for Kweilin, a new adventure with my best friend.

~   ~   ~   ~   ~

George led me to the C-46 transport plane, where a crewman threw his duffle bag into the back of the plane. Ralph drove up in a Jeep with Tom on the seat next to him. "Taking off, huh, George? Couldn't let you go without letting this little guy say goodbye."

George laughed and picked me up, placing me next to my brother. We rubbed noses and sniffed each other. The bandage was off his hindquarters, but he was missing his hind leg. He wagged his hindquarters and barked, nipping at my neck as I licked his face and ears.

"Good luck in Kweilin, buddy." Ralph shook hands with my best friend. "There's always have a part for you in our band."

"Thanks, Ralph. I may take you up on that. We'll meet again." George turned to carry me up the short staircase. He paused in the doorway and peered into the dimly-lit plane. On one side, a crewman stacked the duffel bags against the rear wall. On the other, a few windows along the sides let in a little light. Soon, I could see a few men sitting on long benches along the sides of the plane. George carried me to an open spot next to a window and sat down. He pushed his satchel under the bench, holding me on his lap.

More men boarded the plane, found places to sit, and stowed their gear. Soon the benches filled up, like Cook's tables during chow times. The plane's engines roared to life. The airmen shouted over the noise with conversations and snippets of songs, until a crew member gave directions and told us we were cleared for takeoff.

Putting my hind legs on George's lap, I stretched over his chest and rested my chin on his shoulder to look out the

247

window. Colonel Vincent took off in his sleek fighter, Peggy Two. He shot into the air like a bee in search of flowers and flew through a ring of large white clouds that looked like puffs from Chennault's cigarettes.

Our cargo plane lumbered down the runway, its powerful engines roaring like tigers. Curling up in George's lap while he talked with the others, I felt a tickling sensation in my tummy as the ground fell away from us, like the way Tex Hill held me up in the air when I was a puppy and made airplane noises with his lips. I smiled a puppy smile as he stroked my sides, falling asleep to the rumble of the engines, the voices of the men calling out to each other, and the groaning of the leashes holding the cargo in place.

~   ~   ~   ~   ~

I woke up to hear George yawning. He stretched his arms and legs, and I shifted on his lap. "Nearly there, Gremlin. It's been almost two hours. How're you doing, tiger?" He ruffled the fur on my neck and back. I stretched, sat up, and yawned. *Pop*—went one of my ears, and the sound of the engines grew louder. I yawned a second time. My other ear popped, and I shook my head.

I crawled up George's chest to rest my head against my best friend's shoulder. His hand held me steady as I looked out the window. We flew over hills that looked like bumps and lumps in the landscape, like the anthills in the sandy beaches of the Dai River where we'd gone fishing with Charles.

The plane circled through puffy white clouds and came in for a landing on a large airfield ringed by green hills, wheels bumping a few times when we touched down. The engines became noisier until we rolled to a stop. Their roar turned into whirring and gradually faded. I sat on George's lap and scratched at my ear, then shook my head and sighed, ready to relieve myself. I stood on his legs facing him, wagging my tail and whining now and then to tell him I wanted to go outside.

"Everyone, please wait while we secure the aircraft." One of the pilots opened the side door, unfolded the staircase, saying, "Welcome to Kweilin." George picked up his satchel and held me in his arms as we waited our turn. I wriggled again, but he had taught me to wait, and I did.

Once we stepped out of the plane, I felt a warm, moist breeze. I squirmed in George's arms and slipped down his side... past his satchel... toward the ground.

"Okay, buddy. Have a go." He knelt to let me down, and I didn't even sniff around before peeing on the tire.

The ground crew unloaded the baggage, but George waited for me before picking up his duffle bag. A tall man with a big smile approached us and saluted. "Welcome, Lieutenant Haydon."

"Hello, Master Sergeant," George said, returning the salute.

"Robert Landgraf." The sergeant nodded and pointed to a Jeep. "Everyone calls me Bobby. I'll take you to HQ, such as it is. Here, let me take that." He threw George's duffle bag in the back of the Jeep against the tailgate, and I heard the muffled clanking sound of my metal bowls.

"Call me George. Good to meet you, Bobby." George put his satchel on the floor of the Jeep and held me as he sat in the passenger's seat. "Where're you from?"

"Sheboygan, Wisconsin. The Badger State. Joined up in June of '41. About 2 years and three months ago." Bobby

249

started the engine, which sputtered and wheezed before grumbling to a roar. Soon we bumped down the road alongside the airfield. George held onto his hat in the breeze, and I raised my nose, smelling the warm air of Kweilin laced with hints of decomposing plants I might want to roll in.

Bobby shouted, "How about you?"

George raised his voice above the engine and the noise of planes taking off, landing, and taxiing. "I'm from California, joined a month or two before you. Been with Casey Vincent since I joined up, even sailing from the States on the same ship. A good man. Worked with him in Kunming, Operations, since September last year. Just got my orders this morning to transfer here."

"With the military, we always hurry up and wait. Sometimes, it's just hurrying and other times we just wait." Bobby drove away from the airfield and hangars toward other buildings in the distance. "I got to China in July. Stationed in New Jersey before that—Atlantic City. But things are happening quickly in Kweilin, you'll see."

Bobby slowed the Jeep when we came near a cluster of buildings. He dodged the crowds of workers crisscrossing the gravel road carrying equipment and supplies. He paused near one of the structures and turned off the engine. "These are the new barracks."

I blinked into the afternoon sun. Several big buildings were covered with poles. George shaded his eyes. "I'm amazed to see those bamboo scaffolds on the outside of the buildings. I had no idea bamboo could be that thick, looks like six inches or more in diameter." He whistled softly, and I perked up my ears, hoping we'd go for a walk, but he didn't pick up my leash. "What a massive workforce."

250

I watched the crews climbing bamboo ladders, passing wooden boards and boxes from the ground to the workers above. Sounds of sawing and hammering filled the air as they shouted at one another in Mandarin and other languages I didn't recognize.

"We expect to have these barracks and new office buildings completed before the monsoons hit. In the meantime, we're using the original buildings the Chinese built a few years back." Bobby started the engine and drove slowly along the crowded road, nodding to the workers. "My dad and brothers are in construction. Can't wait to tell them about this."

"What facilities are ready now?" George asked.

Bobby drove through flat land dotted with small trees and brush. "See those ramshackle buildings near those hills? Well, while we're getting up and running, we're using those tired old buildings for HQ, Ops, the mess hall, and sleeping quarters."

Bobby parked in front of a low building with cracked walls and windows. "In fact, here's our bunkhouse, such as it is. Most of the comforts of home." He chuckled. "You'll find one or two bunks available toward the back. Help yourself. Mine's near the door."

George set me down, and I wandered around the front of the building while he took his duffle bag inside. Bobby sat on the step, elbows on his knees. Many airmen smoked cigarettes while they waited, but he didn't. After I sniffed around and left my scent, he called me.

"Gremlin? Here, buddy." Bobby clapped his hands and I ran to him, wagging my tail. He let me smell his fingers. Sniff, sniff—no smoky smell. I sneezed out of habit as he picked me up and licked his smooth chin. He tickled both sides of my belly with his fingers. I tumbled into his lap, rolled onto my back and snorted, wiggling my legs in the air.

When George came out, Bobby's smile grew wider. "If you've got a camera, George, why don't you take a picture of me and my new little friend here? One for me to send to Freida—love of my life in Atlantic City—and one for you to send to your folks back home, huh? I'll chip in to get the film developed. We've got a photo lab in the back of HQ."

"Sure. It's a deal." George reached over the passenger seat and took his camera out of his satchel. "I'll be sure to get that chimney in the picture. Bet your family will love seeing the way it was installed."

"Yep, that's a real howl. I can't afford a camera. So, they'll love getting this." Bobby picked me up and stood in front of the barracks while George took our picture.

"Thanks, George. They just won't believe there's a dachshund puppy with me in China. Seeing is believing." Bobby put me down and gave my leash to George.

He pointed to a tiny building surrounded by a few short trees and the large, rounded hill behind it. "On with our tour. We'll walk from here. That small building by itself over there is known as General Chennault's shack. In the early planning stages for the air base, the Old Man stayed there instead of in the barracks. More private, I guess. Colonel Vincent's using it now for his personal quarters."

We stopped in front of a cluster of buildings with rusted metal roofs facing our barracks. "The Chinese Air Force gave us these old buildings for our original Headquarters, close to the Command Cave."

"Command Cave?" George wrinkled his brow. I scrunched up my nose and shook my head.

Bobby chuckled and pointed to a path that led to an opening in the hillside. "Right. During air raids, we evacuate into the Command Cave. Just high-tail it up the hill."

"I hadn't been briefed on that. Makes sense, though." George nodded.

"It's on a need-to-know basis. Colonel Vincent's here in HQ. Your desk is next to his. Mine's by the door—I like to make quick exits during air raids."

"Okay, thanks." George shifted his satchel from one shoulder to the other.

Bobby pointed to the corner of the building with a smile. "Oh, and the latrines are attached to the back of the building. Three wooden seats, the lap of luxury out here."

George laughed and touched his fingers to his forehead in a salute to Bobby, who returned it and headed back to the Jeep. My best friend took a deep breath, a smile on his face as he climbed the creaky steps of our new HQ. I scampered next to him, eager to begin our duty in Kweilin.

Chapter 21: Command Cave

陳納德將軍

觀戰石

陳香梅題

The rock on which
Gen. Chennault stood
to watch air combats

Rubbing of the Commemorative Rock
Outside Kweilin Command Cave (2015)

The only true strength is a strength that people do not fear.

Lao Tzu

"Come on, Gremlin. You can do it," cheered George. He and Colonel Casey Vincent paused above me on the muddy path. George took a few deep breaths and wiped his brow in the warm afternoon sun. I stuck out my tongue and panted, catching the scents of damp leaves and unknown animals. Thick trees crowded the steep hill; between their trunks I could see parts of the air base below us and the airfields in the distance.

Feeling a gentle tug on my leash, I prepared to climb. My

small paws and claws gripped the moist, cool earth. We picked our way along a path, a long uphill climb over rocks and dirt. Soon the colonel was far ahead of us. I slid backwards in the slick mud, scratches from my claws leaving lines down the slope. Taking a deep breath, I bunched up my muscles and pounced on the hillside the way I'd tackle my brother or sister.

The colonel stopped to greet a Chinese man in uniform where the path widened. He stepped onto a small, flat rock. George and I stood behind him to see the wide valley below with its active air base ringed by hills.

None of the surrounding hills looked alike. Some were tall and pointed like Doreen's pencils. Others had rounded tops like the scoops of ice cream Cook gave out now and then. Some were covered with green trees and bushes, and I wondered if butterflies and crickets lived there. And others had rock faces that looked even steeper than the path to the Command Cave.

Vincent gestured to the busy Yang Tang airfield below. "General Chennault always stands here to check out the operations. No doubt we'll see the Old Man in action the next time he visits." Buzzing planes zoomed over the hump-backed hills to the landing strips. Air crews and builders bustled around the air base.

Casey Vincent lowered his voice; I could barely hear him. "No one can imagine General Chennault's vision and leadership unless they stand—right here—to see what he's accomplished. This rock should be his monument. By God, we've got to win this war over China's skies."

Propellers whirred as a squadron of P-40 Warhawks took off with a roar and disappeared into the sky. The deep humming of the bombers grew louder as they took off, rumbling down the runway almost to its end, slowly following the fighters over the ring of hills.

"Wish I could be on that mission." Vincent sighed. "Well, let's hope the weather holds at the bombing site. Otherwise, it's a waste of gas—and when it runs out, we won't be able to fly any missions."

Vincent stepped back, and I edged forward to peer down, a funny feeling in my tummy when I saw how high we were. I had never seen anything like it and let out a *wwwiffff— wwwoofff* of amazement.

I stood for a moment in Chennault's footsteps, my head up, ears cocked, tail wagging, with my best friend behind me. Against the backdrop of plane engines, faint voices from the air crews reached my ears. The ringing and pounding of hammers on nails from the construction sites sounded far away. The Chinese workers spoke in musical tones as they moved building materials from heavily-laden trucks and swarmed up and down the ladders. Hundreds of laborers crushed rocks with hammers while the huge rollers on the new airstrips were pulled by more men than I could count. The mingled sounds reminded me of the music George played with his friends.

"George, turn around. This is the entrance to the Command Cave, our post during air raids." Vincent gave a thumbs-up signal to the guard, ducked his head, and disappeared into the hillside.

Was he playing peek-a-boo? Would he come back? I sniffed around the opening, wondering who had dug such a big hole. A dog bigger than Private Rex? I ran behind George, so he could protect me. Then I ran in front of him—I was supposed to take care of my best friend.

George signaled the guard and bent over to go into a big black hole. I pulled back on my leash. *Arrrufff*? Would he disappear into the mountain, too?

George held my leash tightly. "Heel, Gremlin," he commanded, but I braced my legs and stood my ground to stay in the sunshine.

The guard smiled. "It is A-okay, little tiger." He kneeled and gave me the thumbs-up signal, something Ralph did when the fighters took off. I whimpered and licked his thumb.

George picked me up, whispering, "Come on, buddy. Low bridge." He held me against his chest and took me into the darkness.

I heard a motor thrumming somewhere in the dark as Casey Vincent warned, "Watch out for the electrical cords coming from that generator."

Strings of lights lit the area below us. We went down a steep slope, like the riverbank where we'd gone fishing, but I didn't smell fish, just the aroma of many humans in one place. Cigarette smoke made my nose twitch—*krrrchh*. I sneezed and picked up a familiar scent from Headquarters and Operations in Kunming—typewriters.

Once my eyes adjusted to the dim light, I saw an office, much smaller than Kunming's HQ. The ceiling melted away into blackness. The Command Cave suddenly made sense to me. We could hide there and be protected from enemy bombs. I barked to tell George I understood—*bbbrkkkk-bbbrrkkkk-bbrrkkk*—but my voice was swallowed by the cave.

George put his thumb and finger around my muzzle to

remind me we were at work. When he let go, I licked his fingers to tell him I was sorry. I knew my mission.

A large part of the cave was filled with desks, equipment, and boxes of all sizes. George placed me on the dusty wooden floor where my toenails clickety-clacked like George's fingers on his typewriter and clarinet keys.

"Here's your station, George." Colonel Vincent sat at one desk and pointed to the desk facing his, as if they were one big desk in the crowded space among tables and filing cabinets. George clicked on the lamp, lighting his desk like the spotlight at a USO show.

Vincent continued, "You'll set up administrative offices here and at HQ." He smiled. "Same as you did back before the war at Hamilton Field. You've never let me down in the two plus years we've travelled the globe to get to this point—Australia, Burma, India, Kunming. Do whatever needs to be done as chief clerk. We're looking at a huge expansion of operations in the next few months."

"Yes, sir. Understood." George chuckled. "I'm to be chief clerk and bottlewasher. No complaints, sir. Glad to assist."

~   ~   ~   ~   ~

The next morning, we hustled from breakfast in the tiny mess hall to the rickety old building housing Headquarters. George didn't give me much time to explore the scents on the roads, bushes, or buildings.

He snapped his fingers, and I hopped into the drawer with my good morning towel, yawning as Vincent called from his desk. "Set up a briefing at 0900 today for my squadron commanders. You'll take notes on my directive for operations. Then inform Kunming and Chungking."

259

The pilots crowded into HQ for the meeting. I sat by George's feet while he took notes. Vincent stood tall and unsmiling as he informed the men, "The Japanese are making headway in their raids and attacks throughout Southeastern China. We've got to push them back—or lose the footholds we've gained so far."

The colonel scratched the back of his neck. "You all know that we're outnumbered. Always have been. The Japanese have more planes, ships, fuel, personnel, resources."

A deep voice growled, "Colonel Vincent, what's the point? The tide has turned and we're fighting a losing battle. Let's all just give up and go home."

Vincent frowned at the crowd, then broke into a grin. "Well, I see the legendary Tex Hill has joined us at last. Let's give him a warm welcome."

I ran to my old friend from Kunming, and the tall, lanky Ace scooped me up in his arms. I licked his face and chin, ignoring the cheers and applause. Did he have a treat for me?

"Let's continue, shall we?" Vincent cleared his throat and pointed to a map on the wall. "The Chinese are putting in longer air strips in Chengtu for the B-29 Superfortress bombers. This circle indicates their range, all the way to Japan. Japs are worried about their homeland being attacked. We'll break up their forces in the Pacific when they take a defensive position."

The pilots took a deep breath all at the same time. The colonel scrawled across a blackboard; the screechy sound made my ears hurt. "Meanwhile, we've got to protect Chinese ground forces and defend our eastern airfields. Bombers, you'll attack the south China ports to disrupt Japanese shipping and supplies. Fighters, you'll escort the bombers and halt troop movements."

Vincent pointed to different marks on the board. "Here's the crux of the matter. We might lose all our air bases in the Forward Echelon, as well as China's wartime capital in Chungking. Let's hit 'em hard so we can all go home."

I felt the temperature in the room rise. Vincent wiped perspiration from his forehead with the back of his hand. "We're gonna knock 'em out of the sky, gentlemen. George here will keep you updated on your missions and weather conditions. Dismissed."

~   ~   ~   ~   ~

A few days later, rain pounded on the metal roof of HQ. Colonel Vincent paced around the office and paused to respond to the radio. A deep voice crackled on the radio, "Vincent, when will you get that air support out for the Chinese ground forces in southeastern China?"

"General Chennault," Vincent shouted over the static. "Can't send out the bombers with the weather over the target area. My pilots are ready to go. I'd send them out gladly, sir, but have no control over the weather." He glared out the window as if his scowl could stop the storm.

The next day started with another rainy morning. A tall, thin man with short hair and big eyebrows arrived at HQ. George showed him to the colonel's office. When they came out, Vincent told George, "Get on the horn for an announcement. Colonel Eddie Rickenbacker wants to talk with our men. Airfield, in fifteen minutes."

George spoke into the microphone, and I heard his voice over the loudspeakers. "Attention, all personnel." I ran to the speaker in HQ and looked back at him. How could he be in two places at once?

"Repeat. All personnel. Assemble at the airfield in fifteen minutes. Colonel Eddie Rickenbacker will give a talk. Repeat—airfield assembly in fifteen minutes."

George drove the two colonels to the airfield, holding me in his lap. We joined the airmen, who snapped to attention when Casey Vincent introduced Eddie Rickenbacker, a World War One Ace with twenty-six confirmed aerial victories. Ripples of energy ran through the group.

That afternoon, the skies cleared and Colonel Vincent led the long-awaited mission with fighters and bombers. When he returned to HQ, his face was pale. "Close one today, George," he said. "Success on our strafing mission. We neutralized enemy troops on the move. Looks like they're retreating. Bombers hit their shipping targets." He shook his head. "But my plane's got seven bullet holes. Ground fire. Just missed my legs."

"Glad you're okay, sir," George said. "I'll get on the horn with the mechanics to follow the repairs. We'll get Peggy Two airworthy again. Even if it takes chewing gum and duct tape, which is about all we have now."

"Thanks," Vincent said. "I'm turning in early."

~   ~   ~   ~   ~

Over the next few weeks, Colonel Vincent came in and out of HQ between missions. George and I established our daily routines. The mess hall was like the one in Kunming, but smaller, and Chinese cooks served noodles and vegetables. I liked the carrots and meat best, but during the long days of spring and summer, I ate anything and everything to fill my tummy.

We stepped out of the mess one warm summer morning. My nose twitched and itched. I sneezed several times. George stopped. "Gremlin, do you smell smoke? Find the fire, Gremlin. Where's the fire?"

I raced past HQ, pulling him along. *Bbbrrkkk-aawwrrkk.* A plume of smoke streamed out of Chennault's shack. We raced across the field to the little building as George yelled, "Fire— get some water here!"

George opened the door, and smoke billowed out. He covered his mouth and nose with a handkerchief, and we dashed inside. He tore open a tall locker and took out Vincent's duffle bag, where he stuffed uniforms and pictures from table, then ran out of the building, coughing and calling for me. I crept under the smoke that rolled up to the ceiling and dodged the crackling, scorching flames climbing the walls of the small room. The wood stove in the barracks was never as hot as this fire.

I saw a large envelope on Vincent's bunk and jumped up to grab it but fell onto the floor. George's letters were important to him, and I knew the colonel would want his letters. Cinders and ash fell on me, and I shook off little burning things that landed on my fur. Standing on my hind legs, my paws tingled from the heat. I tugged on the blanket with my teeth, blinking from the smoke in the room. The big envelope fell to the floor just as George shouted, "Come on, Gremlin. Out—heel—now!"

I wouldn't leave without Casey Vincent's envelope. Grabbing it and clamping my jaws shut, I dragged it backwards out the door and collapsed into George's arms. Both of us coughed as George crawled away from the burning building, holding me with one arm and the duffle bag in another. I held on tight to the colonel's envelope.

Bobby drove up in the fire engine, and the crew shot water onto the building.

"No use," George shouted. "We got everything of value."

"Let it go, boys," Bobby ordered, turning off the water.

We took Colonel Vincent's belongings to Headquarters. Soon I heard his steps—*tap-tap-tap*—and he burst through the door, out of breath. "George, I saw it from the air. Chennault's shack… my personal things… burned," he stammered.

"We couldn't save it, sir," George said. "But we—"

"All gone up in smoke." Vincent's voice choked.

George showed the colonel his duffle bag. "We got everything, sir. Uniforms—"

"Not important. Replaceable." Vincent sat down, head in his hands. I whimpered and nudged his leg, but he pushed me away.

"We saved your photos, sir."

Vincent sat up, his brow wrinkled, eyes filled with water. "My pictures… photos of Peggy and the kids?" He let out a loud sigh. "Thanks, George."

George took the big envelope out of the duffle bag. "Gremlin's the one who saved this. Don't know how he got it off your bunk." His hand shook as he wiped his eyes.

"Gremlin? Your little dog?" For the first time ever, Casey Vincent picked me up and hugged me against his chest. "Peggy sent me a movie of our baby. Photo lab hadn't developed it yet. How in the world?" His chest shuddered as he took a deep breath. "Never understood why Chennault wanted dogs in the Air Force—but I'm a believer now. Maybe

I'll get my kids a dachshund when I get home. Family pet to remind me of you."

~   ~   ~   ~   ~

Bobby and George took Colonel Vincent's things to our barracks. Since the new buildings weren't ready yet, the big room was overflowing. Bunk beds were stacked two and three high with cots tucked between them. Some airmen slept on the wide covered porch or outside on the ground. Whenever it rained, they filled the spaces on the floor.

George always opened the window in our little nook before we went to sleep. I burrowed deep under our blankets to avoid the smells from so many men, uniforms, boots, and socks.

Bobby set Vincent's duffel bag on his bunk near the door. "I'll give the colonel my rack."

"It's not very private." George picked up the bag. "I'll give him my spot around the corner. It's got a window. I don't mind sleeping outside." They hung the colonel's uniforms in George's locker and changed the bedding.

After chow, Bobby, George, and I crowded into the tiny space to show Colonel Vincent his new quarters. "Very smart," our commander commented with a grin. "I've got two whole feet of extra storage space at the foot of my bunk. Not that I need it. I'd rather spend more time on missions anyway." He picked me up and sat on the bunk. Opening his duffel bag, he placed his family photos on the tiny table next to his pillow. "I won't forget what you've done for me, buddy." He rubbed my ears and nodded at each of us in turn.

The next day, Vincent left early on a mission. When he returned, he walked slowly into HQ, his face gray. "George, seems like I've got dysentery. I'm heading to bed but might be up most of the night."

Colonel Vincent didn't go to chow that evening. George made a bed for us on the porch. He went to sleep, but soon I heard Vincent hurry by. I followed him and waited outside the latrine to walk him back to the barracks. Early in the morning, he took fewer trips to the latrine, and his body odor turned sour. Vincent stumbled onto the porch, and I woke up George with my whining. He put his arm around Vincent's waist to help him back to bed.

George woke Bobby and asked him to stay with Colonel Vincent. We hustled to HQ, where he radioed Andy in Kunming about Vincent's health. At sunrise, we took a Jeep to the airfield. The sky brightened, the long shadows of the hills gradually shrinking away from the airfield. My tummy rumbled for breakfast; I heard George's stomach growl, too. A moment later I picked up the familiar engine sounds of Luke's small passenger plane. I barked an alert.

"Good boy," he told me, patting my back. He lifted me out of the Jeep, where we waited. "Sit. Stay." Luke landed and pulled the plane up to us, giving us the thumbs-up signal from the cockpit.

General Chennault climbed out and helped Pop onto the ground. George greeted the general as Joe Dash inspected the tires and relieved himself. He stood on three legs, something I couldn't do.

The black brim of the general's round hat shielded his stern face from the sun. Chennault pulled off his gloves one finger at a time. "Heel, Joe," he commanded. They approached us. I quivered with excitement, ready to pounce on Pop and the general, but I remembered George's instructions to sit until told otherwise. Finally, the commander said, "At ease." When he looked down at me, his eyes twinkled.

When George snapped his fingers. I ran circles around Pop, jumping up to lick his muzzle. Pop sniffed me all over and gnawed at my shoulder as our tails wagged wildly.

As the propeller stopped, Dr. Tom Gentry stepped out of the plane. The doctor's bag smelled like the hospital, and I shook my head to clear my nostrils of the sting.

"Well, looks like your nose healed up nicely. A little broader than before, but the incision didn't leave much of a scar. Any problems?"

"Sir, you d-did a fine job. I'm b-breathing easier now. No pain at all."

"How's Casey Vincent?" Dr. Gentry wrinkled his brow.

"Up and down all night." George motioned to the Jeep. "Gremlin alerted me that Colonel Vincent needed help getting back to bed after a trip to the latrine. The quick-step quickies, you know, we called it in India. Really slowed him down."

"All right. You're a good watchdog, Gremlin." Dr. climbed into the back of the Jeep. I would have licked his hand but knew it wouldn't taste good.

Luke shook hands with George. "Knew I'd see you here sometime, buddy. Didn't think it would be under these circumstances." He turned to General Chennault. "I'll stay here with the plane. Let me know when you're ready to fly out."

"Thanks, Luke." Chennault climbed into the passenger's seat with Pop and lit a cigarette. George held me as he drove toward the barracks. He shouted over the chugging engine.

"Frankly speaking, sirs, between Colonel Vincent's missions and overall command, he's exhausted. He won't admit it, though. Too determined to win the war and get home."

"Understood, son," Dr. Gentry shouted. We passed through the construction area where Chinese workers were painting the buildings. The general lifted his massive chin, motioning to the new barracks and HQ. "Nearly ready, I see."

George smiled. "Yes, General. Proceeding on schedule. With the influx of pilots and crews, we're bursting at the seams."

When we arrived at the old barracks, Chennault dropped his cigarette on the ground and crushed it with the toe of his boot. I led the way to Colonel Vincent. Bobby left the little room when he saw us coming.

"What's this? A house call?" Vincent's eyes were half-closed.

"Heard you're under the weather, Vincent." Chennault crouched next to Vincent's head. "Doc Gentry will check you over, son." The general and I followed George into the barracks. After a few minutes, the doctor joined us and explained the treatment for Vincent.

I trailed Chennault to Vincent's bunk. "Doc says you'll be fine in a couple days. We've cooked up a good mission for tomorrow, son—but you're not going. Doctor's orders."

The colonel turned his head toward us and moaned. "What?"

"That's right. But the good news is you'll stay here in Kweilin as area commander." Chennault patted his arm. "In time, you'll command the entire composite wing for the Forward Echelon. First, get well. Doc thinks you'll be fine in another day or two. We're heading back to Kunming, expect good reports from George about your health."

Vincent smiled weakly as Chennault cleared his throat. "The bad news is you won't be flying any more missions. Try to be patient, Casey. We'll win this war, and you'll get back to your family. For now, you need to throttle back, get well, and assume your command."

"Hot dog, General," Vincent muttered and rolled onto his side toward the wall.

"Watch the colonel," George told me as he put me on Vincent's bunk and left.

I curled up against the colonel's back. After snoring in different positions throughout the day, he sat up and placed me on his tummy.

"You're a good watchdog, Gremlin. And a good friend." He sighed as he stroked my head and ears. "Well, there's something I need to get off my chest."

Vincent sat up straighter and adjusted his pillows. "I've written to my wife about it, but the words just don't come across the way I want them to. Maybe I can tell you."

He coughed, making me rise and fall on his stomach. He took a few sips of water from the glass on the table next to his bunk. "I came out here to fight. Do what I could to end the war. I've missed anniversaries and births of our children to do the right thing. Dropped bombs and strafed enemy troops."

He groaned and lay on his side, facing me. "Combat fighting—it's thrilling and exciting when I'm in the middle of it. Later though, it's a different story—remembering the results of my actions. Injured people running on the ground, planes on fire, hurtling down through the air. How in heaven's name will God forgive me?"

Vincent fingered the fur on my back, soothing my muscles from my neck to the base of my tail and back again. "I've tried to keep my feelings separate from my military perspective. I can't forget what the enemy did, killing my friends. Pearl Harbor. The Bataan Death March. Attacks here in China and in Burma. I've gotta feel justified that it was all for good."

I heard the door open. George's familiar footsteps rang out on the wooden barracks floor.

Vincent sat up, rubbing his hands over his face. He pulled me onto his chest and stroked my ears. "Let's just put an end to this awful war, huh, Gremlin?"

My best friend poked his head into the tiny room. "Colonel, you're awake. Feeling better?"

"Raring to go, thanks to Gremlin. I might need to get a dog like him when I get home. Kids would love a pet." A deep dimple appeared on Vincent's cheek when he smiled. I licked his chin to tell him I understood and jumped off the bunk to follow George.

~   ~   ~   ~   ~

General Chennault returned to Kweilin a couple weeks later without Pop. George and Vincent walked with him through the new Headquarters building and settled into the chairs of Casey Vincent's large corner office.

"Finally got your new digs, huh? The Chinese do good work." Chennault leaned back in his chair. "Brief me on the current situation, Vincent. I can't get the full picture of the situation over the airwaves."

270

I sat by George's feet as took notes in shorthand, stretching out my full length on the sunny floor with a *whhhfff.*

"Japanese are encroaching on the Forward Echelon, General." Vincent pointed to the map on the wall. "They've made three air raids in the past week. No sooner do we move back to HQ, but we hafta hustle uphill to the Command Cave again. Our men and the Chinese crews scatter to the caves closer to the airfield. At the all clear siren, the locals make repairs on the runways and buildings. We couldn't do without them."

The general lit a cigarette. "I hear the Japs may be developing a new fighter. Have you seen anything out of the ordinary?" He blew the smoke above Vincent's head. The white trails floated out the door, and I heard someone in HQ cough. I twitched my nose to keep from sneezing.

Casey Vincent leaned forward. "Yes, sir. Saw an odd plane when I was out on patrol earlier this week—not a mission—I've followed your orders, sir. Just a local sortie in Peggy Two. I caught a glimpse of the red circle on the wings and gave it the gun."

Chennault nodded, chin in his hand. "Any special modifications?"

"This one had a faster diving speed, caught me by surprise." Casey snapped his fingers. I perked up my ears, thinking he wanted my attention, but he didn't look at me. "It took more hits than the older Zeros before exploding."

"They've got heavier armor now. All right." Chennault turned to George. "Notify the Chinese intelligence service and our Office of Strategic Services about this development. Find out what they know. We'll vary our aerial tactics to outmaneuver whatever the Japs throw at us. Once Vincent and I develop combat instructions, send them out to all our fighter squadrons."

"Air raid!" Bobby shouted from the main room. His voice echoed throughout the speakers on base as sirens wailed. "Repeat—air raid! *Jin bao*! All personnel, take your posts." George grabbed his satchel, saying, "Sirs, Bobby, you're with me." He drove us across base and parked at the bottom of the trail to the Command Cave.

I raced up the path, leading the way. From the distant airfield at the other side of the base, I heard our planes revving their engines as we climbed. The men ran after me, panting to catch up. Chennault stopped on the rock near the entrance to the Command Cave, breathing heavily. "Gremlin—stay with me. I want you to see this. Get used to the noise. Anyone have field glasses?"

"Yes, sir." George opened his satchel and handed the general his binoculars. "I'll be in the Command Cave." He disappeared past the guards into the cave. The Flying Tigers took to the sky, one after another, like a swarm of bees. Chennault tracked our planes as they rose into the midday sun. The invading fighters poured over the hilltops into our valley, and our P-40s dove quickly among them, *rat-tat-a-tat-tatting* at the enemy.

I heard the low hum of bombers. Since I knew Chennault was deaf, I pawed at his leg. Grabbing his pantleg in my teeth, I tugged on it to tell him where to look, and he turned that direction. The bombers appeared a few moments later, dropping explosives while our fighters attacked the invaders.

What about gremlins? I had to scare them away from our

planes—protect the Flying Tigers, just as our Chinese guards watched over the Command Cave. Bracing myself on the flat stone next to our commander, I showed my teeth, snapping, growling, and snarling. My muscles tensed, and the fur raised and rippled on my back as I barked ferociously.

The battle for China's skies raged above us. Bombs hit the runways, leaving black holes where our aircraft would need to land. Smoke rose from several buildings on the air base. General Chennault stood silently, as still as the rock he stood on, above the diving, moaning planes, flashes of fire, and deafening explosions.

Chapter 22: The Sun and the Star

Shoulder Patch on George's Flight
Jacket from WWII

Anticipate the difficult by managing the easy.

Lao Tzu

Several days later, Colonel Casey Vincent strode through Headquarters, past the neat aisles of tables and desks without greeting the airmen. He disappeared into his sunny office. George and I followed him.

"Good afternoon, Colonel." George placed a handful of small papers on his desk and sat between the door and Vincent's massive desk. "Here are your messages."

I sneezed several times from the smell of fresh paint and sat on the floor next to Vincent's feet, hoping for a pat on the head, but he leafed through his notes without noticing me. The colonel set the papers on his desk and folded his hands.

George and I waited. Vincent leaned forward. "Glad to know Chennault sends his compliments about our work here. But because of our strong offensive bombing missions— General Stilwell believes the Japanese will rally against us. Sounds like the Japs are planning a major operation. Waiting for details."

"Yes, sir."

Vincent shifted in his seat. "I have something else to talk over with you, George. I'm pushing Chennault to let me go home on leave." I perked up my ears and inched forward on my belly to the colonel's feet, whimpering. *Aawwrrrrr?*

George nodded. "You've been looking forward to seeing your family."

"Sure do miss Peggy and the kids." Colonel Vincent finally reached down to rub me behind the ears. "How about you?"

"I d-don't know when I'll get home, b-but then again, I— uh—don't have a family of my own. So, I'm glad to continue here with the war effort." Vincent opened a drawer.

"Right. Chennault sent me a bottle of bourbon in that last parcel. It's nearly quitting time. Let's have a taste." He took out two small glasses. I heard a crinkling sound as Vincent twisted off the top of a bottle. *Glug-glug-glug.* He poured the amber liquid into the glasses. With a *clink* as they toasted, just as they did in banquets with Chinese officials. George sipped from his glass, coughed once, and blinked his eyes.

"War is a mixed bag. The Chinese undoubtably appreciate our support of their ground forces. And our missions disrupting enemy transportation." Vincent held his glass under his nose and took a slow breath. "But I'm still sorting out that mess from last week when our bombers accidently hit a Chinese town—the absolutely wrong target. No excuses for that."

The colonel lit a cigarette and took a deep drag, letting the smoke siphon out of his mouth toward the ceiling. He took a sip of his drink and shook his head, setting his glass on his desk with a thud. "The weather out here stalls everything. Couldn't run missions. Delayed moving into our new facilities. At least I can tell Peggy I haven't been wounded. Just a close call."

George swirled the brown liquid in his glass and held it up to Vincent. "You're being awarded the Distinguished Flying Cross; several of the men as well. Congratulations— and you're recommended for the Distinguished Service Medal."

"Must be because your paperwork is in order. What matters most to me is flying—and if we don't get administrative citations, I get to fly." Vincent chuckled, but didn't smile. "I think I'm making a difference in the war. We're hitting the Japanese hard. Shipping, supply lines, troop movements; we're raising hell all over. Unfortunately, now it looks like the Japs will pay us back."

Vincent leaned back and put his hands behind his head. "I'll be stateside for about a month. Hope I'll see you around again, George. You've done good work here. Much appreciated—I put you in for some commendations, too."

Their glasses clinked once more.

~   ~   ~   ~   ~

One afternoon, Bobby called from his desk, "Hey, George." I jumped out of my drawer and shook all over to wake up, from my nose to my tail. I put my front legs in front of me and bowed, with my hindquarters and tail in the air, a big stretch. Yawning, I lay my belly lay flat against the cool linoleum floor.

"Word just came in. It's official." Bobby set the phone's receiver into its cradle. "The canteen's opening tonight. Next building over from the mess hall. How about that? Next thing you know, we'll get the USO shows out here."

George stopped typing. "What about Gremlin?"

"Sure, I checked. That's fine, as long as Gremlin stays out from underfoot." Bobby smiled at me, and my tail thumped the floor. "Word is that some of the top brass may pop in, too."

"Okay, sounds good." George continued typing.

"There's another thing." Bobby waited until George looked up. "Colonel Vincent wants us to knock off for the afternoon and head into Kweilin. Seems there's been a discovery the locals want to show us. We're the official representatives to report back to HQ about it. Here's the map. We're to go to the Reed Flute Cave. Bring flashlights and extra batteries."

Bobby jingled the keys to the Jeep and we went on our way down the bumpy road to Kweilin. George held the map and gave directions. "That's the Peach Blossom River. Go over the old stone bridge, the Flying Phoenix Bridge."

Bobby stopped in front of a tall mountain and parked next to another Jeep. Two slender Chinese men in uniform greeted us. "Thank you for joining us, gentlemen," the taller man said as they saluted. "I'm Lieutenant Li and this is Corporal Hsiao. I'm a geologist and he's my assistant. We're the team that checked out your Command Cave for safety when General Chennault set up his post there."

He motioned to an opening in the steep mountainside. "We just received reports of this cave. During the last air raid, people ran along the mountainside and found this opening to hide from the bombs. Let's head in."

George and the others turned on their flashlights. Inside the cave, the ground felt moist of the pads of my paws and the air smelled musty. Trickling sounds of water echoed everywhere. I stepped on a sharp rock and yelped. George picked me up, and I draped my long body over his arm as he shined the flashlight around the dark spaces.

We moved quietly from one part of the cave to another. The men slipped on the slick ground, squeezed through tight spots, and climbed over boulders. The cave opened into a larger space with no end to the ceiling. They all breathed in quickly and made sounds of amazement.

In another big cavern, Lieutenant Li knelt next to a wall. "This inscription was painted here over twelve hundred years ago." The men murmured, "These formations are fantastic." "Never seen anything like them."

They passed their lights over the rock formations. Li pointed out shapes. "Look at these stalagmites and stalactites." I growled at a room full of lions in the flickering lights to protect George in case they charged us, but they didn't move.

The flashlights grew dim, and the other men changed their batteries. As we walked through the cave their whispers were hard to hear and I couldn't tell who was speaking. "Do you think this goes out another way?" "Let's keep going. No one's been here for centuries." "What a find—it needs to be shared with the world." "Once the war is over, this will be one of China's national treasures."

Eventually we worked our way through the cave and came out blinking into the afternoon sun, not far from where we entered. The Chinese and Americans shook hands, their eyes sparkling with excitement at their discoveries.

~   ~   ~   ~   ~

After evening chow, we walked to the Kweilin canteen, which wasn't as big as Mac's in Kunming. George, Bobby, and their friends told stories and laughed while sipping their drinks. The men talked about missions and the weather, when they might go stateside, and who was back home waiting for them.

I stayed near my water bowl, next to George's feet under the big round table. Now and then he dangled little treats of dried meat and cheese, which I licked and nibbled gracefully from his fingertips, smacking my lips and running my tongue around my teeth to find every morsel.

All talking stopped when the door opened. A fall breeze flowed under our table. The canteen became so quiet I heard the skittering sound of dried leaves on the cement porch. Bobby pushed back his chair, stood at attention, and announced, "Attention." Everyone rose at the same time, just as squadrons of P-40s took off together. I scrambled to stand by George's boots.

Major General Claire Lee Chennault entered the canteen and saluted. "At ease, boys. Enjoy your evening. You deserve it." He went to the bar. After talking with the bartender, he took a bottle and two glasses to a table.

Everyone took their seats, but the conversations were quieter. I remained standing, looking for crumbs. The room became dark and a man came to the front of the canteen. A bright light shone on his face. He introduced himself as Don

Barclay. "I'm on the USO circuit, in the spotlight this evening to say thank you and give you a few moments of entertainment. Welcome and let the fun begin."

Don told stories that made the audience howl with laughter. George's belly shook as he wiped tears from his eyes. When the show was over, Don Barclay sat at a table and drew pictures of the commanders and other airmen. The crowd roared with laughter when he showed them what he drew. He signed his name to each one and gave them away without taking any money for his drawings.

George and I waited in line until our turn. "Thanks for the entertainment tonight, Mr. Barclay. I've never laughed so hard in years. I'd like a caricature of the Old Man—General Chennault."

The artist sketched, his pen scribbling and scratching across the slick, shiny paper. He held it up for us— *wwwrrrrffff?* How could General Chennault be on the paper when he was in the canteen with us?

Don Barclay's caricature of General Claire L. Chennault (1943)

Bobby said, "George, the general's signaling. Looks like he wants to talk to you."

George picked up his picture, thanking Don Barclay. We walked to the table in the corner. He saluted Chennault, who nodded and motioned to a chair. George sat down and put the drawing on the table. The general chuckled. "Pretty good likeness, if I say so myself."

I stamped my feet and smiled at the general, wiggling my hindquarters to greet him. The general bent down and gently rubbed my neck and ears. "Looks like Gremlin's growing up nicely."

"He's a good dog. Coming along," George shouted. "Can't thank you enough, sir. He's a good mascot; keeps morale up. He even helped me get over that stutter."

"Glad to hear it, son." Chennault sat up and crossed one leg over the other. He lowered his voice to a rumble. "Listen, I want you to be my aide-de-camp."

George took a quick breath. "Me? I d-d-don't—uh— know anything about b-being an aide." Alarmed, I pawed the leg of my best friend. His hands shook as he reached down for me and lifted me into his lap without taking his eyes off the general.

He stroked my back, ruffling my fur up and down my spine as he spoke. "How could I—uh—leave Colonel Vincent now? We just g-g-got operations running smoothly, moved into the new buildings, established office protocols." His light blue eyes glistened in the soft lights of the canteen. I reached up to lick his chin to comfort him.

"You've proven yourself capable of beating the odds, as we all have, far from home." Chennault rubbed his chin and cleared his throat, then took a sip of his drink. "Casey Vincent runs the show for all our bases in eastern China. But no one is irreplaceable. I'm sending him home on leave. He's got replacements. Who have you been training?"

George rubbed my paws gently, one by one. He took

several ragged breaths. "Tech Sergeant B-B-Bobby Landgraf's b-been—uh—shadowing me. He's a g-good man." He sat up straighter and took a deeper breath. "A few others, but Bobby's the best. Deserves to be promoted. He's officer material, sir."

Chennault poured drinks into the glasses and slid one across the table. I sniffed the glass, sneezed, shook my head, and rubbed my nose with my front paw. The men chuckled and sipped their drinks. I shrank away from the table and curled up on George's lap.

My best friend leaned forward and put his elbow on the table, his chin in his hand. "I must confess, sir. I know nothing about being the aide to a two-star general."

"Sure, fellow, it's all right. Tell you what, though... nobody knows much about what an aide-de-camp is or does. We're both in new territory."

Chennault leaned toward us. "Here's the thing, son. We've got the enemy approaching us from multiple fronts; limited supplies airlifted over the Hump, as always. Stillwell's Ledo Road from Burma will take months to complete, if not years. Fact is—our forward echelon is precarious, even under Vincent's very capable command."

"I'm not sure I'm the best man for the job." George looked down at his hands.

The general chuckled. "We all have things to work on. I've gotta quit smoking, so my wife and Doreen tell me. You've got something with the way you speak sometimes. But we all do our jobs, get the work done. We will win this war."

"Thank you, sir." George's hand rested on my back, trembling.

"You got this base operational during its expansion. That's the kind of man I need in our theater command post."

George blushed but kept his gaze level with the general's dark eyes.

"All indications are that we're losing our footing in eastern China. Operation Ichigo—that's what the Japanese call their major campaign—spells that out clearly. This push will rival the Allies' D-Day—Operation Overlord—and our own Operation Matterhorn, staging the B-29s from India to bomb the enemy homeland from northern China. I need you in HQ immediately. You'll be on the first plane to Kunming in the morning. Understood?"

George nodded. "Yes, sir. We'll be ready." *Ching-ching.* They clinked glasses and drained the liquid. George set his glass down and held me as he rose.

Chennault placed three shiny silver bars on the table. "You're out of uniform, First Lieutenant Haydon. Wear these when you—and Gremlin—report tomorrow." He winked at me. "There's an extra bar for your pup's collar."

~ ~ ~ ~ ~

When we landed at the Kunming airfield, we walked from the plane to Ralph's Quonset hut. He picked me up, holding me on my back as he rubbed my tummy. "Hey there, buddy. You like riding in my airplanes, huh? Good boy—you chased away the gremlins." How did he know? I panted, licking Ralph's hands in agreement. I forgot—they were covered with black stains and smelled like oil. *Snnfff*—I sneezed—*kkchnnnkk.*

Ralph laughed. "That's okay, buddy. Tom likes the stink of oil, but you never have gotten used to it." I wiggled in

Ralph's arm to get to my brother. He set me down, and I ran to Tom, wagging my tail furiously.

George kneeled next to us. "Here, Tom. Good boy." He petted my brother's head. Tom stood upright. How could he do that? I remembered his terrible accident. Did his leg grow back? I sniffed Tom's side and hind end. He sat on something made of wood and metal. *Sniff. Whiff. Sniff.*

"We made good old Tom a wheelchair," Ralph told George. "Put my boys to work whenever we had spare time and this is what we came up with. Tom gets around pretty well now."

Brrawruff. I barked at the wheels. Tom ran from me and I chased him, almost like when we were puppies. Except he paddled his front feet and rolled his hindquarters.

Andy picked us up in the Jeep. When we arrived at Headquarters, I spun around with joy when I saw Mom and peppered her face with kisses.

Doreen shook George's hand and knelt to cuddle me in her arms. "Well, I declare, my little friend—you're getting so big. Almost as tall as your mother." I licked her ear and nibbled at it. She crinkled her nose and giggled like golden bells in the morning breeze.

Our old friends greeted us and introduced us to new people. Andy showed us George's desk, right outside General Chennault's office. A shiny new typewriter sat in the center.

My best friend beamed. "Thanks, Andy. You shouldn't have. Say—who's got that old Remington from the AVG?"

"We still give it to the new guy to see how good he is." The men laughed, and George organized his desk. He took my Good Morning towel from his satchel and put it in the bottom drawer as he and Andy talked.

Something smelled different in HQ. I padded around the big room, sniffing under desks and dodging people's feet. Following an unfamiliar scent from Doreen's desk to a bundle under Andy's desk, I poked my nose into a small blanket. *Hhhhnnnrrrff?*

Two narrowed eyes opened in a nest of long gray fur, reminding me of Sadie the kitten, but ten times her size. A paw with knife-like talons slashed out as the creature growled, hissed, and yowled. I fell backwards with a yip to avoid the claws.

Andy caught me and held me close to his chest. "So, Gremlin, you remember Sadie, my little lady?"

I wiggled out of his grip and ran to my desk drawer, tail between my legs. Vowing to avoid Sadie, the demon cat, I curled up into a tight ball. Was Sadie a lady? No—not at all like Doreen or Mrs. Liu.

~   ~   ~   ~   ~

We settled into a new routine, busier than in Kweilin. We walked to the mess hall, HQ, Operations, the airfield, Mac's canteen, and the barracks. I visited Mom and Doreen every day. Officers with stars, eagles, wings, and colorful ribbons on their uniforms came and went. George talked to everyone before they met with General Chennault. He took notes in the meetings, and I sprawled under Chennault's big desk with Pop, sunshine streaming through the windows.

One day, General Chennault called us into his office. "George, get Casey Vincent on the horn."

"Yes, sir." George turned to go back to his desk. "I'll patch him through to you."

"Just a minute, First Lieutenant. You're the one to deliver

this message." The general motioned for George to come back. "Have a seat." I waited by the door, all ears.

"Yes, sir?"

"Since Vincent gave you a field promotion, it's only right for you to notify him—he's earned the rank of brigadier general."

My best friend beamed. "Yes, sir."

When George called his former boss, I heard cheering over the phone. Casey Vincent shouted over the noise, "What a day, George. We flew several missions—big success. This tops it off. Staff is going wild, telling me I'm the second youngest general ever, at 29 years old. Bobby's brought out the bourbon and is pinning cardboard stars on my shoulders. Thanks for the good news."

"My pleasure, sir. Congratulations, General Vincent. When do you head to the States?"

"Any time now." His voice was replaced by a loud, steady dial tone, and George hung up the phone. I licked George's hand.

That night, we returned to George's bunk in the Tiger Den. Luke was still in his small room near the creaking, old wood stove, reading and smoking his pipe. Soon Luke flew George and Chennault to meetings at other bases, and I stayed with Mom and Doreen. I longed to be with George and wondered why he didn't take me with him, but he always came back to me, and I smothered him with puppy kisses, like the times we played peek-a-boo.

~   ~   ~   ~   ~

One sunny day, Luke went with us into Kunming. He held me on his lap, his long legs crammed into the small space. As

George drove under the carved gates of the village, the thick smoke from Chinese cooking fires and scents of roasting meats and vegetables made my mouth water.

I guarded the Jeep while the men ran their errands. I accepted pats and strokes from people stopping by, but if anyone's hands got too close to our bags or gear, I charged at them, teeth bared, snarling as if they were gremlins.

George and Luke returned with bags and a long stick with sharp points on one end. The gear they'd bought rattled around as our Jeep bounced on the uneven gravel road to the base.

Luke held me in the passenger's seat. "Okay, we picked up the fishing gear Charles ordered for us and everything the general asked for. Hope we didn't miss anything. By the way, what on Earth is that long spear-like thing? Looks like it belongs to King Neptune, twenty-thousand leagues under the sea."

George laughed. "Hah, I thought you'd never ask. Fortunately, Charles found a place that had one. Your eyes were as big as saucers when the clerk hauled it out. It's a trident, known in the States as a gig, for frogging."

"What? That's a lethal weapon there. And—why would anyone want to kill frogs?" Luke shrugged.

George swerved around oxcarts and bicyclists. "Don't you know they're good eating?"

"Naaaah." Luke's eyes bulged out, making him look like the carving of an angry dragon on the Kunming city gate. "I can't imagine eating amphibians. And all those bones? Slimy skin? Little front legs and wide mouths? How can you even think of eating that? No thank you." He wrinkled his nose, stuck out his tongue, and shook his head.

288

"You only eat the hind legs. At any rate, I'm glad the general's taking a couple days off to take us frogging."

Luke scratched my sides. "For someone who works non-stop, that old buddy of mine can camp out a couple days and bounce back like he's been on vacation for weeks."

I wondered if we were going back to the river to fish. *Mmrrmff?* I whined in anticipation of finding smelly riverbank treasures to roll in. To my surprise, we passed the MPs and Private Rex at the base gate. George dashed into the mess hall and returned with a box, then we stopped at Headquarters.

Chennault stepped out of HQ, wearing his flight suit under his jacket. Pop walked with him, carrying his water dish in his mouth. Luke stepped out of the Jeep to grab his duffle bag and put it in the Jeep.

"Joe, Gremlin, in the back," the general commanded. George signaled, and I scrambled into the back seat. Chennault placed Pop next to me, and climbed in. "I'll sit in the back. Andy filed the flight plan to Kweilin, and Casey Vincent's expecting us. Luke, ready to fly?"

"All set," Luke said, hopping back in. "I see we've got a father and son outing today. Right, Gremlin?"

Brrrkk! A-brrrkk! I replied, tongue lolling out of my mouth to catch any new scents on the breeze. We bounced down the rutted dirt road until George stopped at the flight line and handed the keys to a waiting private. Ralph and Tom came up to say hello. Pop peed on the tire. I squatted to pee, and so did Tom in his wheelchair.

"Time to go, Grem." George tugged on my leash as I scratched the dirt onto the pile I left for Tom. I quickly licked Tom's nose and gave him another ear tussle.

Chennault climbed the short staircase. Joe Dash hopped up the steps after him so quickly he seemed to be a blur of black fur, toenails clicking on the metal steps.

George carried me into the airplane that smelled of leather seats, oil, and sweat. He held me firmly as he sat in the back next to a small window. Ralph poked his head in through the door. "Bye, Gremlin. Remember, I tune up engines like violins. This one'll sing for Luke when you soar in the sky. Listen for it." He and George put their thumbs up at the same time. Ralph folded the steps and closed the door.

Luke started the engine. From our seat, I watched Luke push buttons and pull switches. Joe Dash sat with Chennault. While the two men in the cockpit shouted back and forth, George talked to me in a quiet way. I focused on his blue eyes and wide lips. Everything else melted away as his big fingers stroked my ears. We cuddled during the short flight to Kweilin, the droning of the plane's engine a deep harmony below the bass voices of the men.

My best friend wrote in the little book he kept in his pocket. When the plane descended, he pointed to the green snake below us. "There's the Li River, Gremlin. We're back in Kweilin. Next we'll go over the little mountain range to the Yang Tang airfield."

We circled the huge airfield surrounded by the familiar ring of round-topped hills. After landing, Bobby welcomed us. I ran circles around his legs, yapping with joy. I recognized the scents of Kweilin, the new buildings bustling with Chinese and Americans, and the distant path leading up the hill to the Command Cave.

We hopped into the Jeep. Bobby called out to Luke, "Going with us this time?"

"That's fine for y'all," Luke said. "No caves for me. Think I'll stay out in the daylight. Check in with the crew chief on the flight line. I'm not one for dark creepy places. Prefer the fresh air."

"Okay, Luke." George chuckled. "You know where to find us."

"Sure," Luke to us called over his shoulder. "But don't take Gremlin spelunking without leaving a trail of breadcrumbs to find your way out."

~ ~ ~ ~ ~

Bobby stopped the Jeep at the bottom of the hill and escorted us past the guards at the entrance to the cave.

Brigadier General Casey Vincent shook hands with Chennault and George. "Good to see you again, George. You know, we argued over you. Chennault pulled rank and finally got you."

George blushed. "A privilege to work with you both."

Vincent cleared his throat. "Now—down to brass tacks. The major offensive, Japan's Operation Ichigo. Bobby, we'll need lots of coffee. Schedule personnel to rotate through specialized briefings by unit in 20-minute intervals."

Chennault and Vincent huddled around a table while George took notes. Pop lay under a nearby desk watching his best friend. After sniffing around the cave for treats, I flopped onto the floor next to Pop with a sigh.

A group of Chinese men entered the Command Cave and greeted the generals. They wore uniforms, except for one man in a suit. He wore glasses and carried an umbrella. I sniffed my way over to him and sat by his feet.

291

"Well, hello there, little dog. You must be related to Joe Dash. I see the family resemblance." He knelt and rubbed my head and ears. "I am Dr. Tong, from Chungking. Go lie down now, we have matters to discuss." I panted with happiness on my way back to Pop, wagging my tail.

Chennault pointed to squiggly lines and patches of colors on what they called the map of the world. "Glad you could join us, Dr. Tong. Gentleman, on the European front, Operation Overlord—the Allies' massive D-Day Invasion—turned the tide of the war. The Red Army's Operation Bagration crushed the Germans in four weeks. But the war against Japan is not over."

He pointed to a map of China and Japan. "Operation Ichigo is the biggest Japanese offensive of nineteen forty-four, probably the most critical for the outcome of this world war. Vincent, what Intel do you have?"

Casey Vincent stood at attention. "To recap, Ichigo is their number one priority, sirs, hence the name. The Jap's long-term plan to take over China commenced in mid-April, as you know, retaliation for knocking down their shipping and railways and neutralizing troop movements. We're now in September, so they're nearly six months into their campaign. Operation Ichigo has three primary objectives. Dr. Tong will brief us."

My new friend cleared his throat. "The first is to secure land routes for supply lines, basically from north to south, from Pei-ping to Hong Kong and French Indochina."

Vincent motioned to the map of China. "Since China's road system is underdeveloped, the Japs can't stray more than 50-60 miles from railroads and rivers. Hard to move their artillery overland. Go ahead, Dr. Tong."

"Japan's overall objective is to defeat China, of course. Remember that China has been fighting these invaders since nineteen thirty-seven, as well as in earlier campaigns. Our people suffer from famine. Japanese soldiers steal what little food we have and burn every farm before they leave."

Dr. Tong raised his voice. "Our soldiers wear rags and must bind straw around their feet for shoes. They carry outdated rifles." He paused, rubbing his forehead. "Still they fight, protecting Henan Province until it fell in May. Our soldiers held Heng-yang for forty-seven days until the walled city was breached last week."

Vincent tapped the map. "Their advance to the south will bring them here, to Guang-xi Province, in the next few weeks." The men in the Command Cave shifted in their seats. They sat forward, frowns on their faces.

Dr. Tong nodded. "Of course, the third objective is to take over American air bases." He wiped his brow with a handkerchief. "The Flying Tigers are our heroes. We do all we can to support your efforts, but the Japanese have overrun half of your American air bases in the past four months."

"Next in line are Kweilin and Liu-chow." General Vincent pointed to places on the map. "Probably November or even October at this rate. Our best chance of ending the war is sending B-29 heavy bombers out of Cheng-tu to hit the Japanese homeland, unless there's something else cooking."

The men in the Command Cave remained silent; they didn't seem to breathe as they waited for Vincent to continue. "The enemy's putting most of their ground troops into Operation Ichigo. And they've recalled their navy ships and artillery to protect Japan, limiting their forces in the Pacific, to our advantage. We expect our Navy and Marines will make headway there."

General Chennault rose from his chair to stand between Casey Vincent and Dr. Tong. Pop and I heeled quietly, without his command, and stood at attention on either side of him. "Our Operation Matterhorn was to have begun at the beginning of this year but was delayed until mid-year. We'd intended to fly the B-29 Superfortress out of Kweilin, but because of imminent danger to our southern bases, we're basing the operation out of Cheng-tu in the north."

Chennault cleared his throat and lit a cigarette, while I stood tall to guard our commander, hoping I wouldn't sneeze. "We've got to fall back from eastern China, men. Defend the Chinese wartime capital at Chungking and our Headquarters at Kunming. Protect our remaining air bases and divide the enemy's offenses in China and the Pacific. Flying Tigers, we will prevail. Now—let's work out the details."

~   ~   ~   ~   ~

Pop and I lay around on the floor, occasionally going for a walk with a guard, who held our leashes while we sniffed around the lush-smelling vegetation on the hill outside the Command Cave. Morning turned into afternoon. Bobby came and went, bringing food and coffee as the officers worked throughout the day.

In what seemed to be the evening, Dr. Tong asked George if he could take me for a walk, and George gave him my leash. He and General Chennault strolled to a side tunnel of the cave, Pop trailing behind us. Something stirred on the ceiling of the cave, startling me. Huge flying things with big wings screeched high-pitched noises as they flapped and fluttered along the top of the tunnel and out the main entrance. Gremlins? I shivered.

"Bats." Dr. Tong picked me up. "A Chinese symbol for many blessings— good luck, happiness, prosperity, and living to a ripe old age. No need to worry, Gremlin. They're looking for insects and fruit. Something smaller than you are." I licked his hand and relaxed as he rocked me the same way Andy did.

Chennault pulled two chairs into the chamber, scraping the legs along the dirt floor. "I've never minded bats. Maybe they'll bring us the good luck we need. Now, what's the latest from Chungking? Remember to speak up so I can hear you."

The men sat, and Dr. Tong stroked my ears. "General, you've heard of the infighting between the Communist party and the Kuomintang—KMT—Chiang's Nationalist party?"

"Of course." Chennault snapped his fingers, and Pop sat by his feet.

Dr. Tong ruffled my short fur with his firm touch. "When Japanese troops move on from the provinces they've gained, they'll leave a void. They cannot afford to maintain a presence and continue their offensive. Therefore, the Communists are gaining footholds in certain provinces."

"Well, we're fighting a common enemy, aren't we?" The general leaned over to scratch Pop's chest.

"Certainly, but I want you to be aware of this. The KMT are rife with corruption and greed among the ranks."

"Why should that concern us now?" Chennault scratched the bristles on his chin.

"These factors most likely signal additional civil unrest at some point in the future." Dr. Tong set me down. "Only time will tell."

I wandered over to see if Pop wanted to play with me, but he was sleeping. I snuggled next to him and dozed with my head on his back leg as the men's voices droned into the night.

~   ~   ~   ~   ~

Chennault's loud, gruff voice woke me. "Bobby, alert Luke to get the plane ready. We've got a meeting on the Li River." Pop and I stood and shook all over, jingling the metal on our collars.

Casey Vincent walked us out of the Command Cave, past the Chinese guards. I held up my tail high to show them I belonged there, since I couldn't give a thumbs up. Vincent chuckled. "Gremlin, you keep George out of trouble, you hear?" I wagged my tail and blinked at the early morning light as the sun peeked over the distant hills.

George told me, "Heel, Gremlin." I put my head up, like Pop, and trotted next to George as we led the way, slipping and sliding down the hill. Bobby took us to the airfield. We said goodbye, and Luke flew us skyward into the morning sun.

Chapter 23: Li River

Guilin and the Li River (2015)

From wonder into wonder
Existence opens.

Lao Tzu

"*Hoo-weeee*—look at the Li River," said Luke, as he flew the plane between tall skinny mountains. "And all these fantastic shapes."

George picked me up to hold me near the window. Being scrunched into the back of Luke's plane with our gear felt more crowded than riding in a Jeep. George's knees buckled up almost to his chest, reminding me of the way we puppies barely squeezed into our basket once we started eating big dog chow.

I saw a long green snake below us. *Brrkk! Gggrrrww!* I needed to protect everyone in the plane from this kind of monster. Maybe a gremlin hid inside its coils.

He laughed. "Down, boy. That river is so far below us, nothing there can hear you. Especially over these engines."

I blinked twice. A river? With fish? I licked my chops, sniffing the air for any scent of my favorite scaly, slimy treats.

Chennault turned toward us from the cockpit and shouted over the engine noise. "I hear the Chinese have creative names and stories about these mountains." He pointed out the front window. "Luke, make a three-sixty around that hill. Let's get up close to see the horses."

George had warned me to stay out from underfoot around the horses, water buffalo, and yaks we saw in Kunming and in the countryside. Horses were even bigger than Private Rex. They let people ride on them and pulled carts with heavy loads. Why would horses be on top of these tall, steep cliffs? Maybe they wanted a view of the Li River. I wondered—did horses like fish?

My ears felt funny as Luke flew us down toward the mountains surrounding the Li River. I batted at my head with my front paws.

George made his mouth big and wide, like Tom did when he was sleepy. I opened my mouth up, too, took a deep breath and heard a pop in one ear. The noise of the engines became louder on that side. I sat up and yawned again, and the other side opened with the full roar of the engines.

"Yawning helps relieve the pressure when you descend," George said, plugging his nose and crinkling his eyes. "Ah, that's better. My ears just popped. Looks like yours did too, Gremlin." He rubbed my ears and I closed my eyes, leaning my head against his tummy.

"There they are," shouted Chennault. "Eleven o'clock. Horses on the cliff face. See them?"

I'd seen pictures of mountain goats on cliffs, but never horses. *Hrrrmmff?*

George pressed his nose on the window, squinting his eyes. "No… are you sure? Eleven o'clock. Hmmm." His eyes opened wide. "I see it—them. They blend in with the cliffs, like a Chinese sketch or one of those watercolors all in black ink. How many are there?"

Chennault motioned to Luke, who turned the plane at an angle so steep that I nearly fell off George's lap. Soon the white cliffs came back into view. I saw squiggly lines and then… the shapes of horses.

"Are they painted on?" Luke slowed the plane.

Chennault grunted. "Hardly. That's what they call a natural phenomenon. Incredible though, isn't it?" He pointed to the riverbank. "Luke, let's land there. Darn good runway. The sand on the riverbank will hold us."

Luke flew up and over the cliffs, circled around, and straightened the plane so it flew toward the cliffs again. He set the plane down on the beach of the river, startling big black birds. They flapped their wings so fast and so hard that they splashed the water with their wingtips before they flew up into the air.

George said, "Those are ducks, Gremlin. Ducks."

Luke's plane bounced a few times and then slowed down. He turned the plane around so that it faced the way we came. He stopped the engines. I could hear the swish of the propellers as they slowed.

"We'll make camp here," Chennault as he led the way out

of the plane. "Two nights in the open, and I'll feel like a new man. Come on, Joe."

Pop followed the general. I smelled the ground, sniffing where Pop made puddles and piles. I squatted in the sand, making smaller puddles.

Chennault chuckled. "George, you'd better teach that little guy how to pee with his leg up."

"Never had a doxie before, General," said George, shaking his head. "My other pups had no trouble."

Luke laughed as he unpacked the storage area of the plane. "Well, if he doesn't figure out how to hunt and fetch and pee by watching his pop, I guess he'll need you to help him."

Chennault grunted. "Huh. Between the three of you, he'll come along fine. Ah—fresh air." He took out a pack of cigarettes and lit a match. "Li River. Good spot for hunting, fishing, and frogging." Smoke puffed out of his mouth and nostrils.

I turned my head sideways to look at him, thinking about the firecrackers and dragons at the Kunming New Year's festival. Did the general want to be a dragon that breathes fire?

I helped George with his sleeping bag, burrowing inside to chase away any bugs or snakes.

Luke built a fire and cooked something that smelled like Cook's Spam and beans and Hungarian goulash. I sniffed the cans and crept closer; sticking out my tongue to taste anything that was left inside.

George stopped me. "No, buddy." He pushed me away from the fire. "That's too sharp. You'll cut yourself. Go sit with Joe." I huddled next to Pop sprawling on the general's sleeping bag while the men discussed their plans.

"We'll fish early in the morning. Tonight, we'll see how Gremlin can hunt. After all, it's his birthday." Chennault lit another cigarette and blew the smoke toward the burning logs. "September seventh. The youngest and smallest of Hedda's first litter. He's a year old today—let's see if he takes after hunting like his pop. Ever eaten frog legs, George?"

I hadn't heard anything about my birthday. Or hunting. And I didn't know what frogs were. I sat on the sleeping bag and scratched behind my ear.

He nodded. "Yes, sir. On several occasions, General."

Chennault breathed out smoke, like a dragon. "Dad-gum-it, George—we're in the middle of China, no one else around. Let's dispense with the salutations, son. No need to bother. In fact, Luke and I are on a first name basis. Right, Luke?"

"That's right, Claire." Luke puffed on his pipe, cradling the big end in his hand the same way George used to hold me when we first became friends. But Luke didn't tickle the belly of his pipe the way George tickled me sometimes.

"We go way back," said Luke, a cloud of smoke around his head. I put my nose against George's leg and snorted, so I wouldn't sneeze. "And now you're a member of the club, George, out here." He pointed at the river with his pipe. "We're all equal out here in God's wilderness."

Chennault said, "That means you, too, young man." His dark eyes focused on George; his mouth set in a straight line. I could almost picture the scary shark's mouth of the P-40s on his face.

"Sorry, sir." George sat up straighter. I thought he might salute, but the general had told him not to. I looked back and forth at the two of them, cocking my head to one side as I tried to figure out what they would do next.

"Well, tell you what, son." The general closed his eyes for a moment. "Army training is hard to shake off. You can still call me sir, but anything goes out here, all right?"

I took a deep breath and turned to George. He kept his eyes on the commander of U.S. forces in China. "Yes, sir, sir." He blushed, and the men laughed. I jumped up, wagging my tail and barking, joining in with them as they chuckled.

"Sir, sir," Luke said. "That's a good one, George. Anyway, you were saying—about eating frog legs?"

"All right." George patted my head and neck. "Whenever my dad had a break from the farmer's cooperative in Watsonville, he and Ma would pack up the buckboard, hitch up the horse—or later the Model T Ford—with the old cast iron Dutch oven, our poles and gigs. We'd head to Big Basin or Yosemite, just my brother Chet, my folks and me. Two weeks fishing and frogging. Our old dog Arthur was pretty good at finding frogs. Part cocker spaniel, always getting burrs in his fur, but a darn good retriever."

I heard something from the river, like another chuckle far away, a kind of *ggggiiibb* coming from the water's edge. Who— or what—was it? A gremlin? Dragon? I froze, listening intently. I glanced at Pop, but he lay quietly, curled up next to the general. He perked up one of his ears, then lowered it again next to his muzzle. Didn't he sense danger?

"What's that, Gremlin?" The general sat up taller, his eyebrows raised. He pointed in the direction of the noise. "Didja hear something? Over there?"

The fur on my neck stood up, and my hackles rose along my backbone. I listened, scanning the waterline of the river, my ears high, my eyes wide.

"What's out there, Gremlin?" whispered Luke. I turned my head toward him. His eyes were round as he peered into the dusk beyond our campfire. I wagged my tail to comfort him, but I sensed the presence of something unknown to me. Did the men knew what was out there? Did they know if it was an enemy? I had to find out to protect my Flying Tigers.

Gggrriiibb. I heard it again. I spun toward the sound, all my muscles tensed. I was ready to pounce—once I knew what it was. On alert, I rumbled a warning deep in my throat, a soft growl. *Gggrrrrrff.*

George lightly petted my back. "What is it, Grem? Something out there?" I leapt forward on my short, stiffened legs.

Grrwfffftff, I answered him. I lifted one paw after another slowly and deliberately. Off the sleeping bag. Onto the sandy beach. Keeping my head up, I snuffled and sniffed the evening air, catching the scent of water plants and fish, but I knew that plants didn't make noises like that. Neither did fish. What did I smell in the air? What called from the water?

Chennault shifted as he leaned his back against a log, whispering, "Goin' huntin' there, little pup? What do ya suppose is out there?"

I wagged my tail in response, then stopped, concentrating. The men waited, too. They seemed to be holding their breath. Were they frightened of what might be out there making those terrible noises?

Pop rested his head on the general's knee. Chennault stroked his ears with one hand and tapped the end of his cigarette onto a rock with the other. He took another puff and said in his southern drawl, "What is it, Gremlin?"

Grrrruff, I said back to him, stamping my feet. My eyes searched the riverbank, waiting, listening. Would I hear that sound again? Why were all three men waiting for me to do something? Why wasn't Pop worried?

My job was to protect them, no matter what. Were they testing me to see if I really could be their guardian? But what was out there in the murky mysteries of the Li River?

The skin up and down my back quivered as I ran toward the riverbank. "*Gggrrrrr.*" I stood between my Flying Tigers and this unknown enemy.

Gggribb. Gggribbb. I jumped backwards at the sound and fell onto my bottom in the sand. The men laughed. I stood up again, panting to mimic their laughter. Maybe whatever it was couldn't be anything to worry about, especially since Pop was still snoozing. Maybe I was still just a silly puppy.

Chennault chuckled. "He's never heard one before."

Luke threw a stick into the fire. Little lights like tiny, frantic fireflies flew into the darkening sky. "Hey, Gremlin. They sure grow 'em big out here. It sure sounds like they are bigger than you'll ever be."

"Sure hope they don't eat you," the general teased. "Right, Joe Dash? You're worried about your pup there, aren't you, boy?"

Pop raised his head when he heard his name, then rolled over with a grunt. Was Pop sick? Should I protect him, too?

"Full moon tonight. That should help us out with the hunt." George pointed to the large round light rising over the uneven hills. The dark shapes of trees looked as inky as the smudges on his fingers when he changed his typewriter ribbons. Moonlight shone along the river, the ripples of water resembling a long white pagoda on the water.

Ggggribb-bibb came from the edge of the water. I hunched down and crept toward the sound. *Gggribbb. Ggribbit* came from a different direction, and I turned, sniffing the air. I detected the scent of fish, but something else filled my nostrils.

Something crawled out of the water. What could it be? I stepped into the cool, shallow water of the riverbank, up to the top of my short legs, the bottoms of my ears dragging along the surface of the water.

A third *gggggibbbitt, ggrrrribbbitt* sounded close but I stood still and pointed my nose toward it. My front paw lifted. I tensed my whole body, holding the pose in concentration.

"Well, looky there," said Luke. "We've got a pointer. I never knew of any other little sausage dog that could point out a frog—other than Joe Dash."

While Luke spoke, I heard plopping noises in front of me. Were more of them coming out of the water? Or did they jump in? I held my position.

Gggribb-bibb, grrrribb-bibbitt, grrrummm-bibbitt filled the air, up and down the river.

Chennault whispered, "Look how Gremlin's still holding that point, wouldja, George? He did that tracking a caterpillar as a pup. A born hunter. Now, boys. It's time. George, you put on the headlamp. I've got my gig handy."

George and the general came up alongside me. I barely heard their quiet footsteps in the soft sand.

"Good boy, Gremlin. Hold steady. Stay," George murmured. My legs trembled as I held my point.

"Now," said Chennault. With a click, a bright light cut into the night, shining onto the face of a hideous monster. Brown mottled skin over a pointed nose. Bulging eyes. No ears. Thick throat. No fur. The monster balanced at the edge of the river, captured by the light as if on a leash.

I wanted to catch it by the throat, except George had told me to stay. I saw a flash of movement as a shiny stick landed just in front of me. I jumped back. The creature was pinned. The world was silent except for the lapping of gentle waves over my feet. Then I heard the men breathe again.

"Ha ha—gotcha." The general held up the gruesome creature on the end of his spear. "First Chinese eating frog of the night. Come here, Joe Dash."

Pop appeared by my side, growling at the dead thing that Chennault called a frog. He must have been waiting for a signal. No wonder Pop wasn't worried when he first heard the frogs' groaning.

Hunting frogs? Chennault lowered the spear and put his foot on the hideous thing and pulled out the gig. Pop opened his mouth wide, like he was yawning. He put his teeth around the frog's neck and dragged the limp body up onto the beach dropping it near the stones around the fire. I wondered what they would do next. How do they eat frog legs?

Pop came back and licked my muzzle. What? I closed my eyes, feeling his long, wet tongue all over my face. I must have done something right—he'd never licked me before. I rolled onto my back and nipped at the underside of his neck. He growled at me and pretended to run away. I chased him, then he chased me, and we ran in circles around our best friends.

Soon I was tuckered out and wandered over to George's sleeping bag to lie down. Pop stood near Chennault, panting, his eyes bright, wide awake.

"Tell you what." Chennault held up a knife. "I'll start

cleaning these, get them ready for dinner. You get back out there and teach Gremlin about finding frogs. He's got some talent there. Here, Luke, take my gig. It's a two-man job."

"Nah, tell you what, Claire, I'll be the cook tonight. You and George work with the dogs. Best chance for father and son to work together."

"All right. Ready, Gremlin?" George slapped his leg as he called to me. "Find the frogs, Gremlin." I ran to him. When I touched noses with Pop, my head came up to his shoulder. I was one year old and getting bigger. We ran to the water's edge.

George encouraged me. "Come on, let's see what's out there, tiger. Show us you can find more frogs. Find the frogs."

At times that evening, the frogs were silent. Gradually, as we stood still, the croaking chorus rose in volume like the symphonies George played on the phonograph, until it seemed there could never be any other sound in the world. No typewriters, no telephones, no P-40 fighters, no bombs or bombers. Everything else went away—but we remained, focused, waiting, moment-by-moment.

Chennault and George took turns wearing the headlamp. The frogs took turns surrendering themselves to the gigs, sacrificing themselves for dinner. Pop took the frogs up to Luke. And I perfected pointing them out in the dark.

After George speared more frogs, we followed Pop to Luke. "I'm just following the general's orders." Luke held a bowl and a sharp tool, something Ralph would have in his Quonset hut for repairing planes. "Flour, salt and pepper. No butter, though. Cook gave us some Crisco. The hardest part is taking off the legs, but these wire cutters work well enough to keep the pairs of legs in one piece."

"I see you're soaking them in milk first. Just the way Ma does it, too," said George. "I'm getting hungry, and I'll bet the dogs are, too."

Sniffing around, I found a pile of frog heads and bodies. The smell wasn't quite as strong as fish guts, but I felt tempted to roll in them to test how squishy they felt.

George caught me around my middle. "No, no, Gremlin." He pointed at my nose, and my tail curled between my legs. "You're not going to get a BAA-A-ATH tonight, because you are not going to get yourself in that goo." He put the leash on my collar.

We joined Luke and Chennault at the fire. Luke rinsed his hands in a bucket of water and shook them, causing the fire to hiss at the droplets, like Sadie hissing at me. "Been soaking these frog legs in the milk about an hour now. Well, it's just reconstituted powered milk, but it should work."

"Good show, Luke." Chennault lifted a dripping set of frog legs with his fingers. "Now I'll dredge them in flour with just a little salt and pepper, just the way my ole pal Joe did when he cooked up frog legs. Is that pan hot, Luke?"

Luke shook off a few drops of water onto the black pan nestled over the coals in the firepit. "Seems like it, Claire. Here goes the Crisco."

I heard a loud sizzle and backed into George's leg. He put his hands on my shoulders. "It's okay, Gremlin. Soon we'll have dinner."

I sat up straight, watching as Chennault placed several of the frog legs into the pan. Hearing a louder hiss with each addition, I licked my lips and whimpered. *Hhhnnww?*

Since the general seemed to enjoy cooking so much, I

wondered why he didn't work with Cook in the mess hall. Steam rose from the large, black pan, mixing with the smoke from the fire, drifting upwards one way and another in the shifting breeze from the river. As the wind blew the smoke my direction, I sat up and let out a loud sneeze, then rubbed my nose with my front paw.

"Smells good, doesn't it, Gremlin?" The general chuckled. "Smoke follows beauty, I hear. Don't know that any of us is that much of a beauty, but I tell you what—I haven't had frogs' legs in a month of Sundays. Not since, well, who knows when." He lit a cigarette and added more smoke to the air around the campfire. I crawled beside George, hoping he would keep the smoke away from my itchy eyes.

Chennault turned over the browning frog legs with a long, shiny fork. "Luke, where's that chow for the dogs? They must be getting hungry."

"Well, I've got the Spam ready to warm up, and some cold Hungarian goulash from Cook in the ice box back in the plane. I'll get it for them. They deserve it. But why aren't they eating the frog legs?"

Chennault tapped his cigarette against a rock and the ashes fell into the fire. "I don't let Joe touch the frogs until I've checked them and give him a command, since they look so much like toads. Some toads are deadly poisonous to canines. Foaming mouth and all that. You know that, don't ya, Joe."

Pop wagged his tail as he looked up at Chennault. "And you make sure your pup doesn't get into those frog parts, y'hear? We don't want him to get sick."

I followed Luke down the path to the plane. Passing the pile of frog heads and bodies, I decided not to be tempted. I didn't know what a foaming mouth was, but if the general said no, I wouldn't disobey him.

When we came back to the fire, George held a metal plate while Chennault piled frog legs onto it. George passed plates to each of the men, and they sat on nearby logs, almost like the benches in the mess hall.

Luke put his plate down near Pop and poured warmed goulash and Spam onto it. Pop jumped up and ran to eat it. I watched him and waited, remembering that my sister Wench always ran to eat first. If Tom or I got close to her, she would move between us and the bowl, showing her teeth and growling. I didn't know if Pop would growl at me, but since he was bigger than Tom and me put together, I didn't want him to growl at me. I sat next to George, my tummy rumbling.

"Tasty, Claire." Luke held up a leg that looked like a chicken drumstick. "Can't say as I've ever had any kind of amphibian before."

Chennault licked his fingers. "Gotta give credit to my man Joe, the one who taught me to hunt and fish and fight. And frog. Always wanted me to learn about learning. Teaching school taught me lots of things." Pop perked up his ears and walked back to the general, wagging his tail. "But Joe taught me how to live. I always name all my dogs after Joe: Joe Dog, Joe Dash. Huh, buddy? You're a good one, you know that?" Pop sighed as he looked over his shoulder at the general.

"Got to hand it to you, sir." George finished one set and picked up another. "These taste better than the way my folks cook them—but don't tell them that."

Chennault wheezed as he laughed. "I wouldn't dream of

it, son. But I would hope to see you again, back in the States. Sometime when you settle down with a little woman and start your family."

George took a handkerchief from his pocket and wiped his eyes. "That would be an honor, sir."

I crawled to the bowl and sniffed it. The big dog didn't challenge me, and I gobbled up every bit of what was left. I licked the bowl, pushing it toward the campfire each time my tongue pressed against the inside.

"Whoa, boy. That's far enough." George lifted the bowl out of my reach, placing it on the top of the log. "You've licked it clean. I used to lick the bowl like that when my Ma made the batter for my birthday cakes. Ha—that's been awhile."

He took a package out of his pocket and unrolled it, tossing a bone to me and one to Pop. "Happy birthday, tiger. A little gift from our old friends—Bobby and the Chinese cooks of Kweilin." I lay down and chewed on my bone, watching Pop as he crunched on his.

"Permission to ask a question, sir?" George looked at Chennault.

"Of course, George. What's on your mind?" Chennault leaned back against the log and lit another cigarette.

"Oh, I have a million questions for you, sir. And I don't know if or when I'd ever have another chance to ask you. What was it like back in the '20s when you and Luke Williamson were on active duty? How did you come up with those flying maneuvers?"

The men talked about the times that Luke and the General flew together in the U.S. Army Air Corps. George ran his thumb through my fur while he listened, eyes on the two officers as he listened to their stories.

"You've heard of the three men on the flying trapeze?" Luke asked.

"Legendary. I grew up with the newsreels of your aerobatics. Couldn't believe it." George scratched his head.

Luke grinned. "Claire planned it all out. We choreographed the maneuvers first, mapped them out, then flew with our third pilot. Once we got it down, so to speak, we tied our planes together and ran it again." I became dizzy watching his hands move through the air.

Chennault lit another cigarette from his first one. "We tried for all the show-stoppers. Barrel rolls, loops, stalls, spins. But behind it all, I wanted the top brass to see the potential of aerial combat—in formation, not dogfighting one-on-one. The War to End All Wars was over, but we had to plan for anything that could come next."

"What did they say?" George scratched my side, and I rolled over with a long grunt.

"Not impressed. They set us up as a side show, a recruitment effort." The general rubbed the back of his neck. "I lost my hearing, flying those noisy, old open-cockpit biplanes. Kept getting bronchitis, too."

Chennault looked at his cigarette and took another puff. "Might be this old habit of mine. Anyway, I took retirement. Lost confidence in the system. They just wouldn't listen. Still don't. Fortunately, I seem to be of some use here, at least for the Chinese people."

Their voices droned on into the night. When George and Luke shouted at Chennault, I woke up and chewed on my bone, until Chennault's hypnotizing voice soothed me back to sleep.

~   ~   ~   ~   ~

In the morning, I woke up inside George's sleeping bag with his arm curled around me. The air smelled fresh. Chennault was already up, and Pop danced around his feet. Luke rustled around the fire, warming the pot of coffee and pans with sizzling bacon and eggs. George woke and rubbed his eyes.

I walked toward a tree and put my leg up. I fell to the side and heard the men laugh. Trying again, I had a little more success. By the time that I trotted back to the campfire, they had their fishing gear. I nipped at George's boots as we walked down the sloping beach to the river. At the beach, I ran alongside Joe Dash, jumping and barking with joy.

"Don't scare the fish, Gremlin." Luke shushed me. Fish? If they didn't catch any fish, they wouldn't have breakfast. Plus, they would need to gut the fish before cooking them. That's the part that I waited for—rolling in smelly fish guts, my favorite thing to do.

The men found places to fish and put out their gear. In no time, General Chennault's pole bent toward the water. "I've got one!" He pulled up on his fishing rod, reeling in his line with the wriggling fish fighting in the river.

Luke captured it with a big net and removed the hook from its mouth. To my disappointment, Chennault put the fish in his creel, that basket with a lid keeping me away from the fish they caught. They kept fishing, while I waited for my best chance.

Meanwhile, Pop sat quietly on the riverbank with his eyes

on Chennault. He looked upstream and gave a low *wwwrrruuff*. What did he see? I trotted back up the beach to get a better view. A woman and a man drifted toward us in a long boat made of bamboo. The man used a thin pole to move the boat along the river. Three large black birds with rings around their necks perched on the side of the boat.

The couple waved at us as the drifted by, shouting, "Nǐ hǎo." They continued downstream to a sandy spot in the middle of the river. The man threw something in the water, and the boat stopped. The woman let the birds go.

Chennault gestured with his arm. "They're cormorants. Just watch. They'll dive and catch fish but will bring them back to boat instead of swallowing them, because of that ring around their neck."

Pop and I watched the cormorants bring their catch back to the boat to the woman. The man stepped out of the boat onto the sand, wading into the water with something stringy in his hands.

"They're anchoring on that sandbar. Is that a net?" Luke took out his field glasses.

"Sure looks like it." Chennault didn't smile. "Hope they leave something for us."

George used his hand to shade his eyes, almost like he was saluting the couple. "Looks like there's plenty of fish for all of us. I've never seen anyone use a net like that, though."

The man threw the net but kept ahold of one side. It shone like silver in the bright morning sunlight, landing in the water. I waded into the water to learn more. Did the net smell like fish? What would they do if they caught lots of fish? Would they give me the heads and guts? I barked to ask them and startled the cormorants. George held out his hand. *"Shhhh,* Gremlin. Quiet."

I sat down in the shallow water, watching as the birds soared and dived. The man gathered his net and shook it into the boat. The woman raked her fingers down the fishnet, shimmering like a spiderweb after the rain. Shiny fish bodies plopped and wiggled into the boat, their scales glistening in the early morning light.

The man hopped into the boat, pulled up the anchor, and pushed his stick into the sandbar, shoving their boat into the river again. They waved at us again as they floated downstream, cormorants perched on the bow, their heads bobbing with the motion of the boat.

"Well, they caught more with that net than we did, but we have enough for breakfast. George, you're on KP duty this morning." Chennault looked down at me. "For your benefit, Gremlin, that means Kitchen Patrol."

I licked my lips when George cleaned the fish and buried the guts and fish heads. "Gremlin, we don't want a stinky dog in camp—or on the plane. Leave this alone!" Pop watched me, too, and I wisely ate the Hungarian goulash and Spam Luke gave us, although the scent of fried fish tickled and teased my nose.

All too soon, we packed up everything and headed back to the plane. I made one more pass by the buried remains of the fish. Pop ran back and growled at me, nudging me to the plane. I ran to catch up with the men, who joked and laughed on the trail back to the plane.

"The best rest I can get is a day on the river," said Chennault. "That'll keep me going for a few months."

315

Chapter 24: City of Heroes

Autographed Portrait of Major General Chennault by
Tom Lea (1943)

The one who respects others is respected by them.

Mencius

A few days after our trip to Kweilin and the Li River, I fell asleep in my drawer. Soon I dreamed about flying in a Curtis P-40 fighter, high above China's sky, engine running perfectly, guns blazing, shooting down enemy bombers to save lives on the ground. Barking and pawing in my sleep, I woke up when I heard General Chennault call for both of us to come into his office.

317

George grabbed his pencil and tablet, and I hopped out of my drawer and trotted along, wagging my tail. With my tongue on one side of my lop-sided grin, I greeted Pop and sat in my usual spot to watch and listen.

General Chennault sat behind his massive desk and swiveled his chair toward George. He put his hands behind his head and leaned back. "Son, I have a mission for you. You'll be my liaison to Madame Chiang Kai-shek, head of the Chinese Air Force. I usually meet with her, but with the build-up of our military, I need someone I can trust to take messages and supplies to her. I want you to make a very good impression. Take our Air Force pup with you. Madame knows Joe Dash. She'll be very pleased to meet one of his fine puppies."

George leaned forward. "Yes, sir."

"Soong Mei-ling is known as the First Lady of the Republic of China. Her family is powerful, Shanghainese. Studied at Wesleyan College, Macon, Georgia like her sisters, but finished her degree at Wellesley in Massachusetts. Her brothers are all officials of high rank. You've heard of T.V. Soong?"

"Harvard and Columbia. Mover and shaker in finance."

"Right. Madame's brother." Chennault lit a cigarette, and smoke drifted down from the desk. My eyes burned, but I didn't move, except to blink several times. "T.V. Soong really came through in getting Roosevelt to back my plans here in China. We planned to get B-17s flown by U. S. pilots, but with the paint of the Chinese Air Force. We had the deal ready to go a month before Pearl Harbor, but Marshall stopped it—for criminy's sake. Anyway, T.V. is in Washington working with us and Great Britain. He's gotten funds to keep us flying. A true friend of the Flying Tigers."

Chennault finished his cigarette and smashed the butt into an ashtray. "The Chinese say she and her sisters married well. Ai-ling married H. H. Kung, big in finances. Soong Ching-ling married Sun Yat-sen, who toppled the old dynasties and warlords. The country's first president, father of modern China."

I perked my ears as George cleared his throat and spoke almost breathlessly. "And Soong Mei-ling? I saw her photo on the cover of *TIME* magazine recently. She's called China's Joan of Arc."

"That's her third time on the cover. Well, she married for the love of her country. Influential with our Congress and the United Nations. She translates for the Kuomintang, the KMT, led by her husband Chiang Kai-shek. I don't agree with Stillwell on much, but as he once said, she really ought to be the Chinese minister of defense."

"Thank you for this honor, sir," George stammered. "I'll—uh—d-do my best to serve as liaison for you,"

Chennault handed him a packet of papers. "George, you might run into the Generalissimo. You may discuss progress on Operation Matterhorn and our mutual preparations in defense of the Japanese Operation Ichigo. Madame or Dr. Tong will translate for you."

"Good advice, sir. I know a little Mandarin, b-but not enough to serve as liaison without—uh—b-b-botching the job." George blushed.

The general took a long drink from his coffee cup. "You need to know about the civil war between the KMT and the

Communists. Here's a briefing. You've already met Dr. Tong in Kweilin, the Generalissimo's ambassador. He'll meet you in Chungking at the air base and explain the details."

"Yes, sir." George took notes. The loud noise of his pencil scratching against the tablet seemed to fill the still, smoky office, accompanied by the din of rumbling trucks outside and the clattering of office machinery in the building. A small electric fan whirred, sounding like Sadie's purring.

"Now, you've heard of Stillwell's disrespectful behavior toward Chiang, calling him 'Peanut' for his shaved bald head." Chennault took a deep breath through another cigarette, blew the smoke toward the ceiling, and rested the white stick on the edge of a dish. "I know you'll be respectful. I've seen you in action. Good toast at the banquet and all that."

George blushed. "Thank you, sir. I won't let you down."

"Give the Chiangs my best. Madame, especially. She calls us her air force, and I'm not embarrassed to say she's a princess to me. Okay, Andy and Luke will fill you in. Dismissed." The general peered over his desk at me. I attempted to sit up with my front paws in the air as I'd seen Pop. Instead, I lost my balance and rolled onto my side.

The general chuckled. "Those first lieutenant's bars look good on Joe Dash's pup. He'll impress the Generalissimo — sharp military attire."

I got back onto my feet and shook myself with a last look at the general, whose craggy face was surrounded by cigarette smoke. I padded through the door of his office, walking even taller.

George asked Andy to type up the general's orders for us to fly to Chungking and back. He packed his satchel and picked up his orders from Andy. I growled at Sadie and walked away with my head and tail in the air. She couldn't go on our mission.

We stopped at our bunkhouse, where George brushed my coat until it glowed like a new copper penny and buffed my leather collar and leash. He shined his shoes, and I sniffled now and then from the smell of shoe polish on leather. Putting on his flight jacket and round officer's hat, he picked up the satchel.

Luke came out of his bunkroom. "Ready, George? Gremlin? Well, look at you both in those first lieutenant's bars." He whistled and I licked the air between us to thank him. We piled into the Jeep. "VIP service today, George. You and I are taking the general's plane."

~   ~   ~   ~   ~

George cradled me in the co-pilot's seat for the long, noisy flight. From time to time, he held me on his shoulders so that I could look out the window. I whimpered to let him know I wanted him to open the window so that I could smell the clouds up close, but he never did.

Luke pointed through the front windshield. "Hope those are some of our boys. Looks to be four of them." He peered into the sky. I could see little black dots in the blue spaces between the clouds.

As they got bigger, I trembled—would they run into us? The planes made a pass in front of us, clearly showing the shark mouths on their noses. One of the planes tipped its wings from side to side.

"They recognize the general's plane, Gremlin." George stroked my feet. "No need to worry." The lightning-fast P-40s dove in front of us with their loud, rumbling engines, and we all ducked instinctively. I barked just in case any gremlins were on board, to scare them away from making mischief.

Luke looked over at us. "Here, George, want to take the yoke for a bit?"

"Well, sure—okay. For a minute."

Luke said, "All right. Put your hands on the yoke. Remember what Chennault and I do to share the yoke? I say out loud that you have the yoke."

George grabbed it tightly and said, "I have the yoke."

Luke raised his hands, and the plane began to drop its nose. I could see the ground far below us. George's chest became warmer all of the sudden. His heart pounded as he pulled back on the yoke. The plane's nose rose toward the clouds. I held still on his shoulder, not wanting to take his focus from flying the aircraft.

"Gently, buddy." Luke motioned with his arm. "Now lower it just a tad. There you go. Level off. Take a look around, tiger. Bet you thought you'd never be flying yourself over the provinces of southwestern China, eh?"

George let out a grunt and smiled. Little drops of water trickled down the sides of his face.

"All right, now. I'll take the yoke again." Luke motioned with his hands.

"You have the yoke." George's voice shook.

"I have the yoke. Well, buddy, you'd better put that handkerchief to work before it looks like you've been out in the rain."

I crept down into George's lap and fell asleep to the moaning and growling of the engine and the slight ups and downs of the air currents. George woke me and held me up to look out the window to see a sprawling city along a big river.

Luke's big hands shifted on the yoke as he opened and closed his fingers. "We've got a little weather here. Ah— there's the Jialing River. Tributary to the Yangtze. We're close."

I felt the wind pushing on the airplane, up and down and from side to side. Luke stayed in control, shifting the yoke in response to the weather's push and pull on the aircraft.

At last, we landed on the well-worn runway. Slowing, he turned the plane onto a taxiway toward a building with flags flapping in the wind. After the propeller stopped and Luke shut down the aircraft, I squirmed in George's arms, letting him know I needed to make a puddle. He carried me down the narrow staircase, along with his satchel and officer's hat. He gave me a moment alone under the plane's wing for a little break. After sniffing the rubber tires, gravel, and mud, which made my whiskers twitch, I found a suitable spot to squat and let go.

Feeling friskier, I ran to my best friend. He picked me up and tucked me under his arm as we headed toward the pilot's shack, where Luke talked with other pilots. "Good luck, tiger," Luke told me—and George.

A big black car arrived, with flags on both sides. My Chinese friend from the Command Cave welcomed us with a bow of his head. "Lieutenant Haydon, good to see you again."

George bowed, and I tucked my chin next to my chest. "Glad to be here, Dr. Tong."

"And welcome to my friend Gremlin. I'll take you to meet Soong Mei-ling, up on Huangshan Mountain. It's a little bit of a ride to the provisional capital and command center where I serve as Minister of Information."

We sat in the back seat of the car, and I stood on George's lap, balancing my front paws on the window. The driver whisked us away from the air base and into the city, where the busy streets were filled with cars, rickshaws and bicycles, ox carts, water buffalo, and people walking in every direction.

I heard a loud patter on the car's roof, and the windshield splattered with big drops of rain, its wipers slapping back and forth. The driver honked as he passed trucks, cars, and motorcycles. He let his breath out loudly now and then, never looking in the rear-view mirror as he turned the steering wheel back and forth to avoid vehicles and pedestrians.

The pounding rain on the roof grew louder, and the swish of the wipers clearing the drops on the windshield went faster. Having gotten used to the turbulence in airplanes, this ride didn't concern me, but the occasional thunder and bright lighting made me shiver. I whimpered and retreated to George's lap.

"It's okay, Gremlin." George's low voice rumbled, almost deeper than the thunder. "We're in the City of Heroes." His voice calmed me, and I stopped shaking.

Dr. Tong cleared his throat. "That's correct. Chungking is known as the City of Heroes. People travel here from the east, south, north, and west of China to protect our wartime capital city. The population has more than doubled to nearly two million. Troubling times, many factions, but here there is support for Generalissimo Chiang Kai-shek and his wife, Soong Mei-ling. All these people are heroes."

"I can't imagine what they've sacrificed. Leaving their homes. Traveling miles by foot. My family has it bad in the States with rationing, b-but here… I've seen some things I will never forget. If you don't mind my asking, where are you from? How did you learn to speak English so well?"

"Both the Generalissimo and I are from Chekiang Province. I was born into a poor family near a tiny farming village. A slow learner, my teacher often punished me for not learning my characters quickly enough, hitting me with a plank of wood, pulling hard on my ears, or rapping my forehead with his knuckles. In hindsight, maybe I was what you Americans call a knuckle-head." He and George chuckled.

Dr. Tong rubbed his forehead. "Life was hard on the farm, and so I decided I must apply myself to my studies and become a scholar if I were to have opportunities in life. I began to enjoy learning, especially without the beatings."

George shifted on the seat to face Dr. Tong. "How did you get away from that life—to this wartime capital?" I sat up and looked out the window to see a ribbon of river next to us.

Dr. Tong had a faraway look in his eyes. "I grew up in the time of the Manchu emperors and wore the queue—my hair shaved in the front and the long braid down my back. My mother had the custom of bound feet. Very traditional, except that we were Christians, which turned out to be an advantage for my father, who eventually got a job in Shanghai. I attended various schools there, usually getting into trouble. But just as I completed my high school studies, he died—so suddenly. I needed to grow up and go to work to support the family."

George took a deep breath and shook his head. "I'm so sorry to hear this. Forgive me—uh—for b-b-bringing it up."

"No matter, George. As fortune would have it, I returned to my ancestral homelands and taught school. I was close enough to visit my mother, walking only twenty miles from my school. One of my students became... the future president of the Republic of China."

George sat up straighter. "Chiang Kai-shek? You were his *Lǎoshī*—his teacher? What was he like back then?"

"Very good. You understand Chinese. He kept to his daily routines and academics, taking English from me and studying Japanese as his third language. An athlete, avid reader of every newspaper delivered to the school. He decided to study in Japan. At the time, Japan was the place for Chinese to study military science. He wanted to be of service to China for his lifelong career. And my career took a turn when I married a teacher, for love."

Dr. Tong paused and showed George two small photos he took from his wallet. "Here's our wedding picture. And this is our little girl."

George nodded, saying, "B-B-Beautiful family."

Dr. Tong put the pictures away. "My wife preferred to live in Shanghai. To make ends meet, I worked for a printer, and we both taught English every night. I took lessons to become more fluent in English."

He took a deep breath and sighed. "Then I went to college in America. This was a few years before the Great War, and it meant leaving my family for several years. I had to cut my queue, our traditional hairstyle, much to the dismay of my mother, who wept when she first saw me with a western haircut. Later she acknowledged I made a good choice to earn my degree in journalism."

The car climbed a steep, winding road, and he continued, "I returned to Shanghai. To make a long story short, I have been close to Dr. Sun and the Kuomintang since the early 1900s. I am now serving my former student as his ambassador. Ah, here we are—our Headquarters for the allied forces. We'll have a chance to chat more later."

The car turned into a long driveway, and I saw a big gray building set in lush greenery. Ah, a good place for me to explore. I danced in circles on George's lap to let him know I wanted to go out.

The driver stopped the car, and a soldier opened the door. George climbed out and set me down as a few big raindrops fell onto my back. The rain stopped, leaving a fresh smell in the air. I pranced in circles around his feet as he twirled around, unwinding my leash from his legs. Stepping among the short green plants that came up to my belly, I shook my head and breathed in the unfamiliar aromas. Sniffing and snorting, I ran as far as my leash would let me. Pressing my snout into the greenness of it all, I forgot about our mission. Until I heard Dr. Tong laugh.

I stood and shook from my nose to my tail to wring the rainwater from my fur. George's mouth was open as he stared at me. Rolling his eyes, he said, "Please forgive my b-boisterous puppy, D-D-Dr. Tong. This is Gremlin's first time to experience such a big lawn. The Kunming airbase is mostly rocks and d-d-dirt—and one pathetic grassy area." He chuckled, shrugging his shoulders.

"Understandable. Let him enjoy it," said Dr. Tong. He held out his hand. "Oh, on second thought, we'd better head inside." Huge droplets fell from the sky, followed by streaks of rain pelting my head and back. He opened a big black umbrella, and the men hustled toward the building. I trotted behind them, trying to keep up, feeling my paws dig into the moist, silky grass with each step.

Several guards on the long, covered front porch carried guns. They reminded me of our MPs, Sarge and Jimmy, but they didn't have a big dog like Private Rex. One of them waved us to them. Stepping onto the dry cement, Dr. Tong lowered his umbrella and left it open to dry with others, like huge dark flowers waiting for the sun to return.

"You'll need to leave your sidearm here, Lieutenant." Dr. Tong motioned to the pistol at George's waist.

"Of course." George unbuckled his belt and took off the holster with his weapon, leaving it with a guard. Another man motioned for him to open his satchel. George opened the leather pouch and held it open. The guard nodded.

George took out my Good Morning Towel, bent down, and wiped my neck and back and each of my paws. The guard smiled and murmured in Chinese, "*Duome ke'ai.*" I remembered Mrs. Liu teaching George how to say that something was cute and panted at the guards in a smile with my tongue hanging over my bottom teeth.

George put my towel away. He picked me up, and I hung over his arm, sniffing the air and looking around at our new surroundings, nothing like the air base in Kunming.

Dr. Tong escorted us through an entry hall, where George took off his hat, and into a large room with high ceilings. Our guide motioned to a set of chairs along the wall. "Have a seat, Lieutenant. You'll see many people milling about. This villa serves as the Chiangs' residence and as the national capital, our headquarters for the Allied Forces. Please wait here." He left through another door.

George sat in a straight-backed chair like Dr. Liu's. I sat on his knees and we looked out at a garden through rain-streaked windows. Civilians and military personnel passed through the room, from one side to the other, speaking in Chinese.

"Hmmm." George sighed, and I felt his arms relax around me. As my eyes got used to the dim lighting, I looked up and around, backing into his tummy when I noticed two dangerous-looking animals guarding the doors. Bulging eyes stared at me. The fur on the back of my neck rose.

Frightened, I considered hiding behind one of the huge painted scrolls with Chinese writing. Or slinking under a table with a big vase of flowers on top. Or running behind a large rock with holes in it, where I could peek out at the monsters.

No, I decided to stay with George and protect him, in case these animals might be gremlins, though I puzzled briefly over why the Chinese would have gremlins in their governmental offices. *Gggrrrrff*—I made my face into the same angry expression as the dragon. Then the next one, which had wings and looked more like a bird than a dragon. When they didn't move? Or growl back at me?

"I'm going to talk with you, Grem, so I don't stutter when I meet Madame," George said in a low voice. I stopped the rumbling in my throat to listen, his voice calming me. "The dragon means the emperor is in power, and the phoenix—see the one with wings—that means the empress is in charge of the country."

He pointed to two pieces of cloth on the wall. "The flag of the Kuomintang is that one with the white sun, next to the U.S.

stars and stripes. My flight jacket has a shoulder patch with the sun of China, the star of India, and the stripes representing the U.S."

George smoothed his hair. "Now I'll be able to say that I worked with Soong Mei-ling of the Chinese Air Force. Who would have thought that a shy musician from Santa Cruz, California, would get this far?" He shook his head slowly, looking around with his mouth slightly open. His hands trembled, but he rubbed them together and then slowly stroked my back. His fingers became steady and his blue eyes blinked in the soft light of the reception room. "I sure want to stick with General Chennault to see this war through, Gremlin. And you're a big help, too."

I felt puzzled—war, enemies, fighting planes, guns. I still felt like a small puppy in a big world that I didn't understand.

Reaching up to lick his chin, I wanted George to know I would help him with his meeting. I would be brave and stand tall. But the Generalissimo and Soong Mei-ling sounded important, like the dragon and the phoenix. I felt nervous that I might make a puddle in a palace.

Chapter 25: The Dragon Wall

Watercolor Portrait of Generalissimo Chiang Kai-shek by
Tom Lea (1943)

We must decide on what we will not do,
And then we will be able to act with vigor
In what we ought to do.

Mencius

Dr. Tong returned and asked us to follow him. I heard the
distant ticking of a clock. *Tick-tick-tick-tick.* As we came to a
doorway, Dr. Tong stopped. I saw a Chinese man in uniform

writing, sitting at a desk with an alarm clock in front of him, bigger than the one George had. A man dressed in American civilian clothes moved a black pencil on a large piece of paper. On the paper was the likeness of the man's head, brown, round, without hair. Could this be the man Stillwell called 'Peanut?' "

Dr. Tong whispered, "Mr. Tom Lea, the esteemed American artist, is drawing the portrait of the Generalissimo, but our leader's time is limited. So, the Generalissimo set up that loud clock to remind the artist to mind the time. The Generalissimo must return to matters of state." He held up a finger. "One moment."

I squirmed in George's arms, because I wanted to let Generalissimo Chiang Kai-shek see the Lieutenant's bar on my collar. He should hear about my purpose in serving the Flying Tigers and that I would do everything I could to help the Chinese people. But, since George held me firmly in my place, I thought better about barking or whimpering. The tick-tick-ticking of the clock in that office was a reminder that people do what is most important, and for me not to be a distraction.

The artist asked Dr. Tong, "Ten more minutes to finish my portrait?"

I recognized Mandarin as Dr. Tong translated for the Generalissimo, who took out a small notebook and scowled at it, looking as mean like as dragon. He nodded and resumed writing. Tom Lea bent over his drawing and moved his pencil quickly across the paper. Dr. Tong motioned for us to follow him down the hall.

The clock's ticking became fainter as we headed up the stairs. A guard stood at attention at the top of the steps. Dr.

Tong and George walked halfway down the hallway and sat on a bench. My best friend set me down next to his satchel. I sighed and laid my head on my paws. The cool air from the open windows smelled clean and fresh from rain. I let out a big yawn—*aawwwwunng?*

I sat up, hearing someone coming up the stairs. George and Dr. Tong stood at attention when the Generalissimo arrived—without his clock. He had changed from his uniform into a long silk robe. I hoped he hadn't caught me yawning, afraid I'd spoiled my first impression. He extended his hand to George and spoke to him in Mandarin. They shook hands, and the Generalissimo breezed past us, the sound of his footsteps receding down the long hallway.

Dr. Tong motioned to the closed door. "He says that Madame is not quite ready for you yet. He will introduce you to her later. We will walk in the gardens until he summons us. I think Gremlin will enjoy that, and we have many things to discuss."

Dr. Tong led us downstairs and outside into a maze of paths with a million tantalizing smells and sounds. We climbed over a low arched bridge above a trickling stream. George let me wade into a shallow pool to drink the clear water. Dragonflies hovered as I cooled my paws.

Dr. Tong called to me, "Come along, Gremlin. We have more to see."

A squirrel scampered under the trees, reminding me of the way crickets hid in their holes on the road to Dr. and Mrs. Liu's home. I charged after it, barking, but George held onto my leash. The furry animal with a long, graceful tail disappeared.

We followed Dr. Tong through a wide opening in the wall, shaped like a giant vase. Flowers bloomed everywhere in the courtyard, crowding my nose with their perfumes. I sneezed and shook my head. Huge stones with holes in them stood straight up as if they were searching for the Flying Tigers high in the sky. George and I approached the tallest stone on a little hill in the center of the garden. It towered above us, hiding the midday sun. He looked at it from every angle and ran his hand along its sides and into the holes.

I sniffed along the base of the big rock's stand, made of polished wood. The scents were faint, as if no four-legged animal had been there for a long time. I left it alone, as an unmarked place, special somehow.

Dr. Tong said, "You are admiring the scholar's stone. Monumental. Have you seen such a thing before?"

George knelt and petted me, saying, "Only in certain places. Our national parks. Yosemite, especially, has huge cliffs and rocks. This rock reminds me of the potholes where shallow river waters flow over such rocks. Inspirational, peaceful."

"I have not had the pleasure of seeing your Yosemite, except in photographs." Dr. Tong patted the side of the rock. "It is an ancient tradition among monks and scholars to bring such stones from the mountains into their studios. These larger ones are most admirable and provide a meditative influence in the garden."

"I can understand that," George said, standing. "My grandfather likes to bring rocks home to remember our camping trips. We have quite a collection of stones bordering our flower beds. None as magnificent as this, though."

A young man approached us from one of the bamboo-lined paths. Dressed in a military uniform, he spoke with Dr. Tong in Mandarin. When he left, Dr. Tong said, "It sounds like Soong Mei-ling's other pressing business will take a little longer than she thought. We'll have a chance now to enjoy the Chungking gardens as we get acquainted."

I sniffed grasses of many colors and textures feathering the edges of the path, stopping now and then to leave my scent. Just in case Dr. Tong forgot the way, my marks would guide me in leading them back to the offices.

Our path was made of dark pebbles and light gray square tiles in diamond-shaped patterns, uneven textures under my paws. Smooth rocks were embedded in the walkway, forming the shapes of flowers, but unlike the living flowers edging the path, they had no scent. Tall bamboo with thick, black stems swayed high above me in a light breeze. Birds squabbled and fluttered around their narrow leaves and the flowering bushes. Small green vines climbed the white walls surrounding us. Inside this courtyard, I felt quiet, calm, and safe from the war.

Shrubs and low vines covered the ground. I stopped, hearing the rustling of dead leaves under a bush. I stiffened and pointed to the spot.

"What did you find, tiger?" George came closer and bent down beside me. "Good boy, Gremlin. You found a toad."

"Don't eat it." Dr. Tong chuckled, shaking his finger at me. "It could be poisonous."

I backed away, leaving the yellow toad with its bumpy skin and beady eyes, and followed the men down the path. We passed through an opening in the wall into another courtyard where the small rock patterns in the path were made into shapes of animals. The first design looked like a duck, with yellow pebbles for the beak. I stepped over the wings of dragonflies and butterflies and the petals of flowers. The long, narrow stones in between the designs reminded me of the black bamboo leaves.

George bent down and picked me up when we came to the far end of the courtyard. "This gate is shaped like a four-leaf clover," he said, turning to Dr. Tong. "Our family is Scots-Irish. We think it's lucky to find one among the shamrocks. And we entered the gardens through a round opening."

Dr. Tong nodded. "Our gateways have meaning, too, luck, prosperity, long life. We call the round one the moon gate, the best way to see the rising full moon. Our Chinese gardens have curved lines, representing connections with nature, inner peace, and harmony."

My friend walked to the gateway, running his fingertips along the smooth tiles. "These gates make me think about the transitions we make in life. I like to stop here at this one to reflect on my personal transformations as I move physically from one part of the garden to another."

George stepped over the threshold of the gate and stopped as we faced into the huge courtyard. He took a deep breath and stood up straight, holding me as we gazed around the scene. He let out a long sigh. "This looks like a fairy tale—carved columns, the bright paint on the columns and ceilings, red lanterns. I've never seen anything like it. Except maybe in the Reed Flute Cave of Kweilin."

Our host said, "This is a national treasure, the garden's ornate pavilion. Breath-taking, isn't it?"

"I can't believe it," George said, finally putting me down

on the wide path, paved with large flat stones, easier on my feet than the pebbled walkways.

"Yes, I see you understand the connections between nature and our landscape architecture." Dr. Tong motioned to the pavilion and the flowers and plants surrounding it. We walked along a narrow covered walkway to approach the building. I heard trickling water and glimpsed parts of a large pond beyond the bushes.

My nails tapped on the cool stone walkway as we circled around the pond and came closer to the pavilion. What I saw made me stop and pull back against George's grip on my leash.

"Come on, Gremlin," he said. "What is it?"

Perched on a low wall were dogs with wide mouths, sharp teeth, and pushed-in noses. I didn't know whether to bark in joy, growl in warning, or hide behind George. I froze, keeping my eyes on them in case they attacked George.

Foo Dogs in Jiading District, Shanghai (2015)

"It's okay, Gremlin," said Dr. Tong. "Please meet our guardian lions, made of stone. They are often mistaken for dogs, popularly called *foo dogs*."

I walked forward, stiff-legged, and sniffed around the first one, then the next. They smelled alike. Since they didn't move, I snorted in relief, but barked at the next one to see if it might come to life and play with me. No luck.

337

We climbed a few steps into the large pavilion. A set of carved furniture was set back from the pond on a low platform. Painted lamps hung from the tall ceiling above the tables and chair, their long tassels swaying in the breeze.

"Dr. Tong, the furnishings are incredible. I've seen only one chair that's even remotely like it. My Chinese teacher, Dr. Liu and his wife have an ancestral chair, but it's not nearly as large and ornate as these."

"Many important conversations have been held here in this pavilion, much contemplation and planning." Dr. Tong motioned a round table with drum-like stools under a painted roof. "This old porcelain table and seats are hand-painted with depictions of the immortals. The circular shape symbolizes good relationships. I must add they have seen many morning conversations, as well as informal nights over good drinks with pleasant company." He chuckled. "Let's have a seat, George."

They sat on the small seats, conversing as they faced the water. Their low voices were muffled by the walls and the greenery around them. I lay down on the cool stone floor and sniffed at a shiny beetle rambling through the pebbles.

"You'd asked about Dr. Sun Yat-sen," Dr. Tong said. "One of our greatest leaders. He fought against the feudalist society and led the transformation of China into the modern era. Education, transportation systems, especially our railways systems. We vow to rebuild once we win the war and reclaim our country."

"And how does Chiang Kai-shek fit into the picture?" George asked.

"Chiang joined the Chinese Nationalist Party—the

338

KMT—after becoming a military leader and succeeded Dr. Sun as leader of the Kuomintang after his death."

George nodded. "And Madame Chiang? His wife?"

"She is usually addressed by her own name, Soong Mei-ling," Dr. Tong advised. "But she seems to consider "Madame" a term of endearment from her Flying Tigers, whom she holds in the highest regard."

"What is the best approach I can take for today's meeting?" asked George.

Dr. Tong shifted on his stool. I moved toward him to sniff his shoes. Nothing interesting. I yawned. "She will want to confirm certain things with you, especially whether General Chennault has the same interpretation of the latest intelligence that she has. She may want to address the next steps, both in the short term and for the long term."

I stood and followed the beetle along the patio and peered over the edge into the pond far below. Two black birds paddled across its green water. Fish swam below me—their wonderful scent filled my nostrils. I wagged my tail and whined, backing up and looking for a way to get down to the pond. George hadn't secured my leash, so I ran between his feet and dashed along the path. I had to find a way to get closer to the fish.

Splashing into the shallow water, I felt George's hands

around my middle. "Oh, no you don't, Gremlin," he told me, taking out his handkerchief and wiping my paws as he stood up.

I whimpered, wishing he had his fishing pole. If he caught and cleaned even one of those big fish, I could roll in the guts and impress everyone with how I smelled. But in Chungking, the City of Heroes, it seemed like George wanted me to smell like I'd just had a BA-A-ATH.

Dr. Tong laughed. "That's right, Gremlin. You'd be in big trouble if you ate one of our koi. Those big white and gold fish are many years old, treasured by all, but food for none. That includes you, little tiger."

"Plus, they're bigger than you are, buddy." George chuckled.

Dr. Tong paused to point out a white wall with a narrow tile roof along the top, which seemed taller in some sections and lower in others, like a wiggling snake. A dragon's head stared at me with huge, bulging eyes, its tongue and teeth poised to eat me. I barked—*bbbrrrkkk-bbrrrrkk*—to protect George.

"It's okay, Gremlin," he said, petting my head and shoulders. "It's not real."

"Our treasured gardens typically have dragon walls," said Dr. Tong. "There are many meanings for the dragon in our culture—good luck, power, and strength. It is better to be considered a dragon, capable of achieving good things, rather than a worm." He bent to hold me under my chin. "Gremlin, the dragon will give you strength to do your part and complete your mission in life. Embrace the dragon within you."

George set me down, and I shook myself from nose to tail,

340

releasing my fear and standing up tall with the power of the dragon. We wandered through a long courtyard until we came to a tall hill of rocks.

"Let's go, tiger," George said, pointing to a narrow path between two boulders. I scrambled up the stone steps, into little caves, and finally stood on top. I smelled the wind and thought I could feel my dragon wings on my shoulders. Dr. Tong caught up to us and stood panting as we admired the view of the pond and the pavilion.

In silence, we walked down the steep path and ended up on a walkway under the shade of tall trees with the dragon wall on one side. George picked me up, and we looked through a window in the wall. I smelled scents of flowers on the breeze wafting from the next courtyard.

Dr. Tong stood next to him. "The windows of these outdoor rooms seem like picture frames, don't they? We can look out at living pictures and reflect on where we have been."

"I never knew..." George shook his head. I licked his chin and he smiled. "Now we do, right, Gremlin? When we go back home, the word 'garden' will have a completely new meaning."

We followed the dragon wall until a crowd of workers blocked our way. Baskets of rocks were balanced on either side, hung from poles across their shoulders. Others carried tools and buckets of white paint.

"I want you to see something unforgettable, Lieutenant Haydon. This courtyard holds our garden of harmony. But we need to go around. This way," Dr. Tong said. I hung my head over George's shoulder for a better view of the gardens.

Dr. Tong steered us to a side path into a tall bamboo

forest. "Unfortunately, bombs fell on this part of the garden during the last air raid. It barely missed our headquarters but took out the tail of our dragon wall."

They climbed onto a stone bench. Below us, workers passed broken tiles and stones from one person to another, clearing rubble from the wall and several deep holes in the garden. Men sawed broken trees into chunks, and workers carried away the wood and scorched plants, using baskets balanced on poles slung over their shoulders.

"This is a sign of the resilience of our people. In adversity, we gather. We rebuild a better place for a new day, for new generations."

George's chest grew warm. He stood, silent and motionless as the workers made repairs. I wondered why people would destroy a garden of harmony. The Flying Tigers pledged to stop the enemy who bombed China. And I pledged to use my dragon wings to chase away the gremlins and stop the war.

Hearing the shuffling sound of footsteps on the path, I turned and gave a short bark. The messenger returned, out of breath, and spoke with Dr. Tong. It was time to meet Soong Mei-ling.

Chapter 26: Golden Earrings

Watercolor Portrait of Soong Mei-ling
by Tom Lea (1943)

To be able to practice five things everywhere
Constitutes perfect virtues...
Gravity, generosity of soul, sincerity, earnestness, and kindness.
Confucius

When we returned to the stairs, George took out my Good
Morning Towel from his satchel, saying, "All right, Gremlin.

We want you to be most presentable when you meet Soong Mei-ling." Another BA-A-ATH? I hoped not.

George picked me up and wiped my paws again. Once we climbed the steep staircase, he held me up to a window at the top of the steps to see the garden from above, with its rustling treetops, ponds, bamboo, and pavilion. Dr. Tong knocked on a door and spoke in Mandarin. A woman replied, and he opened the door, bowing slightly as we entered the room. The space was filled with light from large windows on two walls, so bright it made me blink.

"Welcome, Lieutenant Haydon." A woman with hair as black as a cormorant's wing smiled at us from a big chair. "So glad to meet you at last." Her voice drawled like General Chennault's, sounding as if it dripped with honey.

Dr. Tong left the room and quietly closed the door. George stood at attention. I sat up in his arms to be respectful as well, my eyes on her, my ears ready to listen.

"It is my honor. So nice to finally meet you, Madame Soong Mei-ling," he said, bowing his head. I curled my chin down to my neck, following his lead. I wrinkled my brow and looked at her with big eyes, hoping to look wise.

She reached out her small, smooth hand and George shook it with his big fingers. I felt his arm tremble as he held me tight. Her hair was pulled up gracefully at the back of her head. Her eyes reminded me of my mother's, large and brown.

"Call me Madame." She raised her hand gracefully, as if slowly shooing away a fly. "It wouldn't sound respectable in some places in America, but that is what your Chennault and other Americans call me. No need to use my full name in conversations where it's just the two of us."

"As you wish, Madame." George bowed again.

The beautiful woman looked at me, then back at George. "Or, rather the three of us. Now, please, Lieutenant, I would like to make the acquaintance of this charming young friend of yours."

I raised my head, sniffing the air between us. Madame's pastel gown smelled like the clothing Dr. and Mrs. Liu wore. Mrs. Liu always gave me treats, so I wiggled in George's arms to see if maybe Madame had something for me to eat.

The head of the Chinese Air Force reached out to scratch under my neck. I stuck out my tongue, trying to smell her hand. Madame turned my collar around to touch my first lieutenant bar. "Delighted, Lieutenant Gremlin. I see your rank on your collar. Very clever."

She put her hand back into her lap—without giving me a treat. "I think Gremlin is a terrific name. I remember the good manners of your papa, Joe Dash, when he sat up for us in Kunming. A black beauty. Shiny coat, magnificent, regal dachshund. You look more like your mother with your chocolate and tan coat."

Madame motioned for George to sit in the chair next to her, saying, "Please have a seat." He sat and placed me in his lap. Cocking my ears forward, I watched Madame closely, hoping to remember every word. Plus, my tummy growled, and I wondered again if she had any food for me.

"My apologies for the delay in our meeting, Lieutenant Haydon. But I trust that Dr. Tong has had a briefing with you."

"Yes, Madame Soong—Madame. He d-d-did," George stammered. I licked his hand to remind him—he could do this. He rubbed my back with his knuckles and took a deep breath, letting it out slowly.

Looking down at me, he smiled, then turned back to Madame with a determined expression on his face. "Dr. Tong did brief me on current events, as did General Chennault before I left Kunming. But I look forward to hearing from you directly."

She nodded. "It is well that Chennault's liaison should become well-versed in our troublesome times, from multiple perspectives. The Kuomintang and the Communists have resolved to defend China together against the outrageous aggression of the Japanese invaders. Although my husband had desired to wipe out every faction of Communism, he was prevailed upon to spare them and join forces against a mutual enemy. Of course, now they have a stronger position than before. But, be that as it may, without the support of Chennault's Flying Tigers, along with the British, Koreans and Russians, we would be at the mercy of even more unspeakable horrors by the Japanese invaders."

George replied, "We're here to support you and avoid more casualties of war."

Madame raised her voice. "As you know, I will not permit our people to be doomed to lives of slavery, for the enemy to pillage our people and our resources, in their bid to overpower the world."

He lifted his chin. "Madame, how may I be of service?"

Her eyes softened, and she reached toward me. "In a moment. May I get to know Gremlin better? I do so love having pets in the home, but here we have mostly cats to keep away the mice. Our stone lions, those foo dogs in the garden have no warmth and affection, not like you, my little friend." How did she know what Doreen called me?

"Yes, of course, Madame." George lifted me into the air and bent toward Madame.

I was so excited when she placed me in her lap that I forgot my manners. I wagged my tail, and my whole behind wiggled. I reached up with my nose to lick her ear, as I did with Doreen. Her large golden earrings looked like the shells I played with at the riverbank where George fished. I nibbled on one to see if it tasted like fish.

Then—I smelled her perfume. I sneezed, and the spray spotted the neck of her fine silk dress. A silken web of doggie drool connected my mouth with her dress. She seemed as surprised as I was. George quickly picked me up and held me to his chest, breaking the silver thread glimmering in the sunlight between my muzzle and her neckline. He fumbled in his satchel and pulled out my muddy Good Morning Towel, wiped my chin, then started to hand it to her.

When Madame waved her hands, he blushed and stuffed the dirty cloth into his satchel.

"I'm so sorry I have no tissues to offer you." She placed her hands gracefully in her lap while I whimpered and licked the droplets off my muzzle. "And no need to apologize for this adorable puppy."

I couldn't believe she smiled at me. "He's still young. But I can tell he'll be a fine little Flying Tiger—someday...."

George rose when Madame stood and said, "Excuse me for a moment. I must change for my portrait with the American artist Tom Lea." She walked toward another room and said over her shoulder, "Just relax now. My amah will bring you refreshments. Mrs. Deng is a devoted servant who has been with me since my childhood. She'll bring you my favorite walnut cake with lemon icing, freshly made this morning. I'll be back in a few minutes."

Soon, an older woman, like Mrs. Liu, came into the room with a tray. George placed me on the floor, where I slunk under his chair with a sigh. She set the tray on the small table next to him and stood nearby. He took the lid off the cup, and a warm, silky bouquet of scents came down to me. I sat up tall and held my nose as high as I possibly could, watching him and licking my lips. The fragile-looking cup did not have a handle, and when he picked it up, it disappeared in his big hand. It didn't smell as good as fish to me, but he closed his eyes as he sipped, seeming to savor every drop.

"Mmm—exquisite. *Xièxiè*, Mrs. Deng," my best friend said to the amah, who smiled, bowed slightly, and left the room. Setting the teacup back onto the tray, he gingerly picked up a delicate-looking plate and used a tiny fork to nibble at the small cake. He didn't offer any to me, probably thinking that it might come right back up and I'd make more of a mess.

I lowered my chin onto my front paws and made my eyes as big as I possibly could. When one crumb of cake fell off his plate, I slowly reached out with my tongue to capture it, proud that I had saved the soft rug. Wonderful and nutty. I licked the air, hoping more niblets would fall from George's lap. I watched and waited without success.

Madame returned, wearing a white gown. George stood in greeting, and I sat up to apologize, lifting one paw, but she didn't look at me. She sat on a small couch and covered herself with a blanket, the same color as the purplish-blue scales of the fish George caught from the river. But my nose told me that

Madame had nothing to do with fish, so I sighed, sat back on my haunches, and listened.

Madame spoke in her beautiful, high voice. "I'm so pleased you'll be the liaison between General Chennault and myself. As the head of the Chinese Air Force, I'll depend upon you to keep me informed about how the General plans to work with us."

George's eyes were riveted on hers. She continued, "I am eternally grateful for any and all supplies you can bring us. With the invasion and no access at all to our coast on the east or the south, we struggle to find essentials, as you well know. We are desperate for equipment, gas and oil, ammunition, and food for our people." I looked up at her, and saw moisture building behind her dark eyelashes as she locked eyes with George.

"Operation Ichigo," Soong Mei-ling said, "was launched by the Japanese months ago. We had intercepted intelligence that a huge counteroffensive was planned to counteract our victories in the forward echelon, the Chinese and American air bases in eastern China, led by the esteemed General Casey Vincent. I understand you know him well. Is that correct?"

I sat at attention near George's feet. Now and then I snuffled through the rug to see if any crumbs had fallen near me. No luck yet. I lay down and sighed.

"Yes, ma'am," George said. "I've known General Vincent since the spring of 1941, before we shipped out for China. He trained at West Point, is an Ace with six air victories, and is well-versed as the commander for air operations in the forward echelon. And I must confirm with you that your intel is correct. General Vincent has been so successful in his strategic operations—bombing shipping and transportation along the Chinese coast and in occupied China—that the Japanese are retaliating with this Operation Ichigo."

Soong Mei-ling smoothed her gown over the couch where she sat forward, leaning toward George. "It appears to be inevitable that we must fall back from our eastern bases. Would you agree the timing is critical now?"

"I do," George replied. "Chennault and Vincent acknowledge that Japanese ground forces are closing in on Kweilin and the other bases. We've had such bad weather our planes can't get off the ground to make bombing and strafing runs. General Vincent has sent orders to fire on our bases, destroying them before the advancing enemy can take them over."

"Very well." Madame pulled a finely woven silk scarf over her shoulders. "The whole scenario gives me a chill. But we must prepare to save China, even if it means giving up what we have worked so hard to reclaim. We will make a comeback, once the air base in Chengtu is completed. Our Chinese and American composite wing of B-29s, the Superfortress, will allow us a longer reach. We will conquer and banish the Japanese intruders and reclaim our land, our ports, our freedom."

George replied, "This campaign Operation Ichigo, as you know, has two fronts. First, as we've discussed, they're neutralizing our southern airbases, working from the perspective that our air bases in eastern China could launch bombing raids on their islands."

"True." Soong Mei-ling sat back on her couch. "That first air raid by the Doolittle raiders shook them up."

"Right," George said, scratching his head. "Even though

Jimmy Doolittle thought the raid was a disaster, the Japanese learned that we have the capability for long-range missions."

"Yes, indeed." She raised her voice again. "And with the threat to their homeland, they pulled resources from other areas in the south Pacific and allowed the U.S. substantial victories."

"And the second front is strategic," George continued. "They're linking railways from the north to Canton. It appears they plan to move resources by train from the sea ports in southern China to up to Peking and minimize the shipping lanes that are more vulnerable to our attacks."

"We will relay this sensitive information to the leaders at the Pentagon, but not just yet." Madame pointed at him, her fingernails polished like stones in the river. "When the time is right, you will be the bearer of news about these developments. Let General Chennault know what we have discussed. This operation and our counteroffensive are of the utmost importance."

"Yes, ma'am. Will that be all?" He reached toward his hat.

"No, just a moment." She tilted her head. "Have you been to Chengtu? I mean, off the air base to see some sights, enjoy the food?"

"As a matter of fact, ma'am, I have. I picked up some jewelry at the Street of the Silversmith," he said.

"Ah, I know that street. What did you get there?" She leaned forward.

His eyes twinkled. "I found a heart-shaped locket for my mother, Pearl. It was made of finely-worked silver filigree."

"Does she appreciate our Chinese craftsmanship?" She smiled.

351

"Definitely. She belongs to a charitable society and wears it there. Even with the war going on, she finds ways to help others less fortunate than we are." George lowered his eyes and reached down to pat my back.

Soong Mei-ling said softly, "Your mother Pearl does sound like a gem. I hope when you make it back to the States on your mission that you will give her my best. She has raised a fine son, one who thinks of her while he's in a war zone."

George blushed, and Madame said, "All right, that's all for now, Lieutenant. I hear my husband approaching, meaning it's my turn to have my portrait done."

Generalissimo Chiang Kai-shek opened the door and stepped into the room. His gown draped over his shoulders all the way to his feet. Ah, the scent of fine silk. I knew better than to sniff him closely, tempting as it was to smell the fabric made from silkworms, but I didn't want to sneeze again. However, I turned my neck so that he could notice the polished captain's bars of my collar. His eyes flickered past me as he turned away to talk with his wife in Mandarin.

Soong Mei Ling looked up at us under her dark, feathered eyelashes. "You'll need to excuse me, my dears. My husband just informed me the artist is ready to do my portrait. Come often, George, to continue our discussions. But maybe Gremlin had better stay at the U.S. Headquarters in Kunming next time. It seems that he's allergic to my perfume, and I really don't want to bother him."

I wanted to hide under the chair because I let everyone down, but George picked me up and held me firmly, my front paws hanging over his arm. "I understand. Thank you for meeting with me. Madame, Generalissimo." He saluted smartly, and the Generalissimo returned the salute.

"I look forward to continuing our good relations between the U.S. and China, minus the puppy sneezes," said Soong Mei Ling. She reached out to me and caressed my worried brow. "You take care of George, Gremlin, and say hello to General Chennault and Joe Dash for me."

Halfway down the hallway, Dr. Tong stopped and introduced George to the man we'd seen downstairs in Chiang Kai-shek's office. "Lieutenant Haydon, this is the venerable American artist Tom Lea."

George held out his hand, then dropped it. "An honor to meet you, Mr. Lea. I see you've got your hands full."

"The pleasure is all mine," Mr. Lea said. Since he was so close, I leaned over George's arm to smell what he was holding.

"George is stationed with Chennault in Kunming," said Dr. Tong. "He's the new liaison between the U.S. Air Force and Madame Chiang, who heads the Chinese Air Force."

"Impressive. Maybe I'll be invited to do the portrait of General Chennault while I'm here in China."

"We can certainly make arrangements to provide you with a ride to Kunming," George said. "I'll show you around if I can. And as a painter, I think you'd be impressed with the landscapes in Guilin and the Li River, if you get a chance to go down that way."

"That sounds intriguing." Mr. Lea shifted his portfolio. "I'll see if I can swing it. I've heard that the landforms in the southeast of China are absolutely stunning."

George nodded. "I was stationed at Yang Tang airfield in

the area and went back recently with Chennault on a fishing trip. The scenery will take your breath away."

"You talk like an artist." Mr. Lea held a glass of water with brushes in it. Realizing I was thirsty, I reached over to get a better look.

George shook his head. "Me? Oh, nothing like that. I'm a musician. But my relative, Lockwood Moss, is a painter. Landscapes and portraits, like you."

Unable to resist any longer, I pushed the brushes aside to get my tongue into the water. Mr. Lea leaned away from me, his paints and papers falling to the floor. George held onto me as he bent down to pick up the papers, and he and Dr. Tong knocked their heads together with a clack. Oh, that must have hurt.

George said, holding his forehead, "Please allow me, Dr. Tong. I'm so sorry for the inconvenience."

Generalissimo Chiang Kai-shek walked past us, head erect, a smile on his face. He spoke to Dr. Tong.

Dr. Tong stood up, rubbing the top of his head. "My apologies as well, Lieutenant. Mr. Lea, we'd best not keep the Chiangs waiting." He pointed at me. "George, please wait here, with the puppy, of course. I won't be but a moment."

The artist chuckled and said, "No major harm done, Lieutenant. Your pup there surely has a mind of his own. Really cute little fellow. I've known a few like that myself. See you two in Kunming sometime soon."

We could overhear the conversation in Madame's apartment. Chiang Kai-shek spoke in Chinese and Dr. Tong translated for Mr. Lea, something about the Generalissimo wanting to be present with his wife for a proper introduction.

The Generalissimo walked past us again, nodding his head as George saluted. He smiled and laughed, showing his gums, no teeth. I licked my lips, then made a smile as best I could by panting with my tongue hanging out. I raised my paw to scratch at my right ear, saluting like my best friend. I couldn't imagine taking out my teeth. How would I gnaw at the bones Cook gave me?

While we waited for Dr. Tong, I heard Madame say, "I wish my husband would keep his false teeth in his mouth. He's much more handsome that way. But, men, you know, they will do what they will despite appearances." I could picture her waving her hand to one side. Nothing seemed to bother Soong Mei Ling, even puppy drool on her silk dress.

When Dr. Tong returned, we went down the stairs and I had a chance to roll in that wonderful grass. A guard handed George his sidearm. Dr. Tong's car drove up all too soon, and the driver opened the door for us. I snorted as I ran to George, who had my towel out to wipe my muddy paws.

Dr. Tong and George chatted as we returned to the air base. When George opened the door, he said, "Farewell, George. Goodbye now, Gremlin. I'm so glad to know you. You have reminded me not to take everything so seriously. There is always a time to take a break from our work and enjoy the moment."

George saluted, and I rubbed a paw across my eye as a salute to Dr. Tong, wondering if we would ever meet again. I wanted to remember his kindness during our walk in the beautiful gardens of Chungking.

On the flight back to Kunming, Luke pointed to the hills. "See there? Can you find the silhouette of the sleeping princess?"

"No..." George shook his head. "What am I looking for?"

"See that rainbow forming? It's just over her head. The princess is lying on her side. Head, neck, shoulders, hip."

"Oh—yeah." George smiled. "Like Madame, graceful and elegant." He took a deep breath. "If I ever find someone and have a daughter, I'll tell her about this sleeping princess."

"And about meeting Madame, too, I imagine. General Chennault's princess." Luke, George, and I all sighed as Luke flew us over the hills through a shower filled with evening sunlight.

Chapter 27: Fall Back from Kweilin

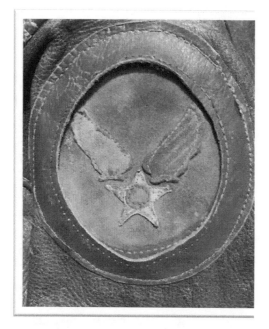

U. S. Air Force Shoulder Patch on George's
Flight Jacket (WWII)

A thousand friends are good,
One enemy is more than enough.
War Area Service Corps Diary for 1944 — China

"George!" General Chennault roared from his office, waking me from a dream about fishing. My best friend stood and gathered his stenographer's pad and pencils in a practiced, smooth motion. I jumped out of my drawer and followed him.

We sat to the side, toward the back of the warm room, filled with officers, including Casey Vincent. Pop sat as always near the general's feet. I started to trot toward him but paused with my front paw in the air. General Vincent's face was flushed as he stood in front of the Chennault's desk, hands clenched at his side. I licked my lips and stood next to George's feet as he sat at attention, his pencil poised for his shorthand duties.

"General Chennault," Casey Vincent shouted. "We've got a strong air offense in eastern China. But with the enemy's Operation Ichigo, our situation is going to pieces. As you know, we're preparing to evacuate our forward echelon bases. Our missions and air raids are successful, but the Chinese army has little chance against the Japanese ground forces."

"Understood, General Vincent." Chennault swiveled his chair to scan the faces of the other men. "General Glenn agrees with your plans to keep up the offensive bombings. How are the evacuations going?"

Vincent scratched his head. "Chinese citizens are evacuating. By rail, trains are so full families are riding on the cow catchers and on the roofs of the cars. Stations are overcrowded. Cars and trucks are piled high, and roads are jammed. Our warning net has failed—none of the phone lines are intact—so we're sitting ducks—on top of a powder keg, sir."

"Military personnel?" Chennault's face looked more drawn and wrinkled than ever. He sat motionless, a wheezing sound coming from his chest each time he breathed.

"We'd hoped to stall the Japanese before they got this close. The new P-51 fighters help, but they came too late to make a real difference. Looks like the enemy troops will get to Kweilin before the week is out—three, maybe five days. I've sent all nonessential personnel to Liuchow, keeping demotion crews and a handful of officers."

"Tex Hill?" The general rubbed the back of his neck.

"He'll stay with me when he's not out on missions. We'll be the last ones to fall back from Kweilin. The Chinese army is retreating—and falling apart. I'm requesting twenty C-46 transports to move the remaining squadrons. I respectfully request your presence in Kweilin, General Chennault."

Chennault coughed several times, cleared his throat, and took a sip of coffee. "Stilwell and I will be there tomorrow."

"Thank you, sir. Chinese demolition teams are already setting charges in the runways. We're ready to demolish the structures and airfields, leaving nothing to the enemy's advantage."

Casey Vincent's face dropped as he looked at each man in the room. "Just a shame though, sir. I started my command in Kweilin when those airstrips and buildings were under construction. Now it's November, a little over a year later, and our teams will destroy what so many men, women and children built by hand for us."

"Understood, Vincent." The officers saluted Vincent as he stormed out of HQ.

~ ~ ~ ~ ~

The next day, Chennault asked George if I could go with him to the airfield. George nodded and smiled. "Certainly. He'd like that, sir."

"We've got to get you out into the fresh air, Gremlin. You and I are spending too much time in the office. Let's see how you're shaping up, huh? You just had your first birthday when we went frogging and fishing, remember?" He held my chin for a moment before snapping the leash onto my collar. He beckoned to Pop. "Joe Dash, come. Heel."

Pop charged out of the office and stood by Chennault's leg, in the place where George usually wanted me to stand. I felt puzzled. Where should I walk? I wagged my tail and walked in front of Pop, but it didn't feel right, so I stood behind him. Shaking my head, I wrinkled my brow and whimpered— *hhhnnnff*? As if he understood my dilemma, Chennault told Pop to sit and stay with George.

I stood next to his heel, ready to go with the general. I pulled on my leash, and he tugged back gently to guide me next to his leg. "Gremlin, heel." I took a deep breath as we went out the door and onto the porch where we had watched the air raids many months before. I paused between each step he took. We walked to Andy's Jeep. The general picked me up and held me on his lap.

"Where to, sir?" Andy asked, bringing the Jeep to life. "Airfield?"

"Roger that, son." Chennault coughed into his handkerchief.

Even though the cloudy morning's breeze wasn't cold, I nestled against the familiar leather of his flight jacket, which matched the brown, furrowed skin on his face. I recalled Andy telling George about Chennault being called "Old Leatherface," but never when he could hear it.

Looking back and forth from his collar to his chin, I reached up to lick his cheek. Salty. I licked his jacket, just to try it—*bbbllukkkk*—*thhh-thhh*. A bad taste. I licked his cheek again.

The general chuckled. "Yes, tiger. Old Leatherface—you bet." He held me away from his face, mouth set in a line.

"Gremlin, we need your good luck, tiger. Send away those gremlins. Out of the engines, out of our lives. Gotta keep every plane in the air." He stroked my head, chin, and ears. "These evacuations could signal the end of the war, but not in our favor. I wouldn't want to see China fall to the Japanese. Looks like it could, with the ground forces on the run."

He turned to Andy, who tugged the steering wheel back and forth to dodge puddles in the road. "Don't mind us, Andy. Just a little conversation here, to get all the help we can."

Chennault rubbed my neck, and my muscles relaxed. I sat up, looking into his calm eyes. "Can't believe this offensive. Retaliation for the bombing raids we did on shipping and transportation. We had a good run, Gremlin, but now they're getting their revenge. As good a leader as Casey Vincent is, we don't have the resources to keep going. I'll go out to Kweilin to take a look, but it seems the wisest option is to fire the bases—destroy them—and fall back from all the progress we made. Hate to say it."

Andy pulled the Jeep to a stop near Ralph's Quonset hut as a large plane landed and taxied to a stop. General Stilwell stepped out of the plane. Ralph, his mechanics and several pilots greeted him. The Commanding General of U.S. Forces in China stood tall and lean, his face unsmiling as he looked toward us.

Chennault got out of the Jeep, leaving me on the seat. "Thanks, Andy." He pointed a tobacco-stained finger at my nose. I sniffled. "And Gremlin, remember your mission. We're counting on you." He saluted me and greeted Stilwell under the plane's wing before I could put up my paw to return his salute.

Standing on the seat, my front paws on the dashboard, I

followed Chennault's orders to warn the gremlins, any gremlins anywhere, to leave our planes alone. I barked to the P-40s and transport planes on the airfield, to the sky, the Quonset hut and hangars. To all the mechanics and pilots. To General Chennault and his Flying Tigers in western China and in the forward echelon of eastern China. To the Hump pilots bringing our much-needed supplies over the Hump. To our Composite Wings with Chinese and American crews working together to defeat the enemy.

Chennault and Stilwell saluted the men gathered around them and stepped into the plane, which took off immediately.

Andy took me back to HQ, telling me, "You're a good boy, *mi hijito.*"

Aaarrrwwwggg, I agreed with him, whipping my tail back and forth.

"You tell those gremlins. Over and over." Andy shifted gears, and gravel spun out from beneath the tires.

Aaooorrrgg-aarrwwwgg.

"We don't want them; they are not welcome here or anywhere." Andy laughed, pounding the steering wheel.

Rrrrwwwoufff-rrrwwwwoooof.

"You did it, tiger—they are long gone." Andy ruffled the fur on my back. "Gremlin, you're the guardian of the Flying Tigers. How does that feel, *mi hijito?*"

Thinking of Chennault's words to me, I sat back in the seat, lifted my head, and howled. My chest felt full and peaceful. The fur on my neck and back bristled as I put my soul into my song. I saw little bumps like chicken skin rising on Andy's arms.

Later in the afternoon, George's phone rang. He picked

up the part of it that looked like a bone. But I knew from experience it was not a bone. The one time I got close enough to nibble on it, I left teeth marks. I couldn't get a grip on it because it was too slippery, but it did not taste or feel like anything I'd want to ever try again. George could keep it.

"Kunming HQ—Haydon speaking."

Chennault's loud voice crackled through the line like the sound of gravel under the wheels of Andy's Jeep. "Copy this down, George. I'm in Liuchow. Kweilin is evacuated. Transport planes departed with all personnel. Tex Hill and Casey Vincent took the last two aircraft out. Demolition crews fired the airfields as the planes took off and will follow in land vehicles. Observers report thick clouds of smoke over our air bases. Multiple columns of Japanese forces are on the march a couple miles away."

"Copy that, sir." George held the bone between his shoulder and ear, his voice forceful.

"And George," the general added. "Off the record. Tell Gremlin he did an outstanding job."

"Sir?" The phone nearly slipped off George's shoulder. He caught it and looked at me, his eyebrows raised. I smiled at him, my haunches rising as I leaned forward in excitement, my tail rotating like a P-40 propeller.

I heard Chennault's low, rumbling laugh. Then a few coughs. "Uh—George, after evacuating all our aircraft from Kweilin, Liuchow is jam-packed with planes. We're under attack as usual. Waves of enemy planes in the sky. Non-stop assaults on the base, but we've got our tigers above them fighting like hell to protect us."

He cleared his throat and lowered his voice. "Tell

363

Gremlin—uh—Casey Vincent can't figure out why the Japanese haven't hit any of our planes. But I know—it was Gremlin guarding all of us from any and all gremlins they could possibly throw at us. Do you copy?"

My best friend was speechless when I pranced and danced around George's feet, barking to General Chennault that I got his message, loud and clear.

Chapter 28: War and Loss

General Claire Chennault Pinning the Bronze Star on First
Lieutenant George Haydon (1944)

Our greatest glory is not in never falling,
But in rising every time we fall.

Confucius

The next morning, after breakfast, a crowd of people
assembled in the narrow briefing room in Headquarters.
George held me on his lap, leaning over me as he chatted with
Charles. Light streamed in through the narrow windows and
the hanging bare light bulbs, illuminating the cigarette smoke
drifting into the bare rafters of the ceiling. After our brisk walk
in the cold air, I could barely take a full breath in the hot, stuffy
room and stuck out my tongue, panting.

Chennault came from his office, a cloud of smoke spilling

out of the door. Everyone stood, screeching their chair legs on the wooden floor, and shuffling their feet to stand at attention. George draped me over his arm as he saluted the general in unison with the other airmen. I squirmed in his arms and felt his heart beat faster.

Chennault returned their salute. A rustling sounded across the room as everyone dropped their arms to their sides. The general cleared his throat and addressed the group with his southern drawl. "All y'all know I'm proud of each one of my Flying Tigers. Today we honor exceptional service. Be seated."

Another wave of sounds echoed throughout the room as everyone sat down again.

"The list please, Lieutenant Garcia," Chennault said.

Andy stepped forward from the side of the room with a clipboard in his hand. He read many names. My ears perked up when he named my best friend and announced, "Will those whose names I called please rise and come forward."

George handed me to Charles. He rose to stand in line at the front of the room. From Charles' arms, I could see Andy lead Chennault down the row of men and women and address each person, but I couldn't see everything. A tall man with a big head sat in the chair in front of me. I swayed from side to side to see what they were doing. It looked like Chennault pinned something on the front of Red and Ralph's uniforms, shook hands and moved to the next person in line.

Soon it was time for General Chennault to meet George face-to-face. I whimpered and wiggled on Charles' lap, freeing myself from his grip. Once my back feet hit the floor, I slipped out of Charles' hands and rushed through the blockade of chair legs and human legs to stand at attention with George. In front of the general. Head up and tail wagging.

Chennault nodded at me with a glimmer of pride in his eyes. Andy handed him a small green box. The general opened it and pinned something to George's uniform, saying, "For meritorious service in the China-Burma-India Theater of Operations and as liaison between the U.S. Fourteenth Air Force and the Chinese Air Force Headquarters of Madame Soong Mei-ling, Captain Haydon is awarded the Bronze Star Medal."

The general and George saluted one another, smiled, and shook hands. "Congratulations, George. Glad you're at Headquarters." He knelt next to me, petting my neck and back. "Wish we had one for you, too, Gremlin. You have done your part as well. You're a fine Air Force dog, a true Flying Tiger." I licked his hands to say thank you, and the general rose to address the next one in line.

After the ceremony, George held me as his friends gathered around us. I welcomed the pets and pats by sniffing every hand and giving a few licks of appreciation. Several of George's friends from HQ walked with us to the mess hall, where Cook had a special lunch of Spam for me, with potatoes and extra gravy. I licked the bowl so hard that I chased it under the table to get every morsel.

"You've got your orders," Andy said to George. "All the arrangements are in place for you to have three week's leave after you make the delivery to the Pentagon."

We went to the barracks, where George dressed in his best uniform. I sniffed his pant legs. Usually they smelled like him, but this time they smelled the way I did after a BA-A-ATH. I sneezed and backed away.

"Come on, Gremlin," George told me, tugging on my leash. I followed him to General Chennault's office. He saluted. I sat and attempted to sit up with my front paws in front of my chest, as Pop could do. I fell sideways against George's leg before landing on my side.

"At ease." Chennault chuckled. "Have a seat, son."

Pop came to me from under the general's desk. We sniffed each other, wagging tails. George leaned over to rub Pop's head and neck. I pawed at George's leg, and he picked me up.

"All set?" Chennault asked. He slid a large envelope across his desk to George. "You know you're the right man for this job. And I expect you to take full advantage of leave at home. Going to California?"

"Can't wait to see my folks in Santa Cruz."

"Don't you have a brother in the service?" said Chennault.

"Right, sir. Chet's in the Merchant Marines. Made it once around the world so far. I'm not sure if he'll be at home when I am, though." George shrugged his shoulders. "But it'll be good to see family and friends for a couple of weeks."

The general lit another cigarette. I sneezed. "Oh, I forgot. Sorry, buddy." He dropped the smoky thing into a cup on his desk. "Any other plans?" I sighed and scratched my neck with a back paw.

"I'm going to check with my college about completing my business degree. Heard they're allowing GIs to count their war experience. I only needed one year to finish college. Since I've served overseas in Karachi, Kunming, and Kweilin, a total of almost three years in Headquarters, I'm fairly confident they'll grant my degree."

"Good luck with that, son. Now, I'm mighty proud of the work you've done as my Number One Aide-de-Camp. Besides, I've watched you raise Gremlin from a pup. He's growing into a fine Fourteenth Air Force dog."

Courier Envelope George carried from Kunming Headquarter to the Pentagon (1944)

George sat up straighter in his chair, and I perked my ears, licking my lips. "Thank you, sir. Truly an honor to serve with you."

"Now, if you happen to find some lucky young lady while you're on leave, wherever you end up when this war is over, I want to meet your first-born child."

George laughed, his cheeks blushing. "Yes, sir. I'll see about finding someone who can help me with that." He called for Pop to come to him and scratched behind his shiny black ears. My best friend whispered, "Bye now, Joe Dash." Goodbye? Were we going on a mission? Pop licked his hand, rubbed his muzzle against mine, and strutted around the desk to flop next to Chennault's feet.

George stood and saluted Chennault. "Thank you, Sir. All my best. Always an honor to serve with you." We left the general's office and stopped at Doreen's desk.

Betsy K. Haydon

"Better hold him by the leash, Doreen," George said. "Thanks for taking care of him while I'm away. Should be back in a month or two between Air Force business and my leave at home, but I don't think he's going to understand."

"Hedda and I will take good care of Gremlin. Safe travels, George," she said, taking my leash.

What? Somehow, I felt this trip would be different from the trips he took with General Chennault. Why was George leaving me? *Hhnnnff—hhhnnn*? I whined, not understanding. My best friend was supposed to be with me—always.

He knelt next to me and rubbed my ears and chin. "Goodbye, Gremlin. I'll just be gone a little while. You'll see, tiger, I'll be back." *Hnnnwwrr*? Where was he going? Why was he leaving me? I gave him wet kisses all over his chin and cheeks to tell him not to go.

"We'll get the new guy settled into your position. John worked for General Hap Arnold, so he'll know how to keep the general in line." Andy held two shiny metal things. "Let's get these handcuffs on to secure the general's documents." George stood and held out his hand. Andy put one metal ring around George's wrist and the other around the handle of his satchel. George put the key in his pocket.

After a round of goodbyes, my best friend in the whole world lifted the satchel and walked out the door of HQ—without me. I watched the door, expecting him to come back with a big smile. Just another game of peek-a-boo, right? I barked softly twice. *Bbbbrrwwff—bbrrwwwff*? Doreen pulled me onto her lap. She rubbed my chest and neck. "It's okay, Gremlin, George will come back."

But he didn't come back. I watched the door. Where was

George? *Hnnnwwrr?* Why did he leave me? I twisted and growled in her lap, but George didn't come back. I yelped and yowled — *Yyyipppp-yyipppp-ippp* — *owwwrrllff-rroowwwwlfff* — at the pain of losing my best friend, but she held me firmly.

"Sh, hush, Gremlin. Be a good dog, remember?" I stopped squirming to listen to her comforting voice and licked her smooth, gentle fingers. "Okay then. Good dog — you'll be fine. He'll be back. Now go lie down." She put me on the floor. "Go to Hedda, Gremlin. Lie down."

I ran to the door, pawing at it so hard I left deep scratches in the wood. Someone opened it, and I would have flown out the door after George, except that Andy grabbed my leash and brought me back to Doreen. She tied my leash to the leg of her desk.

Tail between my legs, I lay down in our old basket. Mom crawled in next to me and licked my ears. I rolled onto my tummy for her to lick under my chin, the way she did when I was a puppy — when I was so tiny, I could fit under her ear.

But I wasn't a puppy anymore. I rolled onto my feet, stood, and growled at her. I was becoming an Air Force dog. General Chennault said so. Why couldn't I go with George?

"Stop that grumbling, Gremlin," Doreen warned, tapping my bottom.

I sighed. Why did my best friend go away? When would he come back? The war was not over. The world was a dangerous place for airmen like George. How could I protect him if I was left behind?

~   ~   ~   ~   ~

Doreen closed her book with a thud, waking me from dreams of George, fish, and frogs. I lay under her chair in her room at the women's barracks. Mom rested nearby. Doreen's chair creaked as she shifted to pick up her teapot. I heard her pour tea into a cup, the fragrance soothing as I breathed in its scent.

"Mmm. Oolong tea from Formosa, Gremlin." She leaned over to pet my head. I gazed up at her, listening, thumping my tail against the floor. "Remember, we got a huge shipment a year or so ago in those large wooden packing boxes? I don't have much tea left. I'm rationing it to last the duration of the war. It certainly is comforting on this chilly night."

She took off her slippers and rubbed my back with her bare toes. "And your friend George, resourceful soul that he is, took three of those huge boxes to send home all kinds of gifts from China and India to his folks before he left."

I rolled over, and she rubbed my tummy with the bottom of her foot. I missed George terribly. Even though Doreen and Luke reassured me that he would return to me, I had given up hope.

The next day, a new airman named John sat at George's desk, next to General Chennault's office. He cleaned out the drawers and threw my Good Morning towel into the garbage can. I whined and whimpered, but he didn't pay any attention to me. Jumping against the side of the short metal can, I tipped it over and grabbed the ragged towel in my teeth, carrying it under desks and chairs, past Sadie and her claws.

"What a mess." John sighed as he pushed papers and old typewriter ribbons back into the waste basket and set it in place. "Don't know why the general allows dogs in HQ."

I jumped into Mom's basket, lying on top of my prize, warning everyone not to take it away from me. George's scent had faded from the worn towel, which was way too small to keep me warm anymore. Would I recognize him if he ever returned?

Sadie walked by, swishing her tail. I glowered at her, baring my teeth and growling softly. She began a low yowl and reached out a paw to touch the basket, until Andy told us to knock it off. Sadie tiptoed away, and I rolled into a ball, tucking my Good Morning towel under my chin.

I followed a never-ending routine of walks to and from Headquarters, planes roaring overhead when they took off and returned from missions, smoke from the general's cigarettes in his office, the chit-chat of Andy and Charles and John.

One day blended into another. Sometimes I stayed with Luke in our bunkhouse, but whenever he flew General Chennault somewhere, Doreen and Mom took care of me.

I wasn't allowed to visit my brother Tom and his human Ralph anymore. Doreen said that I couldn't see Tom again until my manners improved. I pawed at my eyes, trying to forget how much I missed Tom — and my best friend.

Wench and Nurse Red were gone, shipped out to a different Air Force base in China. From puppyhood, my sister would always let me catch her, and I would tickle her by woofing into the places humans call armpits. Her puppy giggles made me happy inside, and I used to lick her face to tell her how much I loved being her littermate — except when she hogged the food.

Whenever I stayed with Andy, I had to tiptoe around Sadie the cat, who eyed me with her snake-like eyes and slashed at me with her sharp claws. I never knew who I'd be with. Most of the time, I'd crawl under a bunk and moan, wishing George would come back.

One evening, Doreen took care of me in her cozy room. She reached down and picked me up. "Oh, you're getting so big. Look at your long muzzle now, almost like your papa's. Your legs used to be as tiny as my little finger. Now, you're as strong as Hedda and Joe Dash. You've grown up to be a handsome dachshund, Gremlin, my dear."

She stroked my back, making rippling motions with her fingers from neck to tail. "So, I hate to tell you this, my little friend... but your mama and I are moving to the States in a few weeks. I'll join my husband there and become a U.S. citizen... there's packing and... oh, there's something I set aside for George..." She picked up a silver bottle on the table and put it down again, sniffled, and lifted a handkerchief to dab at her eyes. "Oh, Gremlin, I'm no good at this. But someone will take care of you until George gets back."

Doreen? Mom—leaving China? Leaving me? Like everyone else. And George—would he ever come back? Who would I guard if everyone left? I slid from her lap and crawled to the doorway, curled up, and sighed, waiting for my best friend.

Chapter 29: When Shall This Pass?

Flying Tiger Shoulder Patch on George's
Uniform (WWII)

The mechanic who wishes to do his work well,
Must first sharpen his tools.

Confucius

After an endless time of separation from my brother, Doreen finally decided we could visit. She drove me to the airfield. "Be good, Gremlin. You stay with Ralph today. Stay." Doreen set me down and handed my leash to Ralph. I sat at his feet, staring at the gravel in the road.

"Thanks for taking him today." Doreen and Ralph stood near the Jeep.

Ralph scratched his chin. "I'm worried about the little guy. How is he?"

"George has been gone so long now I'm afraid Gremlin is losing heart. He hardly eats and is quite grumpy." Doreen hopped into the Jeep. "Well—back to HQ. I'll pick up Gremlin after work." The Jeep rumbled away, and Ralph walked me into the hangar, where the airmen used to play music. Until George left.

Tom barked when he saw me and trundled over in his wheelchair to lick me all over. I sat patiently, trying to be a good dog. He wanted to play, but we couldn't play like we used to because... I knew his accident was all my fault... since I had distracted him... he didn't see the big Jeep speeding up to us... I got out of the way, but he...

George must have been so disappointed in me that he left me behind—forever. I just felt like howling all the time.

Ralph talked with a crew working on a transport plane inside the hangar. I followed him around, my breath creating little clouds of smoke in the chilly air. Tom followed us at his own pace. Several mechanics repaired holes in the sides of a fighter plane.

Ralph rapped his knuckles on the snarling shark's mouth of the Curtiss P-40, which looked like it was sneering at me. "Put them back together with chewing gum and duct tape, boys. Use whatever we've got to get them back up into the air."

The men grinned and one shot back, "That's all we got, boss. Doing what we can with what we have. And that ain't much." They laughed and kept tinkering, their tools clinking, hammering, buzzing, and squeaking. All the noise hurt my ears.

Tom caught up to me in his wheelchair, too close. I growled at him in warning. One of his wheels rolled over my hind paw. I yipped and nipped him in the neck. He gave a sharp, high-pitched yelp.

Ralph reached down and tapped me on the nose. He didn't notice I was limping. "Stop that, Gremlin. You be nice to Tom." He took me back to the Quonset hut and tied my leash to a post next to a smelly tire. "Stay," he commanded, pointing to my nose. I burrowed into a pile of old rags and sneezed several times before falling asleep.

Tom woke me up too soon, balancing on his three legs without his wheelchair, nudging me with his head. Sleepy, I didn't want to play. I shook myself, stood up, and lunged at him with my teeth bared. He yipped and backed away from me. His back leg collapsed and he rolled onto his side. I snarled and pushed my muzzle toward his throat, lips pulled back from my gums. He yelped and pawed the air, showing his teeth, eyes wide with white rims.

"Back off, Gremlin—what's with you these days? Huh?" Ralph kneeled and pulled me away from Tom. I snapped at his hand.

"Hey there. You trying to bite me? Come on, little guy, you know me." He picked up Tom and stood as the glaring winter sun in the window behind him burned into my eyes.

"Let's give your brother time to cool off, buddy." Ralph shook his finger at me, and I bowed my head. "Stay, Gremlin."

When Doreen returned, Ralph told him what I did. They talked in low voices as Ralph pointed at me. I lay in the dirt, my head on my front paws, ashamed. Doreen didn't talk to me on the ride back to the barracks.

~   ~   ~   ~   ~

I didn't see Tom for a long time, and I felt worse for scaring him and nearly biting Ralph. One day, Luke took me in the Jeep, saying, "There's someone you're going to want to see today, little tiger." He smiled at me, as I lay curled up on the passenger seat, too sad send him kisses or to smell the air breezing by.

He stopped the Jeep and picked me up. I hung limp in his arms but noticed he had pulled up near the hospital where George had been for his operation. The walls and roof had been fixed from the bombing, but I didn't want to go inside. I pawed at Luke's arm and whined—*hnnnnnnff-hunnnff*—to let him know I was afraid to go in there.

Luke held me firmly. "Look, Gremlin. Someone's here to visit with you." To my surprise, he walked away from the hospital, across the road to a building that looked like Doreen's barracks. On the steps sat Red and a big, beautiful dachshund. She looked like Mom, but her fur was darker and her eyes were smaller. Could it be—Wench?

My sister barked in greeting. Red held tight to Wench's leash. "Aww, Wench—you remember your little brother."

Luke lowered me, and I wiggled in his grip, my legs paddling the air in excitement before I touched the ground. Wench and I touched noses and sniffed each other all over. I nipped at her shoulder, and she growled—while wagging her tail. We played like we used to, like no time had gone by.

"Hi, Red. Glad you called to say you'd be here on temporary duty and could take The Gremlin. I've got a couple trips to make with the Old Man." Luke smiled at us. "Gremlin needs some company since George's been gone a couple months so far. Too long for this little guy."

"Sure thing. How's Tom?" Red stood and put her freckled hands in her pockets. Wench and I ran in circles around her feet.

"The same. Gets around okay in his wheelchair. He and Gremlin had a falling out, so... watch him. Separate them if Gremlin gets moody." Luke gave her my leash. "Well, I'd better get going. See you in a few days."

"Will do. Come on, Gremlin. Let's get reacquainted." Red led us to her bunkroom in the barracks, a small room like Luke's.

I danced around Wench, happy to see her again, but I was afraid Red would give me another painful shot in my hind end, like she did when we were little. I hid under the bunk, whining, and didn't eat anything she put out for me, especially because Wench hovered over the food bowl and growled at me. She always was a bully around food.

Other nurses took care of us when Red worked. After two or three days, I growled at Wench and nipped at her. I didn't want to play anymore. I was hungry and tired.

That evening, Red called Ralph, and he picked me up and took me back to the air base. "Doreen, sorry to trouble you, but Gremlin's acting up again. Still not himself these days."

"Poor baby. He's so attached to George—no one else will do. Will they, my little friend?" She took my leash and led me into her barracks. Mom greeted me by licking my face and smelling my behind.

"Sure, I can keep him tonight, Ralph. I'll drop him off with you tomorrow morning. General Chennault and I have a meeting at another base. Andy will be too busy to take him while I'm away. He's got his hands full with Sadie, and you know she and Gremlin don't get along—at all."

"Okay." Ralph rubbed his hand over his face, leaving streaks of black on his cheek. "I guess that's the best plan. See you then." He didn't pet me before he left. I slumped to the floor.

After Doreen fed us and took us outside, she sat on her couch with a book, a blanket over her legs. Mom and I lay side-by-side near her feet. When Mom licked my ears and muzzle I wanted to growl and snarl at her but finally relaxed, giving in to her comforting touch, even though I wasn't a puppy anymore.

I knew it was wrong of me to threaten Tom and try to bite Ralph. I wanted George to come back. I rolled over, wishing George could be there to pet me and tell me I was a good Flying Tiger dog. Maybe I wasn't a good dog anymore. Would he ever come back?

~   ~   ~   ~   ~

Doreen carried me to the Jeep, where Chennault waited in the driver's seat. Once she was seated, he drove us to the airfield. Ralph and Tom greeted us in front of the Quonset hut. Tom stood at attention, his hindquarters resting in his wheelchair. His eyes zeroed in on mine as he licked the air between us. Did he forgive me for being mean to him?

Doreen opened the Jeep's door. "Oh drat. I forgot Gremlin's leash." Before she could stop me, I jumped from her lap onto the floor and down to the ground. Running to Tom, I gave him kisses and licks on his face. He licked me back, and we snorted at each other. I nipped at his front legs then danced away, like old times.

380

"We'd better get going. Plane's ready." Chennault shut off the engine. "See that someone gets the Jeep back to HQ, will ya?"

"Yes, sir." Ralph nodded and gave a quick salute.

I stopped playing with Tom to make sure the general's plane was free of gremlins. I barked and growled at any gremlin that might cause mischief with the engine. *Bbbbbrrrkk-brrrrrrkk.*

Ralph shouted orders to two mechanics, and they came running. "Mike, take the general's Jeep back to HQ. I'll need you back here to finish that oil change on that P-40 so it's ready to go. Dave, take that old AVG Jeep so Mike won't have to walk back."

"Got it, Chief." Dave started the Jeep, which lurched forward. "I'll get on top of fixing the clutch and tranny."

I barked as the general's plane taxied to the runway. Once the mechanics left in the two Jeeps, Ralph turned to me. "And what's that with your barking, Gremlin? Is the plane's engine okay? Tuned it up myself, so everything should be all right." He scratched his head. "But Chennault seems to think you're some kind of good luck charm. So, have at it, buddy."

I continued barking until the plane took off. Tom and I played in front of the Quonset hut under a tree, growling, barking, and play-fighting. He rolled circles around me, and we took turns chasing each other, but I was careful to keep my paws away from his wheels.

Dave and Mike returned in the old AVG Jeep. I could hear the engine sputtering before they came around the side of the Quonset hut.

"That thing's a relic from before the States entered the war." Ralph kicked a tire after they skidded to a stop next to him. Mike hopped out. Tom and I stood next to Ralph. "Put it next to that P-40 you're working on, Dave. You can check out the transmission and work on it there. We need every vehicle we can get our hands on."

Tom rolled forward to pee on the front tire. He tried to back up when the Jeep's engine started but lost his balance and fell over. I stepped toward him, but before Ralph or I could help him, the Jeep jerked forward, the back wheel spinning toward us. Tom couldn't move. He couldn't get up.

I barked furiously to warn them my brother was in trouble, jumping back and forth next to the huge vehicle, its metal and rubber looming over us. How could I save Tom when I was so small? Tom needed help—*BBBBRRRKKK—BBRRK—BBRRKKK—BBRRRRKK!*

The engine died suddenly, and the Jeep jumped as high as my head, lurching forward. I rolled backwards, away from the tires spinning over the dusty road. Tom yowled in pain, but his cry was cut short.

"Tom—Tom!" Ralph reached out to him. Men came running from the airfield and the Quonset hut.

"Are the dogs all right?" Dave jumped over the front door and stood by the rear of the Jeep, his hand on Ralph's shoulder.

"Gremlin's okay. But Tom—oh, Tom..." Ralph's voice broke as he knelt next to the back wheel of the Jeep. I nosed my way through the mechanic's legs and crawled to Ralph. A dark liquid seeped out from under Tom's head. His wheelchair lay crumpled beside him.

No one spoke as Ralph picked up Tom and carried him to his bed in the wooden crate. The airfield was silent. No tapping of tools on metal. No murmuring conversations under the engines. No propellers whirred. No planes took off or landed.

Climbing into the bed next to my brother, I licked his face. He didn't move. I whimpered and pawed at his shoulder, curling up next to him to warm his body, as we used to—when we were puppies in our basket. But he lay still and cold.

Ralph, Dave, and Mike dug a hole under the tree where Tom and I had played just a little while earlier. Ralph wrapped my brother in the oil-stained towels from his bed and placed him in the ground, his shoulders shuddering. Rivers of tears streamed down his face as he scooped up the soil with his hands and sifted it through his fingers to cover Tom's lifeless body.

For the rest of the afternoon and into the dark of night, I lay on Tom's grave, hoping he would come back. Ralph played his violin, the music rising from inside the Quonset hut like the sad melodies from Mrs. Liu's huqin. Hoping George would come back. I sat up, lifted my head to the starry sky, closed my eyes, and howled until my throat ached.

Chapter 30: The Silver Flask

George's Silver Flask (WWII)

We live, not as we wish to, but as we can.

Mencius

Gusts of wind pushed on the walls of the Tiger Den. Cool drafts of air whistled through the screens and windows of the barracks Andy shared with several other men, two of whom were snoring in the back room. The square black stove creaked as the burning wood crackled and popped, warming the chilly room with its high ceilings. Coffee percolated in the tarnished blue kettle on top of the stove, its aroma filling the air.

Andy filled his mug with coffee and moved the kettle to a back burner. He sat in a chair next to the stove and blew on the coffee, slurping and sipping slowly as he returned to reading his book. Sadie the cat jumped into his lap and purred loudly.

Since Doreen left, I stayed with him. Sadie and I weren't

friends but had stopped growling at each other. She hadn't tried to scratch my nose in days. I curled up under Andy's chair with a sigh, losing interest in the bone Cook gave me at lunch. Soon it would be time for our evening chow, but I had no appetite.

Raindrops pounded on the metal roof, interrupted by a loud knock on the barracks door, interrupting the pounding of raindrops on the metal roof. My head shot up; I scrambled out from under Andy's chair, nosing his feet out of my way. A low growl started deep in my throat. I stood guard in front of him, wondering who would be out in the storm. But this was wartime—it could be an enemy or a gremlin, and I needed to be on duty.

Andy said, "*Silencio, mi hijito. Shhhh*, don't wake anyone." I crawled under his bunk and peered out.

"*Un momento.*" Andy placed his coffee mug on the table with a clink and pushed Sadie off his lap. She landed on the floor on all four paws with a solid thud and a loud *mmmroww*.

Andy stood, buttoning his jacket as he stepped across the bare floor. Sadie quickly took his spot, turned around once and plopped down. When Andy opened the door, a chilling breeze crept over me and I shivered.

"Welcome back, airman." He opened the door wider. "Come on in and get out of the cold. Can't believe it's you."

The man on the covered porch took off his raincoat and shook the drops off it, just as I shook out my fur after a BA-A-ATH.

"Hey, Andy. Good to see ya." The voice sounded like George's, but lower. *Mmmrrffff*? Was that George? No—he left me and never came back. My best friend forgot about me because I was a bad dog.

386

He wore a flight jacket like George's—I perked up my ears. But everyone had a flight jacket in the winter. I put my head down and sighed. He looked a little like George—I opened my eyes wide. Could it be? No... he was far away. Gone a long time. I sighed. Again.

Andy closed the door while the visitor draped his raincoat over a peg next to where my leash was hanging. A low growl rumbled in my throat because George used to hang his jacket on that peg.

"Ralph told me Gremlin was with you." The man stood next to the stove, took off his gloves, and stuffed them into his pocket. "Gremlin? Where are you?" He turned toward the bunk. "I see you, tiger. Come on out." He clapped his hands.

I eased my head out, sniffing. I crouched and inched toward him as carefully as tracking a cricket. He held his hand under my chin the way he did when I first met him. *Sniff, sniff*—yes! I smelled the back of his hand and licked his cold fingers to be sure.

"Gremlin? Remember me?"

George? My tail spun into motion like a P-40 propeller. I thought I'd never see my best friend ever again, but here he was. I tumbled into him as he fell backwards onto the floor. *Wwwwrrruff? Wwwrooooo?* I asked if he was home for good.

My best friend came back! I wiggled everywhere—head, neck, shoulders, back, tummy, legs, paws, and tail. I jumped up, whining—*wwwrrrrfff-wrrrggh?*

"How are you doing, tiger? Yes, I'm back. We're together again." He put his arms around me and stood, scrunching up his face as I placed doggy kisses on his chin, neck, face, eyes and ears. "Hey, buddy, feels like forever, huh? It's okay now, Gremlin."

387

"He's so glad you're back." Andy brought over a chair. "Have a seat."

George sat down. "It's swell of you to take care of Gremlin. You're my first stop." I whimpered and licked him, unable to stay still, not knowing where to kiss him next.

"He's just fine." Andy picked up Sadie and sat back into his chair. "Had a few ups and downs while you were away. This here is Sadie. Found her as a kitten about the time you left. You've been gone so long she's turned into a cat."

Uh-oh—I hoped he wouldn't tell him I had been a bad dog. But I wouldn't have hurt him if George hadn't left me behind. And what took him so long to come back to me? *Arrrwggh? Wwrrragh?*

George stroked me under my chin. "Sorry, buddy—got held up in Florida on my way back. Waited for weeks in Karachi before they let me catch a flight over The Hump to get back to China. Always seemed to be some kind of hold up."

Andy pointed to me. "He's so much bigger now, isn't he?"

George laughed. "I'll say. Look at how long his muzzle is. Those big ears and paws." He touched my ears and each paw then scratched my neck and back, just the way he used to when I was tiny. I panted with joy and licked his fingers, wiggling in his arms.

"How was your trip?" Andy leaned forward in his chair.

"Just fine, indeed. I took care of business for the general at the Pentagon. And while I visited my folks in California, I saw an old friend from college. We got married!"

Andy slapped his knee, startling Sadie. "You did it—you found your queen? Tell me about it. When you left, you didn't even have a girlfriend."

"Her name's Sara, sweetest person. The one I've been waiting for all my life. And I never realized it, but I've known her all this time—met her nine years ago, in fact, in our college orchestra. Boy, she's the one for me. Wish I'd figured that out earlier."

"Well, congratulations. I wish every happiness to you and your bride." Andy scratched Sadie under her chin. She purred loudly and kneaded his leg the way Cook kneaded bread dough. "Where is she now?"

Sara Haydon (circa 1944)
(Mrs. George A. Haydon, Jr.)

George shifted me on his lap, and my ear pressed against his chest. I could hear his heartbeat, strong and slow, calming me. "She's in New York City. She's going to be the first of her sisters to get a master's degree. Columbia University— Teachers College, no less. Sara's studying the education of young children, a new field in education. Something called preschool. Here's her picture."

George reached into his pocket and showed us a picture of a woman with brown curly hair and a graceful smile. She wore wings like the ones on George's uniform. And I saw the jade piece from the family whose children George saved from a Japanese attack on a small village. I sniffed the paper and stuck out my tongue to lick her ear. Would Sara giggle like Doreen did? George lifted it away from me and showed it to Andy.

"Smart. Talented... and beautiful. You did well, George." Andy smiled and took his wallet from his pocket. He pulled out a picture of a woman and baby, the photograph faded and worn, as if he'd kissed it a hundred times. Blinking his eyes, he said, "I know, because... I found a good one, too."

"Say, Andy, I'd like to catch up on the news, but we'd better head over to chow." George held his stomach. "I'm starved."

I looked up, adoring him as he stroked my front paws. George was back. Really.

"I'll head out in a minute," Andy said, tying his boots. "I'll let Charles know you're back, and we'll meet you at the mess hall."

George opened the door, and the cold wind blew around the barracks. "Just happened to come back during a cold snap, huh?"

"It's usually not this bad. We've been hit by a monsoon and lower temperatures this week. Welcome back." Andy closed the door behind us.

~   ~   ~   ~   ~

In the morning, I licked George's checks help him wake him up and get out of bed. We walked over to the stove to warm up. Andy carried the coffee pot into the bathroom to fill it with water from the sink and brought it back to the little table near the stove. "Coffee, George?" He opened a can and spooned the fragrant coffee grounds into a blue metal pot and closed the lid.

"Sure smells good. Thanks." George yawned. He pulled on his clothes and took me outside to take care of my business. When he let me in again, he sat next to Andy in a chair near the stove, and they spoke in low voices. The aroma of freshly brewed coffee filled the barracks.

George pointed to the coffee pot. "Where'd you dig up that blue pot? Looks like it's Navy issued."

Andy stroked his forehead. "Yeah, well, you know it was a long boat ride over from the States."

"Uh huh," George said, making a circular motion with his hand. "Well? Keep talking."

"I made friends with one of the crew. Expressed my admiration for their coffee. When I arrived in India, I found this in my duffle bag," Andy explained, rubbing his chin. "Couldn't very well send it back, could I?"

George laughed. "I see 'USN' written on the side. Couldn't be plainer. Makes a great story."

"Let me tell you my secret for brewing good coffee." Andy moved the coffee pot from one place on the stove to another as he gave directions. "Get the water to a boil, then let it cool. Not long, maybe a minute or so. Stir in your coffee grounds and get the water to simmer, not boil. Then take the pot off the heat for the grounds to steep a couple minutes, no more."

George nodded. "Uh-huh."

Andy took the coffee pot outside, speaking over his shoulder. "Take off the lid and get fresh air into the pot. Come here. Look, the grounds are sinking."

George went to the porch. "Well, I'll be."

They came back into the barracks and closed the door. Andy continued, "Now, if I had crushed eggshells, throw them in. Makes the last of the coffee grounds settle. Removes the bitterness. Best with cocoa for a Mexican hot chocolate, but just coffee out here will do."

"How did you learn that?" George held out a mug; Andy poured the steaming liquid slowly into it.

"My *abuelito*. My grandfather was a *vaquero*, a cowboy. He taught me." Andy poured himself a cup and set it on the small table next to his chair.

George nodded, smiling. He picked up his flight jacket from the foot locker next to his open duffle bag. He put the jacket on his bunk next to me. Pulling a small red book from the pocket, he flipped through it and showed Andy a page. "You'll get a kick out of this."

"Your flight log? November fifth." Andy held the little book up to his face in the dim light. He chuckled. I wandered next to him and placed my feet on the side of his chair. Andy showed me the book, pointing to lines and dots in pencil,

Andy smiled. "That must be your wedding day entry. I remember those feelings at my wedding, feeling happy and perplexed at the same time."

George blushed. "Best decision I ever made." He seemed surprised and happy about marrying Sara. But my head ached with worry. Would he have room for both of us in his life? What if George went back to her and left me in China again?

George's War Diary
(Entry on 11/5/1944)

I jumped onto the bunk and crawled into George's flight jacket, putting my front paws into the inside pocket, but discovering I was too big to fit into it. I turned around and poked my head out, sighing. George came over and sat next to me, putting his coffee cup on the little table next to Andy's mug.

Andy brought a small cardboard box from his room. Was it a treat for me? I raised my head and licked my lips.

"You heard about Doreen, didn't you?" Andy asked George, who nodded. "She left this for you." He handed it to George and sat in a chair. I sniffed it but didn't smell fish or bones with marrow. Probably nothing to eat.

"I got a postcard at my folks' place from her. Said she was in Washington, D. C. What's the story?" I crawled out of his flight jacket and rolled over for George to rub my tummy. He scratched my chest and belly, and I grunted with contentment, remembering the light touch of his big fingers as he ruffled through my fur.

Andy brushed the back of his hand across his mouth. "Well, Doreen headed out to New York a few weeks ago. Something about dual citizenship in Britain and the States."

I closed my eyes, remembering the day Mom and Doreen left us. A light breeze swirled a few leaves around our feet as we walked to HQ on a muggy Kunming afternoon last September. I chased a leaf, then remembered Doreen had told me to heel. White, puffy clouds rolled past, high above the buildings on base. The American and Chinese flags in front of HQ fluttered now and then, as their ropes tapped out a rhythm against the flagpoles like a pair of drums. We climbed the steps to HQ, and Doreen paused for a moment, looking around the base as the growing winds lifted the branches of the trees and displayed the undersides of the leaves. "A leaf-turner," she said under her breath, holding the door open for Mom and me. "A storm's brewing."

Doreen put a few things from her desk into a box and rearranged the pens and notebooks in the drawers. She dusted her lamp and straightened the phone and typewriter. The room grew darker under the passing clouds. Mom stood next to me. When she nuzzled my head and licked my neck, I noticed we were almost the same height.

A bright flash lit up the windows, and thunder rumbled overhead. All the lights went out. The whirring of the machines and static of the radios stopped. I could sense everyone holding their breath. Was it another air raid? Lightning flashed again; another clap of thunder roared, louder this time.

I felt a pressure in my ears, the same feeling I got when our plane descended for a landing—*wwwrrrrhhh*? Doreen sat in her chair and picked me up. She held my chin and looked into my eyes, showing her teeth as she smiled. "Just a storm, my little friend. You have really grown up, Gremlin. From a newborn pup to a Flying Tiger dog." She held my face against her cheek. "Hedda and I are so proud of you, and George will be, too. He'll be back. Don't fret now, my dear. Andy will take good care of you."

Andy? I whimpered again—*hhnnnfff-hhhmmmff*? Doreen said she was leaving long ago. Everyone I loved was leaving me. Would Mom stay with me or go with Doreen?

I nuzzled Doreen's ear, something I did when I was a puppy. She laughed—the laugh that reminded me of the tiny tinkling Chinese bells at Dr. and Mrs. Liu's home, where George and I learned about China.

The power came back on again, radios chirping to life like crickets. The ceiling lights glared down on the desks and chairs; staff members blinked at the sudden brightness. I looked over Doreen's shoulder, out the window. She turned, and we watched the sun shining and the gradual formation of a rainbow in a double arc across the hills surrounding the Kunming airbase.

Doreen and Mom were gone, but George had returned to me, finally. I took a deep breath, let it out in a sigh, and climbed out of the flight jacket. I sat on the bunk at attention, facing him. When would George leave me again? I shook myself to clear away that awful question. The buckle on my collar rattled in counterpoint to the snoring of the men in their bunks and the creaking of the old black stove.

George tapped the little box. "Well, Andy, Doreen wanted dual citizenship all along. I didn't have a chance to see her stateside, but maybe she and Sara can get together sometime, since they're both on the East Coast."

George scooted toward at the head of our bunk and switched on the gooseneck desk lamp with a click. He rubbed my head, then rocked the cardboard box around in his hands and shook it. "What is it, Gremlin?"

I perked up my ears but only heard the rustling of paper inside it and a soft thud as something solid hit the inside of the box. He used his pocketknife to open Doreen's gift under the light from his desk lamp.

I sat up and shook my head as he broke the tape and opened the flaps. George pushed aside the crumpled newspaper—looking and smelling like the stack of papers Doreen gave George long ago to housebreak me—and pulled out a kind of bottle that sparkled and gleamed. Brighter than a newly washed Jeep. But much smaller.

"A silver flask?" George blinked, holding it with his fingertips. He read the inscription out loud. "To George. Grand working with you. Doreen. 1942-1945." He sighed, shaking his head. "So many friends in the AVG and CATF have come and gone. Doreen may have been Chennault's secretary, but she kept the pulse of HQ going, like a steady heartbeat. A friend to everyone, especially you, Gremlin."

"True," Andy said. "Seems to be the way of it—the only constant is change. Especially in the military. And in wartime."

Andy took an envelope from his pocket and handed it to George, who put his finger under the outside flap and tore it open. He pulled out a photograph, paused and chuckled.

"There she is. Listen to this, Andy. 'George, my fellow sufferer.' Isn't that the truth?"

Andy scratched behind Sadie's ears when she paraded past him. She arched her back and walked around the room. "Doreen's been part of this place since I got here. This little guy was there, too, though *mi hijito* could fit in one hand back then. Now he's nearly as big as Joe and Hedda."

George smiled, wiping his cheek with the back of his hand. I jumped down from the bunk to George's duffle bag, lying open on

"George, My fellow sufferer! Doreen."
(circa 1944)

the floor. Nosing my way inside, I found a handkerchief and nipped a corner, popping out to offer it to him.

"Thanks, Gremlin. How'd you know?" George took the handkerchief, wiped his eyes and blew his nose in the musical fashion I'd missed while he was gone. I jumped down and curled up on top of his feet. He wasn't going anywhere without me.

"Tell me about meeting your bride." Andy sat back in his chair. "I've gotta hear this story."

"After spending time with my folks, I saw Tom and Edie, my old housemates from San Jose State College. Edie's sister, Sara—we called her 'little Sara Bond'—just five feet tall. I was

397

first chair oboe, and she was second. She sat next to me in rehearsals and concerts for three years. She went off to her teaching career and I joined up in the spring of forty-one."

"How'd you find her again?" Andy asked. "Oh, you want some coffee?"

"Thanks, no, Andy. Might get something stronger later." George chuckled and I rolled over. He scratched my belly. My back leg pawed the air, and I grunted with satisfaction. "Edie told me her little sister Sara was in San Francisco. Said I should look her up. Told me where to find her, living with a maiden aunt."

Andy picked up his coffee mug and took a sip, his hands curled around it. "OK, so you went to San Francisco—and?"

"She'd taken a break from teaching and was doing secretarial work in the city. I drove up to San Francisco for our first date on Sunday. I guess it went well, because Monday we walked and talked up and down those hills. So poor I couldn't come up with fare for the cable cars. On Tuesday we walked and talked. And on Wednesday I asked her to take the train with me to New York City."

"And she said…?" Andy sat forward in his chair.

"Not unless we're married." George smiled.

Andy laughed so loudly I sat up. "Good for her—my kind of gal," he said.

"I bought her a ring, on credit, just a little gold band with tiny red rubies—July birthstone. All I could afford, but you should've seen her smile, warm enough to melt an iceberg. Well, Friday we called up our folks and asked them, 'Whatcha doing Sunday? We're getting married.' Everyone was positively floored."

"I bet," Andy said, setting down his coffee mug. He wiggled his fingers, and Sadie sauntered up to him, sniffed his fingers, and walked away again.

"Our families made it work." George scooted back on the bunk to lean against the wall. "Tommy and I spiked the punch with bourbon. My father always said, 'Liquor has never touched these lips.' But I'll tell you, he thought that punch was the 'most delicious refreshment' he'd ever had."

"Wish I could have seen that." Andy smiled. "Did Sara get on the train with you?"

"Yep. We took that tee-rain from San Francisco to New York City. I had orders to fly down to Florida to wait for transport back here, but first we settled her into an apartment near Columbia. And they gave her a job at Teachers College. Can't believe I'm a married man."

The men sat in silence. Sadie and I curled up with our best friends. I sighed and couldn't lick and nuzzle George's hands enough.

After a while, Andy cleared this throat. "Well, George, hate to tell you, but Gremlin's been in trouble." He sat forward in his chair, raising the toes of his boots and lowering them again. I slipped off George's lap and crawled under his chair, curling into a tight ball and tucking my legs under my body. "He and Tom got into fights. Tom got into an accident—hit by a Jeep—and died, poor little guy."

"Oh... no..." George got out of the chair and knelt beside it, calling to me. "Gremlin, come out." I put my head down and closed my eyes. I sighed but didn't budge.

He sat cross-legged on the floor and gently pulled me into his lap. "How's Ralph?"

399

Andy's voice choked. "Still pretty shook up. Those two were inseparable. He blames himself for the accident."

"Gremlin took it hard, too, hasn't he?" George put his hand under my chin. "Yeah, tiger. What a raw deal. We need to have a little talk."

He patted my back and stroked my neck. I whimpered as he held me close. "I'm so sorry Tom's gone, Gremlin. There was nothing you could do. War can bring out the worst in us— and the best." George rocked me back and forth, next to his heart, humming the song I loved to hear, "My Buddy."

Chapter 31: The Engineers

Cover of George's War Diary (1945)

All under the heaven for all.
War Area Service Corps Diary for 1945 — China

I led George from Headquarters to the mess hall, leaning into the gusts of wind, shivering in the evening sleet. He hadn't put the leash on my collar, and I picked our way, dodging the puddles at the side of the road, forging a path over the drier patches of gravel. I felt anxious to get out of the cold and didn't stop at my usual places.

"Kunming must be as cold as New York City tonight," George grumbled. "Whoa—" He slid on a slick patch of mud, catching his balance with his arms outstretched. I stopped to make sure he was all right. Breathless, he mumbled, "Wonder how Sara's doing, Gremlin. Been two long months since I left her in New York."

Mud squished between my toes. I raised my feet up to my knees and shook them with each step. After a while, the gritty slop accumulated on the bottoms of my paws and I slipped, falling on my side, muddy from neck to hindquarters. I whimpered. *Hhnnnhhh?*

"Uh oh, tiger." George knelt and picked me up, getting mud on his pants and jacket. "It's all right." He pulled out his handkerchief and rubbed my side, smearing my fur.

I whipped my head up when I heard the roar of trucks. The vehicles lumbered around the corner of the barracks, and a line of mud-spackled trucks and construction vehicles headed toward us. George fell forward, landing on one knee, catching himself with his hands, while I tumbled out of his arms and skedaddled farther away from the road and its rolling thunder.

Shaking my head, I realized I had to protect George. Running back to him, I grabbed his pant leg with my teeth and pulled. The trucks' wheels came close enough to tower over us. He scooped me up as he rose and ran. The tires splashed water from the puddles and sprayed the roadsides, drenching his pants.

"*Yingle-yangle*—we're okay, Gremlin. How could I miss the fact that a convoy's arriving?" George mumbled while attaching the leash to my collar. "Haven't heard any news about cargo being brought into base. The Ledo Road is still under construction. Except—" He stopped.

"Come on, Grem." George broke into a trot, tapping on the door of a nearby truck. The driver rolled down the window, slowing the truck to a crawl. He had black curly hair and very dark skin.

"Did you drive over the Ledo Road?" George shouted.

The driver grinned. "Yeah, all the way from India. First battalion to bring our equipment over the Ledo Road. Twenty-four days from Assam."

"Which outfit?" George panted to keep up, walking quickly beside the truck.

The man grinned. "We're the Eight Hundred Fifty-Eighth Engineering Aviation Battalion. Negro unit. You should have seen the crowds and flags in Kunming—treated us like heroes."

"Welcome. Glad you made it." George slapped the door twice and backed away. Andy and Charles walked up to him with a group of men I hadn't met before.

Andy introduced George to the men, who looked like the driver we just met. They stood in a circle alongside the road. "These fellas built the Ledo Road, George. They're the engineers from the States, arrived earlier than expected. All the way from Ledo to Kunming. Allow me to present Louis, Julian, Ira, and Michael."

George shook hands with each of the men. His hand looked like a white key on the piano between two black keys. "Can't believe it's done. Two hundred some miles, right?"

Ira nodded. "Yes, sir, two hundred and seventy-one miles, point-to-point—and our battalion connected India to the Old Burma Road, over a thousand miles total."

Charles whistled. "With a second transport line into China we can finally win the war. More supplies and equipment. More gasoline. We can run more missions."

"That'll complement the air transport over the Hump," George said. "Well, let's go to the canteen to celebrate. First round's on me." He started walking to the canteen, with its bright lights blinking through the chilly night.

Everyone was quiet until Andy broke the silence. "George, we're just gonna pick up some beers here and take these guys to our barracks for a little get-together."

George stopped and faced the group. "Aww—come on. I'll buy all of you a beer. Least I can do for all you've done. This is remarkable."

The other men looked at each other. Charles said, "George, have you ever seen Andy and me in the canteen?"

"No, come to think of it." George rubbed under my chin and stroked my neck.

"Well, my friend… it wouldn't be a good idea for us to go in there," Andy said.

Louis stood at attention. "That's the way the world is, sir. It's the same in the States. We don't want to cause any trouble."

"Trouble?" George frowned. "You've done the hard work. We're in China, for crying out loud. It's bad enough that segregation is allowed in the States."

"No argument there, sir," Ira said.

"Sure, but you know that bartender—Mac. He's set in his ways." Charles pointed to the canteen. "Doesn't want anyone but whites in his domain."

"Time for Mac to change." George moved to the stairs of the canteen. "Take the Red Angels, Tuskegee Airmen over in Europe. Remarkable record for fighters escorting bombers. Without their support on bombing raids the Germans wouldn't have surrendered as quickly."

"Sure." Julian put his hand on the railing of the staircase. "At first none of the bomber pilots wanted a Negro unit, but once they learned the Red Angels never lost a bomber, the pilots only asked for them as escorts."

"How about Dave Brubeck?" Andy chimed in.

"Jazz man—he's good," Ira said. "I play string bass, would love to play with him. He's white, but if anyone says his colored musicians can't play a gig or eat with the band—he cancels the whole show."

"Well, I think that you all will go down in history, too." George raised his voice. "I'm going to make sure you all get a drink. You deserve at least that, and a helluva lot more. Come on, let's go." He scraped the mud off the bottoms of his boots on the edge of one of the stairs.

Still carrying me, muddy paws and all, he stepped through the door. The room was full of people, sounding as noisy as a transport plane. It felt as warm as summer inside.

"Let's set up a round for these fine gentlemen, Mac," George said to the man behind the counter.

Mac looked from one face of our friends to another and folded his arms across his chest. "Can't do that."

"Yes, you can." George spoke slowly and clearly. "A beer for each of us."

"Won't do it," Mac said. "Wasn't the way I was raised."

George motioned to Michael to step up to the counter. "Michael, when did you ship out from the States?" he asked.

Michael took a deep breath and let it out slowly. "Louis, Julian, and I started on the road in December 1942."

George looked at Mac. "Mac, how did you get out here from the States?"

"Shipped out on a luxury liner. *SS Mariposa*. Swimming pool, good food and drink," Mac said with a smirk.

405

"Okay. Michael, how did you get here?" George asked.

"Same ship, but our experience wasn't like that. Rooms below the water line. Just cold pork and hardtack to eat. Only water to drink. And we had to shower with seawater." Michael shook his head. "We weren't allowed to get off the ship in Australia. Watched the other passengers get off and stretch their legs. I regretted joining up, except for my buddies."

George's face paled. "Oh, my lord. I had no idea…" He closed his eyes for a moment. "So, Mac rode in style for weeks, not knowing what was happening with you belowdecks. And now, Mac sits in his comfortable canteen here in China, while you've spent over two years in the mountain passes, swamps, jungles. What were the conditions like, Michael? What kind of equipment did you have to build that road?"

Michael cleared his throat. "All second-hand, sir. Tractors and scrapers needed repair before we could use them. Shovels and picks flew off their handles. Had to fix those, too, when we could find them in the jungle. That's besides the snakes and mosquitoes."

George mopped his forehead with his handkerchief. "Any opposition from the Japanese?" I felt his arm stiffen as he held me against his chest.

Ira stepped forward. "All the time, sir. We had no military escort. You know the enemy didn't want us to complete the road, our only possible pipeline for supplies, so they strafed us every week. Lost over a thousand of our men."

"We say that road cost us one man for every mile." Louis frowned. "Lost some good friends building that road."

Julian added, "Equipment fell off the uneven ground. Crushed anyone downhill."

Ira said, "The typhoid, malaria, dysentery. Not to mention the air raids." He shrugged. "I'm just ready to go back stateside. Our job is done here."

"Set 'em up, Mac. A round for a job well done." George glared over the counter at Mac, who kept his hands on the top of the bar.

"Nope." Mac didn't move.

George said, "I heard the States put nearly one hundred fifty million dollars into building that road. Quite impressive... Don't you think so, Mac? Our country has invested a lot in the work our friends have accomplished. Not to mention—now you'll be getting more supplies for the canteen. Maybe more liquor's coming in on the next convoy."

Mac shook his head. "Not buying it, George."

"Don't make me pull rank on you. As General Chennault's aide, I can give him an earful about how you treat our guests." George set me down on a tall stool next to the bar. He took off his jacket and rolled up his sleeves, clenching his fists. "Criminy, Mac. We have a chance to make a difference here."

"Never seen you like this, George." Mac scratched the back of his neck.

George pounded his fist on the counter. "*Agghh*—you know our composite wings are Chinese and American forces working together. We're overcoming segregation in China to defeat a common enemy. Can't you see that? How can you revert to outdated thinking when we have a chance for unity?"

Charles unbuttoned his cuffs. "I'll back you up, George. Chinese Americans like me are making contributions, interpreting at the wing level so that international relations go more smoothly. Mac, we've got to build lifelong partnerships. You know we're not that different from each other."

"Oh, buddy—there are lots of differences between us." Mac slammed his palm on the bar, his face purple. People at the tables stopped talking, their heads up.

"Wrong, Mac." Andy frowned and spoke in a low voice. "Now, listen to me. My parents came from Mexico to make a better life for our family. We have a right to serve in the military—I'm proud to wear the Flying Tiger patch on my sleeve—and be treated with respect, just like our friends here from the Negro division."

Andy and Charles moved next to George, their faces stern. The engineers moved closer behind them. I could hardly breathe, wondering what would happen next.

"Come on, Mac." Charles stood at attention, his head up. "We've been patient for too long, taking our bottles back to the barracks because you can't stand to look at the color of our skin. Just get it through your thick skull—we're Americans, too. Part of the war effort."

Andy nodded. "We've had enough of being boys. Mac—we're men. We fight like men, pull our share. Same for the engineers. You might think calling them 'Negro' or 'Colored' makes them less than you are. We are all equal."

"Yeah, we're men, just like any other." Ira stepped up to the bar next to Andy. "Jobs, families. I've got a little daughter I've never met, Mac. She's going on two now. How about you?"

"A son. He's three." Mac's face softened for a moment, then he frowned. "Haven't met him yet, either. Just a few photos now and then." He shrugged his shoulders, his eyes misty. "I been gone so long my wife left me. Took up with someone else. Sent me a Dear John letter last month." He blinked rapidly and blushed, his mouth turned down.

"Hey, buddy." Ira lowered his voice. "Sorry to hear that. That's rough, especially after giving up everything to come out here. See, we know what that's like, Mac."

"Yeah, well... guess we got more in common than I thought." Mac bent down and brought his hands up, full of glasses. He set them down in front of me and poured liquid into them. "What the hell. A round for our engineers. And Charles, Andy, you're welcome here any time." I sniffed the glasses as he passed them to waiting hands, but my nose burned and I sneezed.

Mac shouted, "First round is on the house. Let's give 'em a toast for a job well done."

"Thanks, Mac." The men slapped George on his back, saying, "Attaboy, George." "Here's one for you, Charles." "Andy, well said." "Welcome to the Eight Hundred and Fifty-Eighth."

I barked in agreement—*rrrrawwrkk-rrraawrkk*, wondering why someone would treat people differently because of the color of their skin.

I thought about the different colors of people and animals. I admired Pop's glossy black coat and his abilities to hunt and retrieve. Rex was stronger and braver than any dog I'd met—and his fur was black. The cormorants on the Li River could catch fish no matter what color their feathers were.

I was proud of George for doing what was right. Whenever I followed George's commands, he gave me treats. The engineers had completed their jobs and deserved to have their treats, too.

409

George swooped me up in his arms and sat at a table with three of the engineers. Ira exchanged a glance with Julian, then tapped Michael's arm and nodded toward the door. The two of them left the canteen.

Julian pointed to the stage in the corner of the canteen. "You think my men could play some tunes?"

"Sure, buddy. I just got back, brought a new clarinet with me. What do you have in mind?" George bent his head bent toward Julian's.

"Well, we just so happen to have some instruments we picked up in various places—somewhere between the States and China. Put together a sort of a band. Think Mac would mind?" Julian pointed to the bartender.

"Anything to draw in more customers would be fine with that barkeep. I'll let him know." George smiled. "Mind if I join you?"

"Well, how about that? It would be a pleasure, George, my brother." Julian sat back in his chair, sipping his drink.

George stood and took me to Andy, asking him, "Would you watch Gremlin? I'm going get my horn and call Ralph to bring his."

Andy rocked me in his arms as he and Charles sat at the table, talking with Julian. Michael and Ira returned a few minutes later with cases of different sizes and shapes. Julian joined his friends.

When George and Ralph came in, everyone took out their instruments, and the group tuned to the piano. The rich tones of Ralph's violin melded with the brass and reed instruments, punctuated by rhythms on drums and cymbals.

Julian told the group, "Let's start with 'It Don't Mean a

Thing.' Key of B Flat." He counted off, snapping his fingers. "A-one, two—a-one, two, three."

The band played all night. More and more people jammed into the canteen, laughing and dancing. Andy joined the band and sang "*Cielito Linda,*" rocking me in his arms and singing out like I'd never heard him before.

Red arrived with the other nurses, holding my sister Wench in the crowded room. Andy took me over to greet them. They set us down under the table, and we played around their feet, chasing and nipping at each other.

Red sprinkled a white powder all over the floor in front of the band. She set the empty box on the table.

"What's that?" Andy shouted over the music.

"Cornstarch." Red tapped out the beat on her knee, her head bopping in time to the music. "Makes the floor slick for the dancers."

More musicians entered the room, holding their instruments in front of them as they looked over the canteen. Mac nodded, a signal for them to come in, and they joined the band. The walls reverberated with sounds of a dozen or more instruments and voices, clicking heels and slushing sounds as the dancers moved around the dance floor.

The women grabbed men's hands and pulled them toward the dance floor. Some of the airmen and engineers shook their heads at first, blushing shyly. Finally, each one smiled and joined in awkwardly, until they were caught up with the beat and danced in rhythm with the pulse of the drums.

Red took Wench and me to a corner of the room, separating us from the flying feet and twisting bodies on the

411

dance floor. We made up our own dances to the music filling the canteen.

People took off their coats and piled them into a heap. Wench and I took turns running through the cornstarch and sliding on our bellies and sides along the slick floor until we plowed into the coats.

All too soon, the band took a break. Julian announced, "My friends, you are listening to the sounds of the 'Biggest Little Band in the Hump' as we were called when we built the Ledo Road. You might fly over it, but we plowed through it."

The room erupted in cheers. Thomas shouted, "As engineers, we can fix anything. I mean anything. So, whenever and wherever we found discarded musical instruments, they went in the truck, got fixed, and joined the band."

Ira raised his glass to Mac, George, Andy, Charles, and Ralph. "And here we are tonight with our new friends."

The crowd cheered when the music started again. Wench and I continued our dances in the cornstarch until we couldn't stand up anymore. We burrowed into the bed of coats, too tired to move. I fell asleep, my chin over her back, and didn't wake up until the bleary-eyed dancers peeled the coats away one by one.

Chapter 32: War Weary

Lt. George Arthur Haydon, Jr. (1945)

Do your work, then step back. The only path to serenity.

Lao Tzu

One cool afternoon we went to the Kunming airfield. George stood in a long line of airmen, holding my leash. Puffy white clouds passed overhead, alternately causing me to shiver in the shade or pant in the sun. George stood at attention, and I followed his lead, now and then shifting my weight slightly across my four legs as a voice droned above me on the platform surrounded by flowers and flags.

I had heard the speaker before but couldn't place who it could be, since I couldn't see the people on the stage clearly. I felt lost in a thick forest of pants and boots.

413

The official announced, "First Lieutenant George Arthur Haydon, Junior." My best friend took a deep breath and stood taller. He motioned for me to heel. I held my head up and walked next to him, jumping up the short flight of stairs in step with his long stride. His shiny boots *tap-tapped* on the wooden platform and my toenails *clip-clipped* in rhythm, sixteenth notes in sync with his measured pace.

"Lieutenant Haydon," the Chinese official said softly as we stood in front of him. "So good to see you again."

Could it be? Dr. Hollington K. Tong from the City of Heroes? Did he remember me? I whined—*wrrrrffff*? He bowed to George and then to me, his hands clasped in front of his chest. His warm brown eyes smiled at me as I put my chest to the floor and bowed to him.

I stood, remembering our long walk in the Chungking garden, wagged my tail furiously, and stamped my feet until George snapped his fingers. I remembered where we were and the crowd below us. I stood quietly at attention but couldn't quite get my tail to be still in my excitement. At least I didn't pee on stage, not even a little.

"This silk banner is presented with great respect and honor by Police Commissioner Li Hongmo of Yunnan Province." Dr. Tong nodded to the man next to him, who bowed to George.

My back itched as a fly landed on it, but I knew it wouldn't be proper for me to sit and scratch on stage. I flexed my shoulder and the insect flew away.

The commissioner motioned to the shiny silk banner with Chinese characters embroidered in fine golden threads, held by two beautiful young ladies dressed in silk.

He read, "For the Allies who protect the territory of our country's skies…"

Two flies attacked my muzzle, and I twitched my whiskers. They flew off. "For your service in the American Air Force… and in commemoration of the thirty-seventh year of America's entrance into the age of flight…" Several flies buzzed around my head. Irritated, I shook my head and snorted.

A murmur of laughter rippled through the crowd. Oh no—had I embarrassed George in this solemn ceremony? What could I do to make up for it?

"May our friend-ship in these times continue with future generations. Thank you for your service, Lieutenant Haydon, and best wishes." Dr. Tong and Commissioner Li bowed, clasping their hands in front of their chests. The women folded the banner and placed it in George's hands. He bowed in response as he held it to his chest. I lowered my head in respect as George saluted.

Sara Haydon Holding George's Yunnan Banner

At that moment, I decided to attempt my own salute to

China, to our friends, our allies. As I had seen my pop, Joe Dash, do so many times, I sat on my haunches. Feeling unsteady, it took two tries for me to lift both my front paws and hold the pose, with my back straight and my head higher than I had ever been able to hold it before.

The laughter of the crowd changed to a collective intake of breath as I raised one paw to my eye. Dr. Tong and Director Li returned my salute.

George's face softened and his eyes gleamed. "Atta boy, tiger. Down."

I dropped to all fours, and Dr. Tong knelt and touched the lieutenant's bar on my collar. "Gremlin, Guardian of the Flying Tigers, a true hero." I licked his hand. He smiled at me, stood again, and George and I faced the audience, who cheered.

We descended the steps as another airman was called to the stage. Luke, Andy, and Charles gathered around and congratulated us.

"I didn't know Gremlin could hold that pose," Charles said.

"He's never done it before," George said. "Guess he just made up his mind and surprised us all, including himself."

"Let me take a closer look at the banner." The men unfolded the banner, and Charles ran his finger across the characters. He asked George for his flight log. "There's mention of an anniversary. What happened in 1908?"

George paused, then said, "Well, the Army Air Corps didn't get started until 1926. Only twenty-nine years. Must have been back when flights first took place."

"Okay, then." Charles wrote in my best friend's notebook and handed it back to him. "Here's a rough translation."

Gremlin: Guardian of the Flying Tigers

For defending the airspace of this allied country
In commemoration of the thirty-seventh anniversary
of America's entrance into the age of flight
      Best wishes, Li Hongmo
      Police Commissioner of Yunnan Province

~   ~   ~   ~   ~

Later that week, after chow, George opened a letter that smelled faintly like perfume. He looked at it a long time but didn't read it to me. My best friend lay on our bunk with his arm over his eyes. I jumped onto the bunk and nudged his hand, but he didn't pet me. I licked George's face, but he pushed me away.

Had I done something wrong? I hadn't made a mess or a puddle inside for weeks. Didn't chew the bones from Cook on his bunk anymore. Or wiggle at night after he'd worked long hours and was ready to sleep. Maybe he was disappointed that I'd never actually captured any gremlins.

Maybe George needed to take a walk. I ran to my leash hanging on its peg next to the door and growled at it, then ran back to him, whining and chewing on the edge of the blanket. He uncovered his eyes and turned his head toward me, saying, "Not now," and didn't get up. We both let out long, heavy sighs.

I wanted to try something else to make him happy. I sat up tall, lifting my front paws for a few seconds before falling over, but he didn't laugh or pet me or tell me I was a good boy. He just stared at the ceiling.

After a few minutes he lifted a paper from his chest and turned onto his side. "A letter from Sara. I didn't want to read it in HQ. Been so long since I heard from her."

417

I listened for more, but all I heard was the fire crackling in our stove. George sat up on the bunk and folded the letter, his shoulders slumped. He looked the way I felt when my tail was tucked between my legs. I knew that feeling. Like I lost my bone, one I really wanted, but I was too tired to look for it.

He picked up a clipboard from his desk and turned on the green metal gooseneck lamp. Sitting up in bed against his pillow, he talked to me as he wrote.

> Dear Sara:
>
> How do you like having a husband and then not having one? I know I don't like having a wife for just a small sample of married life and now being apart.
>
> Rather sorry that we're not going to have a baby yet. But glad too. It's really for the best and much wiser, isn't it?

He shifted from the bed to his chair at the desk. I sat near his feet, then lay down with a sigh. We weren't going for a walk. Maybe writing a letter to Sara would help him feel better. I waited to be there when he needed me.

> The news from China looks worse all the time. If you don't hear from me for a couple of weeks, don't worry, because I'm going to be all right. Just wait for me.

He looked up and ran his hand through his hair. Then he bent his head and wrote some more.

I didn't think it would be as tough as it is to be away from you, but I'm just as lonely as I can be. Not as lonely as when I first got here, because now I know I have you waiting for me. But I guess because of that knowledge I want to go home.

Love, George

He pounded the desk with the heel of his palm. I sat up and whined. George picked me up and hugged me tighter than he ever had before, breathing like he was choking. I felt droplets of water on my fur and snuggled closer to him, licking the salt from his cheeks. I couldn't take Sara's place, but I could comfort my best friend.

George scratched out another letter, reading softly.

Dear Folks:

Sorry if the letters from China haven't been rolling in to Berkeley Way as often as they should—I'm not so busy that I can't write—but after getting a couple of paragraphs off to my wife—can't seem to find anything to say. It's getting so I can't find anything to write to her.

We're working nights again—I hope it doesn't last too much longer because I'm getting pretty tired. In fact, I wish I could be out of the whole thing and come back home. I have fifty months in the Army—

forty of them overseas. I feel I've given my country a full measure.

Guess I'm low tonight—had better sign off.

Love, George

Chapter 33: The Dragon Tapestry

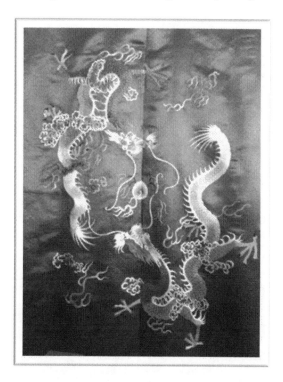

Embroidery of Dragons on Silk
(WWII)

The strength of a nation is derived from
The integrity of its homes.

Confucius

Over the next few weeks, we continued with our routines of walking and working. At HQ, George returned to his desk by General Chennault's office, and John moved away. My Good Morning towel went back into my desk drawer, which was so cramped I could barely fit into it. I kept my feet together as I spun around on my towel, which had holes in it now and was no longer fluffy and soft.

I could pee with my leg up—balancing on three legs, without tipping over. George taught me by holding up one of my back legs each time I went outside, until I figured it out.

Over time, Sadie and I became friends, often sharing our old basket under Andy's desk. Sometimes she licked my muzzle, and I licked her back, although her long gray fur stuck to my tongue. When she kneaded my tummy, she didn't use her claws. Instead, she purred, like the layers of sounds made by the insects in the trees around Kweilin's Command Cave.

On a hot spring day, I took a nap in my desk drawer. Loud voices woke me. The HQ staff argued over when the war might end. I could hear George's voice clearly. "July fifteenth, my wife's birthday. Here's five bucks."

George (center) and co-workers in China (1945)

Charles said, "You're too optimistic. The Normandy landings were on the sixth of June. It hasn't even been a year. We still have a lot of work to do here in China. I'll bet a five spot on August first."

I heard Andy's voice. "Nah, I think it'll still be awhile. Germany surrendered May eighth this year. V-E Day. Wasn't that your birthday, George? You'll never have another birthday present quite like that. I'm in—put me down for August fifteenth, V-J Day for sure."

After lunch, I lay on the floor of HQ next to George's desk, cooler than in my drawer. George called out, "Charles, let's take Gremlin out for a stroll. Remember Dr. Liu, my *Lǎo Shī*?"

"Sure, George, your Chinese teacher. How old do you think he is now?" Charles scratched his head. I sat up and scratched my ear.

"Maybe 80, 90? He was still pretty spry the last time I saw him, but... gosh, it's been almost a year since I took lessons with him and his wife. Wonderful couple. I just feel this urge to visit them."

I heard Charles reply, "Okay, I'll be done early today. Lots of translating still, but I'm catching up. Let's go see how they're doing."

"We'll still have daylight until late. It's the summer solstice. I'd like to thank them before I'm reassigned. With General Chennault and Casey Vincent both stateside, it looks like I'll need to take whatever comes along. I might not be here much longer."

"Sure am sorry to hear that, George. You're right, though. Orders can come through any time without warning. Who knows if you'll ever see *Lǎo Shī* again? I'll be ready when you are."

"Appreciate it, Charles. They've been on my mind." I heard the clatter of George's typewriter. After work, we left HQ and picked up dinner from Cook. He gave us five packages wrapped in white paper.

"Bones for The Gremlin," Cook said. "Dinner for the two of you. Who gets the others?"

"My Chinese teachers." George took the treats. "We're

paying them a long overdue visit." I jumped up to touch George's knee with my front paws to smell what Cook put in the packages, but he held them out of my reach. I barked and wagged my tail, showing my teeth the same way humans smiled.

"Not yet, tiger," George said. "Let's get going. Thanks, Cook. I owe you one."

After saying hello to the MPs at the gate and exchanging sniffs and barks with Private Rex, we walked off base and down a gravel road into the fields. I ran back and forth on the road, smelling the cooling air. Interesting trails led away from the road, and I wanted to follow all of them, but George and Charles needed my protection. I scouted ahead, smelled smoke, and sneezed.

George called me to him, his voice unsteady and lower than usual. "Here, Gremlin—now." We were at the place where the house should have been, but it didn't look—or smell—the same. I ran to him, dodging big holes in the road.

Charles paused, pointing to piles of rocks and burned plants. "These were beautiful, lush gardens. This should be the village... It was just here... when I came last year."

"Last time we visited, this village had five or six houses, rice terraces, water buffalo... Now..." George walked quickly down the road, gesturing to a big pile of stones and wood, paper flapping loosely around the steps. "Charles, here's the house—what's left of it."

He and Charles ran into a yard full of stones and bricks. Branches of fruit trees with dried leaves covered the crushed flowers in the garden I used to explore before and after George's Chinese lessons. Torn red paper from around the doorway fluttered away in the breeze. The bells were gone.

George shook his head. "Looks like part of the roof is gone. Half the place is in ruin. What happened?"

"Must have been the air raid we heard a few days ago," said Charles. He walked to the side of the house. "My god, the back of the house is just another pile of rocks. Looks deserted, George. Think he's still here?"

George turned his head to one side. I turned my head, too, wondering whether we could find them. George went up to the door and knocked loudly.

"*Lǎoshī*? It's George. Charles and I are here to see you. Mrs. Liu, are you there?" He pushed on the door, but it wouldn't open. I listened but didn't hear anything. George looked down at me and I looked up at him, wagging my tail. I thought he might give me the bones from Cook, since we walked such a long way past dinner time. But he didn't open the package, probably worrying about our friends.

"I'll give it a try in Chinese." Charles stepped up to the door and knocked even louder. He shouted and then we listened.

Nothing. We still couldn't hear any sounds from inside. I looked up at my package again, but George didn't notice. I whimpered and scratched at his leg, hungry for my bone.

"No, Gremlin. Not now," he said. "Charles, could you leave a note in Chinese? In case his family or neighbors come by, I'd at least like them to know about our friendship. And that we checked on them. It's not often military folks get to know civilians that well. Best teacher I ever had."

"I'll help you with that. What do you want to say?" Charles pulled a pen and paper from his pocket. I pawed at George's leg.

Then I heard a raspy whisper from inside the house, "Flying Tigers—*Fēi Hǔ*." I barked to alert George that *Lǎoshī* was inside.

"Stop it, boy. Just a little longer. Then you'll get your bone. Okay, Charles. Dear *Lǎoshī*..." I whined. George shook his finger at me. "No, Gremlin. Quiet."

George took my leash and tied me to a post near the road. I barked and whined, tugging at my leash. They placed the paper under the doorway. When George came back and untied me, I tugged on my leash and it slipped out of his fingers. Running as fast as I could, like my pop Joe Dash, I jumped onto the step and pawed at the door, leaping up to scratch at the handle. I clawed at the bottom of the door. If I could dig for nightcrawlers, I could dig for George's teacher.

George ran to me. "Gremlin—is it... *Lǎoshī*?" He shouted, pushing on the door. Charles helped him open the door just wide enough for my slender body to slip through the opening. I rushed into the room where George sipped tea and we had learned about China. I sniffed the dusty, smoky air—musty, like Luke's dirty socks and underwear, and smoky, like Chennault's cigarettes. I sneezed.

"Bless you, George." I heard a soft voice in the darkness and stopped to listen.

"*Lǎoshī*? Are you here?" They pushed on the door again. George squeezed through and followed me, Charles behind him. They stepped around shattered glass to pull aside the torn curtains, letting in early evening sunlight. The ancient chair was splintered, the rest of the furniture smashed into a jumble of broken wood and half-burned portraits.

I saw a movement under the rubble of bricks and tiles.

Burrowing into the heap, I felt a hand on my head. I licked the hand, then pulled away to dig some more.

"Good boy, Gremlin." George uncovered his teacher. "*Lǎoshī*, we were so worried." George and Charles spoke in English and Chinese.

"*Fēi hǔ.* I knew George, our Flying Tiger, would find us." *Lǎoshī's* voice was high and soft, sounding like Ralph's violin as he played to Tom and me, helping us sleep when we were puppies.

"You're weak. Are you hurt? Let me check—don't try to talk." Charles said, as he lifted the old man's blood-caked head. George gave him water from his canteen. I moved closer, perking my ears to hear his whispered words.

"My dear wife died in that last bombing raid. She was in the back, in the bedroom. Didn't make it. Neighbors came by, but they couldn't hear me. Given up for dead, I guess. No one's been around for days. Just a few stray dogs—not you Gremlin. My old eyes are so glad to see you. All of you." He coughed. His embroidered silk robe fell away in tatters.

"We've got food for you, *Lǎoshī*. We'll get you to the hospital." Charles patted his arm. "I'll run back and get the medics. They'll come with an ambulance. George will stay here with you."

George tore up the food from Cook and fed morsels to *Lǎoshī* the way he fed me niblets when I was little. When I sat up to beg, *Lǎoshī* said in a high, thin voice, "What a good dog you are, Gremlin. You saved my life." He groaned. "My legs must have been broken when the roof fell in."

"Take a sip of water." George pulled his teacher up to lean into his chest.

427

"Thanks, number one son. Now listen, we have something for you. You keep it safe. Promise me?"

"I promise. But you will get better. Just hold on."

"Next to me is a cloth. I don't want you to look at it until you get home safely to your family. Understand?"

"Understood. I'll find it." George slowly lowered *Lǎoshī* carefully onto the floor. He felt under the blankets and pulled out a dark bundle of cloth. It smelled like *Lǎoshī*'s robe with the delicate birds embroidered by his wife, now ruined in the bombing. George pushed my nose away and turned it over in his hands. "What is this?"

"Silk. Embroidered. My wife spent every day during the war of Japanese aggression working on this. She sewed stitches after every invasion—Mongolia, Nanking, Shanghai, Hong Kong. All by hand, each thread. By daylight under this window. At night by candlelight. Year after year of war. Dark threads and fire for the enemy bombs. Light colors and clouds for the protection of the Flying Tigers. Finished it a month ago."

"I can't take this. It's too precious. You must have family who would care for it."

"We have no family, you know—elders gone, never had children. Then you came to us from the Flying Tigers. You gave us hope, meaning for our lives. Mrs. Liu made up her mind to finish this tapestry for you, for your family. We knew you would come back. Mrs. Liu ran to get it when she heard the planes coming, bombs falling. She saved the dragon tapestry and reached out to me. I ran to her and took the tapestry just before the walls came down, burying her. I could not save her." He sobbed. "I had to retreat because of the crumbling roof. She begged me to save the tapestry instead of herself."

George whispered hoarsely, "I am so honored."

"Mrs. Liu called China a pearl." *Lǎoshī* sighed. "She said two dragons fight over a pearl. Tens of millions of Chinese people perish. More than the stars we see." He closed his eyes, his breathing interrupted with coughing. He frowned, and I licked his hand to remind him we were there. "Such suffering and death because one greedy dragon fights another for this round treasure." I curled up against him next to his chest, listening to the soft thumping of his heart, growing weaker every moment.

"I don't understand, *Lǎoshī*. Tell me about it when you're feeling better. Charles will be back soon. We'll get you to the Kunming hospital and they'll fix you up."

"Now, George, promise. You take the dragons home. A message of peace, friendship, hope between your people and ours. Share the message, share the meaning she died protecting."

George held the silk to his chest and touched *Lǎoshī's* shoulder. "Thank you, my teacher. I will... treasure our times together."

"And I thank you, my boy." *Lǎoshī* groaned. "Mrs. Liu— my Li-jing, beautiful spirit, is gone. I go to be with her."

"Stay with me, *Lǎoshī*." George patted his face gently. "There's so much I want to tell you... I married a beautiful woman, a teacher... our plans for a family... I want to thank you for teaching me about China and the ways of your people. I came to say goodbye—but not this way."

The old man stroked my ears with trembling fingers. "Gremlin, you take good care of George."

George took his hand. "My teacher... *Lǎoshī*..."

"You're a good man... George... Flying Tigers... *Fēi hǔ... Yīngxióng...*" The breath escaping his thin chest whistled like the sighing of the wind that used to tinkle the bells on their porch. I held my breath, listening. Where was his heartbeat?

George didn't make a sound until he finally took a slow breath and sighed. The house was quiet. I crawled over to him and rested my chin on his leg. He placed his hand on my back A breeze floated gently in and out of the windows, gracefully moving the ragged curtains across the broken windows.

My ears perked up when I heard the rumble of an engine come toward us and stop. The door screeched open when Charles came in, pushing aside the rubble. Two men wearing white coats followed him, carrying a kit and blankets.

One of them said, "We're the base medics. Charles told us about the bombing."

George didn't look up, keeping his eyes on his teacher's face. "Dr. Liu is gone. An honorable man. *Lǎoshī*—my teacher."

"Anyone else here?" Paul pointed to the caved-in roof at the back of the house.

"His remarkable wife. You'll find Mrs. Liu's remains... there."

Paul felt *Lǎoshī*'s wrist and covered his face with a blanket. "Civilians. Murdered by the enemy. Children. Women. Elders. Babies... So hard to see these precious lives snuffed out by such a treacherous enemy."

Charles helped George stand. "What's that?"

George held the bundle, still pressed to his chest. "*Lǎoshī* wanted me to have this. Mrs. Liu made it... for me—" His voice broke off with a muffled cry as he covered his mouth.

Through the open doorway I saw a Jeep pull up with Private Rex in the back. Sarge and Jimmy jumped over the sides of the Jeep. Jimmy called, "Come, Private Rex." The large Dobie jumped down, landing squarely on all four paws. I whimpered—*wwrrmmff*.

"Wait here, Jimmy." Sarge stomped into the house. "Now—what's going on here?"

"Civilians, casualties of war." Paul shook his head.

"All right." Sarge looked around the room. "The area is secured. Let's all head outside so the medics can do their work." The sergeant looked at the bundle in George's arms. "Lieutenant, are you carrying private possessions of the deceased?"

"Yes, sir," said George. "My Chinese teacher—his wife made this—he gave this to me with his dying... breath."

"Sorry, George. We've gotta check it. Orders."

We went outside. Charles held the package while George fumbled to untie the cord, like my leash but smaller. As they unfolded the deep blue fabric, I smelled an aroma that reminded me of *Lǎoshī*'s robe and shoes. Silk. I stood next to George and watched the faces of the medics and MPs, their eyes opened wide. Everyone took a step backwards, shock on their faces.

"Oh, m-my..." Jimmy's mouth dropped open.

"Well, I'll—I'll be..." Charles turned to look at the tapestry. "George, you have a cultural treasure there, as well as a beautiful gift of friendship. You honor the Chinese people by accepting this gift from Dr. and Mrs. Liu."

431

I looked from the men's faces to the cloth they held. Two snarling dragons stared down at me, orange and white and black like tigers in the sky, with a shimmering white pearl in the center. They looked so real—*yyyiippp*—I sat down hard onto George's foot. Then I stood tall and shook myself from nose to tail to show everyone I wasn't afraid of those dragons.

Rex stepped up to me and nuzzled me with his nose, and I fell again. He lay down and took me in his front paws. I wondered if he would eat me, but he gently licked the top of my head, my shoulders, my back. He treated me the way I would lick a bone before gnawing on it. I trembled, whining with fright, then, submitting to his strength and power, I gave up and rolled onto my back while he licked me under my chin.

"Look at that, would you? Rex, buddy, you have a soft spot for that little dog now, eh?" The sergeant turned to George. "Keep the dragons. One special lady did all that work. I won't report it. None of us will, right boys?" Everyone nodded. George and Charles folded the fabric.

That night, I felt George rolling from one side to the other. I wondered if he was worried about the dragons, now secured in his footlocker. I curled around to face it just in case the dragons came alive and worked their way out, like the ones at the Kunming New Year's festival.

I sighed. *Lǎoshī* told us to think of the silk tapestry as a sign of friendship between our people. But the enemy was still at war with us. What had he said about the stars? I couldn't count the stars, and I couldn't count millions of people. Millions who died because there weren't enough Flying Tigers to protect them all. Especially the dear ones we knew so well, as Doreen might say. What could I do—one dachshund against the Empire of Japan and all the gremlins destroying our planes? *Wrrrrhmmm?* I sighed as George rolled over again, murmuring *"Lǎoshī"* in his sleep.

Chapter 34: At Last

The Gremlin, 1945

A good traveler has no fixed plans
And is not intent upon arriving.

Lao Tzu

One hot morning in July, I lay sprawled at the side of George's desk, opening my eyes whenever someone walked through the door of General Chennault's office. Everyone in Headquarters moved slowly, except for the humming fans barely moving the air and the buzzing flies making my whiskers twitch.

George answered the jingling, jangling phone on his desk, rolling his chair forward. A crackly voice muttered on the line. My best friend sat up, drops of sweat on his brow. "Repeat?" He took out his handkerchief and mopped his face.

The speaker shouted, "Pack up your duffle bag, Lieutenant. You're going home."

"What?" George stood so quickly his rolling chair flew into the wall of General Chennault's office with a resounding whack.

Everyone in HQ looked up, eyebrows raised. General Chennault and Pop rushed from their office.

"Sorry, sir. New orders." He picked me up and held me high over his head. I looked down at his smiling face. "I'm going home!" HQ buzzed with voices like a hive of hornets.

He lowered me, laughing and spinning around. "Sara won't believe I got my orders to ship home on her birthday." My tummy felt queasy but luckily, I didn't throw up on him.

The airmen in the office congratulated him with handshakes and pats on the back. "Good luck, George." "War must be coming to an end." "When's it my turn?" "How much longer 'til we all go home?"

Pop stood next to me, wagging his tail. My eyes were nearly level with his. He licked the back of my neck, and I felt proud to be his son.

Chennault's gravelly voice broke through the voices. "Son, you've done us proud, more than I can say. After three and a half years of service with us—with the Flying Tigers—I recommended your transfer. Give 'em hell, tiger. And let me know directly if there's anything you need. Transport plane over The Hump leaves in two hours. Better grab your gear."

The general shook hands with my best friend and said goodbye. Oh, no—was George was leaving me again? I put my ears down and my tail between my hind legs. I didn't want my best friend to go away. He would never come back.

Everyone got back to work. George chatted with Andy as he packed his satchel. I crawled under Andy's desk. Since Mom wasn't there for me to comfort me, I stuck my head into the familiar basket and nuzzled Sadie, who woke up and rubbed her head against my chest. She purred, reminding me of General Chennault clearing his throat. I jumped into the basket next to her and licked her under the chin. She purred louder.

Andy stuck his head under the desk. "Looks like you two finally made friends." He stood up. "Sorry to keep you out of the loop, buddy, but the Old Man wanted to surprise you with those orders to go home."

"You sure kept it a secret." George's blue eyes misted. "Thanks. Say, look me up in New York City, will ya? Who knows where either of us will be after the war ends? Too bad Charles is out today. Tell him to look me up in Santa Cruz, will ya? Come on, Gremlin, I've gotta pack. I gave Sadie one last lick and jumped out of the basket.

Another wave of cheers followed him, and I whined, stopping at the door to keep George from leaving HQ. Who would take care of me when he left to go home to Sara?

"Come on, tiger. You're coming, too." We stopped to say goodbye to friends on our way to the Tiger Den. Once George turned away from packing his long green duffle bag, I crept across the bunk and burrowed inside it, afraid he'd leave me behind. I poked out my nose, wanting more than anything to go with him. I had to make sure that he got back to Sara safely. And I needed to scare away the gremlins from his plane.

My best friend chuckled when he saw me peeking out at him. "It's okay, Gremlin. Of course, you're going home with

437

me. Let's pack your water dish and food in my satchel with your Good Morning towel. I found a small wooden box for your puddles and piles during our flights. Now, get your leash. I'll write a letter home, then let's see about getting some chow for the trip."

George wasn't leaving me after all—I was going home with my best friend. I hopped off the bunk and grabbed my leash to toss it into the air and pounce on it. I held it in my mouth, sitting like a good dog, ready to go.

But my best friend sat in the chair by our bunk, writing a letter at his desk. He hadn't read to me in a long time, but this time he did. "First, a telegram to Sara—coming home—stop—look for me in New York early August—stop—happy birthday—stop—love George—end."

He cleared his throat and used a new sheet of paper, scratching out words with his pen as I lay down with a sigh and nibbled at my leg. He read to me softly, the way he used to long ago.

> Dear Folks:
>
> Soon I'll be back in India—my old stomping grounds. Looks like I'll be there until about the first of August, but they say once you get started from there you whiz right on through.
>
> I plan to remain in New York until Sara finishes her graduate degree, then we'll migrate back to California by easy stages, seeing the country as we go. Well, that's all several months away.

Will write more when I hear about
getting out of India.

Love, George

He put his pen and flight log in his pocket and finally
snapped the leash onto my collar. We headed out of the Tiger
Den. While I took care of my business, George collected a
canvas bag full of soil and sand and left it on the porch. George
whistled as we walked, stopping to drop off his notes in a
building near the mess hall.

While we had chow, we said goodbye to many friends.
Cook gave George two packages. "Here you, go, George.
Something for you and treats—dried out bones and beef jerky—
to keep the little tiger busy on the plane. Good luck, you two!"

Back at the Tiger Den, George put me in the back of the
Jeep with his duffel bag and the bag of dirt. Luke placed
George's worn satchel, stuffed with my bowl, bones, Good
Morning towel, sandbox, and dog chow, next to me. I sniffed
it to make sure everything was there.

Luke drove us to the airfield. The men talked about
meeting in the States. We stopped at the Quonset hut, where
George and Luke talked with Ralph. I wandered under the
trees where Tom and I used to chase each other and play tug-
of-war with Ralph's oily rags. I left my scent in many places,
remembering the times we played as puppies—before his life
was cut short.

Ralph bent down to rub my head. "We've been through
tough times, Gremlin, but you turned out all right." I covered
Ralph's face with wet doggy kisses to let him know I
understood. His cheeks tasted salty, like tears.

I walked slowly to Tom's grave with my head down, circling his headstone and the small mound of earth where he was buried. I sat, took a deep breath, and howled goodbye— to my brother, to the shark-mouthed planes, to the brave people who worked together in wartime, and to China, my birthplace.

~ ~ ~ ~ ~

I had never felt so electric, from the tip of my quivering snout to the end of my excited tail. We found our transport plane amid the roar of aircraft engines and the hustle of Jeeps, salutes of airmen in uniform, and farewells from the grateful Chinese people wearing big round hats in the summer sun. I said goodbye to the bomb-scarred runways; to the rows of snarling, battered and dented P-40s; and the multi-layered scents of the Kunming airfield.

Luke rubbed my neck. "Well, Gremlin, it's been good knowing you. I hope you take good care of George on the trip home." I licked his hand, which he held out to George. "So long, now. No doubt you'll remember me as the worst roommate you ever had."

George chuckled. "But the best pilot. Had some good times. Flying with you and General Chennault, I never stayed in one place long enough to pick up my laundry. I guess we both still have shirts all over China."

My head up, I stood at attention, alert as an airman awaiting orders. George gathered our gear from the Jeep and took me to the back of the plane, where he shrugged off his duffle bag.

A young crewman loaded it with the others, stacked like firewood ready for the smoky black stove. "One C-46 to go over the Hump." He pointed to George's sleeve. "Sir, you've

440

got six stripes on your sleeve. One for every six months overseas, right? You've been here awhile."

"Should be seven." My best friend stood proudly, and so did I. "Forty-two months. How about you?"

"Just a few months. This is my last trip before they send me back stateside. Not enough time to get a stripe. Bet you're ready to go home."

"You got it, buddy. My bride's waiting for me—and my dog here—in New York City." They saluted, and George looked down at me. "Ready to fly over The Hump, Gremlin?" He carried his satchel and my bag of dirt over his shoulder, while I watered the tire. My last time to scratch the soil of China. I sneezed and shook my head.

"That's it, Gremlin." He smiled, gazing around the airfield with misty eyes. "Say goodbye to Kunming."

The Military Police drove up in their Jeep with Rex. "At ease, Private Rex. Out, buddy. You can say goodbye."

Rex jumped out, landing on all four paws. The shiny black Doberman towered over me, bending his neck to touch his nose to mine. We paused, sniffing each other's breath. I nipped at his pointed ears and dove, yapping at his feet. He growled and pranced away from me, then we ran in circles as fast as we could. My tiny steps pounded the ground as I kept up with his giant leaps in the air. He rolled in the dust, and I jumped on his belly, tugging on the tight skin under his neck. *Grrrrwwwrrr.* He barked back at me with a deep *wwoooff,* sending me spinning across the ground to George's feet. I stood and wagged my tail at Rex, panting and ready to chase him again.

"Gremlin, heel." George commanded. "Thanks, guys. He

needed a good romp before our long flight. See you later." I
licked Rex's muzzle and trotted over to my best friend. The
MPs drove away, with Rex barking goodbye from the back.

George held me while climbing the steps of the plane.
Inside, sharp smells attacked my nose. I squirmed,
whimpering. The air stung like the antiseptic in Red's hospital.
I smelled the fear and panic of a scared dog and whined.
Hhnnnnff-hhhhnnnff?

"Something wrong, Gremlin?" He squeezed me a little
tighter.

A burley airman held out his hand to stop us, barking at
us like Private Rex. "No dogs allowed on the plane,
Lieutenant. Orders. Last one out of here was a big dog. Tore
up the inside of the plane over The Hump. Nothing we could
do but get him off at the next stop. You can see the damage.
Been transporting so many troops over The Hump to go home,
no time to fix 'em."

George's blue eyes met the man's stern gaze as he held
me tightly. "Look, this little dog is well-behaved. He's even
flown with General Chennault. Get the Old Man on the horn
and he'll straighten this out."

I perked my ears forward to look as innocent as I could,
panting in a friendly way and moving my tail back and forth
in friendship.

"Can't risk it happening again. We gotta take off now.
Weather's closing in over The Hump. No time to spare. Get
that mutt off the plane."

The other passengers called out, "Let him on board."
"He's the mascot of Kunming's command center." "Gremlin
deserves to fly home."

Luke appeared at the bottom of the stairs. "What's the holdup?"

George turned toward me; his eyes softened. He looked the way I felt when I left perfectly good fish guts behind on the riverbank. But as much as I liked to roll uncontrollably in the smelly fish, I always stuck with my best friend. When he closed his eyes and his shoulders sagged, I knew I would not be getting on that plane.

I heard George gasp for breath as he opened his eyes and held me out to Luke. "Can you bring Gremlin out to New York, Luke? Maybe when you go out, they'll allow dogs to fly again."

I rolled my eyes in panic, refusing to leave George. I had to keep the gremlins away from his plane—to get him home safely—to Sara.

Luke took me and held me against his chest. "I'll take him home when it's my turn. It'll be all right, Gremlin."

I felt helpless. No, it won't be all right—I struggled in Luke's arms, rolling around to look at George. For the first time ever, I snapped my teeth at Luke, scaring myself and startling him.

"Exactly why that pooch ain't gettin' on this plane," the airman shouted.

Luke put me down, and George dropped my water bowl, sandbox, and bag of soil onto the ground. "Guess we won't be needing these... Bye, buddy." He climbed the steps with his head down.

"Inside, sir," growled the airman as he pulled up the staircase and closed the door, trapping George inside. Luke threw my things into the Jeep.

I had to protect my best friend on his journey—even if it meant I would never see him again. What could I do? The one thing I was born to do—I had to live up to the name General Chennault of the Flying Tigers gave me when I was a puppy, so long ago.

I strained against my leash, planted my front feet on the ground, and took a deep breath. I barked at the plane to scare away gremlins. I barked to protect George. Barked for never, ever seeing him again. Barked my wishes for his happiness with Sara, whom I would never meet.

I saw the silhouette of George's head in the window. He put his hand against the windowpane. The engines of the C-46 Commando plane fired up and the propellers began to turn, startling me. I set off a stream of squirms and piercing yips and yelps.

Ralph ran from the hanger, a frayed oil rag dangling from the back pocket of his overalls, the kind of rag Tom and I played with long ago. He shouted over the roaring engines, "I heard Gremlin. Why isn't he on that plane? Is George leaving without him?"

Luke picked me up and pointed to the plane. "They're not allowing dogs on board anymore."

"I'll do what I can to stall them." Ralph raced to the plane as it began rolling toward the runway. He waved his oily rag, yelling at the cockpit window. He made a sideways cutting motion under his neck.

"I'll get the Old Man." Luke jumped into the Jeep and started it, holding me on his lap. Engines powered down. Propellers gradually slowed and stopped as Ralph's mechanics gathered around the plane.

444

The scowling airman opened the side door partway. "What now? What's the hold-up? We have a mission to run."

Ralph pointed toward the wing. "Some gremlin's been monkeying with those engines. You can't go 'til I check it out. Now lower those stairs."

"Engines sound fine to me." The big man began to close the door.

"I tune these engines like fine violins. This plane isn't going anywhere until I hear them singing." Ralph motioned for the maintenance crew to check the aircraft. The airman opened the door and put down the staircase as the crew swarmed the plane, busy as bees.

Luke radioed Headquarters. I squirmed, ready to bolt back to George. But when I heard Chennault's drawl crackling through the speaker, I sat at attention. "Why the hell didn't that plane depart on time?"

Luke explained the situation. The general barked, "Bring the pup back to HQ." My heart stopped beating. It was hopeless. I would be stuck in China, without my best friend — again. Soon Luke would be gone, too, and I would be the last one left behind. I raised my head and howled.

"Hush now, tiger, we won't let go of you 'til we get you back to George." Luke rushed to HQ, away from my best friend. I was doomed to a life without him. I curled up and stared at the floorboards. All the enticing smells of the Kunming airbase and the distant river passed by, and I didn't even raise my nose to sniff the air. Feeling empty and drained, I had nothing to live for. No George. No hope of meeting Sara. No family with kids. I whimpered. *Hhhnnnngh-hhhhnnngghh.*

As we approached Headquarters, General Chennault

flew off the steps and jumped into the Jeep, lifting me onto his lap, his rough hands smelling of cigarette smoke in the moist, sticky summer air. "Back to the airfield."

Luke made a quick U-turn and sped back to the plane. Before the Jeep stopped completely, the General vaulted out, with me under his arm. He bounded up the steps of the plane. "What's all this about? Our Flying Tiger dog isn't on board."

I whined when I saw George, his face pale, eyes wide. I wanted to squirm out of the general's arms, but I put on my best Joe Dash behavior to prove to the crew that I could control myself. I turned my head to show off the first lieutenant's bar on my shiny leather collar.

The general snapped at the crew, "Look, boys, I understand you've got orders. But I'm telling you, this dog is special. He won't cause you any trouble. My dog, Joe Dash is his sire. Gremlin grew up to be a good Air Force dog. He's helping us win the war."

Ralph stepped into the plane, wiping his hands on a rag. He shouted to Chennault, with a glance at the crew. "If it wasn't for this dog, I wouldn't have caught a major mechanical failure. This plane's engines would have stalled at altitude. You all would have gone down on one of those high passes over The Hump, adding your wrecked plane to that old trail of aluminum. Thanks to Gremlin, we made critical repairs. He saved the lives of everyone onboard. Good job, buddy, you stopped the gremlins from doing their mischief."

What—I saved George's life?

Chennault put his hand on Ralph's shoulder and addressed the crew and passengers. "You understand now what's at stake here. This dog is your hero. The guardian of the

Flying Tigers." He handed a paper to the airman, whose mouth hung open. "Here is my signed dispensation for Gremlin to take this flight. It will override any other orders you have."

He cleared his throat and spoke to George and the other passengers. "You're fortunate to have The Gremlin on board. Along with Ralph's good work on the mechanics, this little pup will keep away any other gremlins. And you don't want any problems when you fly over The Hump, right?"

The crew's cheeks flushed as they looked from Ralph to Chennault, George—and me—in amazement. Luke dashed in with a smirk on his face and handed my water bowl, sandbox, and sack of soil to the big airman.

I licked General Chennault's famous jutting jaw. He chuckled as he handed me to George. I immediately curled up with my best friend, a low growl in my throat. My eyes glared at the crew, ready to snap at anyone daring to separate us again.

The crew saluted. Chennault returned their salute with two fingers. "As you were."

He shook George's hand. "Remember, son, you and Sara are going to show me your first-born child." He winked at me and left the plane.

The pilots returned to the cockpit and started the engines, propellors whirling and whining harmoniously on both wings, like the musicians humming in the hangar. The crewmen raised the stairs and locked the plane's door—again. Everyone on the plane cheered as we took off from the airfield and rose above the rounded Kunming hills with the sweet roar of Ralph's engines.

~   ~   ~   ~   ~

I huddled inside George's flight jacket to keep him warm in the freezing plane over The Hump, where our flight through the Himalayan valleys and passes were overshadowed by snowy mountain peaks. In Karachi we stepped off the plane into the dry heat of India, where George took me shopping for fabrics, a teakwood table, and other precious things he chose to start our life with Sara.

We walked through noisy streets, like the ones in Kunming where people shouted and sold food, spices, and treasures from their small stalls. George shook his head after looking at different things. We walked around the corner and stopped in front of a store with a sign in the window. "Ah, they speak English here."

The store was filled with different sizes and colors of statues—people, plants, and animals—from floor to ceiling. The air smelled of dust and burning incense. I sneezed twice, shook my head, and licked my nose.

George talked with the shopkeepers, a husband and wife who reminded me of Mr. and Mrs. Liu. "I've seen many statues of the Buddha in China and India, but none are right. I want to send home a Buddha. Do you have one that doesn't look angry? One that is happy and loves children?"

"Come to this other room, sir. I think I know what you are looking for." The woman wore long, flowing robes and scarves, which rustled softly she led us through the shop. Her hands were painted in patterns of brown ink, like Mrs. Liu's embroideries of flowers and birds, but without the stitches of different colors. She had more jewelry than Soong Mei-ling, and I wondered if she was the head of an air force, too.

My best friend took a sharp breath as he stepped toward the statue of a fat man with blushing cheeks and a big smile. "This is it. I can't believe it."

The shopkeeper picked up the Buddha and took it to the counter. Her husband dusted it with long feathers, and the dust floated across sunbeams streaming through the window. "This is the happy or laughing Buddha, sahib. Also is the fat Buddha. Sorry, sahib, my English is not so good."

The woman explained, "This Buddha sits in a posture of love. He has a balance between thinking and tranquility. He holds a string of beads, meaning he has pearls of wisdom from his meditations. His smile shows how loving he is, and his big belly is a sign of good luck and abundance, whether for wealth or happiness... or children, in which case, he is a sign of fertility." She blushed, and they all laughed.

George and Sara's Buddha
(WWII)

"Do you have children?" George's cheeks were flushed and he smiled like the happy Buddha.

The couple said at the same time, "Plenty of children." She whispered, "We keep him on a table in our bedroom. When our family was big enough, we turned him to face the wall."

Her husband tapped George on the shoulder. "Remember that in future years, sahib."

~   ~   ~   ~   ~

After a few days in Karachi, we took off early and landed late for a short while to refuel, then took off again at night time. The sun rose and set as our flights took us toward a place called home. But anywhere George took me was home, even in the plane, on this trip of a lifetime. Home was wherever we were together.

Whenever we left the plane to stretch our legs, I placed my scent among the markings left by animals I would never meet. On these outings, George brought along the canvas bag to collect soil for my sandbox. The sand from India smelled of incense, teak, and spices.

During a long stay in Egypt, we saw the Sphinx and the Pyramids. The Sphinx reminded me of Sadie when she sat on Andy's lap. The Pyramids were so big we couldn't walk all the way around them. George collected sand from their base, tiny grains of reddish sand weathered from the stones put in place long ago.

I waded through the papyrus on the banks of the Nile River among camels and cattle, savoring the difference in the taste of the Nile's water and the rivers of China where George used to go fishing and frogging.

Whenever we landed, George wrote names in his small flight log: Karachi, Abadan, Cairo, Tripoli, and Casablanca. Every time I used my sandbox, I sniffed out the scents of incense from India, ancient earth from Africa, and salty sea sand from Santa Maria Island in the Azores.

As we settled into our flight over the Atlantic Ocean, George struck up a conversation with the short, muscular man next to us. His upper arm was bigger around than my body. George shifted in his seat, his left shoulder pressed against the window to face the man.

"Name's Frank, Frank Oprandy. I'm from a small town, not far from New York City—in *New Joisey*, right? Can't ya tell from my accent? Served in the CBI, with the OSS. Say, didn't I meetcha in Kunming?"

"Office of Strategic Services—that's right. I'm George Haydon. Born and raised in California. Thought you looked familiar. You came into HQ to brief Chennault a few times."

I sat up in George's arms to take a closer look at Frank. His face and neck were sunburned. He had a tired look, the way George looked when he sat on his bunk after a big day. I wondered how long their conversation would last.

Our new friend looked past us, out the window as the plane took off. He turned back to George, shouting over the engines, "Got plans when you get back to the States?" His voice carried some nasal tones, like Mr. and Mrs. Liu.

George told him about Sara in New York City at Columbia University Teachers College, finishing her master's degree in education. Having heard this story many times, I dozed upside down, with my head between his knees and my feet against his belly as his thumb stroked my chest. The inside of the plane became dark as we flew into the night, and the voices of the other passengers faded into the endless, droning rhythms of the engines.

I woke, still sleepy, hearing Frank's voice. "See, I'd been a weightlifter before the war, kept up my bulk by lifting and carrying those four-point-two mortar rounds and the M2 that fired them."

He flexed the huge muscles in his arms. "There were five of us from the States embedded in a composite group, Chinese

451

soldiers and medics. I taught the soldiers how to fire the M2. And the medics stitched us up after our field operations."

Frank sat silently for several minutes. "Well, to tell ya the truth, we weren't supposed ta come back from our last mission. Eastern Echelon. Japanese occupied territory, though they were losing ground by then. Operation Ichigo."

"Ichigo? You were there when we evacuated Kweilin?"

Frank gave a half-smile and scratched behind his neck. "Our mission was ta row a boat to an island occupied by the Japanese. A demolition detail, disrupting the railway in the north-south supply transport the Japanese needed. We were waitin' ta leave after dark. Just enough supplies ta get there, but not enough ta return. I'd handle the explosives one last time."

Frank shifted in his seat. "We were about ta start radio silence before pushin' off from shore." His hand trembled as he took out a worn handkerchief and wiped his forehead. "Can't believe it, but we got word by radio a few minutes before we shoved off—we were going home. How's that for timing? Now here we are, on our way to the States. Hard ta catch up with the reality of the situation."

They sat in silence as the plane's engines moaned and groaned like frogs on the Li River. A crewman stepped over Frank's ankles to bring them coffee. Frank cupped his hand around the mug and sighed, breathing in the rich aroma.

George filled my tin cup with water from his canteen. I sat up to lap the water from the cup. He gave me a piece of jerky, and I licked and gnawed at my treat, nestled between the two of them.

My best friend blew into his cup and took a sip. "Different

world back there. When I shipped out from the States in forty-two, I wrote home that I had some fine stories to tell. Now all I want is to hear about home. Get on with my life."

"Understood. Believe you me, some things I'll never tell another soul." Frank tipped his cup toward George. As I glanced back and forth at the men, their faces lined with weariness and the strain of wartime, I wished I could tell them that I understood, too. Their secrets were safe with me. I swallowed the last of my jerky and ran my tongue around my teeth to find every last morsel.

George took a long drink of his coffee. "Hey, buddy, we're going home to our families. Sure am glad I stayed so long, though. Working with Chennault was an experience I'll always feel proud about."

Frank drained his cup. "Seems like several lifetimes ago since I arrived in Kunming. Quite a thrill to fly the Hump over the Himalayas into China. Didn't know exactly what to expect. But I think we all made a difference for our Chinese friends and allies, turning the tide of the war. World's a different place now, for better or worse. Flying out—now—well, let's just say I'll be glad to get home."

I turned sideways across George's lap and licked the back of Frank's hand, covered with oil stains like Ralph's. He yawned and dabbed his handkerchief around his eyes. After a few minutes, the flight steward took their cups. Frank turned his head away, crossed his arms over his chest, and fell asleep, just as I knew he would.

The steward brought blankets, and George placed one blanket over our new friend and one over himself. I burrowed under the edges and curled up between them. Now and then I heard Frank mumble in his sleep and felt his fingers tap out little patterns across my back.

After hours flying, George sighed and stretched, and so did I, stretching, shaking myself, and crawling to his lap. I could feel the weight of the first lieutenant's bar on my collar, reminding me of our missions in China.

Resting his elbow on the armrest by the window, George propped his head up, chin in his hand. Pulling me to the window, he said, "Gremlin, look—there's the U.S. of A." As we flew between the puffy white clouds, I peered out the small window and saw more planes on the ground than I'd ever seen in China.

Turning, he woke Frank. "Hey, buddy, looks like we made it back to the States. Presque Isle, Maine."

Frank leaned over to peer out the small window. The plane banked, and we could see the airfield and buildings, trucks and cars. "Final approach. Hmm. Good to be back stateside," he said, stretching and yawning. "Too tired to tell ya before, George, but I've got a wife and two kids waiting for me. Always wanted a big family. Hope to add more kids right away, half a dozen or so. Take my mind off the war."

He threw off the blanket and stretched his arms toward the ceiling. "You know, I delivered papers as a kid. Maybe my kids'll help me out with a similar kind of business—after what I've been through, I think I'd do pretty well with a highly dangerous milk delivery business. Got the muscle for heaving around those big metal milk cans, right?"

The two men laughed. I let out a *bbbrrkk-bbrrrkk* in agreement, wagging my tail.

Frank scratched me under my neck and petted my back,

his eyes misting. "And maybe one of them will go to Teachers College, like your Sara. Maybe even teach there someday. I've got high hopes, now we're back."

Once we landed, we taxied toward the airport terminal, the stars and stripes flying on the tallest flagpole I'd ever seen. The Chinese flag with its white sun on a flag of blue was missing. What had happened to the sun and the star?

Frank pointed at a large sign near the building. "Well, wouldya look at that? 'Welcome Home Troops.' Nice touch."

Jeeps and trucks bustled around the terminal. George put the leash on my collar and picked up his satchel and my things. He walked down the steps, and I scrambled after him.

"Good dog," the crewmen told me. "Good luck, Gremlin." "Bye, George." "Frank, you take care now."

We walked around to the back of the plane, where George and Frank picked up their duffle bags. Military personnel from our plane climbed onto buses or were whisked away in Jeeps. But I didn't see rickshaws or donkeys or water buffalo here.

An officer approached Frank and they saluted and talked in low voices. Frank turned to shake George's hand. "Off on a quick flight ta the Pentagon for debriefing. Hope ta see you around, George."

"All my best to you and that family of yours." George smiled.

"If you *eva* come ta *Joisey* with a family of your own, look me up." He smiled and waved, walking to another plane with its engines revving up. I barked twice to say goodbye to Frank and chase away any gremlins—*bbbrrkkk-bbrrkkkk*.

George knelt, and I put my paws on his leg. He put his face near mine, cradling my head in his big hand. "Hey, tiger, we made it back to U. S. soil. Seven days from China to Presque Isle, far eastern point of the States. North, north Maine. Edge of darkness."

He stroked my ears. "The good earth of the United States." Sprawling onto the grass, he lay on his back, hands behind his head. I jumped onto his tummy. He chuckled. "Just two more long days by train to New York. What they call it a tee-rain in India. *Aahhh.* We've seen a lot of the world, Gremlin."

George turned onto his side and ruffled the fur on my neck and chest. "China—India—Burma. When I arrived, I wrote home about all the stories I'd tell them when I got home. Impossible to talk about it now. I just want to be with Sara and get on with our life together."

I wagged my tail, put my rear up, and bowed to him, like I used to with my brother Tom and Private Rex. I barked, and my best friend tackled me in a big hug. We rolled and wrestled in the deep, soft grass of Maine, surrounded by flowers and annoying little black flies. I shook them off my head and growled and yipped, dancing away from George and crawling back to him. He laughed and tickled my belly, while I gave him puppy kisses all over his face.

~   ~   ~   ~   ~

George held me tight in his arms, duffle bag over his shoulder like so many men and women returning in uniform. We left my sandbox in a trash can and rode the crowded streetcars and subways of New York City.

"West 113th Street. Here's where we get off." He set me down on the warm concrete, and I stretched, sniffing the air. "No bushes here, tiger. Go ahead and use that fire hydrant."

I wanted to linger around the smells I found around every

fire hydrant on the bustling, noisy streets, but he seemed impatient, pulling me away from the layers of scents from city dogs. Some were stronger than others. I wanted to greet every dog we passed and stop at every tree and hydrant—nearly forgetting about our mission to find Sara.

But George didn't forget, tugging on my leash and urging me to heel. We walked past tall buildings and turned a corner where he stopped, and I bumped into his leg.

"Here we are at last." He walked up to a man at the door, who wore a uniform. He opened the door to a building much larger than the Tiger Den. We walked down a hallway, and George knocked on a door, dropping his satchel and duffle bag and letting go of my leash. I sat like a good Flying Tiger dog, waiting for his orders.

A petite woman with warm brown eyes and dark, curly brown hair opened the door. When she saw George, her eyes widened and became watery. Her mouth opened, like she might say something, but she didn't make a sound. I smelled something burning from inside and sneezed. She cried, "Oh, no!" and slammed the door, leaving us outside.

George and I looked at each other and waited at attention. Soon Sara threw the door open and stepped forward. "Sorry— I just burned supper—George—you're home!" They hugged and made kissing noises for a long time, murmuring to each other. I guarded the duffle bag and waited like a good dog, wiggling while I sat, ready to jump up on them, my short tail thumping against the floor.

I whimpered softly, and he bent toward me. My nails tapped in a dance on the hallway's creaky wooden floor.

George picked me up, and I reached out my nose to Sara

as quickly as I could, my tongue lapping the air between us. "Sara, here's Gremlin, my Flying Tiger dog."

She smiled at me with love in her eyes. She held me close, and I sniffed her neck and licked her cheeks and chin and ear. I heard her laugh, lightly as ripples on the Li River and as sweetly as the little bells *tink-tink-tinging* on a porch that was no more.

I snuggled against her chin, sensing that my days of scaring away gremlins were now over, and my new life had begun.

"You're the first new member of our family," Sara whispered to me, stroking my front paws, and scratching me on my forehead. She and George cuddled me as we came through the door—into our home.

Afterword

George and Sara Haydon (1980s)

Learn to old age,
There is still more to learn.
War Area Service Corps Diary for 1945 — China

George lived to be ninety years old, and Sara celebrated her one hundredth birthday in 2016. They were married for sixty-two years, living the life they dreamed of during their separation in the Second World War.

Brothers-in-law (L-R) Bill Higgins, Tom Eagan, and George Haydon (1950s)

Sara and George were among the community leaders from the "greatest generation" in the agricultural town of Gridley, California, sharing love, laughter, and music with their four children and nine grandchildren. They lived for decades on a small ranch, enjoying their grove of eucalyptus trees, roses, migrating waterfowl, and view of the Sutter Buttes.

George and Sara Haydon
(1980s)

Above all, George enjoyed music, his last means of communication when his words failed.

My Deepest Appreciation To…

My brothers John, Jim, and Tom, for sharing memories of Mother and Dad

Vanessa, my daughter, the only person to hear my heartbeat from the inside

My husband Kerry and our extended families

Dear lifelong friends who became my sisters: Suzy, Charlene, Nashan, and Marjorie

Long-time members of my Pacific Writing Team

My students, colleagues, and friends at the University of the Pacific

Colleagues and friends at Shanghai Normal University, Tianhua College, especially our Pacific Tea Club

Nell Calloway, General Claire L. Chennault's granddaughter and Executive Director of the Chennault Air and Military Museum in Monroe, Louisiana

Larry Jobe and the leaders of the Flying Tiger Historical Organization and the Flying Tiger Heritage Park, Museum, and Command Cave in Guilin, China

Personnel of the Tom Lea Institute in El Paso, Texas

Dr. Jie Lu for translating my father's Yunnan banner

Dr. Jinrui "Crystal" Mone, Dr. Cheng "Cassie" Chen, Dr. Fan "Diana" Yang, former students who have become my *Lǎoshī*

Pam Van Allen for formatting the manuscript

Donna Yee for designing the cover and enhancing my father's vintage, postage stamp-sized photograph of Gremlin

Bibliography

Ayling, K. (1945). *Old Leatherface of the Flying Tigers: The story of General Chennault.* Indianapolis, IN: The Bobbs-Merrill Company.

Binion, D. (11/10/2000). "Man experiences rewards of being in military." In the *Gridley Herald* Salute to Veterans Day: 100 Year Anniversary of VFW; 50 Year Anniversary of Korean War. Gridley, CA: *Gridley Herald*, p. 4.

Bond, C. R., & Anderson, T. H. (1984). *A Flying Tiger's Diary.* College Station, TX: Texas A&M University Press.

Byrd, M. (1987). *Chennault: Giving wings to the tiger.* Tuscaloosa, AL: The University of Alabama Press.

Chennault, A. (1963). *Chennault and the Flying Tigers.* NY: Paul S. Eriksson, Inc.

Cornelius, W., & Short, T. (2004). *Ding Hao: America's Air War in China 1937-1945.* Gretna, LA: Pelican Publishing Company, Inc.

Craver, R., & Margo, A. (ed.). (1995). *Tom Lea: An oral history.* El Paso, TX: Texas Western Press.

Exley, H. (2011). *Chinese wisdom 365: A thoughtful quote for every day – from the wisest thinkers.* Watford, UK: Helen Exley Giftbooks in Great Britain.

Flying Tiger Historical Organization. https://www.flyingtigershistoricalorganization.com/

Ford, D. (1991/2007). *Flying Tigers: Claire Chennault and his American Volunteers, 1941-1942.* Smithsonian Books.

Forman, H. (1945). *Report from Red China.* NY: Henry Holt and Company.

Groom, W. (2005). *1942: The year that tried men's souls.* NY: Grove Press.

Haydon, G. A. (1941-1945). Personal correspondence.

Haydon, J. S. (1991). Personal correspondence.

Haydon, S. B. (1944-1945). Personal correspondence.

Hotz, R. B. (1943). *With General Chennault: The story of the Flying Tigers.* NY: Coward-McCann, Inc.

Jablonski, E. (1977). *A pictorial history of the World War II years.* Garden City, NY: Doubleday & Company, Inc.

McRae, Jr. B. Lest we forget: African American Military History by Historian, Author, and Veteran Bennie McRae, Jr. http://lestweforget.hamptonu.edu/page.cfm?uuid=9FE C43A7-AF1E-F85C-02264804E682227C

McClure, G. E. (1975). *Fire and fall back: Casey Vincent's story of three years in the China-Burma-India Theater, including the fighting withdrawal of the Flying Tigers from Eastern China.* San Antonio, TX: Barnes Press.

Mitter, R. (2013). *Forgotten ally: China's World War II 1937-1945.* Boston: Houghton Mifflin Harcourt.

Shanghai People's Fine Arts Publishing House. *Old Shanghai: A photographic album.* (20140. Shanghai, China: Author.

Tong, H. K. (2005). *Chiang Kai-shek's teacher and ambassador: An inside view of the Republic of China from 1911-1958; General Stillwell and American policy change towards free China.* Bloomington, IN: AuthorHouse.

World War II Database. https://ww2db.com/

About the Author

Sara Haydon holding the author as a baby
(1950s)

At home you look to your parents;
Abroad depend upon your friends.
    War Area Service Corps Diary for 1944—China

Elizabeth Haydon Keithcart, Ed.D., is a former elementary school teacher who loves sharing literature, the arts, science, and history with her students. Inspired by her parents' involvement in music, Betsy became a board-certified music therapist and is a visiting assistant professor at the University of the Pacific in teacher education and music education.

Gremlin: Guardian of the Flying Tigers is Betsy's first historical novel. She plans to continue writing about her family in an upcoming series told from the perspective of her Dickinson ancestors, notably the women, who passed their

Betsy K. Haydon at the Flying Tigers Museum,
Chongqing, China (2015)

musical heritage from one generation to the next.

To My Readers:

Thank you for reading Gremlin's story. Writing this novel has helped me cope with the loss of my parents, the dynamics of the COVID-19 pandemic, and damage from wildfires affecting my community in Northern California.

If Gremlin brought you joy and perhaps a few tears, I hope you'll consider writing a review. The main idea of *Gremlin: Guardian of the Flying Tigers* is to bring people together, and I encourage you to make positive contribution toward this effort.

Made in the USA
Las Vegas, NV
29 November 2021